The BOOK *of* ESTHER

ALSO BY EMILY BARTON

Brookland
The Testament of Yves Gundron

The

BOOK

of

ESTHER

A Novel

Emily Barton

TIM
DUGGAN
BOOKS

New York

Copyright © 2016 by Emily Barton

Published in the United States by Tim Duggan Books, an imprint of the Crown
Publishing Group, a division of Penguin Random House LLC New York.
www.crownpublishing.com

TIM DUGGAN BOOKS and colophon are registered trademarks of Penguin Random
House LLC.

Library of Congress Cataloging-in-Publication Data
Names: Barton, Emily, author.
Title: The book of Esther : a novel / Emily Barton.
Description: First edition. | New York : Tim Duggan Books, [2016]
Identifiers: LCCN 2015038206 | ISBN 9781101904091 (hardcover) | ISBN
    9781101904114 (softcover) | ISBN 9781101904107 (ebook)
Subjects: LCSH: Jews—Ficton. | World War, 1939–1945—Europe—Fiction. |
    BISAC: FICTION / Literary. | FICTION / Alternative History. | FICTION /
    Jewish. | GSAFD: Alternative histories (Fiction) | War stories.
Classification: LCC PS3552.A7685 B66 2016 | DDC 813/ .54—dc23 LC record
    available at http://lccn.loc.gov/2015038206

ISBN 978-1-101-90409-1
eBook ISBN 978-1-101-90410-7

PRINTED IN THE UNITED STATES OF AMERICA

Map by Sophie Kittredge
Jacket design by Michael Morris

10 9 8 7 6 5 4 3 2 1

First Edition

טום בן יוחנן וחנה
טוביה אליהו בן טום ומנוחה
אמת אברהם בן טום ומנוחה

The BOOK of ESTHER

And in every province, and in every city, whithersoever the king's commandment and his decree came, the Jews had gladness and joy, a feast and a good day. And many from among the peoples of the land became Jews; for the fear of the Jews was fallen upon them.

ESTHER 8:17

JPS TANAKH (1917)

BRITANIA

GERMANIA

POLO

EUROPA

Praha

BOHEMY

FRANKIA

MAG

ITALIA

YUGOSI

IBERIA

IFRIKIA

Pontus Hatikho

KHAZARIA
and Surrounding Territories 1942/5702

Petrogradye

THE UYGHUR KAGANATE
AND
MONGOLIA

MENSHEVIKI RUS

PONTIC-KHAZAR STEPPE

Kyiv

UKRAINA

Kharkov

Dniepra

Donets

Don

Atil

Tsaritsyn

Yetzirah

Sarkel

Atil

Khazaran

ANIA

Azovskoye Morye

KRIMYA

Kerch

KHAZARIA

ARIA

Pontus Euxinus

Samandar

KAVKAS

Khazar Sea

Byzantium

OTTOMANIA

PERSIA

N

PALESTINE

MITZRAYIM

CHAPTER 1

Dim pricks of blue light shone through the shutters' decorative punchwork. Careful not to wake her sister, Esther braced her hand against one door while she drew back the other. The wooden panel stuck a moment before popping free, letting in the damp, salty air and a view of purplish sky. To the east, the sun cast its first pink glow over the place where the mighty River Atil spilled into the Khazar Sea. Esther raced through her morning prayers, her voice a sibilant whisper.

From her father's house, high up in the walled city of Atil, Esther could see sailors on the island-sized expanse of an aerocraft carrier's deck. Some worked with mops and pails; some checked the serried rows of flying machines; one hoisted the kaganate's white flag, which hung limp in the still air as it jerked up its pole. The decks of the Khazar warships bustled with activity. Men also worked aboard great Ottoman and Persian merchant ships, moored across the river in Atil's twin city of Khazaran. Fishing boats plied the water. Downstairs, someone dropped a log and swore to her native god. The smell of fresh flatbread rose from the kitchen. Much of the world was at work at this hour, just not the children of the bek's kender, or chief policy adviser, Josephus. Esther's sister, Elisheva, still slept, her mouth open, her dark hair trailing onto Esther's pillow.

Esther slipped out of her nightgown, pulled on the sweater and loose trousers she'd worn the day before, and walked barefoot into the cold hallway and down the stairs. Her boots, like everyone's, waited by the back door.

On her way through the kitchen, Esther filched a flatbread the

1

older kitchen maid, Afra, had just pulled from the oven. The younger maid, Kiraz, looked up teary-eyed from chopping onions, but didn't say anything. Holding the hot bread between three fingertips, Esther scooped into the pot of warm lentils over the fire. Afra began to complain—it had been her, swearing a moment earlier—and Esther gestured an apology and said, "I'm sorry, I'm sorry. I'll clean it up." But she was already at the door, the bread and lentils folded into one hand while she wrestled on her fur-lined boots with the other. When she'd taken them off the night before, they'd been caked with red mud. Someone had brushed them clean.

She had nearly crossed the inner courtyard before Itakh zoomed up beside her, hopping to pull on his second shoe. He carried a rucksack on his back. Mindful not to hit it or knock the Bukhari *kippah* off the back of his head, Esther put her free arm around his small shoulder. The top of his head reached her armpit. Itakh took the opportunity to grab the dripping bread and lentils. He took a big, sloppy bite before returning it to her. "Disgusting," Esther said without meaning it. "You didn't even bless it." He was only about nine years old, but should have known better.

He sang out a quick *Motzi* and wiped his mouth on his forearm.

"Good morning to you too," she said. Then she tore the bread in half. They kept walking, companionably quiet while they ate. The sharp, dry turmeric in the lentils cleared Esther's nose. Lentil juice plopped onto the ground.

At the far end of the inner courtyard, the gate stood shut, held fast by a wire loop. Esther swung this up, then drew the gate open, careful to lift as she did so to prevent the hinges from squeaking. Itakh ran through and she closed it again behind them. A higher brick wall surrounded the house's outer courtyard to protect the whole enclosure from attack. Nestled beneath it were the three small servants' houses—empty at this hour, as the staff was up working—the storehouse, the barn, whose milk goats and irritable chickens were already out cropping and pecking at the grass, and Esther's destination, the mechanical stable. As she strode toward it, Itakh ducked off toward the compound's pigeon loft.

"It's late, we have to hurry," Esther said.

Not bothering to look back, Itakh made a gesture of dismissal behind him. Most of the birds belonged to Josephus and a few to foreign governments, who used them to carry intelligence, but Itakh had a passion for them. He kept and trained some of his own, and cared for the whole loft with Esther's brother, Shmuel. The birds strutted and cooed, excited at his approach. Esther heard the rainlike pitter of scattering feed.

The mechanical stable was as old as any building in the compound. In Esther's grandfather's time, it had housed the strong-boned natural horses one now mainly saw speckling the countryside, their flanks a pleasing motley of browns and grays. Esther had learned to ride one before mastering their mechanical kin. In her father's young manhood, Khazaria had invented the mechanical horse, a war machine to protect the rough-terrained homeland from the Rus to the east, the Ottomanim to the south, and oil-hungry Europa to the west. The machines had stood guard as the conflict that brought down the Oestro-Magyar Empire rolled across the steppe to Khazaria's western border. But the kaganate had not been of interest. A few skirmishes, and the chief combatants had moved on to fight with one another.

In the intervening twenty years, engineers kept improving the horses, which constituted Khazaria's chief defense in the event of a land war. Early models had been big and clumsy as steer, with shift mechanisms so awkwardly placed and requiring such force to operate, people called them suicide shifters. The most recent model was smaller and faster, more aerodynamic, with the shifter incorporated more safely into the left handlebar. The unpredictable terrain of the steppe had for thousands of years favored the skilled, ruthless warrior, the man who could keep his horse while slicing off an enemy's head with his broadsword. A Khazar mounted on a mechanical horse could fight with his ancestors' brutality. The army's few hundred tanks, purchased from the Rus, were rumored to break down as often as they ran.

As Esther entered her father's stable, she knew that most of her country's thousands of mech horses stood ready on the eastern bank of the Dniepra to fight the enemy barreling across Ukraina. She knew the bek had stationed warships in all of Khazaria's seas and her many rivers. But Josephus ben Malakhi's horses remained in his compound: four late-model and one hulking, old-fashioned mare called Leyla. Seleme was the one Esther drove. She liked the horse's idiosyncrasies: the way she might buck an unskilled rider; her general dark temper.

The stable's pungent petroleum smell filled Esther's nose. Though she and Itakh had to hurry before her father noticed them missing, she took a moment to breathe in. Bataar, the stable hand, was feeding one machine a bucket of petrol. He lifted his chin in greeting. Esther touched Seleme's steel muzzle, although the machine could not respond unless she was running. Esther patted her side. A dull, muffled sound emerged.

"She's fueled," Bataar said. "Ready to go. *Iyimiyiz?*" Esther spoke enough Turc to nod and thank him. Bataar put down his funnel and bucket, took a grimy chamois from his pocket, and gave a cursory swipe at Seleme's integrated saddle and stirrups. Steppe warriors could ride bareback when necessary, but a mechanical horse's controls were all in its tack. The shift, throttle, and front brake resided in the handlebars that protruded from behind the ears, the rear brake in the right stirrup, the starter behind it. Esther climbed up and over, hooking her left foot tight to get a good jump on the starter. It took a couple of tries to make the engine turn over. Bataar opened up the choke for her; it was a far reach for a person of her size. As she settled onto the rumbling machine, she felt the pattern of Seleme's riveting rub against the inner seam of her pants. She revved Seleme's engine, shifted her into reverse, and prodded her with one foot as she eased out the clutch with her left hand to encourage her toward the open stable door.

"We'll be back shortly," she said, leaning down so Bataar could hear her over the engine. "*Teşekkür ederim.*" Her thanks.

Itakh came running toward the stable with one hand cupped over a small bulge in his shirt. One-handed and without even a foothold, he clambered up behind her and mounted the back of the saddle. Though mechanical horses had no provision for a passenger, he was small enough to ride pillion behind her. He wrapped one arm around her waist and held tight. The other must still have been cradling the bird she felt adjusting its position against her back.

"What are you doing?" she asked him.

"I promised Jascha."

Irritated, she jerked her braid free of him. Dawn had already broken. The bird struggled before seeming to settle in against its master.

Seleme was not built for a casual stroll. She had a 150cc engine and a foul temper, never a lucky combination in a horse. But to the extent that she was capable of feeling anything, she grudgingly liked Esther, the person who drove her most often, and didn't seem to mind Itakh's negligible excess weight. So she walked almost docilely toward the outer courtyard wall in first gear. The guard said, "*Salaam aleikum,*" pulled the wooden latch, and opened the gate.

Esther said, "*Aleikhem shalom,*" and rolled the shifter forward to click up into second, the lower trotting gear. She heard the gate shut behind them and the drum roll of aeroplane engines turning over on the carriers in the river. Preparing for their daily exercises, she thought; further proof she and Itakh had gotten a late start. Seleme's hooves rang against the cobbled street as stuccoed house fronts, slate roofs, and brightly painted window boxes blurred past.

Past the river and the bridge stretched Khazaran's covered market, onion domes, and the spire of the Nazarene worship house. Moments later, Esther and Itakh saluted a guard at the city's Great North Gate and passed through. He shouted something after them, but they hurried on without hearing. Once Esther shifted the horse up into third, the faster trot, she was in her element. She let her feet dangle in the stirrups, unafraid of where the chugging machine would go. The exhaust vents in the belly blew warm air against her cold legs. When high-born Khazar men practiced horsemanship, they raced to get the horses up to third. Then, though the right hand held steady on the throttle, the left could fire a pistol or wield a sword.

Esther looked over her shoulder to ask, "What did you get?"

"Yesterday's bread. A few other things. I could have done better." A moment passed before he added, "I did remember the bird."

Bat-winged KAF aerocraft took off westward. Esther pictured the river-crossed steppe they flew toward, all the terrain they would cover before they reached Ukraina and the enemy troops. She turned her mind back to guiding the horse. Seleme would have liked to gallop off toward the fields and grasslands but knew the routine. Esther kept her hands firm on the handlebars, and she headed up the riverbank toward the camp.

One couldn't see it from Josephus ben Malakhi's house, or from any wealthy dwelling in the city. When the great, hidden kagan had ordered the bek to give permission for a second camp near the capital, he had mandated its invisibility. Though the kagan never left the enclosure of his palace, he did not wish to see this camp any more than he did the one that sprawled along the banks of the Dniepra in the west. Most people Esther knew agreed with him. Among girls of Esther's station, there had been a fad the previous winter of knitting for the refugees. Not one girl had gone to present her goat's-hair hat or mittens to an actual displaced person. Servants had done it for them. Esther sometimes glimpsed Shimon ben Kalonymos in the settlement performing some act of *tzedakah* or *khesed*, charity or loving-kindness. Once she had overheard him talking to a man about irrigating his meager garden plot. As far as she knew, the two of them were alone in this predilection among people of their rank. To reach the camp, one continued beyond the port and wound around a wooded hill that concealed a bend in the Atil River. Then the camp opened up to view: a flat, haphazard sprawl as large and crowded as the city itself. Unlike any Khazar city or town, its outermost dwellings stood open to view, vulnerable to attack. There had been no time to build a defensive wall, no great interest in doing it.

Immigrant women by the hundreds were already out drawing river water for cooking. Others slapped wet clothes against the rocks. Many wore old-fashioned, Western-style dresses, though some were in Khazar castoffs, others in rags, and nearly all covered their pale or reddish hair with kerchiefs. Esther knew it was impolite to stare, but she was fascinated by their coloring, their uniformly fair skin. Khazars did not even all practice the same religion, and those who were Jews had not descended from a single clan. Under Kagan Bulan, more than a thousand years before, the nation of Turkic tribes had converted in a grand public ceremony. Their ethnic stock was mixed, colorful. Intellectually, Esther understood the refugees' common heritage, yet she still puzzled over it. At that moment, watching the washerwomen in the morning light, their foreignness struck her anew.

Some of the women glanced up from their work when they heard Seleme's engine gutter as she slowed. Most remained intent on their labor. Rukhl alone stood up, her lips pressed into a straight line as she gave a final wring to a heavy brown twist of fabric. She tossed it into one of the reed baskets at her feet, wiped her chapped hands on her dirty apron, and came toward the horse. "*Gut morgn,*" she said, pushing an orange curl back under the headscarf. When she smiled, her face looked drawn and tired.

Esther left the horse idling in neutral and jumped down. "*Gut morgn.*" Two nearby women looked at her again. Esther wasn't sure if they were surprised to hear a Khazar attempting to speak their language or offended by her pronunciation.

"Nice to see you."

Still cradling the pigeon in his shirt, Itakh brought one leg across the horse to sit sidesaddle, then slid down. "*Wu iz Jascha?*" he asked.

At that moment Rukhl's son came running up, shouting, "Itakh! Did you bring her?"

"This is Nagehan," he said, and from his shirt produced what looked to Esther like just another messenger pigeon, a repurposed bullet casing strapped to its back. Jascha murmured a syllable of approval, which made Esther look at it more closely. The bird blinked, tilted its head to one side. On second glance, it wasn't a typical gray or brown pigeon: It was white with delicate gray spotting on its wings and tail. Its eyes were red, but she thought all pigeons might have red eyes. She seldom paid them much mind, though she did admire the cunning fabrication of the message cases, their tiny straps. Jascha and Itakh bent their heads—one light, one dark—together to examine the bird and talk over her attributes. Like other boys in the camp, Jascha wore a loose-fitting cloth cap with a brim, different from the crewel-work pillbox Itakh and other Khazar Jews wore. The single gold earring of Itakh's servitude glinted beneath his unkempt hair.

Esther flicked a finger at his rucksack. "Can you take this off?"

Itakh shrugged one arm out, then transferred the bird to his free arm to do the other. He held the bag in Esther's direction and went back to talking with Jascha.

"Let's see what he got for you." Esther crouched down to unbuckle the straps and her braid slipped forward over her shoulder. She wondered if, wearing a Khazar woman's workday trousers and with her braid visible, she looked indecent to these covered women. She pulled out a pile of day-old flatbreads and handed them to Rukhl, who cleared a space in one of her baskets. Esther opened a heavy cloth bag to see what was inside, then gave it to Rukhl, saying, "Lentils." When she handed over three onions, Rukhl remarked on them, "*Akh, gut: tseibelen.*" Some of their papery brown skin fluttered off toward the river.

"Is that all?" Esther called up to Itakh.

"Kiraz came in. I couldn't get more."

Esther shook her head.

"Don't be angry with him," Rukhl said, "it's an act of *khesed.*" To Itakh she nodded and said, "*A dank.*"

"We'll try again tomorrow," Esther said. Other women observed their transaction. Esther couldn't read their expressions, but imagined them as hostile. When she looked around, she saw how far into the northern distance the camp's densely packed hovels spread. A stream of aerocraft continued to head westward from the port.

Itakh held the pigeon up in both hands, then flung her toward the sky. She wobbled as she climbed, then began flying in tight, fast circles overhead. Both boys looked up, delighted, and Jascha shouted, "*Geyn, toyb! Geyn!*" to encourage her. He was an awkward boy, hands and feet too long for the rest of his body. His interest in the bird lent him a sudden grace.

A puddle seeped from under the basket of clean laundry. In Esther's father's house, the laundress used a hand-cranked machine to do the wash and a mangle to help dry it. Still it took her all day. Though Rukhl would soon have to get back to work, she said, "What's the news? Has your father planned your wedding?"

Without looking at them, Itakh replied for her. "After Simkhat Torah."

"Shut up," Esther said. Jascha had taught Itakh some colorful swears in his native language, which was full of them, and Itakh had passed them on. She couldn't repeat them here.

"Why do you tell him this?" Rukhl asked. "How old are you?"

"Sixteen."

This might not have been the answer Rukhl expected. Her face softened as she drew in a breath, approving. "I too married at your age."

Esther had never bothered to wonder how old Rukhl was. She now took in the lines in her friend's face, the irritated skin of her hands. How old was Jascha? Eight or nine, which put Rukhl in her mid-twenties. She looked older. Esther and her sister prided themselves on their smooth, olive skin and the dark hair that had never been cut. She realized she wouldn't have had either of these had her life been as hard as Rukhl's.

"What are you thinking?" Rukhl asked.

Esther shook her head.

"The chief rabbi's son. Be happy."

"I am," she said, though she couldn't conform her face to the expression people liked to see on a happy bride.

"What flowers bloom at Sukkos?" Though she pronounced the word strangely, Esther understood. "I'll braid them in your pretty hair." Nothing flowered in the month of Tishri. Winter would blow across the steppe by then. Regardless of the expense, her father would import silk facsimiles of orange blossoms from Persia for her hair. If Khazaria's enemies had not breached their borders by then. If merchant ships still sailed free in international waters. She felt a sudden shame at her family's decadence and told none of this to her friend. Rukhl went on, "I'd like to help you prepare. A married woman's duty."

"I'd like that too." Esther would have liked to invite Rukhl to the wedding and the Seven Blessings. But Esther had had so little to do with choosing Shimon ben Kalonymos, she doubted she'd be allowed to choose her guests. *A suitable boy, from a good family*, her father had said, *and you like him, yes?* Yes, she did like him. Very much. She had known Shimon since childhood. He was smart and good-hearted. She would enjoy wearing her mother's scarlet-and-saffron wedding robe. What confused Esther was that today she was some unnamed thing between a girl and a woman, out riding a purloined mechanical horse. In a few months, she'd be Shimon's wife, living in his father's house, bearing his children. Someday, she'd be the *rebbetzin* of Atil. Esther had been raised to expect something like this, but the potential transformation mystified her. And no one had mentioned Itakh, who stood before her now giving exuberant hand signals to his bird. She didn't want to go to Kalonymos's house unless Itakh was part of the retinue. *Retinue*, she thought: a reminder that however dear Itakh was to her, he was her father's slave, having relinquished his nominal freedom at the jubilee.

However long her mind had wandered, Esther was drawn back to the present by an odd jerk in Seleme's head. The horse looked up, then began the rapid, ratcheting head motion mechanical horses made while closing in on a target. The ball joint in her neck ticked. She was tracking something in the sky. Esther looked up but saw only Itakh's pigeon circling, and behind it sparse clouds, like tufts of carded wool. Then the pigeon darted off to the east, toward Khazaran. Itakh shaded his eyes with his hand and peered westward.

"I've got it," he said. By now, a faint hum, as of a far-off swarm of locusts, approached from beyond the harvest plain.

The washerwomen ceased their work, and the girls minding the littlest children began sticking their heads out from their tents and huts. Esther couldn't make out what Itakh had seen.

"It's an aeroplane," he said, but kept scanning the sky. "It's—three of them, flying in a vee, like geese. More than three." Esther could now make them out, dark specks in the bright morning. "By Hashem and the Shekhinah," His Holy Consort, "it's a *flock* of them."

Their engines whined. Khazar aerocraft had lower-pitched voices. Esther said, "Not ours."

Itakh peered at them as they came closer. "The wings are strange."

Rukhl translated for the women, whose children gathered around, clinging to their mothers' skirts and legs. The aeroplanes grew louder by the moment as they multiplied in the western sky. There were more than twenty of them, flying in a phalanx, exactly like geese, except that geese didn't emit an ominous mechanical thrum. By now they were loud enough to have drawn men from their labors and the house of study, all the boys from their books in the *kheder*, their forelocks swinging while they ran. As the aeroplanes barreled toward the capital, their details sprang into view. Each was small, manned by a single airman. Unlike Khazar aerocraft, each had only one set of wings, low on the machine and pointing back toward the tail, like a swallow's. Esther couldn't imagine how they remained aloft. They looked to be sheathed in metal. On its side, each bore a foreign emblem: a bright white circle on a vermilion field, in its center a skewed Byzantine cross. In the moment, Esther couldn't place it, but all around her, people were shouting.

Itakh looked at her and said, "It's them. They're here," and at once she recognized the flag. The enemy. The kaganate whose leader's name no one spoke. Their symbol of rebirth. Were these aeroplanes bombers? If so, it was too late to hide.

As the aeroplanes came closer, they turned their noses toward the ground in unison, but leveled off again to keep from crashing into the houses of the court, up on the hill. Some of the refugees, meanwhile, had sprinted for cover, while others prayed in the eerie rocking motion they fell into when addressing Hashem. Some were shouting to one another to be heard over the roar of the engines, while others shouted and gestured at the aeroplanes. Esther recognized a few of the curses. Boys hurled rocks. Seleme, lusting for blood, reared on her hind legs, her sturdy forelegs kicking in the air, her bright green eyes—made from the same marbles children shot in the alleyways—scanning furiously. The aeroplanes were now so close Esther could smell their exhaust. Each had a sort of nipple in its nose—a machine gun—and some kind of bombing apparatus yoked to the undersides of the wings. She could see the pilots, their faces hidden behind goggles and leather helmets. Some held on to the steering yokes one-handed, the other hand holding the kind of box camera girls like Esther took on vacation. They were snapping pictures of the port and the refugee camp. She kept waiting for their armaments to fire, but nothing exploded, nothing dropped. If the refugees kept weapons in this camp, these would be knives or shotguns for hunting, powerless against an aerial assault. The carriers in the river had to have anti-aerocraft missiles trained on these targets—but the enemy aeroplanes would have to get closer for them to fire.

When the aeroplanes flew out over the waters of the Khazar Sea, they banked and turned and, in formation, headed back the way they'd come, a battery of fire chasing their tails. Esther braced herself for bombs to drop, but as the machines passed over the refugee camp, rustling the women's headscarves and the men's tzitzit in their stinking wake, they gained altitude. By the time they headed off toward the Pontus, they were high enough to resemble birds again. A moment later, a squadron of Khazar aeroplanes raced westward in pursuit. These wooden-bodied aerocraft had the distinctive double wings of all Khazar flying machines, and bore on their sides the kaganate's emblem, a blue, eight-branched menorah crossed on the diagonal by a golden sword. Scores of them flew past, perhaps all that remained aboard the aerocraft carriers she'd seen earlier. To Esther's eye, they appeared to move more slowly than the enemy aeroplanes, but handy as she was with Seleme, she was no expert on flying machines. The percussive patter of their guns began, the sound like that of mustard seeds popping in a skillet of hot oil. Far to the west, two enemy machines were hit at once. They whistled as if in amazement as, followed by their own twisting contrails, they plummeted. When they hit the ground, they rumbled like thunder. Within minutes, both nations' aerocraft were too far west to be seen or heard from the camp. The refugees' furor did not subside. They shouted, gesticulated, prayed, wept. One small girl lost her mother in the ruckus and now stood in the riverbank mud, wailing. Esther reached up around Seleme's warm steel neck and patted her on the withers, hushed her.

"Nagehan!" Itakh called out, but his pigeon didn't respond. He whistled his descending pigeon call. He looked this way and that in the sky while Jascha darted around groups of people to seek her on the ground. Esther could not distinguish the bird from any other white pigeon, but the boys could.

Rukhl's unruly hair had flown out from her kerchief all around her face. As she angrily shoved it back under, she said, "May his name be obliterated."

"Like Haman the Agagite," Esther said. This was the euphemism polite Khazar society used to refer to the enemy leader. That or Wicked Haman. People hissed when they heard either one.

Rukhl looked cross. "You have no idea what you speak of. You can't fend off a modern army with *graggers*." Esther must have given her a blank look, because she translated, "*ra'ashanim*. Things that make noise."

The dry stink of aeroplane exhaust still hung in the air. Rukhl was right. This wasn't a Purim play. "I know that."

"You don't." When Rukhl squinted, her whole face squinted. "My mother and father." Esther imagined grim fates before hearing the rest of the sentence. "First their part of the city, walled in. My father couldn't travel to his work, so they had nothing to eat. Then told to pack their bags to be taken to a labor camp. They sent us a cheerful letter. They looked forward to more plentiful food. But we did not hear from them again before we came here."

"I've heard about the work camps."

"There are none. They take people there to shoot them and bury them in shallow graves."

How many people? All of a city's residents? The shooter's hands and arms would ache from the gun's recoil. The grave would have to be—she looked out over the encampment and imagined it a broad, shallow pit.

Esther's father had a brother who had gone on a diplomatic mission to Praha and never returned. He'd found a wife there, not a Jewess, and her father had rent his clothing, declared him dead. All of this happened before Esther was born. But she wondered now if she could somehow contact him, ask him to corroborate Rukhl's tale. She wondered if he too had been taken someplace to be shot. If he could offer any help.

The sun shone high in the sky. Her father must by now have realized they were missing, and might have learned that Seleme was gone. To Rukhl, she said, "We have more to discuss." To Itakh, "We have to go."

"Not until we find Nagehan."

"We'll find her on the way."

Jascha kept looking for the bird while Esther grabbed onto Seleme's spiky steel mane to hoist herself into the saddle. Itakh then climbed up behind her. As Esther fitted her feet into the stirrups and gentled the idling horse into reverse, she leaned down and said to Rukhl, "I'll tell you what I learn."

"May the Lord bless and keep you."

Esther held the horse in second gear as they circled the camp. She couldn't hear Itakh's soft pigeon calls above the engine's strain. Once they'd completed their circuit, she said, "It's no use. The aeroplanes frightened her." When Itakh didn't respond, she called back to him, "She'll come back on her own. That's what she's trained to do."

Itakh let go of her with one hand long enough to gesture toward home. She wound through the gears, and soon they were galloping back toward Atil. Esther prided herself on being a good driver, better than many of the men at court. They thought horsemanship wasn't for girls, yet their own mounts lurched when they shifted. Even at this moment it crossed her mind what a joy it was to have a late-model horse and a knack for driving it. When a few last Khazar aeroplanes raced westward, a low, booming sound rolling over the ground in their wake, Esther once again felt the sense of violation the enemy and their cameras had engendered, felt the prickle in her scalp that meant all of their lives were in danger. Far to the west, someone—she hoped their own aero force—opened fire, the rapid trill of mechanized guns just audible. Itakh, gripping her waist, ducked by instinct at the sound.

The cool summer morning had become a hot, overcast day. Nervous sweat dried on Esther's skin. Refugees had poured in from the west for almost three years now. The camps on the Dniepra had overflowed, and thousands, tens of thousands, Rukhl and her family among them, had trekked east across the steppe to beg asylum in the capital. Others were mere sojourners, heading south through the perilous mountain passes to attempt the long journey to Palestine. To those who wished to stay, Kagan Eleazar and Bek Admon had given land to settle and till, basic materials to live, and meager food rations. Rukhl never wavered—hungry as her family was, this was better than what the enemy had in store for their kind. They would have liked to make their way to Tzion, but had already traveled more than a thousand *parasangs* on foot to reach this place, through the battle zone of Kyiv, past the fort of Sarkel, and through vast plains of mud as deep as a child's knees. *Dayenu*, Rukhl said, enough. Esther had thought that if the refugees' lives were bleak, at least they were safe on Khazar soil. The last she had heard, Khazaria held this enemy back to the far side of the Dniepra. Now, the dark kaganate—the enemy of Jews everywhere—had flown far eastward, made an incursion on sovereign Khazar territory. The KAF hadn't stopped them until they'd reached the capital. And only now did Esther understand that "work camp" didn't describe the fate her friend had escaped.

As they raced back toward Atil, Itakh kept calling and whistling to his bird. They were within the city walls when her form, difficult to pick out against the pale sky, rushed toward them. Itakh held out one hand and the bird alighted upon it, though Seleme hurtled forward in high gear. From the corner of her eye, Esther saw Itakh gather the bird in toward his body; she felt him alter his position to accommodate it, felt its wings brush her back as it settled.

When they reached Josephus's outer gate, Esther braked hard with her right hand and foot. Before she could shift into neutral, Seleme reared up to scratch at the wooden structure with her front hooves. Itakh grabbed for Esther's waist with his bird hand, and they both managed to stay mounted, though the pigeon flew free and circled overhead. Once they'd been admitted, Esther raced toward the mechanical stable, slid down from the idling Seleme, and hurried through the inner gate. Itakh, she assumed, would return the pigeon to its coop, and Bataar would notice the horse in the courtyard. She had to get to her father.

CHAPTER 2

Josephus's chamber was in chaos. Avigdor and Menakhem, the bek's javshigarim, his top military advisers, had come with everyone who worked for them. Josephus's own staff shouted into the big black telephone, clicked out a message on the telegraph, turned the radio dial—flashes of balalaika music, static—and rifled through the stack of Western newspapers that had arrived by post boat the day before. The room was so loud, Esther could hear no single voice. Her father, in his blue kaftan, paced with a sheaf of typed papers in one hand, the other to his gray head. The back of the rear paper was stippled with small holes where diacritics had punched through. When Josephus saw her standing breathless in the doorway, he strode over. His heavy black brows knit together: never a good sign.

"Esti," he said, putting one enormous hand on her shoulder in a way that half hugged her and half barred access to the room. "*Barukh Hashem*, you're accounted for."

"I went riding. I came back the moment they flew away."

"What were you—"

"I'm sorry."

"Have you seen Itakh? He's missing too."

"I think he's with his pigeons."

"I want to know where you went." His hand grew heavier on her shoulder. When she'd been younger, she'd both worried and been proud that her father could knock her flat. "And what you saw."

She hoped the second question would cancel the first. Her father must have known about her early-morning rides—she burned fuel, which cost money—but she did not think he knew she visited the

17

camp. Josephus had a charitable heart. He had taken in Itakh. But if she had believed he would approve of her actions in the camp, she would have told him about them long before.

"Quickly," he said.

"A squadron of their aerocraft, flying in formation over Atil. The pilots were taking pictures of our ports and buildings. Then they flew westward."

"Not a single bomb," he said, musing, not asking a question.

"No. I learned more about the enemy's camps."

Josephus looked around at his buzzing advisers. Now one was raising a racket on the typewriter as Menakhem shouted at him. "We may ask for details once things settle down. Praise Hashem you're safe. Go upstairs with your brother and sister. I don't want you roaming the streets." He patted her, propelled her out the door, as if he hadn't even heard her.

As she crossed toward the front stairs, she heard Kiraz, in the kitchen, berating Itakh. She saw him standing with his hand on his cheek. Without thinking, she barked, "Don't hit him."

"He's shirked his duties all morning. I found him with his birds. And now the sink is full of dishes and we've got all these people to feed."

To Itakh, Esther said, "I'm supposed to go upstairs." To Kiraz, one finger raised: "I said don't hit him."

"It's all right," he said, and sulked off toward the sink. Esther wondered if having been adopted by her parents had benefited him at all. He hadn't learned to read or write. Because his birth was unknown, he would be unable to enter any of the professions. He'd been raised to love the Name instead of some graven image. That was something. But anyone whose conscience demanded it could convert. Given the choice, she would prefer to be a free Tengri-worshipper than a Jewish slave, if Hashem wouldn't strike her down for thinking that.

Esther raced upstairs to the schoolroom in which she and Elisheva studied. There her sister sat with their brother, Shmuel. The tutor hadn't arrived. "Did you take the mechanical horse again?" Elisheva asked, her tone laced with disapproval. She was two years younger, but tended to uphold the law.

"I was in the refugee camp."

Elisheva opened her mouth to say something, then shut it again, as if to demonstrate her superior self-control.

"They buzzed the house!" Shmuel said. This was going to be his bar mitzvah year—aeroplanes, no matter to whom they belonged, were good. "They were this close." He held out his forefingers a hand's distance apart.

"Why aren't you listening?" she asked, pointing to the floor.

"You're the one who knows how to work it."

Esther, annoyed, walked over to the fireplace. Though she prided herself on being capable, she also disliked the way these two expected her to wait on them. She'd learned where the listening hole was by dismantling the house. Without her, her brother and sister would never have tried. The house, or this part, onto which all the others had agglomerated, had been standing for four hundred years. Any number of amateur mechanics had dwelled here, as all over Khazaria—it was a sort of national pastime—and made modifications to the structure. Their father's study had a wall sconce that, if pulled just so, flipped around a damask-covered panel to reveal a hiding place. There was a larger shelter in the cellar of Kiraz and Bataar's hut. And some devious-minded child (obviously not their father) who'd studied in this schoolroom in the last fifty years had rigged up an elaborate spying device. Concealed beneath four tiles in the face of the hearth was a push-button light switch. When one pressed its abalone top button, a panel in the floor slid aside to reveal an ancient brass ear trumpet, its wide end facing up toward the room, the narrow end invisibly embedded in the coffered ceiling of the room of state below. If Esther's father had known of the mechanism, he would have plugged it up. She locked the door and set to work disassembling the tiles, then pressed the button, which made a satisfying click.

The panel drew aside, revealing the trumpet, black with age. All three siblings gathered around it on the floor.

"—intolerable lapse," their father was saying. "Intolerable! We should have known exactly when they planned to strike."

"They haven't attacked yet," Avigdor said.

"We did know!" Menakhem shouted. "We knew ages ago! What did you think would happen when Polonia fell, when they pursued the campaign in Ukraina, when they massed troops on the Dniepra? They'd change their minds and turn back? We know what they want: territory to—"

Avigdor said, "Menakhem," his tone pleading. "We don't need a lecture."

Upstairs, Shmuel whispered, "They already have their own country."

Esther raised her hand to hush him, then whispered back, "If they also had ours, they'd have a bigger one."

Menakhem had continued talking. When Esther caught the thread of his conversation again, she stumbled over the word "*Lebensraum*," some term in the enemy kaganate's barbaric tongue. Esther lost track of his next sentence, trying to parse it.

"Ridiculous," Avigdor said with a low chuckle. He was calm; a good quality, Josephus often remarked, in a military officer. Esther too could often keep her head, and wondered, if she'd been born a boy, if she might have left her father's lineage of policy advisers and become a javshigar instead. Would his younger brother have done the same, if he'd remained a Khazar? "Any yeshiva boy knows how many tribes swept back and forth across this steppe."

"Then," Menakhem continued, "their desire to eradicate the Jews—"

"It doesn't matter why they're doing what they're doing." This was Josephus. "We should have crossed the Dniepra weeks ago. Driven them back."

"That's not your concern!" Menakhem said.

"We lack the manpower and firepower." This was still Avigdor in his measured voice. "And we have spies everywhere, everywhere, and didn't know they would attack so soon? Someone has failed in his duty." Esther wondered if Avigdor meant to implicate her father. Josephus kept the details of his work as the chief policy adviser private, but one of these men was in charge of the spies. Avigdor paused a moment before continuing. "The most powerful military in Europa. Did you see their aeroplanes just now?" Esther could describe them in detail. "They must have been traveling fifty knots more swiftly than our own. Tanks. Warships and submarines; more soldiers."

As Esther and Shmuel curled in closer to the ear trumpet, Elisheva stood and walked to the window. "I can't listen to this."

Esther said, "Shh."

"I can't. I know what he's going to say." Their tutor, with their father's consent, had taught them more about political topics than most Khazar girls knew: their land's bloody history, the oil wars, other nations' superior industrial production.

"Well, I want to hear it."

Up through the trumpet came Avigdor's voice: "—the length of the Dniepra, and from Petrogradye to Kyiv, down to Krimya. The whole Pontic-Khazar Steppe and through to Tsaritsyn."

"He can have the Menshevikim, as far as I'm concerned," Menakhem said.

Josephus said, "Foolish," as if to himself, while Avigdor replied, "He'll have to take us to get them."

"Let him try," Shmuel said.

Avigdor was right: If the enemy conquered the kaganate, they would round up the people of Atil, just as they'd done to Rukhl's parents in some far-off Poloni slum. The refugees in their unprotected camp—first to go. Esther took a deep breath and said to her brother, in a quiet voice, "We've held off marauding Huns and Alans with crossbows and scimitars. That's not what they're talking about."

Down below, through a momentary break in the conversation, the telegraph clicked out its syncopated rhythm, and someone was running the mimeo. Its crank and drum squeaked, and the dizzying, chemical smell of its violet ink rose through the trumpet. Josephus said, "Fourteen hundred years, wedged between the Ottomanim, the

Yishmaelites, Europa, the Rus, and ravening hordes to the north and east. We've shed our blood to make a Jewish homeland until Hashem fulfills His promise and returns us all to Eretz Yisrael. May His Name be praised."

Shmuel looked confused, his brown eyes big as plates.

"Now they're here," Menakhem said. "Thanks to a massive failure in intelligence."

"An advance party," Josephus said. So Menakhem was implicating him.

Shmuel said to Esther, "I still don't understand. They have their own country."

But they wanted the east, the great, fertile east. She held up her hand to him as their father went on: "Believe me, I'll do my best to woo our allies to help us. But it's your job to push them back from our borders with all due haste."

The telephone rang, and the mimeo stopped squeaking as an assistant ran to answer. Esther heard him saying numbers and yes, then hanging up the heavy receiver, which made the bell sound in the base. "The bek reports they've erected pontoon bridges at the Dniepra, and the Ninth Army, with four tank divisions, has begun to cross," the assistant announced. "Ground forces holding them back under heavy fire. At Kagan Eleazar's request, Bek Admon will see you all immediately to discuss the plan of action."

"The plan," Avigdor offered, "will be to push them back toward Ukraina."

"With twenty thousand mechanical horses—not a few of them belonging to private citizens—and two thousand small aerocraft?" This was Menakhem, growing shrill. "Our best hope is to fend them off until help arrives."

"Who's going to help us?" Esther asked. Shmuel and Elisheva looked startled, Elisheva's mouth pursed shut as if the question were an affront. "The Jewish pioneers in Palestine? Hashem?" She hadn't expected either of them to answer, but the way they shrank back made her anger rise, molten behind her breastbone. She sprang to her feet and pushed the black button by the fireplace. The panel slid shut so that all they could hear of the ongoing argument was muffled voices. Esther usually returned the tiles to their place, lest someone discover their secret, but as she strode toward the door she called to her brother and sister, "Put the hearth back together."

"Where are you going?" Elisheva asked. Shmuel added, "Why'd you close it? It was getting exciting."

She slammed the door behind her, relishing the loud reverberation in its antique frame. She wanted to hit someone, throw something. Instead, though her bare feet made little noise on the polished floors, she walked with purpose down the stairs and flung open the coffered door to her father's chamber.

The telegraph continued to tick, the radio's static to hiss. Menakhem, his face purple with vexation, stopped in the middle of yelling at her father to say, "Now what?"

"I told you to go upstairs," Josephus said, cool as butter.

"You're standing around arguing with each other when you need a plan," she said. She knew she was shouting but couldn't modulate her tone.

"How should you know what we do in my chambers?" If he had suspected the listening device, he would have stoppered it years before. "Go back to your schoolroom."

"First," she said, spittle flying from her lips, "you requisition all the mech horses in private ownership. All the moto-trucks too. Every last one. Bek Admon takes them to the front as the KAF flies westward. You should already have brought the navy up from the Pontus Euxinus into the Dniepra to fend them off; but if you—"

Josephus moved in front of her, blocking part of her view. "That's enough."

"If you bring the navy up into the river, you can encircle them, with land and aero forces arriving from the east."

"He can't control his own daughter," Menakhem said, not entirely beneath his breath, to Avigdor. "And he plans to wheedle help from the Turcii!"

"And you need the Uyghurs," she blurted. She and Elisheva had been studying the syndicate that controlled the Khazar oil fields. They were known to be dangerous, well armed, and fierce.

"What are you talking about?" Menakhem shouted toward the ceiling, as if the Great Name would come witness her ill behavior. "Get out of this room, I command you."

Though Josephus looked offended—Menakhem had just stepped upon his paternal prerogative, Esther guessed—he continued to bar her from the room.

She said, "No." And as they looked at her, angry and confused, a thought bubbled up in Esther's mind, a thought so embarrassing she would have admitted it to no one. An inner voice said, *I am Esther, and like my namesake before me, I will save the Jewish people.* The voice of reason at once tried to squelch it, and she blushed to her ears, afraid, despite logic, that her father and the javshigarim could hear her think. But there the thought remained, clear and quiet, her heart's truth.

"This is no place for you," her father said, firm but gentle. "Go back to your brother and sister."

"I want to fight," she said. "I want to go join the bek."

Josephus let a breath out through his mouth. Let him yell at her. Let him say outright that this was not something a girl or woman could do. Then she could argue. But he didn't say a word.

"Shmuel will be the next kender," she said, her face hot and her voice wobbling in the notch of her throat. "Avigdor, you have no sons," she said, though his youngest daughter was still an infant. Perhaps he would someday. "I can become a javshigar."

Menakhem snorted, but again, no one spoke. Their silence mocked her more loudly than words would have.

"All of this is more serious than you understand."

"Really?" Menakhem asked. She understood his tone.

"You don't even know what the refugees have escaped. You have no idea what kind of fate the Germanii have in mind for us."

Menakhem nodded. "But you do." Not even a question.

"I'll go back upstairs," she said.

24

Josephus lowered his chin toward her, half a nod. "And thank you for your help. It's useful to know what you saw."

She tried to read his expression. He'd barely given her time to talk earlier, let alone to describe in detail what she'd seen and heard. Was he brushing her off? His wrinkled forehead and tight lips could mean he was angry, tired, set to a purpose: all three.

"We don't have time for this," Menakhem shouted as the telegraph burst into a spray of sharp clicks, miniature artillery fire.

Her father no longer looked at her once he seemed confident she would leave.

CHAPTER 3

The tutor didn't come that day. Shmuel's yeshiva canceled classes. Josephus's three children rattled around the girls' schoolroom: After Esther's outburst, their father told the staff to keep them indoors. Soon after, all three advisers left, with their bevy of underlings, for the kagan's and bek's conjoined palaces. The buzz of aerocraft continued at intervals. The house felt uncomfortable and still. Servants continued to discuss in whispers what they'd overheard. None was Jewish but Itakh. Some families now plucked help from the ranks of the refugees, but Josephus was more old-fashioned, preferring nonbeliever slaves. When they'd found Itakh crying outside the compound's gate, the infant had been swaddled in coarse brown cloth and had a menorah drawn over his tiny heart in blue chalk, the Khazar name "Itakh" scrawled beneath it in semiliterate print. Esther's mother, Or'li bat Tuviya, had unwrapped the infant right away and found him freshly circumcised. *"Barukh habah,"* she'd welcomed him, hugging the naked creature to her shoulder. He resembled a plucked fowl, a duck ready for roasting. Esther had watched a stain of urine bloom down the crimson fabric of her mother's dress. She remembered being disgusted and intrigued that her mother didn't seem to mind. Itakh's dark hair and skin did not mark him as Jewish—Khazars came in all colors, and the baby could as easily have been Uyghur or Yishmaelite—but Or'li had trusted the mark on his chest and the mark of the Covenant. She had dunked him in the *mikvah*, then adopted him. Although he then legally became Itakh ben Josephus v'Or'li and a member of Avraham's tribe, his role in the household was that of a well-treated kitchen slave. At all events, servants had as much to fear as Jewish citizens if Atil came under attack. Bombs didn't discriminate.

Elisheva picked at the midday meal Afra brought them. She said her stomach hurt. This was how people were supposed to feel at times of tension, but Esther was hungry. She cleaned her own plate, then scooped up her sister's lentils with her bread. Both of her siblings had their dark eyes fixed on her, Shmuel admiring, Elisheva frowning in disgust. When Esther pushed Elisheva's empty plate from her and reached for the bowl of dates, her sister said, "What were you doing with that mech horse this morning? You're eating like a Tatar."

Esther hesitated a moment before she said, "I took some food to my friend in the camp. Don't tell Father."

"Stolen food," Elisheva corrected.

Shmuel shrugged. "He won't notice."

Elisheva said, "If Shimon ben Kalonymos finds out, he won't approve."

Esther tried to think of a response that wouldn't escalate the disagreement.

Elisheva raised her thick eyebrows.

"He'd do the same thing himself." She couldn't admit she sometimes saw him there.

Elisheva looked proud of herself for her tact.

"You're always worried about Shimon," Esther went on. Even when she knew not to engage with her sister, not to pick a fight, provocations flew out of her mouth before she could stop them.

Dark as her complexion was, Elisheva flushed. "I wish," she said, looking down, "you'd take your duty to him more seriously."

Esther wondered if Elisheva wanted to marry him. Shimon wouldn't want to. She and her sister were similar in form, but otherwise very different. "I do," Esther said.

Midafternoon, Shimon came to the house. Ordinarily, thanks to the laws of *negiah*, which governed conduct between the sexes, he spoke to Esther only in Josephus's company, unless they happened upon each other in the refugee camp, outside the bounds of Khazar society. But old Afra sent him straight up to the schoolroom, either because Shmuel was there or because, in the day's pandemonium, she'd lost track of her employer's rules. The boys clapped each other on the shoulders, though Shimon was a head taller. He bowed to Esther and said, "Are you all right? I heard you got caught out in it."

"I did. I was in the camp with Itakh. They went right over us." She should have tried to sound sobered by this, but couldn't mask her pride. "Where were you?"

"We might have met, had it been an ordinary day," he said. "I was on my way when they flew over." He looked down; he'd revealed a secret to her siblings. If they didn't notice, Esther had no plans to explain. Shimon said, "I hear they were bombers, but that they didn't open fire."

"They were gathering information, I guess." The aeroplanes looked so different from Khazar aerocraft, so much sleeker and more menacing, she wouldn't have known what they were if she hadn't seen the weapons.

"Still," he said. His knitted Bukhari *kippah* was askew over his dark hair, which had grown long enough to develop a wave. He had a bump on the bridge of his nose. Something about this, and the way his eyes were set deep in his narrow face, made him look slightly cross-eyed, often amused. If he hadn't been Kalonymos's son, this would have been counted a defect, which perversely made her like the look of him more. His beard was only now starting to grow in thicker than wisps and patches. When he stood or sat close to her, her heart quickened at his scent: sun-dried, ironed laundry and something darker and sweeter, his own smell. Could they have met that day, as they sometimes did, in the camp? Conversed there, unsupervised? Was it possible to stand close enough together to touch, or even kiss? She wanted to know how he felt, tasted. Esther knew little about the refugees' observance, but assumed they practiced *negiah* too, and would disapprove of such actions. Unless, like servants everywhere, they willed themselves not to see the transgressions of their masters. Or not to remark upon them within earshot.

She would have done anything to hide her attraction to him, the hot, giddy pleasure that overtook her when he came near. At one level, she understood this was ridiculous, as their wise fathers had chosen them for each other, and they themselves had approved the match. At another, some contrarian part of her wanted to deny everyone—her father, her family, the world at large—the joy of believing that she and Shimon were *bashert*.

"Our father's gone to the bek. Yours?" Shmuel asked.

Shimon nodded.

"I suppose all the fathers are there," Shmuel said.

Esther knew some people whose fathers weren't there. She knew Itakh, who had been born to someone who wasn't Josephus. She knew Rukhl and Jascha—and kept these facts to herself. She rang the bell for Kiraz to bring tea. Elisheva continued grimly to work an intricate Noakh's Ark puzzle at the low central table. Many of the bright, stylized animals still lacked something, a tail or paw or head.

Shmuel began to get excited. He paced his sisters' schoolroom with a toy mechanical horse in both hands. "You should have heard them downstairs."

Shimon glanced at Esther. "I can imagine. The most powerful army in Europa stands at our gates."

Shmuel kept galloping his toy horse, his shoulders lifting toward his ears. "Khazaria is the greatest nation," he said in his sweet soprano. "El Shaddai has given us His special favor. We guard His Holy Tabernacle until He returns us to the Promised Land. How can we be defeated?" He glanced hopefully at Shimon, as if the nationalist rhetoric he brought home from school might win the older boy.

"We're neither big nor advanced, as countries go."

"But the Great Name is the mightiest of the gods."

All this time, Elisheva had seemed to concentrate on her work, but now she pushed away the loose pieces and said, "You all sound so unconcerned. They're coming to kill us."

"They're coming to be crushed by our superior fighting skills," Shmuel corrected. "*Their* ancestors never rampaged across the open steppe."

"I think they did, actually," Esther said.

Shimon sat down across the table from Elisheva. "Your father will handle the diplomacy. The javshigarim will strategize our military response. For your part, you need to have faith in the Name."

"When has that ever helped?" Esther asked.

Shimon didn't take offense easily; this had to be part of why her father had picked him. Of course, he was also heir to the rabbinate. He smiled up at her, as if aware that his smile—lopsided and causing his left eye to crinkle as his cheek drew up—was one of the best things about him. She couldn't discomfit him as much as he did her. He always seemed composed. This was another reason to hide the way her body responded to him.

"Well, when He parted the Sea of Reeds. That was helpful. Lot was grateful for his safe—"

"Not his wife!" Esther interjected, but she too was smiling. Her face liked Shimon even when the rest of her grew tired of his references to Tanakh.

"Avraham, then. Yekhezkel and Yishaiah. They all saw the work of His mighty hand."

"What about the last few thousand years? The Temple destroyed. The Second Temple. Our exile from Eretz Yisrael. Expulsions from Britania and Iberia. The pogroms of our brethren in Rus. What the dark kaganate has done to those refugees. Explain that."

Shmuel said, "They close the yeshiva and it starts up at home."

Shimon's smile hadn't completely faded. "I guess I think you can be chosen without getting special privileges."

"You'll make a good rabbi," she said.

"*Barukh Hashem*, you'll make a good *rebbetzin*." This was a simple compliment, but she felt its blunt sexual force. A *rebbetzin* bore her husband as many children as possible. She felt a surge of desire for him. When she looked out the window to calm herself, he added, "I really do think that." He knew nothing. No doubt he had mastered his own body's wants.

"Will you fight?" Esther asked him.

She might have asked a question in a language he didn't speak. "I'm not required to." Her question unanswered, she didn't want to press the point. To Shmuel, Shimon said, "Don't glorify warfare. It's more gruesome than you think."

From the shelves lining the wall, Shmuel took down a game, one Esther had bought from a Mongol trader in Khazaran: a board with shiny, edible-looking tiles. "Do you want to play?" he asked Shimon, turning all the black sides up.

"You aren't listening."

Shmuel shrugged.

"I can't play. No one's supposed to be out. I should get home before my father returns from the bek's."

"He'll be there all night." Esther felt irritated at both of them—how could they speak of war and games when she was so enrapt in Shimon's physical nearness?—and angry at herself for her interest in Shimon when their fate hung in the balance. Angry at him, as well, for not wanting to ride out westward.

"Does your father ever see the kagan?" Shmuel asked.

"Only Bek Admon. You know that."

Shmuel began flipping tiles to white in a pattern. "But the kagan is a person. He never needs spiritual advice?"

"He can get that without showing his face. When he calls my father in, he remains hidden behind a wall. I'll never see him, even when I'm chief rabbi. I don't know. I too wonder about his life. It seems lonely." Lonely, and at the end of his forty-year term, he'd be put to death—drawn and quartered, perhaps by soldiers on mechanical horseback, now that Khazaria had this technology to aid with the grim tradition—and a new kagan chosen. Esther wondered if she could have that job instead of javshigar, then realized she wouldn't want it. As Shimon rose, he kissed his own fingertips and held them up toward Esther as if she were some kind of mezuzah. She wanted to grab his hand, lick his palm, stick his fingers in her mouth and suck them. A highborn girl was supposed to have no thoughts, no knowledge of such things, but Esther had done research. She raised her hand in farewell.

The hours ticked by on the Chinese clock—another meal, untouched by her worried sister, came and went, and still their father wasn't home. Everything worth knowing about was at the bek's palace, upon whose room of state Esther could not eavesdrop. Instead, she had Kiraz draw a deep, hot bath in the basalt tub, and Esther and Elisheva lounged in it until their skin turned pruney. They washed their long hair and pared their waterlogged nails, but Josephus didn't return. Looking forlorn, Elisheva went to bed. Esther couldn't sleep. She should have been frightened, but felt a weird excitement, as if she'd plugged her body into the electrical wiring of the house. Once Elisheva slept, Esther drew up her nightgown and touched herself in the way she'd learned from the small Indian book she'd found hidden behind others in her father's study. She was damp before she even began, and brought herself to a quick, panting climax. The moment the sweet feeling subsided and her breath returned to normal, she was wakeful and restless again. From her room, she could hear Kiraz and Afra washing up earthen plates in the sink. She wanted to talk to them, to anyone, but didn't know what she'd say if she went in. Instead, in her nightgown and sheepskin slippers and an old pullover her mother had long ago knit her father, her wet braid dripping down one shoulder and a whole side of her torso, she paced the dark hallways and waited for him to come home.

The servants had gone to their houses in the outer courtyard. Through the kitchen windows, Esther had seen their candles and lanterns go out, one by one. The main house had modern conveniences— electric lights, an oil-burning furnace, hot water flowing from the taps—but Afra and Kiraz still cooked on the hearth. Esther was sitting on the warm fender when he returned, after ten. He didn't seem surprised to see her there. Even in the peachy glow of the low flames, he looked exhausted, his beard unkempt, his lips and the skin around his brown eyes dry. He sat down beside her, looked glad for the fire's warmth.

"So we're at war," she said.

Josephus tipped his large head first to one side and then to the other, as if releasing water from his ears. "Our troops are being slaughtered at the Dniepra, but Bek Admon will move much of the navy up through Kerch to the Azovskoye Morye, and from there into the Donets and the Don, to try to hold them back there. We will muster all of our forces in our own defense. As you yourself suggested, those of our aero force and our mounted troops who have not done so already will depart for the west tomorrow, your beloved Seleme among them. At last she'll fulfill her intended purpose."

She squelched the impulse to protest his sending her favorite horse. "But will we be able to defend Atil?"

Josephus sighed and got up to look around on the counters. He found a bar of fresh halvah under a small glass dome. "Would you like some?"

Esther didn't answer.

Josephus cut a hefty chunk and gave it to her. "For centuries, we've fought to hold on to this land. I don't know if we have the strength now. You saw the aerocraft they were flying. So much more sophisticated than our own. We'll shoot one down to study it, but we're already too late. We can't—" As if he'd forgotten what they were talking about, he cut himself some halvah, chewed it, swallowed. "I don't see that there's anything we can do."

"Your brother—" she began.

"*Sha!*" he spat toward the fire. "I have no brother."

The candy was so sticky-sweet it hurt her teeth. Meanwhile her heart galloped. "But you do. In Praha."

He shook his head.

"Maybe he's dead to you, but if he's alive, can he help us?"

He looked around the kitchen as if around the stacks of the Great Library, as if the walls held answers. "I don't know."

"What's his name?"

"What *was* his name," Josephus corrected. "Before he became not a Khazar, not a person, not a Jew." She had stumbled into dark territory. "He renounced his citizenship and his faith, Esti. He's dead."

"What was his name?"

"Matityahu," he said, pursing his mouth around a no-longer-familiar word shape.

"Matityahu ben Malakhi." Esther made herself take a bite. When she finished it, she said, "You haven't contacted him."

"I am not a magician, to speak to the dead."

"So will they conquer us?"

"I pray not. But it's in the Holy One's hands."

"The Holy One doesn't have hands," Esther said. "It's the first thing they teach you."

He laid a heavy palm on her head. "I don't want you to worry about this. You have a great deal to look forward to right now."

She finished her sweet in silence.

After Esther had licked her fingers, Josephus said, "Go to bed now. Your sister will be worried."

"She doesn't even know I'm gone." She wiped her hand on her nightgown. "I want to fight."

"Hm." An exhalation, not a statement.

"I want to defend Khazaria." The idea of her nation, yes. The things it stood for. Her religion. But more than that: This city, this comfortable and disorganized old house. Its views of the port. This warm fender beside a nighttime hearth. "I want to be a javshigar when Avigdor and Menakhem are too old."

"That won't be called for. Right now, I have work to do."

He wasn't listening and wasn't going to. If she kept arguing, he might get angry, but she couldn't imagine him changing his mind. She kissed him good night and padded up the stairs to her room as he retired to his chamber. When she opened the door and saw Elisheva bundled in the covers, she kept going along the hallway and back down the kitchen staircase.

CHAPTER 4

As Itakh had been raised in the family's faith, though lacking the privileges of Josephus's blood children, he did not live in the servants' quarters in the courtyard but in a small, windowless room off the kitchen. It had once been a pantry, and all these years later, still smelled of star anise and cardamom. Though the room was no larger than Itakh's rug, mattress, and trunk, its long wall stretched along the back of the kitchen fireplace, so it stayed warm on cool summer nights. Esther opened Itakh's door without knocking and found him cross-legged on the rug. He was shooting dice by lamplight.

"Were you listening?" she asked.

He made a noncommittal shrug.

She sat down beside him and tucked her feet under her. "He doesn't even hear me when I say I want to fight. I hope they know what they're doing."

"Do you think they do?" He shook and shot his dice.

Josephus was a respected adviser, descendant of a long line of kenderim. Though his counsel didn't always accord with Esther's will, she thought him prudent. Now, however, she saw her father in a different light: an aging man, unable to raid a village in the dead of night, and perhaps, she thought, growing complacent. Itakh was only a child, but he was also her friend. She said to him, simply, "I don't know."

He held the dice cupped in his two hands. His dark eyes seemed all pupil.

"They intend to mount a strong defense. But Germania—" she tried out the name of the dark kaganate; her tongue caught on the harsh first syllable, "is so powerful."

"More powerful than Hashem?"

"'Above the thunder of the mighty waters, more majestic than the breakers of the sea is the Lord.'" What Itakh had said was awful. "Of course not."

"The Maccabees defeated Antiokhus, though they were outnumbered. David slew the giant Goliath."

"That's true." But no comfort. "If we have any chance, it's to charge across the steppe like vengeful ghosts. To arm ourselves with crossbows and poison arrows and sweep down upon them as we swept across this land a thousand years ago, leaving a sea of headless bodies bobbing in our wake. We know our terrain, after all; they'll find it as foreign as the moon." She paused. "We have to do it right now. Not wait to see what they do next. And we have to try to contact his brother. He might be dead, but if he's not he might be able to help us."

Itakh threw the dice again. She didn't understand the rules of his game—as far as she could tell, it was just rolling and picking up. "They won't listen to you."

"No. No one follows a girl's advice in a military crisis." She thought for a moment. "People listened to Yokhanna d'Arc, I guess."

"Who?"

How would he know? He didn't go to school. She didn't even know how he'd make a bar mitzvah, since no one had taught him to read. "A Frankish girl. She led their army against—someone. Later she was burned at the stake."

He nodded. "She doesn't make your odds sound promising."

"No." She snatched the dice to make him stop rattling them, but once she had them in her hands, she felt compelled to shake and throw them.

"Hey! Fives, that's pretty good," Itakh said, then gathered them up again.

"If I were a boy," she said, "they'd let me fight." Though the idea of doing so hadn't crossed Shimon's mind.

"Maybe not." His eyes flickered over her face and body. "You could cut off your hair and try to volunteer, but I don't think anyone would be fooled."

Esther pulled the damp braid over her shoulder and examined it. She had never considered cutting it; its length and color were a source of pride. "If I lop it off, I'll be a girl with short hair, an unmarriageable daughter. What I need is to be a boy."

"Why?"

Esther hadn't thought it through before saying it, and realized that to be male wasn't the thing she wanted. But the idea kept insisting upon itself. "Because no one will allow a girl into battle, and into battle is where I have to go."

He said, "I guess you should take it up with Hashem, then."

Esther leaned back against the wall. She could feel the heat of the hearth's embers. "Maybe."

He looked over at her. "I was kidding."

"But maybe it's a good idea." When she sprang up to pace, Itakh's room was too small to go anywhere. "I could find the kabbalists. If anyone can help me, it's them."

Itakh tugged on the hem of her nightgown to bring her back down to his level. The moment the idea had appeared to her, it had flared like a firework in her chest. No doubt Itakh could see that. "Esti, there's no such thing as kabbalists. They're like werewolves and *dybbukim* and all the other things that are supposed to live on the steppe."

She saw he was saying this as much to convince himself as to convince her. "*Volkelaken*, I agree with you," she said, using the fine word the refugees had brought with them from their superstitious home. "That's a *bubbemeitze*." Another of their words. She knew a fair bit of their dialect. "They make these things up to scare children. But Kabbalah is real—it's a body of texts. You can see them way up on the top shelves of Father's library. Kalonymos must know about it too."

He bent his knees to his chest and folded his arms over them. "But the stories can't be true. You hear they have *golemim* to do their bidding."

"Maybe they do," she said. "If they can breathe life into clay, why couldn't they make me a boy?" Whether she really wanted them to: that she couldn't answer. But she couldn't let the idea go.

Itakh turned over the dice in his hand.

It was already the nineteenth of Av. She and Shimon would be married after Simkhat Torah, in a little more than two months, after which such an action would be unthinkable. It was such a short time from now—yet by then, Khazaria might be a conquered territory of the dark kaganate. All of her people might have been rounded up and shot. "If I'm going to do this, I have to go now, before Father sends Seleme to the front. Will you come with me?"

"No." He watched her. "You're really going to go?"

She wasn't sure.

"Off into the steppe, in search of magicians who may not exist, to see if they can make you into a boy so you can fight." He listed the details as if wanting to be sure not to forget something important.

The idea did not, she admitted, sound sane. "I don't know. It's summertime. The steppe is passable. And they're mystics, not magicians. I'm sure they exist." Itakh's face began to flush, as it often did before he cried. "You don't want to come."

He looked away. "I do and I don't. I'm afraid to."

She felt the same. "I'll take care of you," she said, aware that she had no idea how to do that at home, let alone in the open country while the nation prepared for war.

"This is a good place to live. It would be hard to leave. Who knows how Father would view my desertion."

When visiting the refugee camp, Esther had considered the comforts she enjoyed. Because Itakh had been so tiny when he'd been found at the gate, he also had never known life outside this warm house, this place of running water and plentiful food. But being a foundling, she realized, must never have been far from his mind. She didn't take her fortunate birth for granted, yet she also never feared its privileges could be revoked. Itakh—a beloved slave; a slave nonetheless—must always have remembered what might have become of him, if not for the good grace of Or'li of blessed memory. "It will be hard to leave," she said. So hard she might not have the courage to do it. "But for my own part, if I don't at least try, I'll feel responsible if all of this is destroyed." As the words left her mouth, they sounded prideful; yet the Name did not send a plague to smite her or turn her into a pillar of salt. Also, she didn't feel prideful. She felt that something had to be done. Not certain that what she proposed was the exact thing. She imagined Rukhl's mother—Rukhl older, stooped, a rough brown kerchief binding her throat—as she faced a soldier with a gun. Plumes of breath exhaled from her mouth in the still mountain air. "And if our father blamed anyone for our desertion, it would be me."

As if someone had pushed him on the shoulder, Itakh toppled into her lap and nestled in. She stroked his hair, setting his needlepoint *kippah* askew. The lamplight cast their lump of a conjoined shadow on the far wall. Restless energy coursed through her body. She wanted to run through Atil's quiet streets, shout until her lungs gave out. But she sensed that her chance with Itakh was now—that if she left, he would not accompany her. She couldn't go alone. She had only enough courage to propel herself forward if someone came with her. So she did her best to settle, not to grow anxious sitting with him. After a time, Itakh's warmth and the quiet must have lulled her into a doze, because she startled awake when he said, "I'll come with you."

Her heart shuddered. Could she be sure he'd spoken, that she hadn't been dreaming? She leaned over and wrapped herself around him to hug him. "I'm so glad, Itakh." If he came with her, she could go. His hair stank of everything from the kitchen fire to pigeons to the mechanical stables. She wondered who oversaw the boy's bathing.

"When will we leave?"

She would have liked to wait a day or two, give herself the chance to think it over. But right then, everyone was asleep. In the morning Seleme would go to the front; and who knew how soon the enemy would arrive. "Before sunrise."

"I'm afraid," he said.

Esther couldn't advise him not to be. She was frightened too. She wondered if she could change her mind, or if it was too late for that. She stayed curled around him a moment longer to gather strength, then crept out to the kitchen. As she had suspected, it was still deep night. She went upstairs to gather supplies.

CHAPTER 5

As she stood in her own closet waiting for her eyes to adjust to the darkness, Esther pictured Atil's return to something like normal a few hours thence. Early in the morning, the sounds of livestock, the kitchen, and men praying in the synagogue down the street would rise into the air. The muezzins' melodic call to prayer would ring out from Khazaran's mosques across the river. The yeshiva would reopen, and Esther and Elisheva's tutor would arrive at the usual hour to pick up where they'd left off: Mishnah and Gemarah, followed by a lesson on the Uyghur mafia and the oil supply, their current secular topic. Until yesterday, Esther had loved her lessons and blessed her father for providing them. Few daughters received instruction in anything beyond household matters and ritual purity. Those who did might get religious teaching, but nothing like the study of Talmud their teacher allowed. Certainly not secular history and philosophy. Josephus had not encouraged Esther to learn to drive, but he hadn't stopped her either. When she'd hung around the mechanical stable long enough to begin tinkering, he'd turned a blind eye. Esther's father considered her a thinking person. She was lucky in this; lucky that Shimon did too. Which meant she should be grateful for these blessings and give this plan up now. Nevertheless, she waited until she could start to see.

Esther had seldom traveled. When her mother had been alive, they'd spent an annual summer holiday in the south, by the Khazar Sea. They had one time made the long westward journey overland to the Azovskoye Morye, the most beautiful sea in Khazar territory. Her father, who loved the fresh country air, sometimes picked up his walking stick and led his three children on a daylong ramble in the verdant pastureland north of the city. (The route he'd taken to get there in recent years avoided sight of the sprawling refugee camp, she'd noticed.) Beyond that, she'd been nowhere. People of many nations made their way through Atil, so she'd seen varying styles of dress and heard foreign languages and accents. She had seen photographs in the occasional magazine from the West. She liked to think of herself as cosmopolitan, and more mechanically inclined than other girls. She had little experience to tell her what she'd need on a journey. But she had common sense.

Esther took off her nightgown and dressed, adding layer after layer to fight the morning chill. She pulled a fur-lined winter burka over her clothes, and tied her fur overcoat at her waist. She put on two pairs of woolen socks, and hoped her feet would still fit inside her fleece-lined boots. She found many of the things they'd need for their journey inside her own closet: warm clothing, extra bedding. After she stuffed in her nightgown and a sweater, she folded up Elisheva's fur burka and stuck it in the bag. Sheva spent little time outdoors and wouldn't require it until winter, while Itakh might freeze on the nighttime steppe in his slave's woolen coat. Esther took soap, a hairbrush, and a toothbrush from the bathroom, then packed hair ribbons from the dressing table, though she couldn't see any of these things well enough to know if they were hers. She slung the bag across her body by its long strap and stood for a moment in the dark bedroom. Her eyes had adjusted enough to make out her sister's curved form under the blankets. Esther knelt down beside her, willing herself to see Elisheva's features, to know which way she was facing, but the room was too dark to tell.

Esther felt she should tell Elisheva to marry Shimon if she herself didn't return. That was the noble thing to do. Instead, she stayed quiet. Elisheva continued to breathe, unaware that anyone watched her.

"Anything could happen," Esther said. "Take care of Shmuely." Elisheva didn't stir, so Esther wobbled back up, feeling foolish, balancing the weight of the heavy canvas bag against her back.

In the kitchen, Itakh stuffed a bag with provisions: dried beans and rice, nuts and preserved fruit. When he stole for Rukhl and her family, he took what was unlikely to be missed. This bag, he crammed with the family's stores. He filled a water skin at the tap and twisted shut its closure.

"Are you packed?" she whispered.

He inclined his head toward his rucksack on the floor.

"What else?"

"Everything we'll need for the horse."

"All in the stables. Tools to fix her if she breaks down. A feed bucket." Taking the horse would also constitute theft—a large theft. But they had no choice: By the time she and Itakh could cross the steppe on foot, Khazaria would be an occupied territory. "Something for shelter."

"Money," Itakh said.

He was right, though stealing money seemed more concrete, more obviously wrong than pilfering food. She took an electric torch from the storeroom, left him busy in the kitchen, and cast a dim beam through the dark ground floor until she reached her father's study.

Esther revered her father, and rarely entered his quarters uninvited. Doing so while planning a theft felt as wrong as it would have to march out from behind the *mekhitzah* at synagogue, stomp onto the bimah, open the Ark of the Covenant, and start poking around in the Holy Scrolls. But she had to do this. She realized that, if her quest succeeded, she wouldn't have to sit behind the *mekhitzah* again. The idea made her queasy, then giddy, then queasy again.

The wall map of the Khazar Empire behind his desk was too big and unwieldy to steal. She shone her torch beam over it, and saw the kaganate's western border, the whole Krimyan peninsula, the Pontus, and the Khazar Sea, crowded with constellations of colored pushpins: enemy troops and Khazaria's own forces. She pored over the area north of Atil along the meandering, westward path of the river, but did not see the kabbalists' fabled village of Yetzirah.

Could the kabbalists help her, if they did exist? She believed they could—they could make men from clay. Did she want them to help her? That was a thorny question. She pictured herself a young man like Shimon, mounted on Seleme and leading a regiment to attack, but she could not imagine daily life as a man thereafter. She wouldn't be able to marry Shimon; she'd regret that. Would she be able to marry anyone at all? That would depend on her being taken back into society, and that depended on Atil and its way of life surviving. If it turned out that the end was near, that the future was in fact not going to happen, then Esther had nothing to worry about either way. This was no comfort. And when she tried to imagine what it would be like to marry a woman, she came up blank. She had no desire for women. All her life, she'd been a girl, and thought no more about it than she did about drinking water to slake her thirst. She'd never questioned her state—no one would, since there was nothing a person could do to change it. The possibility that she could unsettled her. She dreaded it as much as her heart quickened at the prospect.

In the torchlight's yellow glow, she tried to memorize the shape of the Atil and its fertile delta, the location of Uyghur oil strongholds and other landmarks they'd pass along the way, the relative positions of the country's mountain ranges and the locations of its other waterways, so she could stand some chance of knowing their position as they traveled.

She shone the torch over the spines of her father's books. Their titles, some inscribed in gold, leaped out at her. There would be no time to read on this journey. She let the beam linger over his foreign language dictionaries, behind which nestled the Indian book. She would have liked to take it—its bright, stylized illustrations as beautiful as they were disturbing—but did not think she could stand the embarrassment of being found out in the theft.

She lay the torch down, its beam pointing toward her, and began opening the heavy drawers of her father's desk. Each stuck in the humid weather, sighed, and groaned. From one, she took his compass and a small utility knife. From another, two nubs of pencil and a handful of paper scraps, which she shoved into her coat pocket. From a third, a thousand dinars in paper money and coins—more than she'd ever held in her hands before, but not enough to hurt the household's finances. Then she hesitated. In the dim recesses of the bottom drawer, she knew he kept, in a folded leather pouch, a set of small, silver implements for making Shabbat while traveling: two cunning candle holders that fit together like a puzzle; small tapers to fit them; a matchbox, a salt shaker, a collapsible kiddush cup. Her mother had given this to him for long-ago diplomatic missions. Esther knew he cherished it. Before closing the drawer again, she wrote a note on a scrap of paper. *I swear by all that's holy I will return these things to you. May Hashem and His Holy Consort, the Shekhinah, bless you and keep you.*

Back in the kitchen, she placed what she'd stolen into her bag along with the electric torch, and forced one fur- and fabric-thickened arm and shoulder through the bag's webbed strap. She crammed her double-socked feet into her boots, tucked the knife down the shaft of the right one, and gathered up the bulky store of provisions in her arms. They walked out into the cold night, which would soon become morning. Esther realized with a start that she'd never said the evening *Sh'ma,* the prayer upon going to bed, because she'd never gone to sleep. Thank Hashem the Mishnah had workarounds to safeguard Jews from the perils of non-prayerfulness. She could still say it because it wasn't yet day. She recited the prayer under her breath. Then, lest she forget to say the morning *Sh'ma* when they were out on their adventure, she said that too. The rabbis knew that people sometimes stayed up all night. She was glad they'd made provision for such circumstances. If they hadn't, the world would feel like a place from which the Lord had removed His mighty hand, someplace in which anything could happen. Was this what it felt like not to be a Jew?

Wondering made her remember her father's brother. She knew little about him—his name, his renunciations, the place he'd gone— yet in all the great West, he seemed the only person she could ask for help. It was too late to go back into the house and try to learn to work the telephone.

The sky had lightened just enough for them to make out the

ground in front of them, but the features of Josephus's yard would have been inscrutable had they not known them by heart.

She put a hand on Itakh's arm to stop him, and whispered, "Could your pigeon fly a message to Praha?"

"Where is that?"

She could barely imagine such a distance. "In Bohemya, in Europa. A thousand *parasangs* to the west."

He thought a moment. "A bird can fly that far, but she'd never be able to find it. If I took her to Praha, she could make her way home." When she continued to stand still, he said, "What are you thinking?"

"Could there be a bird from there in Father's loft?"

She heard rather than saw him shrug, heard the creaking of straps on his shoulders. "Birds have been brought here and left by a few foreign diplomats. We care for them until Father needs to send them home with a message." But her uncle had defected. She couldn't think when he would have brought a bird.

The servants hadn't yet awakened in their cozy roundhouses; their fires were dark. Even the neighborhood roosters slept—even the confused one, who crowed at any hour of the day or night, was silent. Yet the sun would not wait as it had for Yehoshua. "Let's see."

They shed their bags in the outer courtyard. Esther took out the electric torch, and they ran to the dovecote.

It stank of ammonia and feathers, and the birds clamored at their entrance, shied from the bright beam of the torch. "How do you tell them apart?" she asked in a panic.

"Tags. On their legs." He picked up a bird and showed her. "But I can't read."

She handed him the torch and grabbed for a bird. It struggled against her as she scrabbled for the tag and read it: her father's. The next one said something in Rus. Again and again this happened. She had checked dozens of birds, and perhaps the same one a few times over, before she began to panic. Every minute they delayed might lead to discovery. "Holy Shekhinah," she said under her breath as she checked another and another.

At last one revealed a name in a foreign *aleph bet*, transliterated into Khazar below: "Lyubomir," she sounded out. Beneath it, the characters *mem bet mem*. "That's him," she said, gripping the bird's legs as it tried to fly free. "That's him, that's him!" Matityahu ben Malakhi. Maybe he and her father had both trained to use pigeons, since both were destined for diplomacy. She had no idea how he'd gotten the bird here, but its moment had come. "Hold it," she said. As Itakh took the bird, he dropped the torch. "Hold the light steady!" As he righted it, the now-calm pigeon in his other hand, she took out a scrap and a pencil stub and squatted to rest the paper on her thigh. In her smallest writing, she told her uncle who she was, what she planned to do, and the dangers Khazaria faced. She begged him for information and help. Then she rolled the note up into a tiny tube and grabbed the pigeon from Itakh. At once it began to fight again. It defecated on her. She could barely get the message in its case and screw on the cap. Dropping the pencil back in her pocket, she ran outside, clutching the bird in her two hands as she had seen Itakh do, its heartbeat plosive in her palms. "*Geyn, toyb*," she whispered to it, then flung it up in the air. It was gone from sight almost at once. She had no way to guess when or how it would reach Praha.

The next moment Itakh ran out of the dovecote with the torch and a sack of meal in one hand. In his other, he held a small rectangular box by its handle.

"What is that?" she whispered. She bent down to wipe the bird's excrement in the dirt.

"Nagehan. In a field loft. It's how I taught her to home. She can sometimes even find it again if I'm not too far away from here when I set her loose."

"Bring the bags into the stable."

They gathered everything up. When they opened the stable's heavy doors, the creak sounded loud enough to wake the whole compound, but no one responded. Itakh kept shining the torch so she could see. Like natural horses, mechanical horses in repose either stood or curled up in beds of hay. She half expected them to awaken, their blue and green eyes locked, unblinking, on the intruders. But they were still as death. Though her mouth felt dry, Esther clicked her tongue soothingly at them, and patted Seleme's withers before hitching bags to the loops on the back of the saddle. She tied Nagehan on last, careful that no other encumbrance hit her fragile home.

She started up the engine—easier when the horse was curled on the floor—and sat the saddle firmly as she maneuvered the machine to a standing position. Seleme shook hay from her legs, emitting the mechanical equivalent of a burr.

Esther kept clicking her tongue. She had ridden natural horses for years before being permitted to ride this mechanical one, and found, against reason, that the tricks that placated one worked for the other. "How are you fixed for fuel? Do you want to eat before we go?" Not that the machine could answer.

"I'd like to eat," Itakh said.

"Shh." She slid down, took Seleme's feeding bucket to the spigot on the wall, and let out a heady rush of petroleum. She managed to turn off the tap before it ran over. When she hung the bucket over Seleme's muzzle, the horse's eyes flickered in what almost looked like gratitude as she began to drink in her fuel. Esther went to the storage shelves to grope for what she should take with them: a wrapped kit of socket wrenches, an adjustable wrench, a screwdriver, a pair of pliers, a coil of hempen rope, a bar of beeswax and a tacky chamois cloth, a mildewed and petrol-stinking tarpaulin, a small oil can for sticky joints. They'd pack the fuel bucket once the horse was full. She climbed the ladder to the loft, where she found the family's tents, derelict and cobwebby. She sneezed as she shook the accumulated dust from a folded canvas, a bundle of supports and stakes. With the unwieldy burden in one arm, she made her way back down the ladder.

Itakh said, "How will we fuel her on the journey?"

Esther had no idea. "There are other mechanical horses in this country. There must be ways."

She couldn't see Itakh's expression, but worried he might regret his choice to accompany her. When Seleme had finished eating, Esther stuffed equipment into the bags, tied the bucket to one of the panniers and the tent poles across both of them, and mounted. Itakh closed the stable doors behind them, then climbed onto the horse's back. The sky was still dark, changing to deep blue over Khazaran, to the east. Esther gentled the machine forward. As they passed the barn, a goat bleated within. Morning was coming.

The guard at the compound's gate darted his electric torch over the horse. He let it linger at their tied-on bundles. "Took more than usual," he said, not looking Esther in the eye.

She reached inside the neck of her burka for the pouch that hung from a leather thong, and drew out a hundred dinars in paper money. She held it toward him. The guard turned off his torch and continued to look at the ground. "I know you'd risk your livelihood if you said you hadn't seen us go," she said. "But I wonder if you could tell them you didn't see where we went?"

He peered around the quiet courtyard. No one seemed to be stirring. "That's your father's money, I'll wager." He stood still, nodding, and blew out a stream of cold breath. Then he took the money and tucked it into his boot.

She didn't know if she had given him a week's wages or a month's. "Thank you."

He continued to lean down, as if inspecting the boot or something on the ground. Esther first wondered if she should wait for him to stand, then realized he was affording her a literal opportunity to leave without being seen.

"*Todah rabah*," she said quietly as they passed. "*Sağol.*"

"*Estağfurullah.*" It's nothing.

Her heart beat faster as Seleme trotted down the familiar road to the refugee camp. The feeding bucket made a dull clang as it bounced against the horse's hindquarters.

Though no one was out yet in the camp, smoke rose from the chimneys of more permanent dwellings. Time was short. Esther could already hear aeroplanes starting up from their berth in the river and heading to the front. She slowed Seleme, but the engine revved more loudly in low gear. Rukhl must have heard the machine's approach. She stuck her head out the flap that served her tent as a door. Though she was wrapped in a threadbare housecoat, her red hair was already covered. Esther wondered if she slept that way.

"What are you doing?" Rukhl whispered, and hurried to shut the flap behind her. She glanced from the laden horse to the neighbors' tents.

Esther turned and looked at Itakh, perched up on the cantle. He didn't say anything. What could she reply? She'd never talked about anything like mysticism with Rukhl. She suspected her friend would disapprove. Of her notion to turn herself into a man, she knew to say nothing. One word of dissent from a trusted person and she would turn back. "We're going off to fight."

Rukhl spat twice on the ground. Then she refolded her robe around her and cinched the belt.

"Khazaria's warriors were once the fiercest in the Kavkas. The Rus and the Ottomanim trembled at our approach. I want to be one of them."

Rukhl reached up to stroke the withers of the restless horse. Like a real horse, Seleme quieted at the touch. "A wife can't—"

"I'm not a wife yet."

Rukhl looked at her for a long moment. Her little daughter crawled out, sat upright, and regarded the giant beast in her dooryard. Jascha, who must have been in charge of her, followed her out. The sky over the Yishmaelite city now glowed purple; the pink of dawn could not be far behind. When the aeroplanes took off, they all flew westward. Esther backed the horse away from the baby.

"You have a lot packed onto that horse," Jascha remarked.

Itakh said, "We're going to fight the war."

His face lit up. "Let me come."

"*Neyn. Vas meynst du?*" Rukhl said. Esther caught her meaning from her dismissive tone. The baby grabbed at her mama's hem.

"I'll send word if I can," Itakh said, gesturing with his chin toward the pigeon.

"She won't home to me here."

"She'll home to our father's house, and maybe back again to my field loft. All you'd have to do is get in. Can you read Khazar?"

"Is it written in the *aleph bet*?"

Itakh looked to Esther, who nodded.

"I can try, then."

"We'll write to you," Esther said.

Esther saw Jascha's close-lipped smile with perfect clarity. Day would soon dawn.

"One thing more." Rukhl reached behind her neck and pulled a dirty leather thong over her head. Esther had often seen it, but since its pendant fell inside Rukhl's modest dress, had never known what it was. She now saw it was a silver *hamsa*, black with age and long, hard travel but done in delicate filigree work, the thumb and pinkie finger protruding identically from the hand. She kissed it and gestured for Esther to lean down from the horse. When Esther did so, Rukhl hung it around Esther's neck. "To keep off the evil eye." With the offhand manner of one who dressed children, Rukhl pulled out the neckline of Esther's burka, tucked the talisman inside, and patted her over the breastbone for safekeeping. The *hamsa* still held the heat of Rukhl's body. Her expression remained fierce. "It was my mother's. Don't lose it."

As Esther sat upright, she reached and felt the small bulge it made under the notch of her collarbone. "I'll bring it back." More fires were burning; the sky grew increasingly pink. With a soggy knot of gratitude in her throat, she asked, "Should I pay you for it?"

"Pish," Rukhl said, though her expression said something harsher. "Friends don't pay to borrow things." Esther heard doubt in Rukhl's voice: that they were friends, or that the talisman could be spared, or that she would return. Rukhl gave Esther's leg a tentative pat as if to seal the contract. Esther knew that had a refugee touched Elisheva, her sister would have taken a bath. "May the Holy One bless you and keep you." This was what people said, not a particular benediction.

Esther took a long look at her friend's round face, her weathered skin. From astride the horse, she could smell her scent of fire and cooking grease. Esther tried to fill her eyes, ears, and nose with her—to see how thoroughly she could take her in. "Thank you," she said. "*Shalom aleikhem.*"

Esther looked over her shoulder to back up the horse. Seleme resembled a pack nag. At the edge of the vast camp, Esther turned and looked back to see Rukhl outside her tent, her arms folded as she watched the horse recede. Jascha had taken off his cap, and waved it in the air in farewell. She could see, even from this distance, that he was wearing a small black *kippah* underneath it. How many men, Esther wondered, had looked over their shoulders, as they left for battle, and seen the people they loved standing thus? Esther was one of thousands, or millions, though different in key regards.

Seleme trotted north through the vast refugee camp, and had soon carried them out of the district of Atil.

CHAPTER 6

A ll that day, Esther and Itakh rode at an open gallop. If Josephus came searching for them, he would make haste, so they couldn't afford to rest. They ate bread Itakh tore from a loaf he could reach in the panniers. They drank nothing because they'd foolishly packed the water skin in an inaccessible position. He gathered a few crumbs in his palm and reached back to force them through the grating of the mobile loft for the pigeon. As the sun rose in the sky, their traveling clothes grew too hot, and they took turns wriggling out of their fur garments, then draping them over their laps, the only place to stow them. When Esther touched her cheeks, she could feel they were sun-burned. They stopped at one point to relieve themselves, then hurried on. A steady stream of KAF aeroplanes flew toward the battle. When the Atil was visible, they saw warships traveling upriver, no doubt toward Tsaritsyn, which must also have been a target. Esther often checked over her shoulder to see who might be behind them, and saw only Itakh's anxious face, bobbing with Seleme's hard motion. "This isn't very comfortable," he said in the afternoon, breaking what seemed hours of silence.

"We'll get used to it." She was so focused on moving forward, she didn't know if she was comfortable or not.

"I mean riding up on the back of the saddle. It makes my bottom ache."

Should they have taken two horses? The thought hadn't occurred to her. "I'll switch with you when we stop somewhere."

"I don't know how to drive."

"*Barukh Hashem*, you can learn."

They traveled a distance off the Main North Road, the grass of the plains green as unripe limes and higher than Seleme's knees. The fertile delta of the Atil stretched for miles northwest of the city, and Esther and Itakh rode through vineyards, orchards of fig and gnarled olive trees, and farms cultivating grains and vegetables—wild and voluptuous, some awaiting harvest while others, facing north, had yet to ripen. Vast fields of sunflowers turned toward the sun. The air smelled wet and fresh from dirt. People weeded, watered, plucked, carted manure. Esther did her best not to attract attention; she kept the horse in a steady, third-gear trot, not her fourth-gear, all-out gallop. She said a quick hello in Khazar, Hebrew, or Turc if someone in his field made eye contact, but continued driving. The ground here was open and level to the horizon—a peaceful, beautiful vista, perfect other than for the steady, westward migration of the Khazar Aero Force and the exhaust of a stolen war machine. If anyone came in pursuit, whoever they'd passed would remember them, even with all the racket overhead.

Esther did not feel safe stopping for the night, but when she saw a copse of trees ahead, lindens and pines, decided to find a spot to rest under cover. Once beneath the first trees, she saw they had entered a forest—perhaps the one she'd seen on the map dividing the city's ring of fertile farmland from the pastureland farther north. Esther downshifted, letting Seleme slow and accustom herself to the new terrain underfoot. Instantly, the world quieted.

"Now?" Itakh asked.

"A little farther." She was so hungry, her hands shook on Seleme's handlebars.

When it seemed safe, they turned off the horse, jumped down, and descended like beasts upon the packs. Esther's hands had swollen from gripping the controls on the long ride. They trembled so hard she could barely loosen the knots. She dug out the water skin and drank until she felt sick; Itakh bit into a squashed loaf of bread without blessing it. "Akh," he said, and lay down on the forest floor, holding the bread on top of him. "It's so good." He said a desultory *Motzi* for it after the fact, and his pigeon paced back and forth in her cage, which rocked from side to side with her motion. Her coo sounded agitated.

"Share."

He sat up enough to gulp water, spilling the excess down his chin; she ripped the loaf in half and inhaled it along with the balsamy scent of pine needles. For three years, Esther, a legal adult, had fasted on Yom Kippur, but that hunger was different: spiritual in nature, for a purpose. And on the Day of Atonement, all one did was pray and rest. Today, they'd ridden like Mongol warriors since dawn. Her back hurt, her legs thrummed, the webbing between her thumbs and forefingers ached from gripping the handlebars, working the throttle, and shifting. Her body needed food. As soon as her hunger began to abate, she wondered if Seleme felt the same way—assuming that Seleme could be said to feel anything. There she stood, her engine ticking, still stinking of exhaust. They had no fuel for her, and Esther knew they couldn't find any before nightfall. She wondered how one even got fuel if not from her father's tank. She'd learn soon enough. Her tutor had taught them all about the Uyghur oil lords' business and scare tactics. Someone around here had to have purchased what they drilled and refined. "Have you had enough?" she asked, as much to quiet her thoughts as to learn anything.

"I guess so." His mouth was full. "I need to pish before we go on, and remember, you're going to ride in back."

"You can't learn in the dark."

"I can't sit on the cantle another minute."

A wave of exhaustion swept over her. "We should go back," she said before she'd thought it.

"What do you mean?"

She shook her head. The idea of continuing to drive exhausted her. And now that they were still, she questioned their mission. She didn't even want to become a man; more like she had a project to finish. "What am I doing?" she asked out loud. "This will never work. I don't want it to work. We have to go back."

Sometimes she forgot Itakh was a child, but at that moment, his expression was veiled, confused, as if he thought she might strike him. "But we can't. We'll be in trouble." He watched her, alert to her cues. "If we give up now, we will have done all this for nothing. At least if we keep going we'll have a chance."

She felt herself frowning at him. He was right. And a chance didn't mean they'd even find the kabbalists. Getting them to do what she asked was another thing. So it made sense to press on. There was no guarantee the kabbalists could work the transformation, and it was better to try than to go home now with all these stolen goods.

Esther stood and began to shorten the stirrups for him. She punched each peg from its slot and reinserted it into a higher one. Itakh went a distance off before relieving himself. She took her turn next—not easy under all her clothing. She'd removed her coat and burka earlier in the day, and even so had to pull down, hold up, and draw aside layers. When she returned, Itakh had torn a filament about as long as his own body free from the rope they'd packed. With it, he slip hitched the pigeon to his arm. He and his creature were already mounted, and she climbed up behind him. The ridge of the cantle dug into her tailbone. "Can you make any more room?" she asked.

He inched forward. Because he was so small, she could slide partway down into the saddle behind him. She tried to get comfortable.

"See?"

She lifted herself up and placed his wadded coat between the saddle and her tail. This cushioned her, but made her seat precarious atop the horse. And as soon as the sun set, he'd want the coat back.

"Do you know how to turn it on?"

Itakh worked his right boot out of the stirrup and jumped on the starter. Nothing happened.

"Roll the throttle forward, toward the horse's nose." In case he didn't know which control was which, she reached around him to tap the right handlebar.

When he leaned forward to follow her instructions, he seemed like he might topple off the horse. The engine still didn't turn over. Esther reached around to the left of him and opened up the choke on the horse's neck, as Bataar had done for her. When next Itakh stepped on the starter, the engine caught and rumbled.

"Hey!" Itakh shouted, fishing for the stirrup with his foot.

"Squeeze that lever to engage the clutch and rotate the shifter one click back toward you." Itakh did this with his left hand. "Now give her some fuel." The engine raced and the machine lurched into a walk. "For second gear, you squeeze the lever again and rotate two clicks away from you. Raise the throttle at the same time." Seleme stuttered and nearly bucked them off, but righted herself into a slow trot. "Holy Shekhinah, you're a terrible driver." Seleme, she thought, cast a peevish glance at them over her shoulder.

"I'm learning. Where's third?"

"One click forward from where you are."

As soon as Seleme's gait felt steady, he upshifted without mishap. "I'm getting the hang of it already."

"Third's easy," Esther said. This was true, but she also felt grumpy on the back of the horse. "Don't forget to steer."

Before long, they had come out the far side of the forest, and the sun was nearly set. "Should we go back in to pitch our tent?" Itakh asked.

"We can't afford to stop. Keep driving." Esther gritted her teeth. Each time Itakh shifted or braked, she tried not to vomit up the lump of bread she'd wolfed down. But once the blue hour had passed, she didn't trust him to guide the horse across unfamiliar, uneven terrain, his pigeon flying above him and yanking on its tether. He stalled Seleme in bringing her to a stop, then swung around Esther without dismounting to ride pillion again. As she slid forward into the more comfortable seat, relief flooded her aching body. They took advantage of the stalled horse to bundle once more into their warm clothes.

Esther worried Seleme might step in a hole, so she kept her trotting along in second gear all night. Itakh's weight pressed into her back as he slipped into sleep. His pigeon crawled up the loose sleeve of his burka, cooed, and settled down. Though Esther herself tried to remain alert, she startled awake at several points during the night, worried as much about their mission as about their present safety. How she had managed to keep pressure on the throttle while unconscious, she didn't know. She supposed she might have slept for the briefest moment. Seleme's night eyes cast a small patch of green light before them, beyond which the world seemed even darker.

When, in the early morning, they reached a stream, they stopped to drink, eat, and stretch. They walked a short distance apart to relieve themselves, and soon started off again, the pigeon enjoying the limited freedom of her tether.

That second day, they steered clear of inhabited property and raced across the open steppe as their ancestors had done. Late in the morning, however, with Itakh once again practicing driving, Esther found that although she couldn't remember crossing any kind of demarcation, they'd ended up in someone's field. A few dozen dirty, longhaired sheep cropped the grass. They let out panicked bleats when the mechanical horse approached. Before long their reptilian eyes regained their customary unconcern, and the sheep went back to their meal. In the meanwhile, Itakh's bird, startled by their sudden noise, warbled a complaint and began to strain her tether. She pulled herself free of Itakh's wrist and circled, close and wobbling, above them. The string dangled behind her. Smoke rose from the chimney of a round, mud-daubed house a distance toward the river.

Itakh braked Seleme with his right hand and foot and she shuddered to a stop, stalling and nearly pitching both of them over the pommel. "I told you, put her in neutral before she stops!" Esther shouted. Almost as an afterthought, she swatted the back of his head. Then, feeling guilty yet unable to apologize, she reached around him to grab the throttle and jumped on the starter.

Itakh ducked away from her. "I can't remember everything. Nagehan!" The bird continued its erratic flight. He whistled a descending tone. The bird didn't seem to hear.

Seleme chugged along in neutral, surrounding them with a fog of exhaust. The sheep ignored them. Esther wanted to try to drive the horse from her awkward, rear-of-the-saddle position, but saw someone—he must have been the shepherd—aim a shotgun into the air. She felt relieved he wasn't aiming at them. Itakh better understood the situation and called out, "Don't shoot! Don't shoot! She's a pet." The man took the gun down from his shoulder, looked at them crossly, and began striding over the pasture, his gun held in one hand as if it were a scepter. Though he wore a fitted cap and a beard like a Jew's, his straight black hair and broad face appeared Mongol. As he approached, he chewed on something that popped his jaw muscles with menace. The pigeon circled in a tizzy. The shepherd came right up to the horse, despite her size and the mean cast of her face. Her ears swiveled forward and she bared her steel teeth. Esther drew straight back on both handlebars to steady her as she strained to bite.

"*Shalom aleikhem*," Esther said. Seleme was big and heavy. Much of the time, the horse bowed to its rider's will; at this moment, Esther struggled to control the machine's thrashing head. Seleme's joints needed oil. They stuttered and creaked, metal scraping metal.

The man stepped back and cocked his head to one side. Who knew what tribe he'd thought they belonged to. It was still early enough in the day that both of them wore their fur burkas to fend off the chill. Itakh's *kippah* wasn't visible under the hood. "*Aleikhem shalom.*" He spat a tight red wad onto the ground; he was chewing a betel nut. "You don't spoil a man's shot."

"She's a pet bird! A homing pigeon. Highly trained."

"Also, no doubt, delicious." With a skeptical crease between his eyebrows, he kept an eye on the horse. "You're frightening my sheep."

"I didn't know sheep were intelligent enough to feel frightened," Itakh said. At the same moment, Esther said, "We apologize, we didn't mean to. We don't know when we crossed onto your land."

"No fences. The neighbors know their bounds."

Seleme tossed her head, her articulated neck thrashing like a snake. Esther kept pulling on the handlebars, but this was difficult while reaching around Itakh's body. Suddenly, Seleme tore her head free of Esther's grip, lunged forward, and bit at the man's near arm. Esther shouted to warn him—as he himself pulled back—and got hold of the horse in time to wrench her head up and back on its universal joint. Yet Seleme came away with a bite of fabric in her teeth. The gun was stowed in one hand, the man's other guarding the place that had been bitten.

"Are you all right?" Esther said. She meant to shout, but her voice came out faint with fear, as in a nightmare. Only as an afterthought did she cut the horse's power. In an instant, she could hear the landscape's natural sounds: the sheep browsing and bleating, insects buzzing, a far-off dog's gruff bark, the man's labored breath. "Did she hurt you?"

He lifted his hand to examine the arm. Seleme had torn a gash in the fabric, grazed the skin. A thin, shiny layer of blood and plasma rose to the surface. "*Barukh Hashem*, no." He spat his betel nut to the ground, took a deep breath, and settled both hands on his hips to examine their bundles of provisions. "You're neither a caravan nor a horde."

"Travelers. Heading upriver."

He glanced around. Sheep meadows and cultivated fields. Beyond them, the barren steppe continued to the horizon. Esther knew that if they continued upriver a few more days, they'd reach the bustling industrial center of Tsaritsyn, but its smokestacks and clamor were difficult to imagine in this peaceful setting. "The boy looks Uyghur."

Esther had known Itakh as a Jew all his life. His coloring was perhaps dark for a Khazar, but the same could be said of her whole family. "Jews," she said, though she couldn't be sure that the shepherd's Hebrew greeting meant he was a member of Avraham's tribe. Though Khazar was the lingua franca of the kaganate, people also widely used Hebrew, the *Lashon Hakodesh* of the ruling classes. People of all ethnicities and backgrounds sprinkled their conversation with it.

"And if I may say so, you look more like runaways than travelers."

She didn't know what to answer. "I'm Ephrat bat Mordekhai," she said before thinking through the lie. Ephrat was a good inadvertent choice, given their mission: as common for boys as for girls. "And I apologize for my horse's ill temper. This is my brother, Yitzkhak."

"Eliezer ben Turbish." So she'd been right on both counts: a Mongol Jew. "It's not your fault about the horse. I hear they build them that way. Ephrat, did you say?" Esther nodded. "I have a daughter your age, starved for company. We'd be pleased to welcome you for a meal. Were you out all night? It gets cold on the steppe, and the *varkolaki* prowl." He used a cognate to the word the refugees used. Apparently everyone believed in werewolves except for ethnic Khazars. "You're from the city?" She nodded again, and the way he shook his head indicated that he resigned her to the Holy One's help. "Where did you get that?"

"She belongs to our father. He's letting us borrow her."

The pigeon flew in and settled on Seleme's head. Lucky for the bird, the horse was turned off. Itakh must have been thinking the same thing, because he scooped up the pigeon and held it to his chest.

"You," Eliezer said to Itakh. "Get down and bring that into the barn." He pointed to a second roundhouse a distance beyond the first.

"It has to be driven, sir. It can't be led."

"Can you leave it in the field?"

"We can," Esther said, "but she's running low on fuel." And Esther wanted to oil the creaking joints. "Can we purchase some from you before we leave?"

"First we'll eat. Then I'll explain." He made two sharp whistles, and a shaggy black-and-white dog the size of a small bear charged from the house. Itakh instinctively drew his feet from the stirrups to huddle over his bird, but the dog charged past and began running circles around the sheep, driving them toward the next pasture. When Itakh climbed down, he placed Nagehan in her cage and tossed in a handful of grain from the sack.

Eliezer's daughter waited by the door, her broad face solemn. She dressed, as Esther did, like a boy, in loose trousers and a shapeless sweater, though her clothes were older and dirtier than Esther's, more often patched. She held out both hands as Esther approached. Esther took them, and they kissed first on one cheek and then on the other. "Sister," the girl said, "I'm glad you've come. Welcome."

Esther glanced back at Itakh, who interpreted the girl's weird formality as a sign to make a deep bow.

"I'm Liora bat Eliezer."

"Ephrat and Yitzkhak b'nai Mordekhai." She gestured behind her. "We are grateful for your hospitality."

Liora brushed the compliment aside with her hand and held the door open. "It is our solemn duty. You are, I gather, our coreligionists. And look at the blessings El Shaddai rained on Avraham for welcoming the wayfarers as guests."

Itakh said, "They were angels."

"As might you be."

Esther didn't want to correct her.

No lamps or candles burned in the single room, dim at midday. The cooking fire glowed in the central hearth; smoke drew straight up the chimney. The two bedrolls were old and colorful, like a nomad caravan. This father and daughter might really have *been* nomads—there were no furnishings besides a few plates and cooking implements and piles of blankets and clothes. The food in the cauldron gave off a steamy aroma of cardamom and cinnamon. Esther's stomach growled, and she covered it with her hand.

Liora gave a grunt that might have been laughter. "You will eat your fill. Father slaughtered a lamb yesterday."

Itakh said, "Thank you."

Esther looked around while Liora ladled the soup and set out a washing pitcher and bowl. Both were made of silver—dented and scratched with age, but gleaming. Once Itakh came back indoors, and everyone's hands were washed and the washing blessed, they gave thanks for their meal, and Eliezer gestured for them to begin.

The meat was good in their father's house, but not as sweet or tender as this. Itakh sighed his pleasure. Eliezer watched them with sharp eyes. When Esther put her bowl down to rest, he said, "Excuse my curiosity, but in twenty years raising sheep on this land, I've seen few travelers. Ravening hordes; oil lords come to extort protection." Esther waited for him to finish. "If you sought pleasure, you might have gone south for a seaside holiday. If you were escaping punishment, you would have run when I approached you."

Liora spilled some of her soup in her lap, perhaps afraid that Esther and Itakh *were* angels, and she and her father about to be cursed. Esther had the impulse to conceal their plans—if no one knew of them, no one could divulge them—but also had only a vague idea where she was headed. "We've heard rumors that on the far side of the river, there resides a village of kabbalists, versed in the uses of magic."

Eliezer leaned forward. "Those are no rumors."

Liora said, "They inhabit a floating village, Yetzirah."

"Floating?" Itakh asked.

"Traveling. The holy men remain within their walls in winter, but in the more clement seasons, they pack up and wander, as Khazars did of old."

"You know they exist?" Esther asked. Her heart quickened.

"We've met them on their migration. They've drunk of our milk and drawn from our well. A mitzvah."

"What were they like?" Itakh asked.

Eliezer asked, "Why do you seek them?"

Liora said, "They dressed in old-fashioned robes and wore knitted *kippot*. They prayed much of the day, and danced to welcome Shabbat. And they brought remarkable things with them."

Eliezer hushed her and watched Esther for an answer. The small hairs on Esther's arms bristled at what Liora had said. "We seek their help in defending Khazaria against the foreign menace."

Eliezer nodded and touched the place where Seleme had bitten him. "The aeroplanes we saw in the sky yesterday."

Esther also nodded. When he didn't volunteer more of an opinion, she asked, "Did you know what it was?"

"No."

"An enemy kaganate. Making incursion upon our territory."

"I know the one of which you speak." Eliezer continued to think and to touch his arm absently.

"The army that drove the refugees across the western border," Itakh blurted out.

"Refugees?" Liora said. Her father said, "Why are they sending a young woman and a child to alert the kabbalists?"

She saw the glimmer of wanting to tell in Itakh's eyes. Esther's instinct was to keep as much of their project secret as possible, although she didn't believe Eliezer would try to stop them. "No one sent us," she said. "We decided on our own."

Liora placed the kettle on the hob. After an uncomfortable moment, Eliezer said, "We can guide you toward Yetzirah."

"We'd be grateful. But we need fuel for our horse. Can we purchase some from you?"

Liora was measuring tea leaves and dried herbs into an earthen pot.

Eliezer grunted. "I've lived forty years and never used a machine that ran on anything but the strength of my hands or my back." To demonstrate, he took an eggbeater from the low shelf behind him and turned its crank, making it whirr and spin. Was this a point of pride? To Esther it sounded backward. The mechanical horses in her father's stable were signs of his wealth and a means of protecting it. She wondered if the others had already left for the front. "I doubt our neighbors can help either, and they're a morning's walk distant. You'll have to go straight to the Uyghurs." Her eyes must have widened, because he added, "The supply line. Where'd you think it came from? Hashem doesn't drill wells."

"I didn't realize the Uyghurs were so nearby."

He shrugged. "Aren't they everywhere?" The way he said it gave Esther a chill.

"I guess we should go find them," Esther said, eager to be contradicted.

"No," Liora said. "You must rest with us until tomorrow morning. The steppe is unsafe for a woman at night." Something about her diction made her sound like a musty scroll rather than a girl. Perhaps she read more than she spoke. There were books among this house's scant possessions, stored on a rough shelf to keep the Name from touching the ground.

"We have to hurry."

Liora nodded. "Then at least you'll drink your tea."

After they finished the fragrant concoction, Eliezer went out to check on how the bear dog—he called it Goliath—had herded the sheep to the far pasture. Then he led Esther and Itakh into the dirt yard, took up a stick, and began to draw: the Latin "X"—two crossroads—to mark their current location, a larger one, a distance south, for the capital, a meandering line for the Atil, branching into its delta. He drew a sweeping arc over the top, and said, "The steppe, in all directions, to the territory of the Ukrainii and the Rus." On her father's map, this area had looked barren, forbidding, devoid of settlement. He crouched down to draw on a finer scale with a smaller stick. "The road falls away half a day's journey north of here. You'll judge your position by the river and the sun."

"We have a compass," Esther said. "Half a day by foot or by horse?"

"By foot. That's a point." Eliezer nodded. "The machine will go faster." Some distance north, he drew the river's course bulging to the right and made a slash across it. "You'll see the beginnings of an oxbow. You'll reach the place tomorrow on the machine. Ignore what the river does until then—this is a broad curve out to the northeast; unmistakable. Toward the southern end of the oxbow is the ford. If the water is high, you'll find a ferryman to take you across."

"I hope he's there," Esther said. Mechanical horses could ride and fight in foul weather, but had intake vents and access hatches in their bellies. When submerged in water, they shorted out.

"Soon after you cross, you'll be within range of Yetzirah. If the kabbalists aren't yet back in the permanent town, people will have sighted them and know where to point you."

Esther stared at the lines in the dirt. In case her father's men came looking, she dragged one foot across the marks to erase them: a shuffling, hobbled step.

"You'll need money for the fuel dealers. Money and"—he ran his fingers again over the superficial wound—"you'll want to look them in the eye, is what I'll say. They're merciless to the fearful."

Itakh went with Esther to rouse the horse. Once they were beyond earshot, Itakh nuzzled close to her shoulder, so she had to put her arm around him. "I want to go home," she said. At the same moment, he said, "This is crazy. We're going to get killed."

"Might. Might get killed. But you were right when you said we had to keep going."

He rammed his small shoulder into her armpit as they crossed the bare yard. "The river can't be forded. We don't know where they are, or if they can help us once we get there."

"Or if I want them to."

"Menacing Uyghurs control the fuel supply."

Right where they'd left her, Seleme stood, turned off, asleep. The pigeon, confined to her loft, looked comfortable, puffed up and napping. A small oil spot darkened the grass beneath the horse's tail. She shouldn't have been leaking, but Esther didn't think they had time to open her up and see what was wrong.

"It won't be easy," she said, "but what choice do we have?" They could turn back. Having never before done anything worse than borrow the horse for a joyride, she had no idea how her father would react. Given the political situation, after a momentary outrage, he might welcome them without incident. He had more important affairs to attend to. She could return at least temporarily to her comfortable life, watch whatever unfolded unfold. She could remain in the body the Lord had given her until Khazaria's enemies came to claim it. "I can't turn back," she said, her stomach dropping lower in her gut. Then she mounted and started the horse. Start-up exhaust steamed out of the machine, soiling the grass further. "You can go home, if you want. I won't blame you."

He laid one hand against the horse's withers, which warmed up as the engine ran. He took a breath so deep it lifted his shoulders. "I can't do that," he said, not looking at her. "My home is with you."

Esther felt as if she'd banged her nose into something. That shock, the sting in the corners of her eyes. Part of her believed her home *was* with Itakh, but for the most part, it was in cosmopolitan Atil, so different from this pasture in which they stood. A chunk of her idea of home had broken off when Or'li had died, and could not be recovered. Instead of expressing any of this, she said, "We're going to run out of fuel." And Seleme, unaware that time had passed since her incident with Eliezer, grumbled and shook out her head. Her steel mane tinkled.

Eliezer and Liora waited at a respectful distance as they approached, Esther on Seleme and Itakh walking beside the machine. Esther felt awkward, saying goodbye. They had offered their hospitality despite having no luxuries. She wanted to give them money. As if privy to her thoughts, Eliezer said, "We wish we could give you a true parting gift, but can only offer our blessing."

Esther said, "I'd like that very much." She left the horse idling and slid to the ground to join Itakh. The thought of money slipped away.

He raised both hands, his fingers splitting like a flock of geese—or a squadron of aerocraft—in flight. Was he a Kohen? A Mongol Kohen? He held the heel of one palm close to each of their foreheads and delivered the priestly blessing: "May Adonai bless you and keep you. May Adonai let His face shine upon you and be gracious to you. May Adonai look kindly upon you and give you peace."

She had heard the prayer a thousand times. Her father said it perfunctorily over his three blood children and Itakh every week at Shabbat dinner. Rabbi Kalonymos led the Kohanim of the congregation in its recitation. He would say it over Esther and Shimon at their *khuppah*, if that ever happened. But Eliezer put his heart into his speech. She could hear his true intent to bless them. She closed her eyes to take his words in better, and she felt the prayer for their safety flying up to El Shaddai. She pictured Him enthroned on the Mountain of Heaven, with His Consort, the Shekhinah, beside him. And then Eliezer was done.

Esther held Liora's hands, kissed her on her cheeks again. Liora smelled of fresh butter. She pressed a skin bag full of dried berries on

Esther. "My thoughts will be with you, my sister Ephrat. I hope you will be able to serve the kaganate." Esther felt a pang of regret about the deception.

As they rode toward the river across Eliezer's land, they turned in the saddle until their hosts' figures disappeared, then their buildings. It was as if the tall, waving grass had swallowed them. Seleme carried her passengers through the sea of grass, which made a rhythmic swishing against her legs and, once the sun began to warm up, gave off a lemony scent. Esther opened the small bag and they began to eat the berries, hard as gravel. They had an odd, smoky taste.

"Ukh," Itakh said around a mouthful. "Can I spit it out?"

"No. The provisions from home won't last forever." Up on the saddle behind her, he chewed dutifully in her ear, the berries making cracking sounds as they stuck to his teeth. She heard their stickiness even above the engine's rumble. "We'd better find the Uyghurs soon. Unless we want to leave Seleme and travel on foot."

"I can't tell which is worse," he said, and at last managed to swallow. He leaned away from her, and when she turned to see what he was doing, he was forcing the berries through the lattice door of the mobile pigeon loft.

"Is she eating them?"

Itakh waited a moment before replying. "Sort of."

Esther was busy thinking about the kabbalists. Eliezer and Liora had seen them, known them. Why had she doubted? She wondered what kind of Jews they were. Even before the refugees had come, there had been variations: those who followed Kalonymos; Karaites, though Esther had never met one in the capital; born Jews who'd strayed from the fold; believers in the Nazarene rabbi; converts. To Esther's knowledge, none of these sects produced mystics. She tried to imagine how such people might practice.

Seleme moved more slowly by the step, the purr of her engine low and gurgling.

CHAPTER 7

There was no good road along the riverbank, but people traveled this route, so they'd beaten a path of clay and mud. Though the grasslands themselves were arid except in torrential rain, the river dampened everything, and Seleme's steel hooves sank almost to the pasterns in the muck. Her proud head hung low. Esther wished the machines were water-cooled. Had Seleme been a real animal, water would have helped her.

All at once came a tattoo of hoofbeats and a terrible yell, of multiple voices, like the shrill of the dead, their graves disturbed. The pigeon skittered in its box and made high-pitched complaints. Seleme lifted her head, too depleted to track the alarming sounds. Esther managed to turn her so that their backs faced the river. At least now they could see who was approaching: five men on late-model mechanical horses, all painted black. The men themselves were also clad in black, but only when they pulled up short, stopping their mounts gruffly to surround them in a semicircle of loud-idling engines, could she make out their peculiar attire. Like Eliezer, their features and coloring looked Mongol, though they shaved their beards, braided their hair, and wore black skullcaps, not Jewish. Unlike anyone she might have expected to meet on the Khazar steppe, they dressed in Western clothing: black, buttoned jackets, with lapels; straight black trousers; pointy black boots with a slight heel. They wore black shirts with buttons and collars. Esther had no idea what this costume signified, but she felt its menace.

"Who are you?" one man demanded in Khazar, with an accent she couldn't place.

When she first opened her mouth, no sound came out. Once she found her voice, she said, "Ephrat bat Mordekhai. Yitzkhak ben Mordekhai." Then she added, "Who are you?"

One sniggered. Another revved his engine for show, his horse baring its teeth. They'd modified the tailpipes to make the engines sound louder. Even in repose, the horses chugged and spat. The man in the center said, "Who do you think?"

So they'd found who they were looking for.

Itakh said, "We need fuel." For the first time, Esther noticed how small his voice sounded.

Another man snorted and said, "Do we look like salesmen?"

The central man eased his horse forward in first gear and appraised them. He himself had a long, shrewd face with a deep crease on either side of his mouth. "Nice machine. Stolen?"

"No." Itakh's high pitch sounded like lying.

This raised a wide smile, which showed that one of the man's teeth was capped with metal. "I asked if it was stolen."

"I said no. Also, it's a she." Esther felt Itakh quaking behind her, his discomfort mirrored by the pigeon's restlessness, but he was doing his best to sound brave.

The four others smiled, nodded. One, she saw, had a sword slung in a scabbard beside his right leg, where it would be accessible to his left hand. Another carried a mace, like a clove-stuck orange on an iron chain. "Look," she said, "we need fuel. We have money. Can you help us?" As soon as she mentioned the money, she thought they might wrest it from her and gallop away.

The leader paced his horse to one side, as if to get a better view. "Depends on how much money."

Esther couldn't guess. She didn't even know the capacity of Seleme's tank. "She's nearly empty."

He thought a moment and replied, "Forty dinars."

"That's ridiculous," Esther said. He'd named a large sum, not a princely one. "We'll give you twenty."

They all laughed.

"You're at our mercy."

Another added, "I'd rather kill you than haggle."

"Thirty-five," said the lead man.

"Take it," Itakh whispered.

But Esther was what Rukhl called a *hondler* by nature. Her heart quickened at the game. "Twenty-five."

"Twenty-five dinars to fuel an empty horse on which your life depends? That's khutzpah." The word in dialect caught on his tongue, though Esther understood him. Where had he encountered refugees?

"Take it with our gratitude. Or leave us and we'll find another dealer."

Most of the henchmen found her funny; she didn't like the way they laughed at her. One—he appeared to be the youngest—didn't laugh, but watched her with naked interest. She held her gaze steady on the leader as he reached into his inner pocket. She thought he might be after a weapon, and prepared to grab her small knife. He only brought out a pipe and a leather pouch of fragrant tobacco. He filled and tamped the pipe, replaced the pouch, took out an engraved matchbox, lit a match. "Two things," he said. "One: There are other dealers, but there's only one mafia." She didn't know what language that word came from, but she noticed he pronounced it more confidently than he had the refugee word. "We all report to the same big boss, and he doesn't like trouble. If he were here, you'd be dead by now. Two: If we refuse your offer, what makes you think we'll let you go?" He shook out the match, which had already burned down, then lit another and took a few puffs to draw the pipe.

Itakh held so tight to her waist, she could barely breathe. The pigeon paced and cooed in its box behind them. Esther took in the deepest breath she could, looked the man straight in the eye, and said, "Because El of the Mountain has sanctioned our mission, and because His wrath is boundless toward those who seek to thwart Him." She pointed southward toward the mountains of the Kavkas, invisible at this latitude.

She saw the henchmen fall back slightly in their black saddles. One gave a curt nod and, under his breath, said, "I respect that." The leader smoked and watched her. She didn't know what religion the Uyghurs practiced—they might have been shamanists, Tengri-worshippers like her own remote ancestors—but it didn't matter. Everyone in Khazaria knew how fierce the Great Name was. The Shekhinah could appease Him, but didn't always. In the past thousand years, a hundred war-like tribes and nations, from the Huns to the Ottoman Turcii, had tried to conquer this kaganate and failed. Khazars prided themselves on a cosmopolitanism that left every man free to practice his faith, although people of all religions recognized the strength of El Elyon, the supreme God. Esther might tempt punishment by saying this, but it seemed worth the risk. Who but the Name, after all, had put the thought of going on this mission into her head? It could have been the Evil Impulse—the same one that goaded her to impure thoughts about Shimon—but she didn't think so. She hoped not.

He puffed on his pipe, his eyes narrowed against the smoke or the eastern sun or with cunning. "Thirty dinars."

Itakh shook behind her. She felt him poised to jump off the horse and run. She kept watching the man. Then she spat on the ground, aiming halfway between Seleme's hooves and those of the leader's dusty black machine. "All right." Esther reached inside her fur burka to draw out her money pouch, and tucked the *hamsa* back inside. She didn't have money in the correct denominations. "I need change," she said, mortified, holding out forty dinars in paper currency before her. She made him approach. He cast an almost bashful smile at his co-hort and touched his hair before he guided the horse forward. Except for the young one, the men's smiles didn't look friendly, and when his horse and Seleme stood nose to nose, their ears swiveled toward the front and they bared their steel teeth. But Seleme was too depleted to attack, the other man's horse too sleek and well trained. The man took and pocketed the money, handed over a filthy coin. He said, "Follow us."

"How? Our horse is running on fumes."

He snapped his fingers and the youngest henchman dismounted and approached. Esther scanned him for weapons, saw none. Off the horse, she could see he was only about her age, a little on the short side, with buckteeth. He removed a battered flask from his pocket and uncorked it. His eyes flickered up at her with a giddy expression while he pried Seleme's metal lips apart and tipped the flask into her mouth. Esther could hear the petrol pour into Seleme's belly. Without Esther touching the throttle, the horse's idle speed picked up. "For emergencies," the boy said, glancing up at Esther again. His slight frown didn't conceal the smile underneath.

"Shut up," the leader said. To Esther, he said, "You'll ride in the middle of our pack."

Itakh said, "Our horse has a bad temper. You don't want her behind you." Seleme lifted her head as if to bite something. Despite his apparent familiarity with the machines, the mafia boy stepped back.

"In front, then. Tselmeg, stay close to her."

As Esther guided Seleme through their parted ranks and onto the path, the boy remounted his horse. Once up, he followed behind them. Itakh nestled the side of his face between Esther's shoulder blades and whispered, "We're still alive."

"For now," she whispered back. She shifted and tried to shrug him off, but he stuck tight. "*Barukh Hashem.*" Anything could still happen.

They rode around a bend in the river—not the one Eliezer had drawn for them; they hadn't gone far enough yet. It had concealed, a short distance to the west, what at first Esther took for a small city. Then she noticed that its spires were empty metal latticeworks. They resembled a pleasure tower, somewhere in the West, of which she'd seen photographs, though these were not so well proportioned. Each contained a kind of mechanical grasshopper that clattered as it drew back, then bobbed its head toward the ground with a thud. A city of oil derricks. Men in indigo work clothes clambered over the rigs, shouting in one of the guttural steppe languages. Isolated words, cognate to Khazar terms, drifted to her ears. Tselmeg, riding a short distance behind her, said, "For your own sake, I wouldn't look too closely."

So Esther cast her eyes down and listened. The noise grew louder, as did the shouts of the men working. Each time a derrick's boring tackle made impact, the ground trembled, and an answering shudder traveled through Seleme's body to the saddle. At each impact, the bird complained in its loft. The sharp scent of crude oil filled Esther's nostrils. A local pocket of shouting picked up as their group approached. The Uyghur words sounded harsh, unfriendly. She suspected the conversation was about her and Itakh and Seleme, though she disliked jumping to this conclusion. Tselmeg guided his mechanical horse in a broad arc, leading them toward a cluster of buildings. Esther didn't dare look around. She straightened up in the saddle. She knew it was unwise to follow these men into any enclosed space, though in retrospect, neither had it been wise to meet them on the open steppe.

Someone in their party shouted something in Uyghur, and Tselmeg drew them up beside a corrugated sheet metal shed—a Mensheviki import, Esther knew, a product that shipped down the Atil from Tsaritsyn. Independence from Mensheviki steel had been one of her tutor's pet topics, before all of this happened; that and what the Jewish presence in Palestine might mean for Khazaria. Whether they would all still someday return to Eretz Yisrael, or whether this very land now constituted the Promised Land. Both topics interested Esther more than they did Elisheva. The leader rode up beside her with a show of trying to control his horse as it bit at Seleme, and said, "What does your machine drink?"

Drawn back from her mental digression, Esther felt her eyes widen, but tried to remain calm. She worried the question was a trick. "Petrol."

"She's a luxury item, I'm sure you'll agree. Which would explain why you stole her. I'm not familiar with the model." His face froze halfway to a smile, as if her stupidity had arrested its progress. "Are you?"

"No, sir," Esther said. At once she regretted the "sir."

"Do you know her preferred octane?"

The word, though delivered in Khazar, meant nothing to her. "No." Her face heated up. "It came out of our father's tap."

He snickered, showing off his capped tooth. When he finally succeeded in smiling, the long, dry creases formed down the sides of his face. "Who is this Mordekhai, to have a tap?"

"A lawyer. One of the kagan's lawyers." The lie slipped out. It wasn't perfect—an imperial lawyer's children would be worth kidnapping for ransom—but better than associating herself with a man as powerful as her father.

The leader turned off his horse and slid down from it with an easy swagger. As he approached, Esther willed her body not to clench in fear. She pressed her boots into Seleme's stirrups and challenged herself to keep them there. The man's scent of sunbaked sweat, stale pipe smoke, and petroleum preceded him. Esther sat steady as Seleme began to track his movements and emit her eerie whine. Itakh drew his legs up into a crouch, preparing, no doubt, to spring and run. But when the man reached them, he only touched one sure hand behind Seleme's ear to calm her and the other to the row of rivets in front of the integrated saddle. He followed the rivets down until he reached the series of letters or numbers etched into the steel. Esther had seen them a thousand times without reading them. He thumped his fingers twice against the horse's girth, which gave a soft, metallic ring like a struck brass bowl. "Good horse," he said, glancing at Esther. He barked a number at Tselmeg.

Esther looked up and around, surprised by the scale of the manufactory. This drilling and refining operation dwarfed any industrial producer in the outskirts of Atil. All the kaganate's petrol—for heating the homes of the wealthy, generating electricity, running the mechanical horses and the nation's moto-trucks; all the oil for export—came from here and from places like it. Some, perhaps, went to the Menshevikim who would require more with Haman the Agagite on the attack. Her father had once mentioned in passing that the Uyghurs supplied oil to the dark kaganate too. Esther couldn't understand the logic of doing so.

"Hey!" Itakh shouted.

Tselmeg jumped back from the saddlebags. He held both hands up in the air. "I was getting her feed bucket."

The leader laid a hand on Itakh's arm to still him, as expertly as he had done to the horse. "Proceed." Seleme reached around to nip at him. He continued to hold Itakh still while Tselmeg secured the bucket, filled it from a hose, and strung it over Seleme's jerking muzzle. The man's smell made Esther want to gag.

Seleme drank in big, shuddering gulps. She drained her bucket in minutes; then, before she'd lifted her nose from the bucket, her green marble eyes began scanning for more.

"Not so feminine, is she?" the leader said. The long-lined grin now seemed permanent. "Give her another, Tselmeg."

"She could kill you if she wanted to," Esther said.

He raised his eyebrows. "She must not want to then."

Everyone watched while she drank her fill. When she was, at last, sated, Tselmeg removed the bucket and wiped her muzzle with an old red cloth. She burred with pleasure. He hazarded another glance up at Esther, who made herself look away.

"So," the leader said. He continued to stand near Seleme, though it would have been more natural to get back on his horse. "You're traveling—how far?"

She didn't know what to tell him. "A distance upriver."

He paced away and back again. She noticed his bowlegged gait. "And how are you planning to fuel your machine?"

"Our expectation has been that we'll purchase fuel from whomever we meet."

"No."

She waited for him to continue.

"We control it all. We fuel every horse in the Khazar Army and every flying machine that went past yesterday."

"That isn't true," Itakh said. "Some of them belonged to the—" He cut himself off before he said the word.

"The Germanii? Them too." It was true, then. A low laugh passed from one to the next as a fire leaps from branch to branch.

"How can you do that?" Itakh blurted.

"I advise you," he continued without even glancing at Itakh, "to cultivate friendly relations with our kind, wherever you find us. Not all the big boss's men are as lenient as we are."

Esther wanted to remind him that he'd threatened to kill them earlier, but this was imprudent. What had made him do business with them instead? She wasn't sure. He took note of the way Seleme looked at him, waiting for the right moment to strike. "If you like, I can give you an insurance policy—a full fuel can. Another ten dinars."

Esther reached into her pouch to give him back his dirty coin.

He took it, bit it as if he had not just given it to her, spat, and stuck it in his own pocket. Then he snapped his fingers at one of the henchmen, who rode off and returned long minutes later with a rusty red metal canister with a spout in one end. Esther thought it looked like a hot water bottle. He tied it to the left saddlebag along with Seleme's feed bucket. She reached back to bite at him, as if at a fly. Alert after the horse's treatment of Eliezer, Esther drew back harder than was necessary on her handlebars. Seleme's head thrashed.

"Why are you doing this for us?" Esther asked.

The leader lifted one corner of his mouth more than he smiled. "Because you stole a little Uyghur in addition to that horse."

Itakh pressed himself up closer behind her. Through all their layers of clothing, she could feel his beating heart.

"That's my brother," Esther said. "Yitzkhak."

The man snorted. "Your father's slave?" He tugged at his own earlobe.

Esther said nothing. In their haste, they had not thought to remove the gold ring of Itakh's servitude from his ear. His sloppy, chin-length hair usually covered it, but she couldn't see him at the moment; the wind

77

might have blown it aside. Even in the midst of her panic at their over-sight, a screed raced through her head about what a ridiculous enter-prise it was to try to guess at a glance who was Khazar and who wasn't. The highborn had converted to Judaism more than a thousand years before, when Kagan Bulan had invited scholars from all the world's great religions to persuade him of their faiths' relative merits. Judaism had won—Khazar children learned this was because the Great Name was the mightiest of the gods, though Esther knew there had to be some political reason too—and Khazars became a people; but up until that time, they'd been members of the myriad tribes that charged back and forth across this steppe, stealing one another's women and claiming the land as their own. Others had converted since that time. Eliezer was a Mongol Jew; she could cite him as an example. But she couldn't make this argument aloud. Instead, she repeated, "My brother."

He gazed at them both contentedly, as he might have at a lovely dinner. "If you encounter any trouble from others of our kind, you can tell them Chuluun is your protector."

"Thank you."

"Eyes down," he said. Chuluun. "Tselmeg will lead you back to where we found you. You can continue on your way." To Itakh, he said something in Uyghur, to which Itakh couldn't respond.

"Thank you," Esther said. He bowed just his head. She had to raise her eyes to turn Seleme, and as she did, she saw a striking man start down the metal stairs from a high, silolike structure. He was taller by a head than the people on either side of him, and his long braid was soft white, like a sheep. Red dust caked everyone else, from the workers in their indigo pants to the black-suited band who'd led them hither. This man was immaculate. The yellowish white of his long hair shone against a sleek, black suit dark as a cloudless night sky. Like Jo-sephus, he radiated the calm of one accustomed to obedience. Esther heard a mechanical whir in the air behind her, and just had time to glance over her shoulder to see three small, peculiar flying machines before Chuluun barked at her.

"Eyes down, I said."

She saw the immaculate person gesture to those around him, who stopped walking to attend. Esther looked down. She was torn between wondering about the man and wondering about the aerocraft she'd just seen. Like all Khazar flying machines, they were made of wood and equipped with doubled bat wings. But these had been a quarter the size of ordinary aeroplanes, large enough to hold a single pilot in the barest suggestion of a basket. Stranger still, they had produced only a sound of gear clicks and the whoosh of what appeared to have been flapping wings.

"No one sees the big boss," Chuluun said.

"Who?"

"Lead them off, Tselmeg."

Tselmeg remounted his own horse and shifted it into reverse. To his leader, he said, "She won't try anything. I've got her."

Esther followed him out of the enclosure, keeping Seleme well back from his horse's tempting steel-wool tail. But once they were away from the place, and the din of drilling and refining began to abate, he said, "Come alongside."

She shifted to a slow trot, guided Seleme in a wide arc around the other machine, and settled in a few neck lengths away from him. Sure enough, though Seleme gave their companions dark glances, she didn't try to bite them.

Tselmeg glanced at her sidelong, nodded, once again smiled. "Good work," he said. When she didn't reply right away, he added, "We really might have killed you, you know." This sounded like a boast, but she couldn't be sure.

"Well, thank you," Esther said.

"People cower when we come riding toward them. But you," he paused, perhaps thought over his words. "You sat so steady. Not what I'd expect from a girl." Someone else might have said this in condescension. His admiration sounded real.

For a few minutes, no one spoke. Esther didn't know what to say. Tselmeg worked his lips, made unnecessary adjustments to the horse. She could see him thinking.

"I'm going to tell you something," he said. She knew not to interrupt. "The big man is named Göktürk. I'll kill you if you tell anyone I told you."

"I wouldn't." Though she thought he wouldn't harm her.

The Uyghurs' leader was so greatly feared, mothers used the mere idea of him as a warning. To know his name was to know a magic spell, to be able to defeat the troll beneath the bridge or to halt the Angel of Death in its tracks.

Tselmeg grinned, showing his rabbitlike teeth. Most Khazars of Esther's standing had such defects fixed with orthodontia, but for the first time she thought this a shame—the teeth gave his face character.

They were approaching the riverbank. He looked up- and downriver a moment before saying, "Really if you meet anyone along the way, anyone who gives you trouble, say you're with the big boss. Chuluun overestimates his own authority."

Esther felt nervous that there were people more menacing than these on the steppe. "Anyone can see I'm not a Uyghur." Or could they? How did their women dress? She added, "Thank you."

He nodded and checked for people again. "Ephrat. Ephrat? Is that your name?"

"It's Esther."

When he swallowed, his whole head bobbed. "Look, I'm never going to see you again. May I ask where you're going?"

He had probably risked his life by telling them his leader's name. "We're looking for the kabbalists. They have a village on the other side of the river."

"We meet them sometimes. You'll find them."

"I hope so."

"You will," he said. "Why do you want their help? What's the mission you were talking about?"

His expression seemed so open, trusting. "We're going to save Khazaria from the foreign menace."

"El of the Mountain sent you on a mission to the kabbalists?" he said, alert in the saddle.

"Not exactly."

Itakh added, "We decided to send ourselves."

"Tselmeg?" Her tongue tripped over the unfamiliar syllables, but she had an advantage she should press. "I have a question. What were the flying machines I saw?"

Once again, he grinned. "You weren't supposed to see those either." She waited, tried to hold a friendly expression. "Aerocycles."

She didn't want to seem too curious. "But what are they for?"

"They patrol the oil fields." On guard for spillage? Thieves? "They never need to be refueled." This seemed ironic, given the abundance of Uyghur oil. He squinted at the horizon and said, "You should go. I should get back before they start to wonder. I wish you luck and health."

"To you as well."

He turned his horse around—it had a tight turning radius: a tricked-out warlord model—and gunned it back toward the refinery. They watched him go.

Itakh said, "You didn't blink."

"Neither did you," she replied, though it wasn't so. She began to guide Seleme upriver.

"I think you might have scared them."

Esther sat a little straighter. His praise felt good.

"I just hope we find Yetzirah in time. I had no idea the journey would take so long." Was the capital already under siege? He set the pigeon free, knowing it would home back to its mobile loft in a short while, and it spiraled off into the air.

"Neither did I," Esther said.

"Aerocycles," he marveled. "Do you think he could be right, that I'm a Uyghur?"

"It's not possible. You had the menorah on your chest—I saw it." Though anyone could have drawn it to ease the baby's passage into a Jewish home.

Itakh didn't answer, so Esther assumed she'd convinced him. She shifted Seleme into a higher gear, hoping to cover as much ground as possible before dark.

CHAPTER 8

They hadn't reached anyplace by nightfall. To the north, south, and west, as far as they could see, an occasional weather-beaten cluster of trees punctuated the grasslands. The waning moon had pared itself down to a crescent, lying cupped on its back, but the many stars reflected in the Atil's waters. They could see their way.

"When do we stop?" Itakh asked. He rode in front again, guiding the horse better than he'd done the previous day. The pigeon slept in its box.

"I don't know. We should have quit before nightfall. It would have been easier to pitch the tent. If we can still see, maybe we should keep going."

They continued on, silent a few moments. Then Itakh said, "I'm hungry."

Esther sighed. "Let's be done. We can leave again at first light."

Itakh guided Seleme westward into the open grass. Her engine whined as he downshifted. It would have been better to shelter by a stand of trees, but the nearest stood a distance off. At what seemed like an arbitrary point, he shifted the horse into neutral before he braked. She drew to a halt without stalling. He turned her off, and the tick of her cooling engine counterpointed the calls of insects. When Itakh released the pigeon from her cage, she began picking for food in the grass. Esther and Itakh dismounted, untied their saddlebags, and laid out the components of their tent: the dark, mildew-scented canvas, the bundle of wooden supports, and a bag of tent stakes lashed to them. Though it had been years since her family had observed the old Khazar custom of spending the summer out in the harvest fields,

Esther knew how to put up a tent. She fitted the wooden supports together, and she and Itakh draped the canvas evenly over the structure. They raised the tent on its guy lines, then used large wrenches to hammer their stakes into the ground. The remaining stakes they worked through loops along the tent's sides. When each anchor felt secure, Esther stomped on it for good measure. She felt pride at her mastery of the contraption, just as she felt about Seleme, and she wished she had thought to pitch it in daylight so that now she could examine the horse's insides. She could use the electric torch, but the task would be easier in the morning.

"We won't find any firewood," Itakh said. "It was nice at Eliezer's."

"It was nice at home." Not only was the starlight insufficient to fix Seleme, Esther couldn't see into the bag of food. She began pulling out provisions at random. They sat down together, with an assortment of bags between them. Not knowing what each contained, Esther didn't know what blessing to say. She thought Itakh might be stalling for the same reason. At the same moment, they decided to sing the *Shehakol*, the catchall blessing for foods that didn't have their own specific blessings. Then they tore into a loaf of hard bread and what turned out, to Esther's pleasure, to be a bag of Afra's dried beef. Nagehan made a running commentary on everything. Itakh fed his pigeon from his cupped hand. Almost as soon as Esther had washed down her first bite with water, she said, "I wish I knew where they were."

"Who?"

She watched him a moment. Then she said it out loud: "The Germanii." The world didn't come crashing down around them. If there were a curse, one would feel it rush through the grass like a storm wind.

Itakh looked up into the peaceful sky. "Maybe they went back where they came from."

Esther snorted. She looked up too. The sky was bigger here than in cosmopolitan Atil. It stretched deep blue from horizon to horizon, a perfect dome. No wonder the ancients had believed themselves to be at the center of things, with Hashem and the Shekhinah enthroned above. No wonder Yehoshua had asked Hashem to make the sun stand still, not the Earth upon which he himself stood. How far had his battle been from where she now sat in the tall grass? Not so far; not much more distant than the Pontus Euxinus. Closer, she felt certain, than Praha. She wondered how much of its journey her uncle's pigeon had completed, or if it had already been shot down. *Lyubomir,* she thought. The name sounded exotic, Rus. "Our aero force can't fly at night. But the Menshevikim can; they have a technology to see in the dark. Where are they?"

Itakh didn't try to answer. His pupils were dilated; when the starlight caught them, they shone.

They splashed some of their drinking water on their faces before retiring—so near the river, they could afford to be profligate—and curled up in their blankets beneath the tent. Its ends were open, but the long sides sheltered them from the wind that cracked in the canvas. Itakh curled up and draped his hand over his bird as if she were a favorite toy. In his embrace, the bird puffed up and tucked her beak beneath one wing. Itakh whispered the prayer to thank Hashem for closing and opening his eyes, then the great *Sh'ma*; Esther whispered along with him. He dropped right into sleep, and she liked the dense, solid heat of him, his warm little-boy smell. This was more pleasant than sharing a bed with Elisheva, and much less exciting than the prospect of sharing one with Shimon, about whom she thought with embarrassing frequency after dark. She had imagined that she might miss her soft mattress and goose-down pillows, the thick, hand-loomed blanket. As it turned out, however, there was something almost magical about the hard ground and the cold, clean air. The sleep Esther fell into was restful and dreamless. And unlike at home, she fell into it without tossing and turning, without sinful thoughts. She barely felt herself drift off.

When she woke, it was deep night. At first, she thought she'd awakened for no reason. Itakh breathed beside her, the only other sound the sides of the tent and the guy lines rustling in a gentle breeze.

She turned over, intending to go back to sleep, but was moving in the blankets when she thought she heard a strange noise. It might have been a dog's howl. She couldn't be sure.

"Itakh," she whispered.

He opened his eyes. When he blinked, they disappeared.

"Listen."

No sound came but the breeze, however. Esther began to suspect she'd imagined something.

"What am I listening for?" Itakh whispered.

Of course, the moment he began speaking, she heard it again, far off. "That."

He nestled deeper into the blankets. "That was nothing."

Then it began again, louder and closer: a frantic baying, like that of a dog tied up and abandoned by its owner. Esther and Itakh both sat upright and threw the covers off.

"That's a dog, right?" Itakh said, as he would not have done had it sounded exactly like a dog.

It kept up its frenzied howls. She couldn't be sure. "It might be a wolf." It fell silent.

"It's a *volkelake*."

"Shh." She wanted to hear it. "There's no such thing." Then, "We don't know what one sounds like."

When it bayed again, he said, "Like that."

Esther started pulling in the blankets to fold them. Her hands shook, but she worked quickly.

"What are you doing?"

"We've got to go."

"Are you crazy?" He was almost shouting now. "I'm not going outside with a werewolf."

She kept folding, and stuffed the blankets into one of the bags. "We're basically outside now, with a piece of cloth draped over us. If we pack up, we might be able to get away. Start pulling up stakes."

Esther hurried from the tent and started Seleme; she wanted her ready to go. As if the horse understood the conversation, she made her

85

whinny, a grating sound, more machine than animal. Esther clicked Seleme's night eyes on, and when she ducked around to the other side of the tent to pull the stakes from the ground, she saw their two green points gleaming through the canvas.

As soon as all the stakes were out, a biting wind picked up. Itakh shoved the pigeon into her loft and slammed the door shut. Together, he and Esther struggled to fold the tent canvas and lash the supports together. Even with their fur coats, the night was cold. Esther had a pair of fur-lined mittens in her coat pocket, but couldn't take the time to get them out. Neither was there time to retrieve the electric torch. As the sounds drew nearer, the cold made her clumsy. Nothing fit as well as it had. Seleme shifted her weight from hoof to hoof, something Esther had not known she could do unbidden. Though her fingers stung with cold and she could see little in the starlight, she hitched the bags and the tent onto Seleme, helped lift Itakh onto the cantle, and mounted. As soon as Esther had raised the horse's idle, Seleme turned to face south, her eyes casting an eerie green glow onto the trampled grass on which they'd made camp. Far in the distance, a pair of round yellow eyes twinkled, low to the ground.

Itakh shouted, and Esther drew back hard on the steering handles, which caused Seleme to rear up and emit her metallic neigh. For a long moment, Itakh clung to Esther's torso to keep himself from slipping off. Seleme worked her forelegs in the air as the weight of her burdens nearly drew them all backward. But after a few seconds, the front of the horse's body dropped toward the ground. With a thud, she regained her hooves. Esther managed to turn her and they began hurrying in the opposite direction. Esther wound her out in each gear before shifting to the next, so frightened was she of losing valuable time. Before each shift, Seleme's engine roared in complaint. But soon they were in a full, fourth-gear gallop across the grassland, a tiny arc of space in front of them illuminated by the starlight and the green glow of Seleme's eyes. The creature howled behind them. Even over the din of Seleme's hooves, the roar of her engine, the clatter of their poorly attached baggage, and the rush of their progress through the grass, Esther heard it running toward them. As it gained on them, Esther could see, when she hazarded a glance back over her shoulder, that it was smaller than Eliezer's dog, a fact that did nothing to quell her anxiety. Its eyes and fangs glinted, and its howls filled the air. She ducked a little in the saddle each time it made the sound.

"It's getting closer!" Itakh shouted. Esther already had the horse in the highest gear; she let out the throttle until the engine screamed. But the beast was closing in behind them.

Seleme had been designed for war: to charge, to do battle, to retreat when necessary. All of her sensory apparatus now engaged. Her ears swiveled to the sides, and Esther was sure the machine could feel the creature approaching from behind. But she stretched her neck out and kept galloping. Esther and Itakh had to lean forward to keep hold of her. In a moment of odd clarity, Esther noticed that they were running upriver, which would be helpful to their ultimate progress, if they didn't get killed.

Seemingly in an instant, the animal appeared right behind them. It growled, and bit at Seleme's fetlock, but though Seleme let out a kind of grunt, the animal's teeth couldn't gain any purchase on her steel leg.

"We should have stolen a gun!" Itakh said.

"I don't know how to shoot."

"Still!"

It bit again, and snarled when it failed to make contact. Then it had the sense to start biting at the load Seleme carried, and her riders. Esther, whose legs were longer, felt its fangs brush against the soft leather of her boot. "Akh!" she exclaimed, and released both feet from the stirrups to draw them up beside the horse. But she couldn't do that for long. The rear brake was in the right stirrup. "Pull in your legs."

Itakh drew into a squat behind her, both feet balanced on the saddle and all his weight thrown forward onto her back. She did the same with her left foot—the one the wolf was nipping at—but had to keep her right foot at least near the stirrup for safety. She leaned all their weight onto Seleme's withers and neck. The balance was precarious, nearly impossible, and her cold palms clutched the cold handlebars so hard, she was afraid she might pop the horse out of gear. She got a good look at the animal as it leaped and bit, and saw that it oddly lacked a tail.

"What are we going to do?" Itakh asked.

"I don't know." She tried to keep an eye on the uncanny creature as well as one on the dim greenish space in front of them. Thus far, they'd been lucky—the ground beneath the grass had been level. But Esther kept a lookout for animal burrows or other depressions that might trip Seleme, and for fallen branches, though the likelihood seemed slim on this treeless plain.

For a moment, it seemed the wolf had fallen behind, but Esther soon saw that it had paused and coiled to pounce, like a cat. When it sprang, it shot through the air, aiming straight at their baggage and Itakh's curled-up body. Itakh shouted and ducked down against her back. Somehow, Seleme had gained enough height in her gallop that, when the wolf missed its target, it became ensnared in the steel tangle of her legs. The horse lurched and swayed—Esther dropped her left foot into the stirrup to keep her balance—and the wolf let out a squeak as Seleme's steel hooves stumbled over it. Esther heard an awful squish and the sound of bones breaking. Within a few steps, Seleme had righted herself and regained her former speed, but Esther drew in the braking lever on the right handlebar and eased her right foot forward in the stirrup. She downshifted to slow Seleme to a walk. The horse growled.

Itakh punched Esther's back. "Are you insane? Go, go, go!"

But Esther still heard the whimpering behind them. She turned around.

The wolf limped after them, one front paw suspended useless in the air in front of it, its belly dragging on the ground. Something shone wet in the grass behind it—entrails. Flattened grass shiny with gore stretched back to where they'd first hit it. Esther felt their meager dinner rise in her throat, but kept it down.

"We have to go back and kill it," she said when she found her voice.

"Oh, Holy Shekhinah!" He hit her again. She barely felt the impact through her heavy clothes and the adrenaline that coursed in her veins.

"It's suffering, Itakh. It isn't right."

She guided the horse back to within a few feet of the animal, then applied the brakes. To Esther's surprise, Seleme lunged her head forward and snatched at the wolf's head with her steel jaws.

"Stop!" Esther shouted, then realized that Seleme was incapable of responding to verbal command. "Stop it! Stop!" she said anyway. The horse shook her fierce head back and forth, worrying the wounded animal as a dog worries a toy. The wolf couldn't fight. "What do I do?" she asked, shrieking now. A thousand times she had seen Seleme respond, of her own accord, with a menacing sound or gesture, but other than the nip the machine had taken at Eliezer, Esther had never seen her in automated attack mode. She tried yanking straight back on the handlebars, but Seleme only lifted the wolf off the ground. Finally Esther pushed the handlebars toward the ground and cut the engine. Seleme's jaws remained locked. The wolf lay whimpering on the ground, its soft cries amplified in the horse's hollow, metallic mouth. The rest of the world seemed silent with the engine off.

Esther was down from the horse in an instant, trying to pry the jaws apart, but she found them too strong and the teeth too sharp. "Help me," she commanded Itakh, then rooted in her pocket for the mittens. She tossed him one. "You take the top and I'll take the bottom."

She put the mitten on her right hand and used it to grip onto the lower teeth. With her left hand, she grabbed onto her right. Itakh mirrored her. Exerting all their strength, they pried Seleme's jaws apart. The wolf fell to the ground with a soft thud. Its panting sounded loud in the quiet. It wasn't trying to get them any longer; it lay on the grass, the sides of its head bleeding, licking its broken paw and watching them with yellow eyes.

"Holy Shekhinah, how are we going to kill it?" Itakh asked. "We still don't have a gun."

"We could trample it with Seleme."

"Ukh."

"It's that, or I slit its throat."

She tossed the second mitten to Itakh and reached into her boot for the knife. She hoped it was sharp enough.

Could the animal know what she was about to do? Its eyes, which had so terrified her from a distance, looked trusting, almost human. Esther had to steady her breath as she knelt beside it. She put her hand on the top of its head and, she didn't know why, stroked its fur. It was thick and bristly like a mountain dog's, with a soft, lighter undercoat. Esther felt she should say something to it. "You were a worthy adversary," she tried, though it sounded wrong, forced. "You're a good dog." She drew back on its head to reveal the pale, silky fur of its throat, and closed her eyes. She knew wolf wasn't kosher—it had paws—and especially not after having been trampled and mauled by a horse, but she recited the *shokhet*'s prayer over it anyway, since it was the only prayer she knew for killing an animal. "*Barukh atah Adonai, Eloheinu melekh ha'olam, asher kideshanu b'mitzvotav v'tzivanu al Shekhita.*" Blessed are You, Adonai, our God, King of all that is, Who has commanded us to do ritual slaughter. Then she closed her eyes and drove the tip of the knife into its throat.

The *shokhet* did this for a living and as a mitzvah. His knife was swift; he made the work look easy. But though Esther had witnessed *shekhita*, she had never done it herself. The wolf gasped, and blood burbled out around the knife, its flow quickening with each beat of the living heart. She was surprised and sickened to have to saw the creature's throat, and at how much resistance the windpipe gave. The creature kept looking at her, and it gave a last, shuddering sigh before it fell still. This was not a kosher killing.

A choked sob rose in Esther's throat as she cleaned the blade on the grass. Itakh reached across the wolf's body to touch her arm. He said, "You did the right thing."

"Thanks."

"Let's keep going."

They couldn't leave it there. She had prayed over it. She knew this hadn't made the werewolf holy, but it had commended it to the Holy One's care. She had made herself responsible for it. "We have to take it with us."

"No," he said.

"Something will eat it."

They both looked around. The sliver of moon had disappeared, but it could be hours before day dawned.

"Or we could sleep," he ventured.

"You want to pitch the tent for two or three hours' rest? With a dead wolf beside us? I'm telling you, something will come for it."

"No," he said, but she could hear in his voice that this was, in fact, what he wanted.

"You can sleep while I drive. In the meantime, help me tie this thing on."

Itakh stood back while she rooted in their bags and pulled out the rope and mildewed tarpaulin. Even in this fresh country air, its sour smell was overpowering. She rolled the wolf up into the fabric like a salad into a flatbread, then struggled to truss the body with the rope. Despite its small size, the wolf's body was as heavy as Esther herself. Grunting, she dragged it to the horse. She noticed that the pigeon, in its small cage, stood alert, watching them.

"I need your help."

Together they lifted it up and hitched the ropes to the saddlebags. It hung in a heavy arc across the back of the horse, like a giant sausage in a butcher shop. The metallic stink of its blood clung to Esther's hands and clothes.

"Let's go," she said.

There was no saying if it was two or four in the morning. Esther hoped day would come soon. She was wide awake, almost shaking with grief and with a raw, animal pleasure that rose out of grief's core. She was ravenous with an energizing hunger. She couldn't get enough of the biting, sweet air or the terrible scents that surrounded her. Each time Seleme's left front foot stepped forward, there was a slight hitch, as if the chase and attack had damaged something. One more thing to fix, when an opportunity came to stop. Slowly, the stars dimmed and the sky lightened to an uncanny lavender. Then the sun began to rise.

As soon as it was light enough to see, Esther stopped the horse and opened up the access hatch in the left belly. She stared into the machine's innards a long while without seeing what was wrong. Then she saw that a wire connecting the engine to the leg had come loose from its contact point, its end frayed. With the crux of her pliers she cut the wire and stripped back its rubber casing. She plied the ends together and curved it to hold better in place. She loosened the screw, rewound the wire, and tightened it back down before closing the access hatch. The problem with the horse's neck, she could examine later. She tried not to look at the bundle when she emerged from beneath the machine.

Itakh, down in the grass, chewed on something. "Check the leak too."

Her glance crossed the bundle to see if the rear access panel, in the belly between the hind legs, was blocked. A black oval stain had formed on one side of the bundle; a larger, paler one, of the sort a healing wound leaves on a bandage, toward the ground. "Later. I can't work on the horse with that so nearby."

Itakh shook off a shudder.

At least when Esther restarted the horse, she found that repairing the loose wire had restored the machine's normal gait.

Before long, daylight was upon them, the strangeness of night replaced by a hazy sky and mild weather. They said the morning *Sh'ma*. Esther looked out ahead at the river and saw it made a sharp diversion to the northeast, as Eliezer had said it would. In the distance, a barge poled its way from east to west, toward them. *"Barukh Hashem,"* she whispered, and steered Seleme toward it.

Farther off, so far it touched the northern edge of the horizon, a fleet of warships clogged the river from bank to bank. They didn't seem to be moving. "Can you see whose flag they're flying?" she asked.

Itakh sat silent long minutes behind her. As he did, Esther kept straining to see. She told herself in turns that she saw the bright white background of the Khazar flag, a subtle lightening of the color of the surrounding sky, and that she saw something red. Red could be two things: the banner of the Rus, Khazaria's sworn enemies for so many generations, or the emblem they had seen on the Germani aeroships two days since. It was strange how, for most of Esther's lifetime, the first would have been a dreadful sight. She hoped for it now. Was there a proper way to ask the Great Name that it be so? She couldn't think of one, and with no schooling in spontaneous prayer, could not invent one on the spot.

"Menshevikim," Itakh said at last. "I see their symbol."

"Better than the alternative." She wondered if they were sailing southeast, toward Atil, or northwest to Tsaritsyn. If the former, they might be going to help in Khazaria's defense; if the latter, to defend their own city. Neither was ideal, but both were good enough.

CHAPTER 9

Quite a day for war machines," the ferryman said. His clear blue eyes took a long look at the Rus fleet upriver. In the time it had taken Seleme to reach the landing, the ships had advanced enough for Esther to make out their banners. They were traveling toward Atil, as the Khazar fleet sailed north toward Tsaritsyn. Who was protecting whom?

"Do you know what they're doing?" she asked.

He didn't bother turning back to her. "Preparing to fight."

"But whom?"

When he fixed her with his icy stare, she felt he could bore holes in her. She had never seen eyes as pale as his. "There's a war on, you know." He eyed Seleme. "Pack animal."

"She's fierce," Itakh said, "you should be careful."

"Officially?" Esther asked. "We've declared war on—who? Or someone's declared war on us?"

"I don't know for certain. We don't get news. But there's been skirmishing up- and downriver. Bombs in the water, farther north. Haven't you heard?"

"Disrupting Rus shipping," Esther said over her shoulder to Itakh. "Or the oil supply."

"That is, if it's the enemy. We could be dropping the bombs."

"I doubt we'd drop bombs on our own waterway." In fact, the Atil—the Rus called it the Volga—and its transport rights were a constant source of tension. The border between the two nations shifted back and forth across it and up and down its length as often as one army could make an incursion into the other's territory. At present, the border stood several hundred leagues northeast of the river, protected, as Esther's schoolbooks said, by a high wall of barbed wire and a plucky force of Khazar fighters on mechanical horseback. The one exception: Tsaritsyn, which sat, fortified by stone walls and cliffs, on the western side of the riverbank. The bek tolerated it because it was a major center of industry, supplying steel to Khazaria. Despite its presence, all good Khazars thought the waterway their own, their birthright. The Atil's waters were those in which their ancestors had sought conversion. This had changed the nature of the water forever in addition to changing the people's future.

"Where'd you get it?" the ferryman asked, still regarding Seleme. Did he never blink?

"Our father. We're on a mission. We wish to cross."

It was clear in the ferryman's expression how little he thought of them. Esther saw how small Itakh was, how overladen Seleme, how out of their element they all were.

"This is not a mechanical ferry," he said, enunciating as if the words were distasteful. "I take people and beasts—sheep, for example."

"This is a beast."

"Too heavy."

Esther watched his expression, but his face remained still as a mask. "What do you do when an army wishes to cross?"

He let out a puff of air: something shy of a laugh. "Armies put up pontoon bridges. They have nothing to do with me."

"We wish to cross," Esther repeated.

When he glanced upriver this time, she got the feeling he was looking for witnesses. "Twenty dinars."

Esther expelled some breath from her nostrils in a way she hoped sounded disdainful, though she worried it sounded like a sneeze. Would they have to *hondel*, as Rukhl said, for everything on this journey? Esther wished she'd spent more time in the marketplace before setting out on this expedition. Her experience bargaining with the Uyghurs had shown her how little she knew the monetary value of anything. "We'd rather ford it."

"You can't, at this season," he said, indicating Seleme's air vents with his chin. "It'll flood."

Esther knew this to be so; she trusted him as to the river's depth. "I'll give you ten dinars or I'll find another ferryman." She had no idea who came up with these pronouncements.

"There is no other. I'll take you for ten." He probably charged one, for a person. As he reached for one of Seleme's handles, she drew back the steel sheath of her lips and swiveled her sharp ears forward. He didn't look frightened, but he held up his hands as if in surrender and said, "Suit yourself." He stepped down off the grassy bank onto his wooden barge and stood aside to let them board.

Once again, Esther lacked correct change. She gave him a twenty-dinar bill and received a ten-dinar coin. Chuluun had bitten the coin with authentic menace. Esther, uncertain she could pull this off, placed hers back in her pouch. She gentled Seleme forward, but the horse seemed uneasy about this bobbing, dipping terrain. She placed her front hooves, then nearly stalled from hesitation. Esther gave her a little fuel and got all four feet on.

"It's strange, how much they're like horses," he mused. "They might have built them any number of ways." Then he cast loose from the mooring and began to pole his way across.

This was the same River Atil that flowed down to its delta south of the capital and past Josephus's house, but it was much broader here, the surrounding countryside more wild. Atil was a city divided by its river. The ruling class, the Jewish Khazars, lived in the city of Atil, while the Yishmaelites, Nazarenes, Turcii, Tengri-worshippers, pagans, and, it was rumored, a small community of Karaite heretics lived across the river in the twin city of Khazaran. This was also where the markets were. To get across—as one did at least a few times a week—one simply crossed the great suspension bridge that soared above the water, high enough for tall ships to sail beneath its span. In all their lives, Esther and Itakh had never been adrift on the open water. Though the ferryman steered their course with the long pole in the river bottom, the barge kept turning around the pivot point and drifting downriver.

Esther wondered how far they'd wander before they landed. The traffic of Rus and Khazar warships—massive as cliffs, high as the capital's tall buildings—had halted a distance from the ferry. They seemed to be allowing Esther and Itakh to cross. In the meanwhile, the barge's lazy spinning gave them a view of all the terrain: the endless grass, a village of roundhouses on the far shore, the Rus fleet upriver. Seleme was heavy enough that her weight submerged the barge below the surface of the water. She stood pastern-deep in it. The ferryman's leather boots were wet halfway up his shins. He didn't seem to notice.

To Esther's surprise, he had guided them well enough to land almost at a mooring. He poled them along the rocky eastern shore, hopped off into the shallows, and fed the rope through a sturdy iron ring protruding from a rock. He pulled the barge in, fed the rope once more through the ring to bind it, and belayed it to a huge iron cleat. Esther urged Seleme onto the muddy shore. It *was* strange how much the machines resembled horses, uncanny. Though Seleme couldn't feel anything a natural horse felt, she nickered discontentedly and cast a withering glance at Esther over her shoulder. The village was only a short distance upriver. Some people were walking toward them to ride the ferry or gaze at the horse.

"Your father sent you on a mission to Malinky Yatsa?"

Esther assumed that was the village's name. "No," she said. "We're looking for the floating village of Yetzirah."

For the first time, a spark of interest flared in his eyes. "What for, a sick parent? You can't be barren; you're too young to be married." Itakh poked her in the back ribs. She kept looking at the ferryman, who added, "I don't know any other reason why a girl would seek out the magicians."

"To save Khazaria," Itakh piped up from the back. Esther wanted to smack him; he'd never sounded so juvenile.

The disdainful expression returned. "You won't find the village floating now. They're back from their wanderings to their permanent home, gathering in their harvest for winter. Doing whatever else it is they do."

Despite her lack of sleep and all they'd experienced the night before, Esther thrummed with energy. "Can you direct us?" she asked. Her brief mental foray into the previous night brought the smell of dead wolf back to her nostrils. Worried, she checked the ground behind them, fearing that a trail of blood might lead to the water. Instead she noticed the woundlike stain on the trussed carcass growing. They had to get away before someone asked about it.

"Head upriver, toward the ships. When you see a walled village in the distance, turn off through the fields. The terrain is hilly and it'll disappear from view, but you'll find it."

"How will we know it's the correct village?"

For the first time, he smiled, a crooked affair that lifted one side of his mouth more than the other.

"We should go," Esther said. Whether or not he was mocking them, the wolf carcass would attract his notice before long. "How far a journey is it?"

"You'll be there soon enough on your war horse. They need access to the river for their," he seemed to search around for a word, "you know."

"Their what?"

"May the Lord bless you, if you really are protecting Khazaria."

She walked Seleme wide around the approaching passengers and tried to smile at them in a friendly, normal way. Still, when she stole a glance behind her, they'd stopped, turned to watch, and made animated gestures to each other as they spoke. They might have been talking about the Rus fleet as well as about Seleme. Heedless of the attention it might attract in this unmechanized place, Esther shifted Seleme into third and gunned it out of town.

When they'd cleared the village, Itakh said, "That wolf stinks. I'm surprised he didn't say anything."

"When we get there, we can borrow a shovel and bury it."

"I'm hungry."

"Grab something. We can't stop."

He rooted around and came back with some dried apricots, for which he hurried through a *Ha-Eitz*. Esther threw a handful into her mouth and choked them down half-chewed.

"I thought they might taste like dead wolf, but they don't," Itakh said.

In the pause between coughs, Esther said, "Stop talking about it. Water."

He passed her the skin. She was getting more adept at doing non-driving activities with her left hand. She wondered if she would ever be proficient enough to use a weapon with her left hand while driving with her right. How could they be hungry when the wolf smelled so foul?

"Let's send the pigeon to Jascha to find out if we're at war," she said, handing back the water skin.

"No. Anything could happen to her, and we can't guarantee she'll find her way back to the field loft, so we can really only send her one time. We have to wait till it's more urgent."

"Needing to know if the enemy has reached Atil isn't urgent?"

Itakh wasn't trained to argue as Josephus's blood children were. "Something could come up."

They were traveling through what seemed like endless fields of steppe grass. "What good is she if she can't bring us news?"

"She's a bird, Esther. They're not all that smart. She'll find us if she can."

The day was idyllic: the sky a hazy gray-blue, the sun warm on their shoulders and heads. They had extra fuel in the can. A battalion of bat-winged Khazar aeroplanes flew westward overhead, thick as a flock of migrating birds.

When the shadows began to lengthen and the sun to dip over the Atil toward the west, a strange, mournful sound became audible.

"What's that?" Itakh asked.

"Shh." She downshifted, and when that didn't help, braked and eased the horse into neutral. Seleme's idle was a low, sputtering hum.

The melody became clearer—that was what it was. Esther could only hear it when the breeze blew from the east. Once the wind stilled, it vanished. The tune was plaintive and in a minor key, like much Khazar music. It sounded like the Yishmaelite call to prayer rolling across the river from Khazaran, or like the kind of folk song in which young lovers die. At first, Esther thought it was a single voice, a low, man's voice, but then it broke up for a moment as if there were multiple singers. She turned in the saddle to see what Itakh thought. He looked spooked.

"We head toward it, right?" Esther asked without conviction.

Esther watched Seleme's ears swivel as she tried to pin down the song's location. It grew louder as they approached, and resolved into a group of voices all similarly pitched and on-key. But for a while, Esther couldn't see where they were coming from. Waving grass, the broad sky. After a time, they reached the top of a small hill and could look down into its valley. There, in a perfect square, stood a field wild with broad-leafed, tangly vegetables, and dotting it were men. All were crouched or bent, weeding and harvesting, each with a plain black *kippah* on his head. She could see little of their downturned faces as their mouths opened and closed in song. Their thick fore-arms, tending to their work, were reddish brown, like earthen pots. The wind shushed in the grass and a sparrow made its sad cry. Beyond this field were others, riotous with growth. Beyond the fields stood a low stone wall—the kind used to pen sheep, not the usual defensive structure—surrounding a miniature city. It was only the size of a no-madic tribe's winter encampment, but the inhabitants had built their closely packed buildings of wood, stone, and brick, and a few reached to a second story. Even from a distance, Esther could tell this place had civic pride—not a stone out of place in the wall, the thatch on every roof a fresh green-yellow.

"Is it Yetzirah?" Itakh asked. He held on around her waist but leaned out to one side to take in the view.

"It has to be." It looked so clean after their days on the road. "Ev-eryone said we'd know it by sight."

The workers must have heard their approach, because at the end of the musical phrase, they fell silent, as if of one mind. In a synchronized gesture, they stood and turned to face Seleme. As they turned with methodical grace, they resembled a field of sunflowers, angling their wide faces toward the changing light. They were taller and broader than average men, more on a scale with Seleme than with people. At closer range, Esther was startled to notice that in place of hair, on top of their heads the same brown flesh of their arms and faces was molded into a hairlike shape. On some it was molded straight and orderly; others had the more fanciful suggestion of curls. She wondered how they kept the plain black *kippot* fixed in place without hair to pin them to. None looked directly at their visitors, but even with their downcast glances, Esther could see that their eyes—pupil, iris, white—were made of the same dull brown material. Each had the word *Emet*, or Truth, incised in a flowing hand across his brow. They bowed, and Esther's heart skittered in her chest, so unnerved was she by the beauty and strangeness of the gesture. She too inclined her head, though they weren't looking. She asked, "Have we reached the village of Yetzirah?"

"Indeed," one responded in its low voice. "Go forward. You will be made welcome."

Esther waited for further instructions. Silent, they all held their bow. "*Todah rabah*," she said, and urged Seleme on.

They were halfway to the gate when Itakh blurted out, "Golems!"

"Shh." Who knew if made things liked to hear this about themselves. She and Itakh had almost reached the town. The pigeon rode the right handlebar, beside Esther's hand. The bird flapped her gray-speckled wings and resettled.

Two men hurried out to greet them. One had gray hair, the other brown. Both wore clean, white kaftans, traditional Khazar garb. They also wore large white knitted *kippot*. Outside the gate, they stopped. Their shining skirts flapped against their legs in the breeze. The younger one glanced at the setting sun before folding his hands in greeting.

"*Shalom aleikhem*," he said.

"*Aleikhem shalom*."

"You seek shelter in our village?" She had never heard an accent like his before, and paused a moment to be sure she had understood him.

"Shelter and knowledge."

Though his beard and mustache obscured his mouth, she could see his smile. "Welcome, then. You've arrived in time to help us welcome the Shabbat Bride."

Esther had lost track of the days. What luck not to have broken the Sabbath unwittingly on the road.

The younger man now moved around the horse. When he saw the awkward, blood-stained bundle on the back, he extended one finger as if to touch it. "What's this?" A delicate hand, like a city dweller's. The golems went back to work without resuming their song.

Itakh shifted on the cantle. The bird cooed to itself.

"It's a wolf. It attacked us in the night, and our horse trampled it underfoot." In the recounting, the events sounded a little off. "She didn't kill it, so I slit its throat to end its misery. Then we worried something would eat it on the steppe, so we brought it with us, hoping to bury it." The younger man remained beside Seleme's rump, a sinking expression on his face. She hoped he'd understood her, and at the same time worried that he'd done so too well. Only now did she notice that their burden attracted flies. "I apologize. I know it's strange."

"No," he said, though he didn't sound convinced. Toward the workers in the field he shouted, "I'll need two of you, both with knives."

Esther could not tell how they chose themselves. Two came toward them. They moved with deliberation, as befitted their great size. The younger man indicated the bundle with an outstretched finger while giving instructions in a patient voice. They cut the bundle loose, shuffled it to the ground beside the idling horse, and cut through the binding ropes.

"That's good—" Itakh began, meaning, she thought, to tell them not to let the rope go to waste, but he stopped short when they began to peel away the fabric. The first thing to come free was a lock of dirty, pale brown hair, matted with black blood. A woman's long hair.

"Oh," Esther whispered. She couldn't think of any prayers.

As her heart pounded and her breath grew tight, the workers revealed the slight form of a person Esther's age. She was naked, battered, and filthy. A huge, jagged gash disfigured her throat and another her fish-gray belly. Tangles of purple entrails hung out. A panic seized Esther, unlike any sensation she'd experienced: the urge to vomit receded behind a jolt of electricity that made her limbs tremble and set the short hairs at her nape on end. She wanted to flee; she stood ready to fight any of these people. Though her mind wheeled, trying to figure out what could have happened, she found the presence of mind to say, "By the God of our fathers, I swear it was a wolf." But her terror rose. She didn't know if they'd understood her, either what she spoke of or her accent, which surely sounded as foreign to them as theirs did to her.

The workers didn't seem moved by the sight, but the two white-robed men leaned over the corpse with interest, gingerly holding back their skirts from the gore. When Esther spoke, the older man rose, put a hand on Seleme, and looked Esther in the eye. "You killed a *volkelake*. Do you know this word? A *volkelake*. It reverted to its human form after death."

"I told you!" Itakh said.

This was no time to call his excitement inappropriate.

"By the God of our fathers," she repeated.

"They are known to be difficult to kill, so you had to have some conviction, perhaps even the strength of the Holy One's hand, to do so."

Now Esther started to shake in earnest.

The man took a deep breath, stroked Seleme as if she were a real horse. To Esther's surprise, Seleme angled her steel neck better to receive his attention. To no one in particular, the man said, "We must bury her before Shabbat." Pale orange tinged the western sky. "Carry

103

her," he said to the golems. Toward the others, still in the fields, he called, "Get shovels and picks. Dig a grave, outside the bounds of the cemetery, before sunset."

They rose with a ponderous grace and walked toward a round-house at the edge of the cultivated fields. One entered and began handing implements to the others as they filed past. The line of them snaked around the village wall toward some invisible point in the west. These beings moved quickly, yet without hurry. The two who'd first come rewrapped the girl before hoisting her up to carry her in the same direction. Esther had calmed down enough to observe them. The likeness in their coarse features struck her. In human faces, count-less variations were possible, but these facsimiles all had similar broad mouths, square chins. As they trucked their burden off with seeming unconcern, the older of the white-robed men stood and bowed to Es-ther and Itakh.

"An unusual introduction," he said. "We do our best to be hospi-table to visitors, as Torah instructs. I am Shelomoun ben Mordekhai."

The other, bowing with equal formality, as if Shabbat wasn't bar-reling down on them while they had a corpse to bury, said, "Dovid ben Gershom."

"Esther bat Josephus." The pseudonym had deserted her. "And my brother, Itakh."

Old Shelomoun's brown eyes twinkled with recognition. "The children of Kender Josephus?"

"Yes."

"I met him once, years ago. His whole family." Shelomoun nod-ded, his lips pressed together in interest. "I look forward to the tale of what brought you here, but now we must hurry. Dovid, gather a minyan."

Dovid sprinted into the village—an odd sight in his formal robes. His bare legs flashed as he ran. Having seen them, Esther took care to avert her eyes.

"For a werewolf?" Itakh whispered. His bird ruffled its feathers and resettled itself.

Shelomoun led them, still mounted, around the perimeter of the village. "I visited Atil when I was your age, Itakh," he said, though he wasn't looking at him. "I have fond memories of the place."

The sun put on a splashy display for the approaching Shabbat. Teased-out tufts of orange and pink cloud illuminated the horizon. The workmen were hard at their labor. Ordinarily, the task of digging a grave occupied one or two men for hours. But eight *golemim* had spaced themselves around a small plot of earth and synchronized their movements. Four wielded picks, and while they raised them up to swing, the other four took up spadefuls of dirt to toss aside. Their machinelike precision allowed them to dig the grave with unusual speed. By the time Esther, Itakh, and Shelomoun arrived, a small berm of upturned earth, full of rocks and smelling sharp with minerals, surrounded the workers. The two who had first come to help stood still, the body at their feet. Esther turned off the horse, and she and Itakh slid down from Seleme's back.

"You have to get a lock of her hair," Itakh whispered.

The idea was so shocking, so inappropriate, it sent a new jolt of electricity through her. She didn't dare look at him. "That's against the Law."

"I know." He was good at whispering; his light, child's voice disappeared amidst the scraping of spades against dirt. "But it's what you're supposed to do."

Esther glanced at the mangled body. "What if she's Jewish? Jews have to be buried whole." It was hard to keep her voice down.

"Jews don't become werewolves. Only gentiles."

"How would you know?"

"Hurry."

His argument didn't convince her, but in her body it felt true. She had more or less by accident defeated this magical creature; it seemed right to take a prize, to hold on to some piece of her as protection. But her religion said to do so was wrong. She would have to be careful.

The golems kept at their labor. Shelomoun watched the sky. Esther leaned down to scratch her leg, and as if she'd practiced such cunning all her life, slipped her knife from her boot up into the palm of her hand. She held its hasp loosely between her thumb and fourth finger and felt the steel blade's light touch against the inside of her palm. The long, fur sleeve of her burka draped over her hand. Esther crouched down to the *volkelake*. A wave of rotten meat smell washed over her, and Esther's heart leaped like a frog in her throat. From this vantage, she could not see the golems' faces, but could keep an eye on Shelomoun. When he looked away, she reached down to touch the girl's body, and as swiftly as she could, pulled a lock of hair taut with her left hand while her right drew the knife through it. The strands fell free in thick chunks. She gathered the hair up inside her left sleeve. Unwashed. Its slick, human texture clung to Esther's fingers and turned her stomach. But she stood, breathing shallowly to keep from vomiting, and managed to pull both the knife and the hair up out of sight inside her sleeves. To the best of her knowledge, she'd done all of this unseen.

Soon, most of the golems stepped back so that two could descend into the deepening pit and work from that more favorable angle. Dovid arrived from the village with a group of white-robed men behind him. One wore a wristwatch on a leather band; the ostentation with which he regarded it made its tick more sonorous. "Thirty-nine minutes," he said. But the gravediggers neither checked the sky nor increased their speed. They tossed dirt up onto the ground.

After a time, the two digging golems stood neck deep in the pit. They lay their implements on the ground and climbed out without effort. Itakh patted his crewelwork *kippah* down over his head. Esther, mindful of the dangerous things she held in her hands, carefully pulled up her fur hood. The rotten meat smell clung to her hand.

An elder, not Shelomoun, began to recite the burial prayers in a matter-of-fact tone. Itakh was trying to catch Esther's attention, but she was doing her best to focus on the service. In various places they had to participate, the *ameyns* and *b'rikh hus* of the Kaddish. They had to pay attention to hear them coming.

Still, Itakh reached his face up toward her ear and whispered, "You pray for a *volkelake*?"

"I have no idea," she whispered back. She followed along with the liturgy a moment. "How else do you bury someone?"

"I would have thought a werewolf was more of a thing than a person." He paused a moment before saying, "Am I wrong that she couldn't be Jewish?"

She turned to him in alarm, but before she could say anything, someone clouted him on the head from behind. His bird flapped and resettled.

After the Mourners' Kaddish, one of the golems held out its spade to Esther. She felt herself blushing. She had attended her mother's funeral, seen her grim father shovel ceremonial dirt over her body. But she'd never done it herself. In her bloodstained, road-dirty coat, she felt hot and conspicuous. Still, sliding the knife up the inside of her forearm until she felt confident it would stay put, she took the shovel and drove it into the pile of dirt the golems had removed from the grave. The implement and the soil were both heavier than they looked. The dirt thudded when it fell onto the body. She shoveled in her three spadesful—a sprinkling of dirt, like cinnamon atop a cake—and handed it to Itakh. The tool was shoulder-high to him; he struggled to wield it as his pigeon took off into the air and strained against its short tether. When he finished, he passed the spade to Dovid, who shoveled three quick times and gave it to Shelomoun. Then it went back to the golem worker, who hadn't moved at all while it went around.

As soon as the final prayer was said, everyone sprang into action. "Twenty-seven minutes," said the one with the watch. To the waiting golems, Shelomoun said, "Fill the grave, change your clothes, and get back within the walls." They began shoveling the moment he finished speaking. Dovid held a hand behind, but not touching, Itakh's back to hurry him toward the village. To Esther, he said, "We need to get both of you in the *mikvah* before sundown."

She ran to catch up to them, saying, "But our horse."

"And my pigeon!"

Dovid, without slowing his pace, called over his shoulder, "Someone drive their horse to the stables and place their bird in the dovecote."

Esther worried that Seleme would buck an unfamiliar rider and that golems might not know how to drive, but overseeing her transfer wasn't possible. One of the creatures bent to receive the tethered bird from Itakh with a solemn grace, then cradled her in the correct fashion against his massive breast. The bird settled as if in human hands.

The whole village bustled. Half a dozen more golems ferried trays of food from houses toward a larger building; one carried an enormous flagon of wine in each hand. Tidy stone chimneys released smoke. Esther smelled khallah fresh from the ovens and wondered when the women who'd baked it would appear. Dovid herded Itakh toward a majestic building of smooth gray stone. Everyone kissed the mezuzah on the doorpost. A golem sat on a bench inside. Dovid said to him: "Get each of them out of the *mikvah* in time for Shabbat. Get someone to remove their polluted clothing outside the walls; you'll wash them after Havdalah." To Esther and Itakh, he said, "*Barukh Hashem*, I'll see you for Kabbalat Shabbat."

The golem shepherded them down an elegant, polished stone hallway, one side of which had an alcove recessed into the walls. At about the height of Esther's chest stood the top of a pool of teal-blue water, the size of a bathtub. This was the *keilim mikvah*, for purifying kitchen implements. At the end of this hallway, a second ran perpendicular, extending in both directions. The golem, the pitch of its voice like the others', asked, "Have you ever before immersed?"

Esther shook her head no. Her first immersion was to be in the month of Tishri, before her marriage to Shimon—about whom, she now realized, she had thought little since the incident with the werewolf. She was anxious about not having yet received instruction in the ritual, and eager to finish before the sun set.

"Wash. Clean beneath the fingernails and inside the ears and nose. Not a speck of dirt anywhere on your person. Go to the pools.

Immerse yourselves twice—every hair on your heads. The prayer is inscribed on the walls. Pray each time." The creature gently pushed Itakh down one hallway and gestured with his large hand for Esther to go down the other. Did these beings also observe the laws of *negiah*? Though shaped like men, they seemed sexless. Meanwhile, Esther found it strange to be divided from Itakh. At home, they sat behind the *mekhitzah* together, she for being female and he for being a child, free to sit where he pleased. Here, their different sexes meant separation.

Esther didn't bid him goodbye. She ran down the hall into an elegant bathroom, its stone tub already full of water. Esther dropped her knife to the floor and balled up the lock of greasy hair into a bundle, which she stuffed into the leather money pouch she pulled over her head. She ripped off the *hamsa* and her stinking clothes and climbed in, only to find the water cold. "Holy Shekhinah," she said. On the tub's rim sat basic grooming implements, a perfect rectangle of creamy soap, its side stamped with roman letters—the kind of Frankish soap she and Elisheva received as a Khanukah gift. In her hurry and excitement, she dropped it into the tub. It bobbed beneath the surface. Her skin prickling, she scrubbed herself down as quickly as she could, using the small brush to work caked blood and dirt from under her nails. She lathered her matted hair, dunked herself under, then used a wide-toothed wooden comb to rake the knots from the tangled black strands. She yanked handfuls of hair from her head in the process. As she emerged from the tub, droplets splashing everywhere, she saw how gray and webbed with hair she'd left the water—but there was no time to worry about being a polite guest. She saw no towel with which to dry herself, but instead a small triangle of white fabric. Not knowing its purpose for sure, she blotted her feet on it, then draped it over her dripping hair. Another door, arched and tall, led out the far end of the room. She ran, naked and shivering, toward it.

The *mikvah*'s pool—square, and blue as polished turquoise—filled the entire small room next door. She stood on a narrow stone ledge. Steps led down into the water. To her surprise, the blue water released curls of steam into the cool air. It beckoned to her. She walked down the steps and into the enveloping warmth as fast as she could move through the water. When she stood neck deep, her long, dark hair fanning out around her on the water's surface like a peacock's tail, she raised her eyes and saw the words of the prayer etched into the stone wall.

Barukh atah Adonai, Eloheinu melekh ha-olam, asher kideshanu b'mitzvotav v'tzivanu al Hatevilah. Blessed are You, Adonai, our God, King of all that is, Who has commanded us to immerse ourselves in the *mikvah.* She whispered the words and heard them reverberate off the hard walls. She lay the headscarf on the pool's edge. Then she drew in a breath and let herself sink under.

Beneath the water, she opened her eyes, seeing the blue of her environment and the gray of the surrounding stone. She saw the steady stream of bubbles rise from her nose. She felt her hair wave like sea-weed, remembered the golem's injunction to wet every hair, and ran one hand in a wide arc over her head to draw each strand underwater. When she ran out of breath, she rose up.

She could hear droplets drip from her head back into the water, but could not hear if Itakh was splashing in a pool of his own in some other room. She didn't know why she had to immerse herself twice, but would gladly have done so more than that. She whispered the prayer again, first in Hebrew and then in Khazar, and submerged herself once more in the warmth.

When she'd finished, she splashed up the steps toward the stone perimeter. Her skin prickled in the cool air; her limbs felt drawn toward the water. A runnel of water trickled off the hair between her legs. She tossed the damp piece of fabric over her head once again. The floor was slippery under her wet feet. Would this be what it was like to be Shimon's wife, wondering all the time if her hair was covered, submerging herself in the *mikvah* monthly to be reunited with him after their ritual separation? Her notion of what that meant allured and alarmed her in equal measure. Back in the washroom, her clothes were gone. In a panic, she tore through a pile of fabric on a low stool she hadn't noticed before. There, beneath a coarse, clean towel and a pile of unfamiliar clothes, sat Rukhl's *hamsa*, her knife and pouch, and in the pouch the lock of hair. She stood a moment dripping, her heart thudding in her chest, before she put her treasures down, dried herself off, and squeezed water from her hair. Her body remained damp in spots, and she had to struggle to get into the clothes: a shapeless white dress that hung below her knees, a pair of white cotton tights—the kind little girls wore and too short in the crotch—and a beautiful pair of slippers—garnet silk embroidered with white and yellow flowers. Esther's hands shook as she secured the buckles across her feet, so worried was she about the time. The slippers were too big, but this didn't matter.

She noticed in passing that someone had let the water out from the tub, leaving behind a gray film and clumps of black hair. There was also a second triangular kerchief, this one embroidered with white flowers. She tied it around her head, tucked the *hamsa* and pouch inside the new clothes, and ran back into the hallway. Unlike the sturdy fur boots she'd been wearing, the slippers had fine leather soles. They slipped on the polished floor and she felt the hard stone through them.

Dovid and Itakh were waiting for her, their eyes trained on the doorway as if they could draw her out. A look of relief passed over Dovid's features, and he glanced westward for confirmation. "Come, come," he said, pushing Itakh in front of him and extending a hand Esther's way. As she ran behind them toward the large building, Esther saw that Itakh was also dressed in white: a clean chemise over loose trousers, too long for him and rolled at the cuffs. His wet black hair curled up around the edges of a Bukhari *kippah*, white with a city embroidered on it in gold.

Dovid led them inside. The building enclosed one large, elegant room, its walls hung with colorful fabric, a long table laden with food in its center. Clustered around it stood perhaps two dozen men in white robes. Around them stood some of the *golemim*. Those who'd performed the burial and touched the bloodied clothes were perhaps exiled to some other place. Esther couldn't distinguish them.

111

"At last," Shelomoun said from beside the table. He held up one hand to welcome them. "And one of you a daughter of Rivka v'Leah, *Barukh Hashem*. Esther bat Josephus, may we ask you to light?"

The sides of Esther's face grew hot. She lit each week in her father's house, but that was in front of her family and occasional guests. This was a lot of people, all but Itakh strangers, and not one of them a woman. All the golems were shaped like men. She had no idea how the kabbalists practiced, if the way they said the prayers was the way her family said them, if they said the same prayers at all. She didn't respond, but approached the table. A murmur of approval passed around her. She heard someone comment, "It would be the one reason to have a woman in the village." She didn't feel like a woman, despite the kerchief on her head. When she married Shimon—if she married Shimon—she would light the candles at his table. She'd been born to this small dominion. Someone dropped a ceremonial dinar in a wooden *tzedakah* box, and now she could begin.

Shelomoun handed her a fancy silver matchbox, its top enameled with a menorah. In her discomfort, she broke the first match by striking it too hard, but the second lit a satisfying flame and brought the familiar, acrid scent of sulfur to her nose. She covered her eyes, and the world contracted to that small, dark space. For the first time, she thought that might be the reason one had to cover one's eyes with one's hands. Her voice wobbled as she began singing the simple prayer—Blessed are You, Adonai, our God, King of all that is, Who has commanded us to light the Sabbath lights—but soon she found the melody and heard her voice resound in the room. Before she took her hands from her eyes, she offered up the prayer of her heart, a brief, incoherent plea for everything to work out right. Then she said, "*Ameyn*," and the room gave back a solemn echo. In the silence, punctuated by an occasional exhalation, she could hear she'd done well.

Three of the men had taken seats on the floor, one with a sitar, one with a tabla, and a third with a pair of flat bells tethered to each other with string. At home, there might be musical accompaniment to sex-segregated dancing after Shabbat dinner, but never before. The rhythm instruments began to play a sinuous, syncopated beat, and when the sitar joined in twanging, Esther recognized the familiar melody of "Shalom Aleikhem," made exotic by the instrumentation. Itakh looked skeptical; she herself found the music strange. There were always songs at Shabbat, all praising Hashem's might, but they didn't sound like this back in Atil. By the third song, when a guitar and a tambourine started to play, Esther found the melody strangely enticing. She might have wanted to dance, if she hadn't been afraid to do so in mixed company. Only once they all began to sing did she realize that this joyful song was "L'kha Dodi," the welcome to the Sabbath Bride, a song that, in Kalonymos's temple and his followers' homes, always had a lugubrious tone. It had never occurred to Esther that the song's joyful lyrics could find reflection in a melody as celebratory as this one. She knew the words well—"God is one and God's Name is one!"—and although she felt self-conscious in this room full of strange men, she muttered along beneath her breath, afraid of hitting a wrong note in the unfamiliar melody. As the song progressed, someone opened the door to the outside. This happened at home too, this opening the door to greet the Sabbath Bride. At her father's house or Kalonymos's temple, everyone would turn and bow to Her, just as if She were a real *kallah*. But to Esther's surprise, the kabbalists streamed out the door, the guitar and tambourine players in the lead. Itakh shrugged at her before following them into the violet twilight. The men didn't stop once they were outside. Instead, their steps skipping into a dance, they proceeded out the town gate into the grassland adjoining the cultivated fields. While singing the verse, "Come, O Bride! Come, O Bride!" they all turned to face east and bowed to the darkening hills and the stars rising in the sky. For a moment the gathering fell quiet, then erupted into an ecstatic chorus, everyone whirling and dancing. Esther couldn't resist. No one was watching. Holding Itakh by both hands, Esther spun in a circle until his feet lifted off the ground. He laughed like the little boy he was. There were no more verses, but everyone kept joyfully *lai-dee-dai*-ing, spinning, and clapping. Itakh begged to be put down, and the world

slipped sideways after they stopped. Around them, people kept swirling. Eventually—Esther wasn't sure on what signal—the song wound
down. When everyone had stopped singing, the only sounds left were
people catching their breath and the chirp of crickets. Esther's heart
surged with joy. This was how Shabbat was meant to be celebrated.
These isolated kabbalists knew something Rabbi Kalonymos did not.
She felt lucky to experience it.

More songs followed, all with dancing, and a few more rhythm
instruments appeared, shakers and something that made a zippy
sound, which made Esther want to twist and leap in the air. When
they'd run through most of the Kabbalat Shabbat liturgy, celebrating as if this really were a wedding, the robed men led them back in
toward the central hall. The golems let them pass and followed behind. The two Sabbath candles Esther had lit glowed on the table;
silver serving dishes picked up glints of their light. With Shelomoun
leading, the assembly said the *berakhot* over wine, hand-washing, and
two gigantic loaves of braided bread. ("Is their oven really that big?"
Itakh asked. If so, it was the kind of oven in which, in fairy tales, one
baked a child.) Then it was time to eat. The serving tables stood at
waist height, but people ate in the normal fashion, sitting on the floor.
Shelomoun beckoned for Itakh and Esther to serve themselves first.
They each took a flowered china plate from the teetering stacks at the
table's near end. Esther tucked a pressed linen napkin and a three-
tined fork underneath it, so she could carry them all with one hand.
Though the dancing had gone on for a while, the food was still warm,
fragrant with spices: a cinnamon-scented tagine of chicken and some
kind of fruit, accompanied by nutty couscous; string beans shiny with
oil and smelling of ginger; the khallah; dishes of apricots and dates.
As a guest, one was supposed to strike a balance between showing one
liked the food and not appearing to be a glutton, but Esther didn't
care. She was hungry, she heaped up her plate. The golems didn't seem
to have the ability to change their facial expressions, but some of the
men chuckled what she assumed was their approval. Shelomoun led
her and Itakh to pillows in the center of the floor, and they sat down

cross-legged, balancing their plates on their laps. Shelomoun must have seen Itakh's anxious expression as he looked at how many people still had to serve themselves, because he said, "Don't wait. Your food will grow cold."

Esther and Itakh ate like feral children, hunched over their food. They couldn't help themselves. Soon all the company sat and ate. The great room grew warm with bodies and conversation, ripe with the smells of people and food. Forks made their pleasant scraping sounds against plates. The meal tasted delicious, separate from Esther's hunger: the chicken juicy and tender, the spices well balanced. One of the golems stooped to hand them stemmed glasses of what looked like wine, but when Esther took a tentative sip it turned out to be fresh grape juice. She drank it down in one long, appreciative swallow, and moments later he was back, crouching solemnly with a pitcher to refill it.

When everyone had eaten, the golems came around to remove the plates. They also passed around the salvers of fruit. Shelomoun started singing the grace after meals. These prayers the kabbalists offered without instrumentation, their cantillations strange to Esther's ear. When the last song, "Yom Zeh L'Yisrael," finished, a hush fell over the room like a contented sigh. Then Shelomoun looked at Esther, his dark eyes lively in the candlelight. Though she was seated only a few feet away, he addressed her in a public voice: "Esther bat Josephus, Itakh ben Josephus. We seldom receive visitors here because of our remote location, so close to the Rus—"

"And the fact that we spend half the year wandering the steppe," Dovid added, which elicited a general rumble of laughter—not, Esther noticed, from the *golemim*.

"And the fact that most modern Khazars concern themselves with worldly things." Shelomoun's remarkable smile lifted his eyes and even his pink ears with happiness. Though his white hair and wrinkles meant he was older than her father, the smile was as quick as a young man's. "Our visitors being few, we repay their fortitude with hospitality."

115

"We're so grateful—" Esther began, fingering the fancy dress; but Shelomoun kept speaking.

"I'm not fishing for praise. We know you're thankful." His eyes remained fixed on her. "And I don't wish to molest you with questions." Esther could feel it coming. Itakh reached for her hand. Shelomoun gave a slow blink before continuing. "However. You are two children of high birth who have traveled a long, dangerous way from the capital in wartime. You've ridden in on a specialized war machine, borrowed from your father at best, at worst stolen. Your machine has required you to have dealings with the Uyghur mafia, who, we know from hard experience, can be fierce. And you arrived with a slain werewolf as a prize." At first it seemed he thought he'd said enough. Then he added, "Some of my brethren call all this portentous. We would be grateful if you'd explain."

Esther gripped Itakh's hand. His name meant "puppy" in Khazar, and it suited him: a small, steadfast, tightly wound coil of energy. Still, at this moment she wished he were old enough to do some of the talking. At home in Atil, she hadn't minded that he was so little while she, at sixteen, was somehow old enough to marry. He was her favorite person, her chosen companion, and everything else fell by the wayside. Now, it would have been nice for someone else to talk. Where could she begin?

"How much news do you receive here of the outside world?"

A faint smile passed across Shelomoun's face, as if he knew she was stalling. "We have no electricity, so we lack some devices you have in the capital. We are too remote to receive mail except on rare occasion by carrier pigeon." Itakh shivered with excitement. The gray pigeon they'd sent west toward Praha flashed through her mind. Even amidst all her other thoughts and worries, Esther hoped it was right then homing to her long-lost uncle. She wondered if Matityahu looked like her father, shared his temperament. She wondered if, when Shelomoun had mentioned that he'd met Josephus's family, her uncle had still been among their number. "But we have congress with the rest of Khazaria. We see our fellows, particularly when we're out upon the steppe. We know the Uyghurs. And the Rus are a dozen *parasangs* distant—we have to be prepared for them to strike at any moment."

She wondered what he meant by strike. "You've heard of the war in the west?"

A ripple of discontent passed through the crowd. "We're not fools," someone said.

Shelomoun put out a hand to quiet him. "We know that Haman the Agagite has annexed Polonia and crossed Ukraina."

"And the refugees?"

"Many driven to New Britania and to Palestine, while others find safe haven within our borders. They fill camps in the west, on the banks of the Dniepra, and a smaller camp near Atil."

Itakh said, "The one north of Atil has a hundred thousand people in it."

"Not that many," Esther corrected. "But a lot. All Jews, to our knowledge." She took a sip of her juice to see if it would give her the strength to speak. "This week, a squadron of enemy aeroplanes swarmed the capital—"

"The whole region," someone interrupted. "We saw them too."

"My first fear was that they'd come to destroy the city, but they were gathering information. Still, their presence does not bode well. My father"—Itakh squeezed her hand—"Our father is the kagan and bek's kender. The bek reports that the enemy has crossed the Dniepra. There are forces there fighting them back, by land and sea and air. But none of these forces is as great as we might wish them to be. The enemy army is powerful."

Shelomoun said, "We have seen aeroplanes of more than one nation. And warships."

In the far corner, a man with a flaxen beard lifted his face to speak. He said, "I don't understand why this brings you to us."

Esther nodded. The good, spiced chicken turned in her stomach. "Because we want to help."

"And what does your father say of this?"

She licked her lips. "We didn't ask."

The blond man still had his chin in the air. He shook it no, looking off in another direction. "*Kabbed et-avikha v'et-imekha.*"

Esther said, "Yes." Honoring her father didn't have to mean obeying his every word. But she wasn't about to argue theology with a kabbalist.

"Your father rules a nation. You should obey him in all things. Not to do so shames him and the Name. Who are you to do this?"

"Gamliel," Shelomoun said, "don't antagonize our guests."

The person beside Gamliel said, "I think he has a point."

"It is a reasonable question," Gamliel insisted.

Esther wished she were back in her well-appointed bed in Atil with Elisheva beside her. Then she remembered how short-lived that world would be unless someone did something to defend it. "We know we must sound arrogant, ungrateful. That you must wonder how our father raised us." She half hoped someone would contradict her. "But he raised us to love Torah and fear Hashem." As she said it, she realized what an outrage it was that Itakh had not been taught to read. He knew the words of Torah because he heard them in Kalonymos's synagogue, but he should have been able to read for himself. "Our father underestimates Germania's power and its disregard for Jewish lives. They have advanced all this way across Ukraina—will they stop before they've crushed the Rus and ourselves?"

"There are natural fortifications," said the person beside Gamliel. He had small black eyes like dried currants. "Our rivers and steppe and taiga have kept invaders out before."

"No," Esther said, surprised at the flat force of it. "Khazars have kept back would-be conquerors. The terrain helped. You know this yourselves, so close to the border with the Rus." All of this sounded right. She could still turn back, but they had come this far. She ventured onward. "We've come to ask you to help me fight for Bek Admon's army." Slowly she let go of Itakh's hand and stood up.

A dozen people began talking and arguing. Someone guffawed.

"Settle down, now," Shelomoun said, but it took a while for people to comply. "It is the bek's work to raise armies, to conscript the necessary soldiers. Furthermore," he continued, nodding his head as did her tutor when he wished to make a point, "you are a girl." His eyes glanced away from her face. "A young woman." Esther thought he might say more, but he seemed to consider that sufficient.

Despite the ambivalence in her heart, her words came out clear. "This is why we've come to you, sirs. To ask you to make me a young man."

For a moment, she had shocked them into silence. Some gaped at her while others looked away as if she were unclean, an abomination. The next second, people were on their feet, pointing and shouting, some at her, some at one another as they argued. Above all these voices, Shelomoun called, "This does no good! *Khaverim*, it does no good! We are like the workers at Babel—no one can understand another."

Itakh stood up and pressed against her side the way a lamb presses up against its mother. The men were arguing with one another; the two of them might as well have been elsewhere. Esther considered slinking out the door.

But Shelomoun continued his pleas, and in time, the hard boil of controversy slowed to a simmer. Then people's gazes began returning to the two gaudily dressed outsiders. Esther thought she might have made their case more forcefully in her bloodstained road clothes. As it stood, she felt like one of Elisheva's Dolls of the World, each bland girl tricked out in her kaganate's native finery. She saw a man nearby tuck his skirt under him and sit back down, a furtive expression on his dark face, as if he'd been caught doing something forbidden.

"Is it beyond your powers?" Itakh asked. Esther could hear his struggle to find his voice.

" 'Mightier than the thunder of the great waters, stronger than the waves of the sea, is the Lord, our God,' " said Shelomoun.

Itakh blinked, then said, "I wasn't asking about the Name."

"A little *vantz*," one murmured, using a word in the refugees' dialect that Esther didn't know but understood. How many refugees had these kabbalists encountered? Those who passed through Khazaria on their way to Palestine either took the western route, along the temperate shores of the Pontus, or traveled through the capital to head southward. Rukhl had never spoken of seeing kabbalists.

Holding out a hand to silence further commentary, Shelomoun told his peers, "He didn't mean it that way." To Itakh, he said, "All that we do, from awakening in the morning to the greatest of wonders, we do by the grace of the Lord. Everything by His Holy Name." Itakh still looked at him, waiting for an answer. "It is not so much a question of what we can or cannot do."

"You can make golems," Itakh said. "From nothing, right? From dirt? And you've given them souls."

"Not souls," Dovid said. "We've animated them."

Esther felt sick, considering what the difference might be. Itakh also looked stunned, so she took up the thread of what she thought was his argument. "Surely, if you can work that wonder, you can work this one?" She half hoped the answer would be no.

Shelomoun frowned with his whole face. His eyes frowned. "Leave aside the question of what we can do. I'm interested in the question of what we should, and of what we will."

That meant they could do it, Esther felt sure. She didn't know if she should feel glad about that. She didn't know how she felt, other than, for the moment, relieved.

"It's Shabbat," Shelomoun said. "As the Lord rested after Creation, so shall all of us rest. It won't happen on this holy day. But there is all the time in the world for discussion. For now, shall we turn to a happier topic?"

Esther nodded. It would have been fruitless to disagree.

No topic presented itself, however. The awkward quiet of all the assembled people reminded Esther of when she and her family had sat shivah for their mother. She and Shmuel and Elisheva had been desperate for news of the outside world, but their visitors seemed bashful to discuss anything besides dead Or'li. At first, perhaps, Shelomoun thought that the conversation would resume its natural course, but people were either too disturbed or too tired to speak and kept shifting uncomfortably. Shelomoun cleared his throat and stood. "We will see you to our guesthouse, then. Come back in the morning for breakfast before services."

Now people rose and made their way toward the door. As they moved around her, most taller by at least a head, she felt them avoid looking at her. That was what they thought of a person who sought to become what the Holy One had not made her. That was what she could look forward to, back in the world, if they were able to work their magic upon her.

Two *golemim*—one of whom, she noticed, had his clay hair carved into a cowlick that stuck out around his black *kippah*—led them silently to the guesthouse, a cozy roundhouse with a sweet-smelling fire in its central hearth: applewood. She wanted to hear their low voices, but how did you make small talk with someone—something—that wasn't human? Two tidy bedrolls flanked the fire. The golems bowed and shut the low wooden door behind them as they left. Esther and Itakh stripped out of the awkward clothes and crawled into their beds.

Itakh breathed deeply and said, "Smell that."

The silken sheets had been dried on a lavender bush, or its leaves had been sprinkled in the storage chest. Both the bedroll and the thick blanket were stuffed with eiderdown, and when Esther settled herself she felt she was floating in one of the day's high, puffy clouds.

"It's wonderful here," Itakh said.

The floating sensation took over. All the muscles that had clenched—Esther's thighs from holding the horse, the arches of her feet from working the stirrups, her hands from gripping the handlebars, her jaw from fear—begin to uncurl, soften. She heard Itakh's breathing slow, but before he fell asleep, he said one last, groggy thing, "I told you it was a *volkelake*." Esther didn't have the energy to formulate a retort. They both slept.

CHAPTER 10

The embers remained warm in the morning, the little house snug and dark. Outside, wrens and sparrows warbled and chirped as if they knew it was Shabbat. Across the hearth, Itakh's blankets bunched around his ears, his black eyes shining out at her.

They dressed and hurried to the main house to find breakfast, not sure if they were early or late. People were eating in the great room, now awash in sunlight. "Our guests, our guests," said someone whom Esther couldn't remember seeing the night before. He rose from his seat and ushered them in, leading them toward the food like an old *savta*. Esther heaped up a bowl of fruit and yoghurt and took a slice of khallah, chewier than it had been the night before.

Esther had not yet seen a clock in Yetzirah, but at a certain moment everyone knew it was time for services. They stood in unison, just as the *golemim* had bowed in the field the afternoon before. They stacked their plates and utensils in reed baskets near the door, and filed out across the well-tended dirt of the square. Three sheep wandered across their path, two white and one brown. The cleanest sheep Esther had ever seen, their wool seemingly picked out with a comb.

She had surmised, from the deference everyone paid to Shelomoun, that he might be this village's rabbi. When they arrived at the shul, however, another white-bearded man chanted at the bimah. Did they all take turns? Esther wanted to stand at the back of this congregation of men, but Dovid reached behind him to point her toward the stairs, up which a tiny balcony stood concealed behind an elaborate, perforated *mekhitzah*. Itakh, as a boy, could have stayed down with

122

the men, but chose to pray in the women's section, where normally there would have been other children, babies nursing, and women whispering to one another about daughters and husbands. Esther and Itakh were alone up there—a good thing, because the balcony could only have held six people. "What was the women's bath like?" Itakh whispered.

Esther shrugged. "Fancy. Why?"

"No women."

"It was big, considering that."

They stood up and bowed at the appropriate times, sat back down. Not having known what tradition the kabbalists followed before she'd arrived, and having been won over by their ecstatic music and dancing on Erev Shabbat, Esther had hoped their whole practice might be mystical, exotic. As far as Shabbat morning was concerned, they performed most of the service the way Kalonymos did—with instrumentation, at least, when songs were sung. The day's Torah portion was *Parshat Re'eh*: kashrut and the three Pilgrim Festivals, and a number of dull regulations. Esther's ears pricked up at the section about slaves. "But should he say to you, 'I do not want to leave you'—for he loves you and your household and is happy with you— you shall take an awl and put it through his ear into the door, and he shall become your slave in perpetuity." Itakh had been only seven when Josephus had asked if he wished to be free. Of course he had chosen to stay. No child would ask to be cast out from the only family he'd known. Josephus had steadied him whimpering against the doorpost while the doctor had held a pneumatic awl against the boy's plump earlobe. With a plosive rush of air, it drove a needle through. Itakh had shouted, then cried; Esther had seen the blood trickle and been surprised at her sudden nausea. The doctor worked the golden ring through the hole, then pressed a shard of ice to each side of the lobe to ease the pain. He was bound to her father for life now, but she felt it was to her. She imagined having the authority to set him free, and whether she'd choose to do so, knowing he might leave. When she brought herself back from this reverie, she felt bored, sleepy, and guilty for feeling bored and sleepy, as often she did at shul. "Is it more entertaining in the men's section?" she whispered.

Itakh didn't answer.

The Torah reading had ended when, at the edges of her hearing, Esther heard a low, distant thrum. At first she thought it might be a trick her ears played, the bass notes of the golems' voices outside. Then she convinced herself it had stopped. Then it reappeared, slightly louder, enough so that she could hear it was the sound of a machine, similar to Seleme's engine. She stood and peered down through the *mekhitzah* to see if others had noticed, but through the pattern of the latticework, which bore a faint smell of beeswax, everyone seemed intent on prayer. Itakh looked up at her, and before they could say anything, they both bolted for the pie-shaped staircase. Esther felt a momentary gratitude for the delicate shoes the kabbalists had given her, which kept her from thundering down the stairs. Heads turned—faces with irritated expressions—but Esther was too preoccupied to care.

Outdoors, the day was as cheerful as before. The summer sun shone warm and bright. The sparrows and wrens had been joined by a pair of bluebirds, so colorful they dimmed the rest of the landscape. They flitted off the moment Esther and Itakh stepped outside. The immaculate sheep grazed on an enclosed lawn, and nearby stood a goat, gnawing with its yellow teeth at someone's flower patch.

"There," Itakh said, and pointed into the western sky beyond the river.

All she could make out were gray specks in the expanse of blue. But the drone was unmistakable. Because no words could sum up her anxiety at seeing them there or the terrible perfection of their timing, Esther said, "No," and stood with her hand shading her eyes to watch them come.

Before long, the specks resolved into a squadron of enemy aerocraft—a smaller one than had flown over Atil, just nine swallow-shaped planes. Esther wondered if she should alert their hosts or allow them to worship in peace. These aeroplanes were particles of dust compared to the power of the Name, and He was a vengeful god, one who demanded His due on Shabbat. Itakh must have worried over the same question, because he twisted as if chained to the spot. "What do they want?" he asked.

Despite the warm sunshine, Esther shivered. She didn't answer—what the dark kaganate wanted was obvious; what this small squadron intended would soon be clear. By now, the sound of the engines droned loud and near enough that men had begun to stream from the synagogue into the square. Though the sun was in the east and the aeroplanes in the west, everyone raised their hands to their eyes because the day was so bright. Scores of men in immaculate white robes stood with their skirts blown against their legs by the wind. The golems stood straight and turned their wide-eyed faces upward. Perhaps, animate but not truly alive, they felt sunlight differently.

The aeroplanes headed straight for Yetzirah. They'd as likely bomb the assembly as photograph it and turn around. Esther saw the military use of both strategies, though she wondered how they knew the location of the village when it was not even marked on the kender's map. Now people were supposed to start running around in a frenzy, like chickens with an eagle circling above. But all around her, the kabbalists stood still. Then someone began to sing, "Shiru L'Adonai Shir Khadash," one of the psalms from Shabbat services the night before. The man had a clear, strong tenor, and his words rang out over the square: "Sing to the Lord a new song, sing to the Lord, all the Earth. Sing to the Lord, praise His Name!" Everyone knew the words. Other voices joined in, the golems filling in the bass notes. Dovid jogged across the square toward the main building, then returned a minute later with his arms full of rhythm instruments, shakers and small drums. These rattled and rang as he handed them around. Esther ended up with a tambourine in her palm; she wrapped her thumb and fingers around it and gave an experimental shake. Meanwhile, the aeroplanes kept coming. As they neared, the ground magnified their sound and trembled. The song grew louder, some voices breaking into harmony. At first, Esther wiggled her instrument from side to side, but as she grew accustomed to its weight and behavior, she started to rattle it, then clap it against her other palm. She tried out a more complex rhythm, aware of how strange it was to enjoy this at this moment. "For all the gods of the nations are idols," they sang, "but Hashem made the heavens."

Now the machines flew near enough that Esther felt their wind on her face, smelled their scent of burned petrol, more pungent than Seleme's exhaust. Normally, with such mechanical din approaching, it would have been hard to hear anything else, but the assembled raised their voices to counter the noise. Soon the aeroplanes were about to pass overhead, and Esther almost forgot to worry about what they might do in the sheer joy of shaking the tambourine and shouting. But the moment they passed over, they opened their hatches and let something drop. She flinched; most around her did too. Not bombs, she could see that almost at once. Something— fluttery. Hundreds of what looked to be moths. She kept up her part of the song, but most of her attention watched these creamy things as they spun in the aeroplanes' wake, then wafted, tacking from side to side, toward the earth. Sheets of off-white paper, settling like falling leaves. Once the aerocraft passed the village, they banked in unison into a breathtaking turn, then headed along a wide arc toward the river. She saw them release a second load of papers over the village of Malinky Yatsa. From there, the fleet continued westward, she assumed to drop papers on every settlement, however small. A moment later a second, larger squadron raced by from east to west. Their shape was boxier than the enemy's sleek machines, less antique than Khazar craft. Esther caught the tail marking on one as it whizzed past: the hammer and sickle of the Menshevikim. Some of the men dropped their instruments to clap and shout *Barukh Hashem!* but most kept right on singing and playing.

Then the song ended. The aeroplanes seemed smaller and quieter as they receded, though their burning stench lingered. Esther only now noticed that Itakh had become the master of a pair of painted shakers. He stood with them hanging from limp arms, and looked like a much smaller child than he was. Dovid put down the rattling instrument he'd been playing—Esther didn't know what it was called, some kind of gourd wrapped in chain mail—and walked off to gather some of the papers, which had scattered all over the village, here stuck on roofs and there pressing against walls. They darted away as he tried to catch them, animate as butterflies. He'd collected half a dozen before he said, to no one in particular, "Pamphlets. All the same."

"What do they say?" someone asked.

Still looking at the papers, Dovid returned to the group. He passed the papers around. Itakh snatched one and crouched down with it. That symbol emblazoned the top, the jaunty cross of the Byzantine Empire. The bottom was a paragraph of strange letters, leggy as a swarm of spiders. "What is that?" she asked.

"Hunnish?" someone asked.

"Germani, of course," said Gamliel, the blond-bearded man to whom Esther had taken such an instant dislike the night before. "They have their own *aleph bet*."

"A barbaric one," someone opined.

Someone else said, "I thought they used the Latin alphabet, as do the other nations of the West."

His fellow kabbalist replied, "You'd think if they wanted us to read something, they'd write it in Khazar."

"'Jews of Khazaria,'" someone read in a halting, soft voice. Esther looked up at him. He might have been the youngest of the group, his curled forelocks as black as Itakh's, his posture already a little stooped from reading. He mouthed the words as he puzzled them through. "'Abandon your idolatrous ways. Cease to circumcise your sons. Give up your refugees and cross the mighty Dniepra, which now lies under our control. You will all be granted amnesty, given work and food. Join us in building a stronger Fatherland. Do this by choice, and we will cease to bombard your cities and tear up your crops.'" He paused, continuing to peruse it. "It goes on. They seem to revere their leader."

After he read, the square fell silent. The smell began to dissipate in the fresh breeze.

127

"What a lot of pother," Gamliel said, and grunted a laugh that seemed intended to cause others to agree with him.

But no one did. "They've already conquered Polonia," someone said. "And torn across Ukraina in a few short months."

"As our visitors said last night, they've interned their own Jews," Dovid said. "That's why so many thousands seek asylum here." He thought for a moment, then added, "They wouldn't grant us amnesty."

"As if we'd be willing to go!" Gamliel said. "As if we care for their Fatherland."

A low voice said, "Jews do not abandon their God for political convenience." It was one of the *golemim* who'd spoken. People nodded wide-eyed, as if surprised at his level of understanding.

Shelomoun caught Esther's eye. Though his whole face was covered in a fine web of wrinkles, a long vertical furrow had gathered between his brows. His brown eyes shone. "Esther bat Josephus," he began, "we had no reason to doubt the words you spoke last night, but this sign, this portent, proves we must act." Esther sensed that she was supposed to say something, but didn't know what. "We will help you in your cause," he went on, "but I cannot say how. I cannot think about it when Hashem and His Holy Shekhinah dwell among us on Shabbat." He cast a worried glance at the shul, as if the service might have been ongoing all this time, although everyone was outside. "We have prayers to complete." He walked off toward the sanctuary, head down. People looked at one another. Then, in small groups, they began to follow him back, the instruments rattling and making joyful sounds, unaware of the living beings' somber mood.

"Could they make you something besides a boy?" Itakh asked as they brought up the rear.

"I don't know." Esther's imagination couldn't stretch that far. Her heart began to hammer the moment she tried. She was glad to be heading back toward the safe invisibility the *mekhitzah* conferred. For however much longer the prayers lasted—if her experiences in Kalonymos's shul were any indication, this might be a long time—she could avoid thinking about any of this.

CHAPTER 11

The problem being that Shabbat was all about thinking. Or about rest, thinking's natural counterpart. If you couldn't write, knit, or carry anything, and if you weren't yet married, what else was there to do? Kalonymos had long tried to explain, to her and to everyone, that a day of rest meant allowing everything to relax, including the mind. "Do you suppose that on the Seventh Day," he once said, a big grin on his gruff face, "the Lord sat around *worrying* about the heavens, the Earth, and all Creation?" The obvious answer was no, and Esther disliked a question that led to only one response. But she was built to worry. After services in Yetzirah came a lovely cold meal of bread, cheese, and more fruit and nuts, but her mind was so busy spinning out dreadful scenarios that Esther found herself exhausted, despite that she could rest on this drowsy summer afternoon. She wanted to hunt Shelomoun down and barrage him with questions about her family, but didn't feel it would be right to march through the village on a mission. After asking a golem to show him the dovecote, Itakh brought back an animated report of Nagehan's happiness amidst the other birds, then retired inside their snug house and took a nap. So she was alone, her mind wheeling through the possibilities of foreign domination, enslavement, mass murder, and above all else, who she would be if she became a man. When, if, the war was won—for there was no longer any doubt there would be a war—she would return to her father's house as a son and have to live out her days that way. She might become a javshigar; she might be banned from society, a kabbalistic misfit. Unclean, forbidden. Which of these scenarios was most terrible? She had never exactly wanted to be a woman, but had taken for granted that she would be. She had never wished to be a man. The whole idea was madness, something she was certain no person had thought of before. The Name created a *neshamah* male or female. There the subject began and ended.

If the mystics were correct that the Sabbath conferred an extra soul on each person, she wished the one she'd acquired that day might have been more tranquil than her own. Her thoughts were more exhausting than running from the werewolf had been. At least then, she'd known that she could focus all her attention, all her senses, on one thing.

Itakh was fast asleep, a rasping, childlike snore at the end of each in-breath. She craved exercise, but much good exercise was a form of work, forbidden on Shabbat. She went back outside and stood in the swept dirt yard. Not a pebble out of place. If only the sun would set.

"You don't look like you're resting," came a soft voice from behind her.

Torn—gratefully—from her toxic reverie, she turned, and saw the young man who'd read out the Germani text. Up close, she wanted to call him a boy. He was no older than she, the faintest hint of down on his cheeks, and about her height.

"I didn't mean to startle you."

"No, I'm glad for the company. My brother is sleeping, and I don't know anyone else here."

"Would you like to take a walk?"

"Very much." Esther worried she'd responded with too much enthusiasm. "I mean, it's kind of you."

"It's a beautiful day," he said, looking up at the sky as if it hadn't recently been disfigured by war aeroplanes. "And you've hardly seen anything here."

"I've seen golems!"

He laughed and gave a shy shrug of his stooped shoulders. "They're only part of it." He started walking toward the town wall. "We haven't met. I'm Amit ben Avraham v'Sarah."

Esther stole a sideways glance at him. Phrased that way—"the son of Avraham and Sarah"—it meant the person had been born into another nation and later accepted Avraham and Sarah, the first Jews, as his spiritual parents. But one wasn't supposed to ask.

Amit must have seen her thinking. "Those are my parents' actual names. You can imagine the jokes." His teeth fit oddly in his mouth, as if they were too big or his jaw too narrow, but this made his smile more appealing.

A few people sat on small rugs or woven mats in their yards, reading or enjoying the sunshine. Through the open windows of houses, Esther saw others sitting and talking together, some laughing while others argued. This must have been what it had been like when Kagan Bulan had invited the sages of the various religions to come persuade him: a long Shabbat afternoon of holy debate.

"I'm Esther bat Josephus," Esther said.

"Everyone knows that."

In the past, she had often thought that Atil, for all its size and grandeur, was a small town, the way everyone knew everyone else's business. Now she knew what a small town was.

"Not much happens around here, you have to understand. Or a lot happens, but much of it is internal. So you've caused some excitement."

"And some anger too, I gather."

He made a noncommittal noise and led her out the town gate into the countryside. Across a small valley and halfway up a gentle rise, natural horses were grazing. Seleme stood in their midst, albeit at a distance from them. Her idle sounded like the growl of an angry cat. Mechanical horses had been designed to mimic some natural horse behaviors, purely for decorative purposes and for the thrill of life-like design. She was, for example, supposed to pretend to crop grass. But Seleme was the only creature whose head didn't bow toward the ground. Instead, she stood in the long grass as if braced against an unjust blow, her sharp ears pointed forward and her expression as peevish as a machine's could be.

Esther hurried toward her, though she hadn't given her much

thought since handing her over the previous afternoon. Seleme's keen eyes tracked her as she approached, weighing the level of threat Esther posed. "What's she doing out here? Why is her engine running?"

"No one knew how she might like to spend Shabbat, so they left her running all night and put her out to enjoy the day with the others. I have to say, though, she doesn't look pleased."

This was a profligate waste of fuel. "She has no knowledge of Shabbat." Esther put her hand out to touch Seleme's steel nose, and the horse blinked. "She's a machine." There was no point in being angry. The harm was already done.

"She is and she isn't."

Amit was right. None of the specifications suggested a mechanical horse should like to be stroked or flattered, yet they did, to varying degrees. This one also took offense at things. Machines weren't supposed to do that. Esther had interrogated Bataar about these issues, but he had shrugged her off, saying that no one in Khazaria understood what had wrought this change in their greatest invention. One didn't question it. Esther was glad she'd purchased the extra fuel from Chuluun, but worried it wouldn't be enough. She turned Seleme's engine off.

"I thought they pretended to eat grass. That's what I've heard."

"They design them for that, but on her, it didn't work. I don't know why."

When Esther looked up from Seleme, she noticed that not all the grazing horses were what she'd thought. Many were steppe horses, and two—one bay and one piebald—had the musculature of fine Arabians, but a few had a more idiosyncratic conformation: shorter than usual, blockier. They were varying shades of brown, and their coats lacked the Arabians' velvet sheen. Esther simply noticed these things. Then she realized how closely their coloration resembled the golems'. These had to be *golemim* themselves. Golem horses! She'd heard of such things in legends—two spiritualists working themselves up a golem calf, then eating it, say; such a tale always had an air of warning about it, as did every golem story she could think of—but had never expected to see one. "Can I pet them?" she found herself asking.

Amit didn't look as if that was the question he'd expected. "They're gentle," he said.

She approached the nearest one, its smooth flanks the color of a newly dug yam. She now saw that it wasn't actually grazing but sniffing at the grass with its mouth open. It was like a mechanical horse in this way, mimicking a behavior that occurred in the given world. It raised its head as a natural horse would do and regarded Esther sidelong from its dull brown eyes. She held still to let the creature snuffle at her hand, then placed her fingertips on its long nose. Incised into the clay between its brows, in clear, delicate letters, was the same Hebrew word, *Emet*, or Truth, that adorned the brows of the golems. She ran her fingers over the letters reading-wise, right to left.

"They all say that," Amit offered. "Man-golems too. It's part of the spell that animates them." She must have glanced up too eagerly, because at once he added, "Not the only part." She watched him, and he licked his lips, then paused. "Women can't study Kabbalah."

"Because it's in their nature, or because it's the rule?" She kept stroking the horse, which she now thought of as being named Emet.

"The official answer is because it's their nature. But I believe it's just a rule. Who better to create things than those whom Hashem has already endowed with the ability to create?"

"I never thought of that." The horse seemed to like her. Seleme had her head down when Esther turned her off, and now looked as if she were glaring at them.

"Best not to mention I said it."

Esther nodded. Amit couldn't know how many secrets she'd had to keep to get where she was—he had no way to judge her trustworthiness. "Why horses?"

"What's that?" He raked his fingers along another horse as if his hand were a currying comb. It lifted and shook its head in enjoyment.

"Why do you make horses and not some other kind of animal? I saw sheep this morning, but they looked like regular sheep." Then she corrected herself. "Regular except for how clean they were."

"The golems bathe them to keep the wool fresh. They use it

to weave some of our garments." He gave the horse a final pat and touched Seleme's muzzle. Esther almost leaped between them, then recalled that the horse wasn't running. "She's a beautiful machine."

"Thank you."

"Golems have senses and faculties—faculties suitable to their kind—but they neither eat nor excrete, and their flesh can't be consumed. A golem lamb doesn't produce meat or wool. A golem chicken won't lay eggs even if we fashion her a golem rooster. They're only good for work. So we make useful creatures, horses, men. There are a few golem oxen. I'll show you, they're out in one pasture or another." The way he regarded Seleme made Esther think he'd never seen a mechanical horse up close before. "The main reason we make them, of course, is as a spiritual exercise. But the man-golems' ability to plant and reap, to cook, launder, and polish the kiddush cups, is a gift to our studies. I doubt we could do such labors without their help. The horses and oxen carry our goods when we travel."

"But they don't work on Shabbat."

He looked puzzled. "No one works on Shabbat."

"One sees gentiles going about their business every week in the capital."

Amit nodded. "I don't know any gentiles. I suppose the golems are Jewish by association. I never really thought about it. To the best of our abilities, we see that our cats keep kosher too. We don't feed them milk with meat, though they then go out and hunt mice. But even if the golems aren't Jewish—and it's not as if I've ever spoken with one about Hashem—it would be wrong to make them work while we ourselves observe a day of rest. That's like hiring the Sabbath goy to do what you yourself are banned from on the Lord's Day."

"It's like the part about slaves in today's *parshah*. You ask if their conscience will allow them to convert. If so, they more or less become members of your family. You don't treat them by a separate set of rules. Is that how you think about golems?"

Amit nodded once, as if punctuating her statement more than indicating assent. Then he said, "Should we keep walking?"

"I'd like to see the oxen." To Seleme, Esther said, "We're going to leave, but you stay here. You'll be safe." The horse was turned off, but it didn't seem right to leave without saying goodbye.

As they continued up the hill and toward the pasture on the other side, Esther asked, "Won't you be in trouble for going off alone with me? At home, I'm not allowed to be in the same room as the person I'm going to marry, unless someone's there to supervise."

"Not trouble, no." He bent down to retrieve a bright blue feather from the grass, hardly breaking his stride to do so. "So someone is waiting for you?"

"Shimon ben Kalonymos, the chief rabbi's son." Even that title sounded diminished under this vast sky. "They expect us to marry after Simkhat Torah."

" 'They' is your fathers?"

Esther nodded, though Amit was inspecting his tattered feather.

"And what do you think?"

Esther shrugged. "He's kindhearted, a good Torah Jew. I like his smile. My father made a good choice. I would have picked him myself." In an ordinary conversation, this was where the person would have asked Hashem to let the blessed day come in good time, but Amit made space for her to speak. "But I don't believe Khazaria will still be standing in Tishri. Not if we don't mount a stronger defense. I have to be part of that." As they walked along, she realized there was more, and that Amit wouldn't stop her from talking. "My mother died when I was a child. Behind the *mekhitzah*, it seems few women study. They don't ride, they don't make war. They raise children; they offer up some of the khallah before baking it. Would I do these things? Even if the world that permitted them continued?" Her cheeks flushed hot. The very moment she had wondered what the laws of *negiah* would make of their aloneness, she thought about flaunting those laws. Amit walked, playing with the feather, but as when she was with Shimon, she felt a powerful desire to touch him. She liked Amit's face too, she realized. He wasn't as handsome as Shimon, but something about him drew her eyes in.

135

"I understand," he said.

There were the cows—real animals, she gathered from their coloring—up ahead, golem oxen interspersed among them. A few of the cows lay on their bellies in the grass, their forelegs drawn in beneath them. They looked like house cats, or like loaves of bread.

"Would you rather be a man?" he asked.

"Not for myself, no." She realized how flimsy her denial sounded. "I guess I can't say I really want to be a woman either. But I've always assumed I would be one. I never thought of trying to escape."

"But if you became a man, would you regret your escape?"

The way he said this made her hopes sink a little. "I don't know." The cows that weren't sleeping looked up at them with big, wet eyes. "Can we visit them too?"

"Don't you keep livestock in Atil?"

"Chickens, mostly. A couple of milk goats. They raise larger animals outside the city walls."

He glanced up to see where the sun was. "We can keep going, if you aren't tired, and still be back in time for Havdalah."

Esther glanced down at her feet. The silk slippers were damp, and rubbed blisters on the backs of her heels. Still, she wanted to keep walking. She didn't want their conversation to end. "I'm not tired," she said.

The way his smile broadened indicated she'd said the right thing. She could have reached out and touched his hand, touched the blue feather. No one but Hashem would have seen.

She said, "We haven't gone too far?"

"I don't think so." He looked around to judge where they were. "Rambam says a Shabbat walk can be two thousand cubits in a straight line." She wouldn't have been able to produce the figure herself. "That's a quarter of a *parasang*. And I wouldn't say we've been walking straight."

She liked his way of interpreting the rule. The beautiful countryside rolled away beyond these few small hills they'd crested. White and purple wildflowers Esther couldn't name dotted the grass. She caught a sharp, bitter scent as they walked past a small copse of evergreen bushes: juniper. Amit didn't ask further questions about her home or her upcoming marriage, but Esther continued to think about them, missing her father, missing Kiraz's cooking, but not sure how to answer Amit's question about escape. If the kabbalists changed her into a man, this would make the marriage impossible. This would mean never being kissed by Shimon, never pressing the length of her body against his. She didn't *want* the change at all, if she put it in those terms. She had no intrinsic desire to be a man, only a conviction that she could not do what was necessary in her present form. Of course, she wouldn't tell this to the kabbalists. Her only hope of convincing them was to express her desire as wholehearted, uninflected.

They'd been walking silently for some time. Amit didn't appear troubled. For someone with such a timid scholar's body, he seemed at home with himself. But Esther felt it was her duty to continue the conversation. A question she'd been considering since the evening before leaped to her tongue: "If there aren't any women in Yetzirah, why is there a women's pool? Atil is half women, but I've heard Kalonymos's *mikvah* has only one pool, to which the sexes go at different times."

"Women come to us, sometimes from great distances. And because we have none of our own here, we take care to keep them separate—a separate pool, your separate guesthouse. We embrace our life here willingly, but some might be tempted."

She noticed he wasn't looking at her. Looking itself was a form of temptation, a violation of *negiah*, though Esther couldn't imagine herself a temptress. The only features on which she had ever received compliments were her station and the great length of her otherwise undesirable dark hair, neither of which was her doing. Women at court plucked their thick eyebrows, used depilatories on their arms and legs, reddened their lips and cheeks. Even had her father permitted such ministrations, she had no desire to perform them. When she looked down to distract herself, she noticed a pale pink pebble at her feet and stooped to pick it up. She was less agile at this than Amit had been with the feather. "Rose quartz," he offered. "If you take it back to the village and put it in a bowl of water, it'll glow. I bet your brother will like it."

"It's pretty," she said, turning the smooth stone over in her hand. Then she added, "Why do the women come?"

"Different reasons. Most are praying for a child. Some seek a husband—" Esther must have looked at him in alarm because, laughing, he put out a hand in front of him as if to ward off the thought. "Not among us! They ask us to plead with the Holy Shekhinah on their behalf."

"Does it work?"

"I don't know." Although he always seemed to be half a pace behind her, he was also directing their route. Now he led them in a wide, sweeping arc across the grassland and back toward the distant village. "Some come because their husbands are drunkards or gamblers, and we ask them to bring the men here. I think the sight of us puts the fear of the Lord in them." He glanced at her sidelong, and they both laughed.

"Do the men ever choose to stay?"

"Not that I've heard of. When they consider the rigors of a life of prayer and celibacy, they seem to feel lucky to leave with the wives they once mistreated."

Esther looked out at the vast landscape. Sky encompassed land, the sea of grass waved. Amidst the wildflowers, birds, squirrels, the occasional rustle of a hopping toad, the gurgle of its call, Yetzirah appeared tiny, and the only habitation in sight. Esther knew the great manufacturing city of Tsaritsyn stood close by this mystical village, but couldn't see even its smokestacks from this hillside. "None of you can have been born here. You must all have come by choice."

Amit nodded. "Hashem calls us to do this work. A man becomes a tinker because his father is a tinker, but no one's father is a kabbalist."

Shmuel would be kender to the next bek because that's what their father did. No one had asked Shimon if he wished to be a rabbi. Esther really would have liked to be a javshigar, if the choice were hers. She wondered what her father's brother would have become, had he not defected to the West. "You heard Him calling?"

Amit thought for a moment. "Not like Avram did, no. But I knew I had to come here to find that for which my soul yearned." He had a clear sense of himself, then. This explained the sureness in his manner despite his unprepossessing appearance. "I'll do what I can to argue in your favor," he said. "All of them are my elders—every one—so I can't speak out if they all stand against you, but I'll do my part."

"Thank you." She looked at the resting village. "Do you think they will? Stand against what I ask?"

Amit said, "I can't say," meaning either that he didn't know or wasn't at liberty to reveal. She didn't ask him to clarify.

The route he chose to return them to the village did not take them by the cattle and horses. Instead they approached the graveyard, past which a small stream wound. An old willow tree presided over the small plot, its long, pale tendrils sweeping the grass. The tree was huge, the biggest thing in the landscape other than the village itself. Esther couldn't believe she hadn't seen it the afternoon before. Two older men sat on woven mats in the graveyard—not on top of graves, but off to the side, near the banks of the stream—talking and laughing. One looked up and waved to Esther and Amit. "*Shalom aleikhem*," he called out. "Showing our esteemed visitor the countryside, are you?"

"We had a pleasant walk," Amit said.

Both men nodded. Outside the bounds of these more ordinary graves, marked with flat black stones, Esther saw the fresh one, unmarked and heaped with dirt, different from the land around it as a new scar from unbroken skin. "Do you want to pay your respects?" the other man said.

Esther couldn't read his tone. "I don't know how without knowing her name."

Both of their faces grew more somber. Amit said, "Perhaps you could call her '*volkelake*.'"

Esther gripped the pebble in her damp palm and walked over to the grave. At this short distance from other people, she felt in the wilderness; the susurrus of wind in the grass filled her ears now that no one was talking. Up close, she could see the dirt crawled with worms. No doubt they were already digging into the unfortunate creature beneath. She couldn't recite the Mourner's Kaddish without a minyan, so she said an inward, stumbling prayer for the soul of the *volkelake*, then placed her pebble on top of the mound. The palm that released it felt the cool afternoon breeze. The greasy feel of the *volkelake*'s hair sprang vividly to mind. She tamped the pebble down into the soil so it wouldn't roll away.

No one had moved while she said her prayer. They watched her return. "Looks like Havdalah will come soon," she said. The sun was in the west, if not yet setting.

"No need to rush it," said one of the men.

They remained quiet until Esther and Amit had moved away, then resumed their conversation.

"Will I be in trouble for carrying the rock on Shabbat?" Esther asked.

"Oh, no." He waved the feather back and forth. "There's an *eruv*, it extends pretty far." As she looked around for the string that defined it, he said, "It's underground. The golems buried it. We're free to carry handkerchiefs in our pockets when we walk on Shabbat."

"All of Atil is surrounded by an *eruv*. But you can see it, a weathered red string. The kagan employs a man whose sole task is to patrol it, in search of breaches."

"I think ours is red too. I've never seen it; it was buried before I arrived."

"How old were you?"

"Twelve. I ran away from my village."

They passed through the village gate, Amit still allowing her to walk in front of him, like a queen.

"And how old are you now?"

"Sixteen."

Involuntarily, Esther let out a snort through her nose. "Four years! Is that all it takes to become a kabbalist?"

"You know nothing about it." His expression remained mild, but his tone was heated.

"I'm sorry." Her same age, and already a mystic. "I'm sixteen too."

"One learns quickly when all there is to do is study." She knew this from her few days on the road. He bowed to Shelomoun, walking toward them, who also bowed as he passed. In that short moment, Esther saw him take in the fact that they were together and how dirty her shoes were, but she couldn't tell if his expression meant that he was puzzled, bothered, or amused. "And it'll be years before I attain mastery. They'd have me be a water boy if the golems didn't do all our manual labor."

Esther wondered if they made just enough golems to fulfill every task, or if they took such pleasure in animating clay that some of the golems ended up loafing. But what she said was, "You became a bar mitzvah here."

"*Barukh Hashem*. A great honor."

They had arrived back at the guesthouse. Itakh jumped off his bedroll. "Esti!" he shouted. "I was so worried!"

"You were sleeping. I had a pebble for you, but it's gone now. Amit ben Avraham led me on the most pleasant walk."

Itakh stayed glued to her arm and looked up at Amit with his black eyes wide and not altogether friendly. He said, "Next time, wake me. And come see the lofts. Nagehan won't want to leave." He kept staring down Amit until at last Amit bowed backward out the door and shut it behind him.

"Why did you do that?" Esther asked.

Itakh shrugged, fiddled with his single earring. He looked out the house's one small window to see if Amit was really gone. "What did he tell you?"

"Nothing. I don't know what we're doing here." He waited for her to continue. "I want to help save Khazaria, if I can. But then what? Do I live the rest of my life as a man? A javshigar, or a unit commander for the bek?"

"You could become the kender. You'd be better at it than Shmuel."

"That's not the answer I was looking for."

He sat back down on his bedroll. "I don't know. There are other ways to be a man."

"What, a rabbi?"

"A merchant. A goatherd. A mechanic. You like fixing Seleme."

None of the suggestions solved the problem. "And I'd marry a woman?"

He lay down, as if her reasoning had exhausted him. "You like Rukhl, don't you?"

"Rukhl's already married," she said, which also didn't solve any problems. "I give up. Take me to the dovecote before you argue me to death."

He was halfway out the door before the sentence had left her lips. She was the one who felt exhausted—she had failed in the primary task of Shabbat, the task of resting. But she followed him out to see the pigeons.

CHAPTER 12

The kabbalists bade farewell to Shabbat as joyfully as they greeted her. They drank more wine and dunked the braided candle in it; they passed around exotic spices, their smells earthy and intoxicating. They sang the songs to welcome back secular time and the Prophet, whenever he might decide to come. Then they ate another festive cold meal. The golems had labored hard to have laid in this much food for the day of rest. When the fruit and nuts were passed, and tea poured from a great samovar into tiny glass cups, each with a lump of sugar on the saucer's rim or a spoonful of compote inside it, Shelomoun blew to cool his cup as if this simple task were his only responsibility on Earth. After taking a sip, he said, "Esther bat Josephus," and she sat to attention. "From the moment you arrived, I believed your story. The slain *volkelake* confirmed to me that you were on some kind of mission. It was a sign." He paused to sip again. Esther's instinct was to say something—anything—to fill the silence, but she held back. "If any of my brethren doubted you at first, the enemy aeroships persuaded them." Shelomoun looked out the door a moment, cradling his steaming glass between his blunt fingers. Then his dark eyes turned back to Esther. "I believe that if Hashem had made you a man, you would lead Khazaria's armies to victory. But as you know, the Lord has not made you a man."

His gaze was so steady, so intimate and kind, Esther had to look away. To hide her embarrassment, she sipped at her cup. The compote contained tiny seeds, which she crunched as quietly as she could between her front teeth. When she raised her eyes again, his inquisitive gaze still rested on her.

"This is why we've come to you," she said. "We don't know of any other way to effect the change."

Shelomoun nodded. His posture, she noticed, was easy yet upright, despite that they were seated cross-legged on the floor. She tried to straighten up.

"But we cannot do that," he said. "We cannot change the will of the Lord."

Esther tried to parse his "cannot," as she had tried and failed to do with Amit's: if it signified literal impossibility, or, more slippery, governmental impossibility, or if it denoted unwillingness. Before she could decide, Itakh said, "Yes, you can. People all over Khazaria know of the wonders you work."

"What you call 'wonders' are the secrets the Name has helped us unfold. The average man, the householder, does not ask if he can breathe spirit into a lump of clay or unlock the gated door to his wife's womb. We study those things, so they are known to us."

"I don't understand," Itakh said. "If you can make a golem out of nothing, or next to nothing, why can't you make Esther, who already exists, into something different?" This question—the result of his age and disposition—made it worthwhile to have brought him along, if she had any doubts. It disquieted some of the kabbalists—there was a rumble of discontent, and she heard someone call him, in refugee dialect, a *pisher*.

"Asked like a true scholar," Gamliel said, grudging approval in his tone. "Do you study Talmud? You've begun your Mishnah, perhaps?"

"I don't attend yeshiva," Itakh said, his tone prideful, envious.

To Shelomoun she said, "You haven't answered him."

"Indeed. The question, Itakh, isn't one of existence, because as the laws of natural science teach us, you can't make something from nothing. A golem is only clay before it becomes a golem, but clay is something—it has weight and a form, however malleable. To make a creature, a beast or a man, from the humble earth is to participate with Hashem at the moment of Creation. It is to eradicate time as we know it and to be with Him in the very first days." He paused to examine a plate of cookies one of the golems held in front of him. Another golem bent to offer Esther a similar plate, and she chose a cookie that contained a glazed cherry. The golems could bake, despite that they themselves didn't eat. "But you see, the Name made your sister as He wishes her to be. He made her *bashert*, in the hope that together, they will be like Himself and His Holy Shekhinah and do their part to further the work of Creation. I and my brethren can, through diligent study, sometimes decipher the mysterious will of the Great Name, but we cannot countermand it."

"But what do you mean by 'can'?" Esther asked, unable to keep the question in any longer. "Do you mean it's impossible, or do you mean you won't allow yourselves to?"

Shelomoun's gaze remained on her and she held it. "You frame those two possibilities as a binary opposition, which they are not."

Esther didn't understand.

He shook his gray head. "You would have to study to know what I mean. But I cannot allow you to study, because you're a woman. It's a pity. You have a great *neshamah*," a great soul, "and your destiny would be different had Hashem placed it in a man's body."

"Then why don't you do it?" Esther shouted. Because they were denying her, her will was clear. All her hesitation vanished for the moment. She wanted to smash the delicate tea glass.

"Easy," someone admonished her from across the room.

Shelomoun's tone remained calm. "You lead me in a circle, Esther bat Josephus. I don't do it because I cannot."

She couldn't think what to say or do. Perhaps the worst part was that beneath her rage at being denied, she felt a rising surge of relief, so clear and giddy that if she didn't take care to suppress it, it would blossom into elation. This was so shameful, she didn't want to admit it even to herself.

"You look stunned," Shelomoun said, with what sounded like genuine concern.

She shook her head. She had no idea how she'd managed to remain seated all this time. "Is there no appeal I can make? Do you speak for everyone?"

"He does," said Gamliel.

"We are not all of one mind," Shelomoun corrected, "but I speak for the majority."

Itakh dropped his face into his hands. "I don't want to go," he said in a small voice, meaning either that he liked it in Yetzirah or was afraid of the perils of the journey home.

"You are welcome to stay as our guests as long as you like. Itakh, should you wish to remain to study, you are younger than most boys who come to us, but we take all who carry a genuine longing for the Almighty in their hearts."

Esther said, "You don't take me." At the same moment, Itakh said, "There isn't time." Esther pulled him toward her and felt the smallness of his bones.

"Think about it, Itakh. Esther, I am sorry to disappoint you. Go home to the capital. I know you will find some other way to serve Khazaria."

"There won't be a Khazaria to serve. We'll be conquered. If the Germanii don't take us, and I expect they will, the Rus will swoop in for the oil fields. One way or another, they'll eradicate us."

"Only a child could be so sure. Believe me, Esther, you'll find another way to help."

Esther drank what remained of her tea, the unmixed compote in the bottom of the glass sweet and grainy enough to make her gag. "We'll leave tomorrow. We'll be grateful if you can fuel our horse." She checked the urge to gripe about them leaving Seleme running all night.

"Of course," Shelomoun said. He seemed calm, comfortable to have them sit there the rest of the evening. But Esther excused herself, drew Itakh to his feet, and bowed out the door. They would pack their few possessions, do their best to sleep, and think of some other way to help Khazaria before it fell. They had no choice.

CHAPTER 13

They had retired, but Esther did not believe she'd ever fall asleep—the shame of her failure to convince the kabbalists was too fresh, her relief over their refusal too vivid. Anxiety over how far the Germanii might progress into Khazaria loomed in her imagination. She heard a knock at the door, and tried to believe it had been some shift in the natural landscape, or something in the house itself settling. She sat quiet, upright and blinking, in the dark and listened to the gentle summer night outside. The second time the knock came, Itakh sat up. They both remained still, however. After the third knock, he whispered, "What should we do?"

Esther went to the door with Itakh close behind her. She opened it a crack and saw Amit, now wearing something darker than his Sabbath robes.

"Shalom," she said, uncertain.

"Shalom. May I have a word with you before you go?"

Her heart skittered under her breastbone. "In the morning? After minyan?"

"Now." He looked around at the empty square. "I feel that with your brother present, we do not risk impropriety."

She opened the door wider to let him pass, and felt stirred by the smell of him—his scent coupled with the lavender in which the *golemim* did their wash—as he passed. Itakh knelt to light the oil lamp, and Esther smoothed her bedroll so Amit would have a place to sit. She knew she could trust him, but *negiah* had its reasons for mistrust.

"I wish I could offer you tea," she said.

They all settled on the floor. In an effort to take up as little space as possible on her own bedroll, Esther perched on her pillow, drew her knees up, and wrapped both arms around her shins. Amit sat with his hands pressed against his thighs. He might have been holding his legs down, keeping them from shaking; he might have been doing it because his palms were slick with sweat. "I wanted to tell you that I disagree with my brothers," he said.

"You're kind."

"You misunderstand me. I disagree with their assessment that what you ask cannot be done."

Itakh began to speak and Esther hushed him.

"To their knowledge, what you ask is impossible. A woman cannot be made into a man, she cannot thwart the Lord's intentions for her. But this isn't true."

The flush that had heated Esther's ears with awareness of his physical presence shot down and warmed her entire body, pooling between her legs. She felt the impulse to bolt outside into the cool air, but held herself to her spot.

"You've asked the elders to change your sex, and they are correct, they cannot help you. But there is nothing to stop you from doing it yourself."

Itakh turned his palms upward in an appeal to heaven. "What are you talking about?"

"Itakh, shh." She reached over and grabbed his sleeve to restrain him.

"Get off," he said, slapping her hand, but he otherwise remained still.

"Think," Amit said. "When two people wed, does the rabbi marry them?"

This sounded like a trick question. "No. The rabbi officiates, but they marry each other by their own consent. Witnesses sign the *ketubah*, which binds them in the contract they've agreed to."

Amit nodded, his lips pressed tight. "And when you immerse yourself in the *mikvah*, who purifies you there?"

She had only done it the one time. "Hashem and His Holy Shekh-inah." Then she thought about it. "I did it myself. I purified myself by the action of my prayer." Esther felt she would make a good yeshiva boy. She'd be good at the debate.

He continued to nod. "What you ask is done the same way, by heartfelt prayer and the cleansing power of the water."

In addition to being hot, Esther felt that her whole body was vibrating, the way it did after she dismounted Seleme. She felt the ghost of movement in her hands and fingers. The lamp flickered as if in sympathy. "But the elders don't know this?"

"Or they choose to overlook it. You phrased your request in such a way that they could say no without addressing the underlying yes."

Itakh looked frightened, his eyes wide and dark.

Esther tried to speak, but her voice wouldn't come out. She cleared her throat and tried again. "But as we were walking today, you sounded as if you thought rules served their purpose. What's confusing me is that you'd tell me how to break one. And how you know with such certainty." This did not emerge as a question.

Amit glanced at the floor before meeting her gaze. "Because I have done it myself."

Itakh shot up, but Esther sat transfixed.

"You can't tell anyone," Amit said.

"No." She stared. "You were a girl?"

He raised his fine eyebrows but didn't respond.

Had he looked more or less the same as a girl? If so, he had been blunt featured. His beard was so sparse she could easily imagine him without it. And was he now a man in all physical respects? Esther hated her mind for darting to that first thing, but she couldn't help it.

"You used to be a girl," Itakh said.

"Until I was older than you."

"What was your name?"

Amit wrinkled his nose; his wire spectacles lifted up. "Amit."

Itakh, now pacing, looked up at the ceiling to think this through, but it had stopped his questions for the time being.

"What made you do it?" Esther asked.

"I wanted to study. And you know what our religion says to a woman with such desires." He watched Itakh for a moment. "I come from a small village close to the border with Ukraina."

"How far distant?" Esther asked.

"More days walking than I could count. They all blended together, after a while. We were on the trade route to Kharkov, so people of various nations came through and some had settled there. This is how I learned to speak and read a little Germani, Rus, Bohemyan, a smattering of all the languages one might need in the marketplace or for settling a contract. There were three marriageable Jewish boys my age in my village, a handful more in the market town. My father would have chosen to make me a farmer's wife or a shepherd's wife, or he could have married me to a boy who'd one day inherit his father's vegetable stall in the market. Had my brother begged, he would never have been made a scholar. We were too poor. I had to change my circumstances. I didn't see how else I could be happy."

Until this journey to Yetzirah, Esther had never seen anyplace as small and isolated as the village he described. She had rarely imagined life outside Atil. "But how did you figure it out?"

"We were a religious family. I'd been schooled in the ways of the Lord. And I saw no harm in trying. The worst possible outcome would have been for nothing to happen, which was no worse than if I remained as I was." He looked so unassuming, thin and hunching on the bedroll. But if this tale was true, he possessed remarkable bravery. "I knew that the *mikvah* was the engine of transformation, that it represented my best chance. The only one was in the market town, half a day's journey. When my mother went for her monthly visit, she left our house at midday and returned the next day after spending the night with her cousin. I packed up my few possessions and stole away in the night. The *mikvah* was empty when I arrived, empty and silent except for the faint trickle of water feeding the pool."

"And?" Esther said. Even after everything she and Itakh had experienced in the preceding week, she was astonished that all this had happened to a real person. A real person she could reach out and touch, if the laws of propriety did not forbid this.

Amit looked aside and gave a shy shrug. "Well, it worked. I emerged from the *mikvah* a boy. I couldn't go home. I couldn't even take shelter with my mother's family, who would have cast me out as an abomination. I wandered the town that night, alone with the feral dogs and cats. Some slatternly housewife had left her wash out drying on the bushes overnight. I stole her son's red kaftan and left my girl's clothes and a single dinar in its place. Then I set out to find Yetzirah in the hope that they would take me and teach me. I was lucky, Esther. It was a mild spring, so although the journey was long, I neither froze nor broiled to death. I was exhausted and thin, with blistered feet, when I found them, but they took me in. I have not, until now, divulged my secret."

Esther felt the gravity of guarding his confidence. It felt like a treasure, like protecting one's own soul from the Evil Impulse. "I'm grateful to you for telling us. We'll tell no one."

"I only told you because I can help you. Or rather, I can tell you what I know, and you can decide if you wish to help yourself."

But Esther didn't know how to decide. Sheer momentum had propelled her to Yetzirah, but ever since she'd arrived, she'd been wrestling, like Ya'akov with the angel, with this single question. "The problem is this," she said, as much to spell it out for herself as for him. "I want to do my part to save Khazaria. If it cannot be saved, I want to know that I did the best that was possible, that I contributed what I could. But I cannot say that I want to live the rest of my life as a man—that I want to take a wife and follow in my father's footsteps, or renounce one and follow in yours." Her chest felt tight. She had to make a decision, and had no idea what she thought. "Of course, there's no guarantee, if I go to fight for Khazaria, that I'll live, but somehow that's no comfort."

"I have a question," Itakh said. He stopped pacing, waited for them to look at him. "Say she enters the women's pool and utters the prayer and makes her transformation. Then, she comes out of the women's pool a man. That isn't right. But if, as a woman, she enters the men's pool to anticipate her transformation—that's not right, either. So I guess I don't see how she can go in the *mikvah* at all. Or how you did it."

She felt a momentary surge of gratitude toward him for finding a loophole.

Amit smiled. "You're bright, Itakh."

Itakh's eyes shone.

"You could be a scholar, if you wanted to."

People kept saying that to him. She wondered if he would like to, but she couldn't give his secret away by asking. Amit nodded and said, "In the *mikvah* in our market town, there was only one pool. Men and women used it at different times. A matter of not seeing something you aren't supposed to see.

"Nevertheless, I considered a similar question. The *mikvah* was never meant, at least as far as I know, for the kind of transformation I sought. But you know, even that rural *mikvah* had a *keilim mikvah* tucked away in a corner, for kashering the villagers' pots and plates and spoons." Esther had seen the one they had here as she'd raced against Shabbat's arrival when they'd first come to the village. "I thought, if it could make a piece of glass into a holy vessel, why could it not make me into a vessel of the Lord? And it did, or I hope it did. That's the water in which I immersed myself."

Esther's skin prickled with gooseflesh. She said, "It had that great power in it, but no one knew, though it was there in plain sight."

"I think that's correct."

Itakh resumed his pacing, though at a less frenzied clip. After a while, he stopped, facing Amit with his arms straight at his sides. He looked ready for a fight. "I have one more question." Amit looked up at him, eyes wide with expectation. "Suppose the transformation is successful. She becomes a man. She leads the army. She survives the war. Can she change back?"

This idea had never occurred to her. It seemed enough—*dayenu*, more than enough—to ask the Almighty for one great change in the course of things. He was a vengeful, an angry god, not like the suffering lamb the Nazarenes worshipped. Though Kalonymos had never said as much, she had the sense that Hashem did not care for ditherers. Avraham and Sarah had received the promise of many descendants, but only one actual child. Two miracles seemed like more than anyone's share, especially hers.

Amit said, "It might be best to assume the answer is no. If she wants to change back, and her prayers are answered, she could praise the Lord then for His mercy and might."

Esther could not continue to sit upright. She flopped onto her side and drew a silken cushion to her chest. She made sure the tips of her toes were clear of Amit's body. She shut her eyes, as if that could wipe away her whole predicament.

"Esther?" Itakh said.

She kept her eyes closed.

Amit was so silent he might have vanished, and Itakh tried his best, though his knees gave a pop as he lowered himself down to sit, and his sleeping mat rustled under him. Esther wanted to go home. She wanted her father; she wanted her mother. But if they went home now, what would be the point of all the courage they had mustered? They had run away, stolen Seleme, killed a werewolf, *hondeled* with the Uyghur mafia. Kalonymos would never permit Shimon to marry her. And who could say what would become of the Khazar kaganate. She would have made forfeit her former life—for what?

"I have to do it," she said, so quietly she didn't know if they could hear her.

After a moment Amit said, "Are you certain?"

"Not certain it's the right decision. Certain there's no other I can make."

"That isn't true. Every moment is a crossroads, and each action one of many possibilities."

Esther sat up. A bright surge of anger flared in her chest, surprised her with its force. "How can you not believe in destiny? That Hashem meant to choose us? That Yosef was sold into slavery so that he could

153

later save his people? That each of us is made for her *bashert*?" She stood up and flung her cushion to the floor. "Without that belief, how could we have survived two millennia of exile from the Promised Land? We would have been broken, assimilated, long before now."

If she'd been yelling at Itakh, he would have been on his feet in an instant, fists and voice raised. But Amit stayed seated. He continued to slouch while he thought. He was quiet long enough that Esther lost some steam. "I suppose I believe that destiny is to make each choice as the Holy One would have you make it. At each juncture, to choose that which is most in line with His plan. And I might argue just one millennium. I believe that, if the Jewish people still mourn the loss of Tzion, we are fortunate to have been given Khazaria in its stead."

Even in her anger, Esther heard the truth in his words. "Fine," she said flatly. "Let's go."

Amit held one hand out as if to show her the state she was in. "You can't make such a decision in anger."

"You try to get yourself here from Atil. I've had time to think." Though most of the thinking she'd done had run her around in a circle. "Are you coming with me?"

Amit rose and brushed the folds of his kaftan out from behind his knees. He pushed his glasses up his nose.

Only a few hours had passed since the kabbalists had retired from their evening meal. The streets of Yetzirah stood empty, and though reading lamps shone amber in some houses, many were dark, their occupants already asleep. Esther supposed they went to bed early if they rose before dawn to make magic. She was glad that her leather-soled slippers fell silent on the path despite the force of her stride.

No serving golems awaited them at the *mikvah*. Esther hesitated at the threshold of the dark building and Itakh and Amit stood close to her. Itakh embraced her, his grip tight and his cheek pressed hard against her breastbone. She hugged him back, surrounding him with her arms. When they released each other, Amit put his hand out as if to touch her. Even the suggestion of such an action was forbidden. It sent an electric shiver down her body, just as if he'd made contact.

"You can still change your mind," he said, withdrawing his hand.

Esther nodded. She wanted to run back to the guesthouse, but something made her stay.

Then he raised his hand over her head, his two middle fingers spread apart in the gesture of blessing. Quietly he said, "May Adonai bless you and keep you. May Adonai make His face shine upon you and be gracious unto you. May Adonai lift up His face unto you and give you peace." After he finished, he released his arm and let it dangle beside him. The village seemed to hold its breath.

"I'll be back soon," she said, as if she knew whom that "I" might be upon her return.

CHAPTER 14

Esther was still a woman. She could use the women's bath. She padded down the cool stone hallway, its clerestory windows letting in dim shafts of moonlight. Although she suspected that what flowed from the spigot would be cold, she plugged the tub's drain and turned both taps on full force. She had to grope around the walls for the linen closet. Once she'd found it, she pulled out a towel and a white napkin to cover her head while on her way to the pool, though there was no one to see her but the Name. Nights on the steppe were cold even in summer, and she delayed undressing as long as possible. When the tub was full, she turned off the water and discovered, to her delight, that it was warm. She sank gratefully down into it. The hard muscles on the tops of her shoulders began to relax. Such a simple but total pleasure to lie in a warm tub. From women who used the *mikvah*, she knew there was a rule about how long one was supposed to soak before washing oneself. Relaxing in the water loosened the dirt in one's hair and skin, in the same way refugee women dunked the soiled linens in the river before scrubbing them in earnest. But Esther did not know the length of the prescribed period, nor did she have a watch or a clock. So she lay in the warm water in the dark. Her eyes adjusted to the gray moonlight. When she moved her hands and feet, the water made a tinkling splash in reply.

Still and calm as her body was, her mind darted from one thought to the next. She had no way to fathom how this night might change her. She looked down the length of the tub at her own form, rippling and dark through the water, and felt a rush of affection toward it. By the grace of Hashem and His Shekhinah, her body was healthy and strong, able to do the things she asked of it from day to day, able to ferry her mind around. She lifted one leg out of the tub, and as water trickled down it, she noticed how the strong calf narrowed toward the ankle, how the water had disturbed the fine black hairs. She examined her small toes and thought how blocky her father's and brother's were. She wondered if the shape of her feet would change, if the down on her arms and legs would coarsen, or if the Almighty would choose to change her in only the most obvious of ways—ways Esther was ashamed to consider, and therefore kept circling like a vulture, waiting for a predator to leave off eating its kill. Her hands under the water, she touched and then kneaded the soft flesh of her breasts, ran her thumbs up the nipples. These would surely change. She reached down to stroke the silky tendrils of hair between her legs. What would these be like, an hour hence? She moved her fingers between her legs, and wondered in passing if this was the last time she would feel their particular pleasure.

By the time she finished and her breath returned to normal, the skin on her fingertips had puckered. It was time to wash. She took the soap between her hands and made a good lather to rub over every exposed surface of her body—another opportunity to notice them all one last time. She worked the suds into her scalp and the roots of her hair, then combed out the knots. After rinsing herself in the bathwater, she pulled the plug, then saw a small hand-held nozzle attached to a length of hose. As the water gurgled down the drain, she showered herself with clean water, then stepped out to towel off.

A mirror hung over the sink. She could see herself dimly, her wet hair shining. She combed it out again, feeling the water drip down her back and torso. Her black hair, above, below, and in downy tufts in her armpits, described the points of a compass rose. The sunburn she'd gotten riding had faded, but her face, neck, and hands still looked darker than the rest of her body. She brushed her teeth, cleaned her ears, pared her finger- and toenails, though they were hard to see in the light. Then there was nothing for it but to go. Esther took a deep breath and exhaled a sigh, which reverberated more loudly than she'd expected against the room's stone surfaces. She draped the napkin over her head, took another clean towel from the linen closet in which to wrap herself, and gathered her clothes in her arms. If she was no longer a woman when she emerged, she could not come back to retrieve them.

Her feet slapped against the hallway's cool tiles. Her heart hammered in her chest, and all the hair on her body pricked up, because the night was cold and because of her fear. She arrived back at the *tevilat keilim*. This pool was no larger than the tub in which she'd just bathed, and set into its alcove at waist height, so that a person purifying plates wouldn't have to bend over too far. Esther dropped the towel, removed the kerchief from her head, and climbed onto the pool's thin outer lip, on which she crouched as would a boy shooting dice in the alleyway. She reached one hand down to test the water, and was relieved to find that, as with the women's pool, it was warmer than the surrounding air. She released from her crouch to dangle her lower legs and feet in the water. Then she slid in.

Unlike the *mikvah* in which she'd immersed herself the night before, this pool was not deep enough for her to stand upright. If she squatted, she could be in it up to her collarbone. Her hair floated like seaweed on the surface of the warm water. As she moved her arms to maintain her balance, she thought of what she knew about this water: that in some cases even without a prayer, it had the power to remove impurity and consecrate an ordinary piece of metal to holy use. A similar pool had made Amit into a man, or Amit himself had done so.

A *mikvah* was a powerful thing. It purified wives of their monthly uncleanness so they could return to their husbands. It cleansed those same husbands after they'd enjoyed their wives. It made the *kallah* ready for her wedding. It transformed the adopted child, whose ancestry was unknown, into a member of Avraham's tribe. It changed the convert from a *ger toshav*, a righteous stranger, into a Jew. When Kagan Bulan had converted this whole nation, three rituals had been required: a mass circumcision of all the males, old and young; an enormous *beit din*, or rabbinical council, to examine each individual on his knowledge of the Law and his level of observance; and a great *mikvah*, in which thousands of Khazars had streamed down to the Atil by night, stripped naked, and submerged themselves in the holy waters. Esther imagined the scene, the riverbank thronged with bodies, dark, wet heads as numerous as tadpoles glinting in the moonlight. What a *mikvah* could do, to body and spirit, was as close to magic as most ordinary Jews believed possible.

She remembered the prayer and said, "Blessed are You, Adonai, our God, King of all that is, Who has commanded us to use the *mikvah*." Then she stopped for a moment. What was the prayer of her heart? Not that the Lord make her a man. That was a prayer that could be granted and misinterpreted at the same time, as in the fairy tale about the person who asked for eternal life without asking for youth or health, without which the blessing became a never-ending curse. "Holy One, our God," she said, then hesitated. Were Itakh and Amit listening at the front door? There was no use worrying. "Holy One, our God, help me to save Khazaria from its present danger. If it is Your will, make me the person who can help lead this country to victory and save the Jewish people. Make me a warrior." She could not bring herself to say in so many words, "Make me a man," because in her deepest heart, that was only the means she desired, not the end. But her words implied that meaning, and who could imagine that He who created all that is could not see into a person's thoughts? Quietly she added, "*Ameyn*," took in a breath, and slid under.

As she exhaled her stream of bubbles, she found it more difficult to submerge herself completely in this smaller space. She had to make her body horizontal in order to let it unfurl enough for the water to touch every surface. She had to corral all of her long hair to get it underwater. Then she was out of breath. She put her knees and toes on the pool's tiled bottom and straightened up to bring her head out into the air.

The ritual of the *mikvah* was to immerse oneself twice. She raised her eyes to the vaulted ceiling and spread her hands wide on the surface of the water as she repeated the standard prayer. Could she be clearer about what she asked? She was asking the Lord's help in saving her people, her nation, her country. She had to trust in His infinite wisdom to know how best that could be done.

Again she took in a breath and went under, again she spread out. She let her fingers and toes go soft so that the water could touch and transform the webbing in between them. As she floated and felt the bubbles rising from her nose, she experienced a flash of understanding, almost a memory, of what it had been like to float in the warm darkness of her mother's womb. She felt the pool surround and nurture her, as Or'li would have done if she still lived. Esther felt the water's love. Was this the moment of transformation, when she became not part of something larger but her own independent self, with sovereign dominion over her own fate? She didn't know. She was afraid to think too hard about it, and afraid for the moment to end.

It was impossible to stay under any longer. Esther lifted herself out of the water and breathed. As she put her hands on the lip of the pool and climbed back onto it, she felt the water pull at her legs, her legs reluctant to leave the water, her body struggling to readjust to the gravity of the everyday world. She stepped down to the floor, mindful not to slip, and picked up the heaped towel. As she extended her arms to wind the fabric around herself, she saw her hands and forearms, their bones the same size and shape as before. Water matted the fine hair to the skin. She glanced down, glimpsed her breasts, and looked away, as if she had seen something *niddah*, forbidden. Her body began to shake with cold. She ran her hand down the coiled hair between her legs, the smooth, rounded, palm-sized bone beneath. Unchanged. Was her will not strong enough? she wondered. Was she unworthy in the eyes of the Lord? Esther had made a momentous effort, and she had failed. Her eyes stung.

She dried herself gruffly and pulled on her clothes. She wondered if it was possible that the prayer took some time to work, then dismissed the thought as wishful thinking. She gathered up the towels, then slapped down the hall in the infuriating silken slippers, which still fit. As Esther rounded the corner to the ladies' bath, she clipped the wall with one jutting elbow. "Holy Shekhinah!" she cried. Her eyes clouded with unshed tears. She shoved the towels and head covering into the laundry basket and wheeled around to head back to the street. She didn't know why she was in such a hurry. All that awaited her there was Amit and Itakh, who would be sorrier than she was at her defeat. But she barreled down the hallway toward them anyway. They would be disappointed, but were also her only comfort.

As she approached the door, she saw them sitting on the front steps, Amit slouching and with his knees tucked under his kaftan, Itakh more straight and alert. They looked happy together, like friends out enjoying the night air and each other's conversation. Itakh responded first to the sound of her approach. He jumped to his feet and, before she'd emerged onto the steps, blurted, "What happened?" Amit also stood facing her by the time she got outside, the same girl in her same, imperfect body.

"It didn't work." Every cavity in her head burned. It seemed a miracle she wasn't crying—which left open the question of why the miracle she'd asked for had not been granted.

"What do you mean, it didn't work?"

"I'm the same, look." She held out her arm for inspection. "It didn't—" That wasn't the right way to frame it. "I must not have done it correctly."

Amit stood with one finger on his mouth and the others wrapped around his chin, that elbow cradled in the opposite hand. "There must be more than one right way."

"I didn't ask sincerely enough, then. Or I wasn't holy enough to begin with."

Still with his hand on his face, Amit shook his head no.

"Look at me." She flung her hands out alongside her to demonstrate. "See? It's Esther bat Josephus, not some Turkic warrior prince." Her voice was loud, but she didn't care.

Amit nodded. "How did you state your petition?"

The question annoyed her, and she was on the brink of blurting

161

a reply when she realized that she couldn't recall her exact words. Details remained vivid in her memory—her arm and hair flashing around behind her in the water, the vision of her ancestors dipping themselves in the Atil, the moment of insight—but her words had vanished, though their sense remained. "I said something about becoming the person who could lead Khazaria to victory. I left it to His will. Should I not have done that?"

Amit replied, "It's not as if you had another choice." He paced off and back again with his chin still in his hand. "You do look the same," he said. "Yet something must be different."

She wondered if he was simply soothing her. "When you submerged yourself in the pool, was your transformation immediate?"

"I stepped into the water a girl and stepped out a boy."

Once again her mind raced to the most obvious meaning of that statement. She was ashamed of herself, ashamed of being so prey to the Evil Impulse. She loved Shimon, so why did her mind go there? "Well, the Holy Name destined you to be a mystic. I don't know what He intends for me."

"We'll find that out, in due time."

"If we're not all killed or taken prisoner."

As if she hadn't spoken, Amit continued, "But for now, we should retire. No matter what tomorrow brings, we need our rest."

"I won't be able to sleep," Esther said, but exhaustion washed over her as the water had done. Her feet felt too heavy to drag toward the guesthouse.

A few short steps from the *mikvah*, a small group of kabbalists rushed toward them and blocked their path. Esther, Amit, and Itakh stopped short. Esther's heart sped up and the hairs on her arms and the back of her neck pricked, alert to danger. Shelomoun and Dovid led the group, both with their hair unkempt under their sober *kippot*. Three others, whose names Esther did not know, stood behind them. Her mind spun as she tried to think up reasonable excuses for their presence here and discarded them one after the next.

"We have continued to ponder your mission," Shelomoun said

without preamble. His breath labored; he had exerted himself to get here. Esther's heart jumped in the hollow at the base of her throat, but she held still and waited. "I spoke truth when I told you that we could not make you a man," he said, then swallowed with visible effort before continuing. "But I lay awake this evening, unable to sleep, tormented with worry for Khazaria's future."

"Many of us were tormented," Dovid added.

They spoke in ordinary tones, but these sounded loud in the quiet night. Other residents of the village began sticking their heads out from their doors, then moving toward the commotion.

"I have seen the enemy with my own eyes, after all. I saw their war machines. What will become of us? Our whole way of life, and the many deeds we hope shine as good works in the Almighty's eyes, will vanish. Then I slept, and in my sleep I saw a vision."

Esther bristled like a cat as she waited for his next words.

"In my dream, you rode at the head of an army of *golemim*. They were numerous as the stars in the heavens. You retained your God-given form."

A shiver prickled down Esther's spine from top to bottom. She saw it reflected in Itakh, whose body also gave a momentary shake.

"I can only interpret this as a sign from the Name. Others of my brethren also saw it."

"A waking dream," Dovid confirmed. "Clear as the light of day."

Esther was as aware of her body, her unchanged body, as she had been at any moment of her life. Every part of it was awake. Her heart leapt like a bullfrog. She put one hand to her throat to still it, but the pressure didn't help. "When was this?" she asked.

"A short while ago. It woke us all."

Esther knew it had been while she'd immersed herself in the *mikvah*. And she knew with unwavering certainty that this shared vision of the kabbalists' was the Holy One's response to her prayer. "I prayed to be given the strength to fight for Khazaria. I think you saw the vision at the moment of my prayer." She was dripping water. They had to know she'd done *Tevilah*. But she chose not to mention this.

"We have not all conferred, but I've reached a decision," Shelomoun said. He folded his hands in front of him. They seemed to shine in the dim light. "The bek needs more than another good soldier, and I have thought of a way to help him and you. We shall raise you an army of *golemim*. A battalion, for you to lead, with golem horses. Neither the men nor the beasts require food, water, or sleep. We will give you a band of nearly invincible fighters. It will be yours to rally more forces around them."

Esther looked to Amit, hoping he could help her understand, but his attention focused on Shelomoun. "I am so grateful to you," she said. She swallowed, but her mouth still felt uncomfortable, full of saliva. "But I leave Yetzirah in the same state in which I arrived here. A woman cannot lead an army."

"Not exactly the same." It took Esther a moment to realize he was refuting her first statement. "Or perhaps you are the same, but it took us a while to see your mettle with our flawed, human eyes."

Hashem had not changed her physical form, but perhaps He had changed, or revealed, something in her deepest nature: what, it was not hers to know. Though the night was dark, Esther's vision began to speckle and brighten. Everything turned a vivid shade of violet. She thought she might faint. "I accept—I gratefully accept your offer."

A murmur of laughter passed through the assembly. "You cannot choose to decline," Shelomoun said. "We are fulfilling your destiny."

Esther balked at the word. She could fail at this, just as she'd failed to transform herself into a man. The question she chose to ask was, "How long will it take to raise the battalion? For all we know, our enemy is already on the march to the capital."

Itakh blurted, "We can send Nagehan. She might be able to bring us news."

"We don't know," Dovid said. "We will give you some of those we have made already, and we will make others for this purpose. Until now, we have always produced golems one at a time, as a spiritual practice. We have never before tried to make large numbers of them." He turned to Shelomoun, as if he might have a better answer.

Shelomoun shook his head, then said, "We must begin tonight. If any of our brethren remain asleep, we must wake them." He seemed to see Amit then for the first time, and though it was too dark to read his expression, Esther thought he might have wondered what this youngest kabbalist was doing out at night with the visitors. "Amit, come. There is work to do."

"I haven't gotten any rest," Amit protested.

Shelomoun nodded again, as if Amit's statement had confirmed some unflattering thought. "And yet we begin our work."

Amit glanced over his shoulder at Esther as he followed his brethren down a side street, away from the square. She saw a glint of moonlight on his eyeglasses, but could not make out the expression on his face.

CHAPTER 15

Esther and Itakh were left alone on the street. "An army of golems," he commented. She didn't know what to reply. "And you'll be their leader! Won't Shimon be amazed when we get back to Atil?"

"I hadn't thought of that." Esther loved Itakh as a brother, a pet, and a friend, but at this moment she wished he were older and could curb his excitement. He was right that Shimon would still be in Atil when they returned. The whole country could be taken before a rabbi in training became cannon fodder.

"How do you think they make them? I'd like to watch."

With all of the kabbalists gone, the village seemed ordinary. "I don't think they'll let you. They wouldn't have their village out here almost among the Menshevikim if they wanted to make golems as an exhibition."

Itakh took a moment to think. "But it's you they're building the army for. Maybe that gives you a right."

Esther shook her head. In legends about the kabbalists, they did their mystical work in the quiet of deep night, the best time for communion with the Almighty. The logic made sense. Would they work wonders in broad daylight, when any number of Atil boatmen, Uyghur oil lords, wandering Khazar tradesmen and tinkers, or warlike Rus might happen by? *Someone* would have seen them by now, and sent the tale downriver. "If I'd succeeded in turning myself into a man, I could find out how they do it."

"Not and lead the army at the same time."

"Afterwards." If there was an afterwards. "I could come back and study."

Even in the dim light, she could see that he wobbled his dark head back and forth, considering. "Maybe I could learn." When she didn't bother to contradict him, he crouched down to gather some pebbles, which he shook in his hand as if he intended to cast them.

"I want to know for myself," Esther repeated.

"Then we'll find out."

She glared at him so hard she felt she could burn a hole in him. He couldn't see this, which was a mercy.

"We've done harder things."

Judging from Itakh's size when he'd been found, he was nine now and would turn ten after the harvest, assuming all the crops weren't run over by tanks and blown apart by mines. As much as Esther loved him, she disliked when he understood something she herself didn't understand. He was so much younger than she was, and had received almost no formal education. She should always be the one to figure things out. Now, however, she had to admit he was correct. They were consumed with curiosity, and would do their best to learn. "You're right," she said. She drew her long, wet hair back into a knot, as if to gird herself for the journey. Her stomach growled. They had eaten a hearty dinner, but so much had happened since then, she was ravenous again. She wished her embroidered shoes weren't so shiny, her borrowed clothes so white. In the light of the waxing moon, they were easy to see.

But there seemed to be no one there to see them. Despite whatever mystical work was being done, Yetzirah was as quiet as any sleeping village. No light burned in any house. Itakh shivered and drew his arms around himself, then whispered, "This is just how it would seem if everyone were dead."

"Shh."

They walked around town, found no one. Toward the gates, they approached the barracks in which the golems resided, all together. The building was larger than most of the houses for people, rectangular. A heavy curtain stirred in the open doorway. Esther pushed it aside and stood on the threshold.

Inside, the house was a single, open space. Unlike other houses, it lacked a central hearth. All around, golems were lined up sitting on the swept dirt floor, their backs against the wall, their legs straight out in front of them. Esther felt a grue shiver over her. Their eyes were fixed open. They looked like dolls, like Elisheva's dolls, sitting watchful on the shelf. Itakh came up close behind her, his warm breath hiding behind her back. "Are they sleeping?" he whispered.

"No," one said. Not a head had turned nor an eye blinked. There was no telling who'd spoken. One of them—perhaps the same one—said, "We do not require sleep."

Inspecting them more closely in the gray moonlight, Esther could see that they sat on the bare floor instead of on cushions. Did they not feel physical sensations? If she were sitting thus on the floor, the sharp bones of her bottom would ache. And did they simply sit all night, every night? Had they worked around the clock, the kabbalists might feel some remorse about driving them too hard; but their repose looked eerie, unnatural.

"We wonder," Esther began, "if you can tell us where your masters have gone."

One turned his head toward them. It was impossible to distinguish them from one another in the dark. "Why do you seek them?"

Itakh chimed in with, "We want to know what they're doing."

The golem, silent, continued to watch them. After a long pause, he said, "They've gone down by the river."

"Thank you," Esther said. She should have known that from the legends.

"Keep hidden. They will not wish to be seen."

She nodded, though they might not be able to see her.

"We should not tell you this."

"No," Esther said. Her curiosity remained. "Why do you, then?"

A few of them let out low, sharp grunts, a spooky sound in the dark night. She and Itakh let the curtain slip shut behind them as they walked toward the town gates. She kept wondering.

The grassy steppe seemed brighter than the village in the moonlight, varying shades of blue and gray that rippled in the breeze. Rodents flitted through it, leaving wake behind them, and night birds, dark against the sky, circled in the hunt. Esther heard the mournful hoot of an owl, and in the far distance, a high-pitched bark that might have been a wolf cub. With a start, Esther realized that, when she'd left for the *mikvah*, she'd forgotten to bring the knife. She must have jumped a little or drawn a sharp breath, because Itakh said, "What's wrong?"

"We don't have a weapon. In case anything—shows up." She was afraid to say the word "*volkelake*" lest the act of speaking conjure one, but she believed Itakh knew what she meant.

Itakh kept walking. She could hear him half singing the *Sh'ma* under his breath.

The walk from the river had not seemed far when they'd ridden Seleme, her engine purring and chugging in the cheerful daylight. On foot, in the dark, it seemed long, the shin-high grass rippling like water. "They travel this far every night?" she asked aloud.

"Some nights, they must sleep."

The moon had risen most of the way toward its zenith before Esther thought she heard a sound. She put out her hand to stop Itakh. At first, the sound vanished, but then it returned—the delicate slap of the Atil's current against its banks, and the murmur of voices. Itakh grabbed her hand and they continued forward, keeping as quiet as possible as they walked. When they neared the riverbank, they crouched down low, and when they saw the gathering, they sat.

All the kabbalists of Yetzirah had gathered by the water, their forms resplendent in the white Shabbat robes they had worn the previous day. A large group stood in a circle, their hands joined, surrounding a smaller group in the center. Those, in turn, surrounded a supine form. Esther could only catch glimpses of it in the spaces between them, but it looked like a dead body, and Esther shivered. Because the kabbalists all faced in toward the circle's center, their voices were difficult to distinguish, but there were so many of them that, when the wind was favorable, the chanting carried. The words at first made no sense. Over time, they began to cohere: "*Samekh . . . ayin . . . pe.*" They were reciting the *aleph bet*, in order. When they got to the end, they started over again at the beginning. Itakh widened his eyes at her, but she shook her head in case he was thinking of saying anything, and turned back, rapt, to listen.

They kept on with the alphabet, over and over. Esther began to be lulled by the repetitive rhythm of these sounds she knew so well. As they came around time after time, she began to feel them, in her body, forming a loop, a circle, like those the kabbalists formed with their joined hands. As they recited, the letters of the *aleph bet* flashed in her mind, pure sound and form, devoid of other meaning. The kabbalists recited the sequence so many times, she lost track of where the alphabet ended and began.

Then the chant began to change. The men called out three letters together, out of sequence. Then they paused, recited three more. Esther could discern no logic to their order, and she noticed that her feet had fallen asleep from the way she'd been sitting on them. She shifted off to the side, stretching her electrically charged legs, and listened to the combinations of letters. The seeming randomness for some reason made her afraid, as if there were no saying what else the kabbalists might do if they came down to the river at midnight to say nonsense. But after what seemed a long time, she thought she heard one of the triads repeat. Her heart yearned for the recitation to go faster so she could be sure, but the chanting kept on at the same slow rhythm. It seemed an age later before she was sure she heard a group of triads a second time, but then she was certain to her marrow. This was a pattern of nonwords, repeating in a very long sequence.

Itakh reached his mouth to her ear and said, in a voice so quiet it sounded like breath, "What is it?"

In a flash she understood: This was the *Shem Ha-Mephorash*, the holiest of the Holy One's names. Seventy-two three-letter names for Him, that all together added up to the Name of Names. Everyone in Khazaria, Jewish or no, knew it existed—it was a part of the ruling culture's lore, like the kabbalists themselves—but Esther had never dreamed of hearing it pronounced. A thick lump stopped her throat, a lump of gratitude or sheer awe, yet she managed to whisper, "I think it's the name by which the Name calls Himself."

Over and over they recited this long holy word, their voices sometimes rising higher. With joined hands, they began to revolve in circles, the inner group turning clockwise while the outer turned counterclockwise. The white kaftans and the moving waters flashed in the moonlight. As the chanting continued, the circles sped up, until the men were no longer walking but dancing a kind of hora. As even this dance sped up further, some spun off either inside or outside the circle, and whirled themselves around, jumping and spinning, shouting, "*Emet! Emet!*" Over time, the long Name began to die out, and all the men were crying out, "Truth!" not in unison but each on his own. In the midst of all this, the supine body convulsed once, twice, and then began to sit up. The men hollered with joy, clapped, praised the Holy Name. Some bowed down to the now seated figure, while another shouted, "*Barukh habah!*" in welcome. One held out a hand to help lift him up as he sat, stunned and blinking.

All of this, Esther thought, for each golem, one at a time. All this joy, despite that one might think that they'd know by now that their work would succeed. She realized that Itakh was gripping her arm so hard with both hands that her fingers tingled. As she shook him off, her hand throbbing, he said, "We saw it. We saw it rise. Who can say that?"

"I wonder if any woman has ever seen it, before me."

His dark eyes shone at her as he thought. "Few, but I bet you aren't the first troublemaker ever to live."

She smiled, more delighted at what she'd seen than that he'd called her this. All her life, she'd hoped to be more than merely dutiful. Still, she feared what might happen if the kabbalists discovered them spying. Was their night's work done? Would they now retire to their beds, dropping this new golem at the barracks on the way so that his kin might inform him about his strange fate? If so, Esther and Itakh sat in their path. She lifted up onto her haunches, one hand resting on

Itakh's forearm as she prepared to bolt and to drag him with her. But as some of the kabbalists prayed over the new golem—commending him to Hashem, she thought; one bent over his forearm, perhaps in a gesture of blessing—others had gone down to the water's edge. They tied the long skirts of the kaftans up between their legs like washer-women and rolled the voluminous sleeves up to their shoulders. Then each took one end of a large basket, positioned it on the ground, and began scooping up clay from the riverbank. She could see from the way their backs rounded and strained how heavy it was.

"They're going to make another," Itakh said. Quiet as he was, she could hear his excitement.

"We should go before we're spotted," she whispered.

They waited to be sure the kabbalists seemed occupied with their work. Then they rose to a half crouch and began moving as stealthily as possible through the tall grass. The closer they got to the village, the less Esther could hear from the riverbank, but the more she thought about what they'd left behind. All the fires were burning low in Yetzi-rah, and there were none of the nighttime noises one heard in Atil, people coughing behind their open windows, or arguing in hissing tones. It was as if the village had been attacked and all its inhabitants massacred or herded away.

She lifted aside the barracks curtain and stepped inside. "Thank you," she said.

None of the golems turned to regard her, but one said, "You have seen the work of Creation?"

"We have."

"You will tell us of it sometime."

Esther had no response. She couldn't be certain, but she thought the low cough that issued from the creature's throat in reply might have been his laughter.

CHAPTER 16

Before dawn, a knock came on the guesthouse door. Esther sat straight up, her heart skittering. Whoever was outside waited a moment before opening the door a crack. It was one of the golems.

"My masters bid you come," he said. Somewhere behind him, an early-rising song thrush sang its loud, crazy, nonrepeating call.

"Give us a moment," Esther said. The golem shut the door.

Itakh had slept through this, his face slack as a baby's. She shook him awake, and he rolled onto his belly and wound all his fingers into his hair. "They're summoning us," Esther said. "We have to get up."

She paced as she smoothed her still-damp hair and plaited it down its great length. Itakh roused himself enough to dress, but his thick hair stuck out in clumps. Esther crammed his *kippah* down on top of it, though it didn't help much, and opened the door. The golem stood closer to it than a person would have, so they had to stop short. His massive body blocked the view. A person might also have pretended to do something else to lessen their discomfort at being waited for. The golem stood squarely in front of the door, intent on his task.

He didn't greet them, but began walking toward the center of town. As they followed, Itakh's stomach growled.

This early in the morning, she might have expected to find the inhabitants of Yetzirah either breakfasting or tying on tefillin. But as they rounded the last corner, Esther saw most of the village gathered in the central square. In the brisk air, curling plumes of breath rose from their mouths and noses. Behind the people and more than a head taller than them, all the town's golems stood crowded together—many more than she had noticed in the preceding days.

Wisps of condensation rose from their mouths too, which meant that they breathed. Esther didn't know why she found that surprising—the wonder, after all, was the bare fact of their existence—but for some reason it chilled her. Toward the rear of their ranks, each held a golem horse by its bridle, and behind these, other such horses stood clumped together, some biting at the dirt, others glancing around at one another. Each creature was rusty or brown in color, and each, like the man-golems, had the word *Emet* scratched into its brow.

Looking at all of these people and made beings, Esther felt small. She was of average height for a woman, but the men, golems, and beasts loomed over her. Itakh must have felt a similar sense of his own diminutive size, because he stood close beside her, his wild-haired head hovering near her shoulder.

Shelomoun stepped out from the gathering and lowered himself into a bow. Before Esther could reciprocate, everyone else did too, men and golems. All that fabric moving at the same time made a gentle rushing sound. One horse blew through its lips as it stamped a clay hoof on the ground. Esther and Itakh also bowed, though the moment Itakh was down he began squirming, just as he did at services, because he was afraid of being either the first or the last to pop back up.

There was rustling, however, to cue him when everyone else rose. Shelomoun said, "Esther bat Josephus," then paused to be sure he had her attention—as if it could wander at this moment. "Behold the core of your army."

The impatient golem horse stamped and blew again, and one of the kabbalists disappeared around the back to quiet it.

"We give you twenty-eight of our own golems and eight more made for this purpose. For now, we can spare them all. If you return them to us at some future date, as we hope Hashem will enable you to do, we will find work for them. We give over to you all our golem horses, as we believe you will find few of the mechanical variety available for your cause, and the natural kind are so often a casualty of battle. We know they'll serve you for transport, and believe they will fight alongside mechanical horses, if not with the same ferocity."

Though the square teemed with beings, Esther knew that thirty-six men was less like an army than a foraging party. These were not men, however.

"Do you know how to kill them?" Shelomoun asked, and, startled, Esther looked up at him. "It may prove necessary, if one is incapacitated or grows unwilling to obey."

There they all stood, soulless as far as she knew. Esther said, "Grows?"

Shelomoun nodded once. "If there is time, you take a damp cloth and hold it to the clay of its wrist until the material becomes malleable. Then you rub out its name. That erases its individual identity. Sometimes this will suffice, for a time. If it doesn't, or when it ceases to, wipe out the *aleph* from the beginning of its '*Emet.*' At which it will cease to be a manifestation of Truth, and will simply be '*met.*'" Dead.

Esther's heart jumped behind her breastbone. If she was, in fact, to help defend Khazaria, she would have to lead these creatures and countless others—mortals—until she delivered them to the bek. Somehow, until this moment, she had thought of this in abstract or spiritual terms, her duty to Hashem, to Khazaria, to the People Yisrael, but in this moment she realized the day-to-day, human responsibility this would entail. She did not feel capable. But they had put their faith in her. She couldn't back out now.

"Your horse is fueled. You are ready to go. We will remember you in our prayers."

"Thank you," she said. This was insufficient, given all they had done for her. "You have put great trust in me, and given me a great gift."

"We give the gift, we hope, not to you but to a future Khazaria. We are patriots in our own way."

"We must provision them," Dovid said as an aside.

175

"Before we do," someone said from within the crowd. It was Amit, passing through the ranks to the front. All of them had been up all night, but he looked worse than some, his skin chalky, circles beneath his eyes. "Before you go, Esther." His curly hair stuck out in tufts, like Itakh's. His brown eyes were wide, and his face wore a desperate expression. Esther shrank back from him, and had a sudden intuition—half terror, half delight—that he had come to declare his love for her. She squared her body to face him, and hoped that although she felt herself shaking, this was not visible to others. Amit stopped, facing her. He drew himself up to his full, unimpressive height. "I wish to join you."

Esther looked at him, standing as straight as he could with his round shoulders, his hair like a bird's nest, his embroidered *kippah* like a colorful bird. "To do what?" she asked, then regretted how dismissive the question must have sounded.

"To fight."

All around them stood grown men, steeped in the study of Torah and Zohar. Not one said a word.

"Amit," she said. "We're going off to war."

"I know this."

Would she have to spell it out? "You're a scholar."

"And you're a girl. You think you're going to gather an army of soldiers? No. You'll gather an army of farmers, weavers, traders in wine and in silks. Have they endured as much as I have to be able to study?" The kabbalists would think he meant the long journey from his village. "Perhaps. Have they devoted themselves to Torah, gone days without sleep to study her mysteries? Again, perhaps. But not all of them will have labored as hard as I. Not all will be better fit for soldiers."

Esther looked at Itakh for support. He kicked at the dirt, an alarmed expression on his face.

Amit went on, "You yourself are a woman, yet you know you have the mettle to lead and to fight. Would you judge of another's worthiness?"

"There is an analogue," Shelomoun said, "in the rabbis' teachings. When asked if men should inquire about the level of their neighbors' observance, they responded that this was the Lord's business, not man's. If a man observes the Law of the Jews, we must treat him as a Jew. By extrapolation, I would say that if Amit presents himself to you as a soldier and has no obvious physical or mental deformity to prevent him from serving, then you must accept him." He wiped his thumb and middle finger down the sides of his mouth and fixed his gaze on Amit. "Despite all of which I must say that your decision surprises and disappoints me, after all we have done for you."

Esther itched to add something to his list.

Amit met Shelomoun's gaze. "It is my hope and prayer to return."

"None of our community has ever, to my knowledge, left. We guard the Lord's secrets. We do not gossip in the marketplace."

"But we can't continue if our country is destroyed. I will pray that you'll all still be here, at war's end, for me to return to."

Shelomoun didn't blink as often as other people, which made his brown eyes fierce and lively. "I give you my blessing, then. For now, I think our most pressing task is to provision you and saddle up other horses, as you can't all ride a single mechanical beast."

"Thank you," Esther repeated. "I need to work on her too, before we set out." Real time, secular time, was catching up to her, biting at her heels. She wanted to ask Shelomoun about her father's family, but not in front of all these people. When the crowd began to disperse, she tried to follow him, but a small group of golems stopped her to say they were going to the stables to fetch Seleme and gather saddles and tack for the golem horses. Itakh went with another one to retrieve his bird from the loft. Dovid sent two golems off to the well with water skins; a third beckoned to Esther and, as Shelomoun slipped away, led her to the storehouse.

This turned out to be an actual house, larger than the one in which Esther and Itakh had been sojourning. Wooden shelves lined the round walls all the way up to the ceiling. Beneath them were waist-high wooden bins for everyday supplies (wheat flour, barley groats, rye), ingeniously curved to the shape of the room and looking like large, truncated slices of a tart. Esther wondered how they'd been built. She asked the golem.

He blinked his mud-brown eyes before responding, "We built them. We build everything."

"Did you design them too?"

"No, Esther bat Josephus. Our masters design. We implement."

"Do you mind that?" He didn't seem to understand the question. Esther added, "Always doing the work others assign you."

The golem stood stiller than a human could. She supposed he had to marshal all of his energy to think, or to do whatever his kind did that was analogous to thinking. "That is our lot and our duty. Our masters created us for work. Your lot is no different, relative to your Master." His voice was low and hollow, like wind blowing across the mouth of an empty bottle. "Will you take dried apricots for your journey? I understand they are fine."

Esther pointed to each item she desired and read aloud its Khazar or Hebrew name. She felt like Adam naming the animals. For each food she chose, the golem took a cotton sack from a bin, stooped his great form to fill it, then held it between his two square hands and flipped the contents around and around, as if the sack were a child's jumping rope. Then he knotted together the two corners he'd held and, without warning, tossed the parcel at Esther, who had to catch it and place it in the carrying basket at her feet. Esther had never seen anyone fill and tie a bag so playfully at market. As she named her foods—raisins, dates, hard goat cheese—she wondered if this was standard practice, or if the little fillip was an expression of this golem's personality.

"What's your name?" she asked him.

He filled, twirled, knotted, tossed, looked at her. Cashew nuts.

"Do you have a name?"

With the same care he'd given to bagging the foods, he rolled up his left sleeve to reveal his wide, flat wrist. When he turned his palm to face upward, she saw a letter incised into the delicate place where, on a human, the webwork of green veins would be. Esther shivered in sympathy, thinking how sensitive her own wrist was. The golem's mark looked like the initials a potter incised in the bottom of a vessel before firing it.

"Your name is Gimmel?"

"Gimmel," he repeated, almost, she thought, with pride.

"Are you all named after letters of the *aleph bet*? There are more of you than there are letters."

"When they run out, they begin using complex numerals, more than one letter long. I was made in the letter cycle." He looked at the basket of bags by Esther's feet. "Are you provisioned for a few days' journey? I have seen the boy eat; you may need more."

She let him choose her an assortment of salted meats, which he placed outside the basket, where they would not contaminate the cheeses by proximity. It seemed strange that a nonhuman could understand the rules of kashrut. When they were done, she bent down to hoist the basket, but the golem—Gimmel—made a sound of discontent, similar to a cow's low. At once she dropped the basket and let him lift it for her. She picked up the smaller parcels of meat. He led the way back to the guesthouse. As she followed, Esther tried to burn his image into her mind, so consumed was she with worry that she would be unable to distinguish him from his fellows despite having learned his name. At the same time, she felt the pressing need to get on with their journey, back to the capital and their mission. A picture flashed into her mind: a speck of gray pigeon flying the vast distance across Europa. She wondered if Lyubomir lived or if someone had shot him, eaten him as Eliezer had threatened to do to Nagehan. She had to talk to Shelomoun before she left.

"Thank you, Gimmel," she said when he placed the basket on the ground beside one of the golem horses. As he did this, a second golem knelt to buckle a pack strap beneath the beast's clay belly. The horse, solemn and calm, lowered its head to accept bit and bridle from another golem. None of these things, she had to remind herself, was alive in an ordinary sense, yet they interacted with one another. She looked back and forth from the provisions to the golem horse.

Gimmel, as if able to read her thoughts, said, "I'll gladly pack these things for you."

She thanked him, and saw Itakh coming back toward her with the pigeon perched on his forearm like a falcon. He stroked its head, and the bird walked back and forth along him, seeming to enjoy the attention.

She went back to the guesthouse, which she'd begun to think of as home. She thought of the bedroll as hers, though some other suppliant would sleep in it soon enough, unless the war kept them all away. Perhaps this next person—assuming there was one—would have her prayer answered in a straightforward way. Esther felt jealous of this, of the ability to ask for something ordinary, for a child or for an ailment to be cured, and to see that wish granted.

Their old clothes were clean, folded on the bedding, which a golem had tidied. She pulled off the fancy dress, glad to see it go, and pulled on her wide black pants, her loose gray shirt, her thick boots. She felt as powerful in these clothes as if she truly had become a man. She folded the dress and left it on the bedroll.

Itakh came in with the pigeon cooing on his arm.

"Don't bring that inside," she said.

"She's fine," he said, and let her go. She strutted around on her red legs while he stripped to his loose underdrawers. "I won't miss these fancy things."

"Me neither."

"But I like it here."

"You can come back, when you're a grown man."

He snorted a breath out. "I'll still be Father's slave."

Other than their clothes, she noticed, all their things were gone. The golems must have packed them. "He might free you for good."

"After I've run away?"

"I'm the one who ran away." She didn't know what it meant to own someone. "Maybe I can be the one to free you." Though she couldn't stand to think he'd choose to leave her.

He shrugged his slender shoulders and pulled his old shirt over his head. His own trousers looked baggy and worn as he tied the drawstring at the waist. Even with his needlepoint *kippah* on his head he appeared somehow tough, like a street urchin or one of the Uyghur mafia. Esther remembered Chuluun's backhanded compliment, praising her for having kidnapped "a little Uyghur." She wondered.

Itakh said, "He's going to be angry. We should send Nagehan home." To the bird he said, "Are you ready?" He made a sucking sound with his lips and the bird flapped up into his hands. To Esther he said, "Can you write a note?"

It was wrong that he hadn't learned to read or write. If they ever again found themselves in Atil in peacetime, she would rectify this. For now, she dug in her coat pocket for a pencil and paper.

Before she even began to write, Esther realized there was a strong chance Jascha could read only block letters. She prepared herself to print, something she rarely did. The pencil sat awkwardly in her hand. *We are returning with a small army. What's the news from the front and the capital?* she wrote, feeling as if she were shouting. *And is Father angry?* That was enough. She didn't need to sign it—Nagehan was the only gray-flecked white pigeon who'd home to Itakh's loft. She folded the message and rolled it up tight.

"Are you ready?" she asked Itakh.

He kept a grip on the pigeon with one hand and unscrewed the cap from the repurposed bullet casing. He stuffed the message inside, screwed on the cap, whispered a prayer over the bird, and kissed her head. "Do your best to find us," he said to her. "Stay safe." About none of this did the animal seem to care. He held the bird close to his heart as they went back outside.

Back in the square, a golem shortened a stirrup on one of the golem horses. When Seleme was led out, she cast a haughty glance at these other made beasts, then turned her head away with a snicker. Esther thought she was right: she'd been modeled after a sleek, Arabian

181

war horse, while her golem sisters, with their blunt muzzles and wide girth, looked cloddish.

Itakh cradled the pigeon in his two hands, his fingers folded beneath it and his thumbs curving over the top. Other than its pert head sticking out, it resembled a turnover. Then Itakh crouched down, still holding the bird tight in both hands, and flung it into the air. The pigeon banked and turned, finding her bearings, and took off like a shot for the south.

"I know she can find her way home," Esther said. "But how will she deliver the message back to us? We'll be a moving target."

"She knows her mobile loft. With a little luck, she'll be able to find it. That and the Holy One's grace." He touched reflexively at his shoulder, as if expecting to find the bird still there.

"Do you require anything, for the mechanical horse?" asked a low voice. She couldn't be sure, but believed the golem who spoke to her was Gimmel. If only she could catch a glimpse of his wrist. Another golem said, "I polished your machine with wax."

Turning her attention back to Seleme, Esther could see how the blue-gray steel shone. "Thank you." She walked around the horse to turn off her ignition before opening her tail access hatch. She wanted to see where the oil leak was coming from. "I'll check her." She still wasn't sure she knew to which golem she was speaking, but she was ready to guess. "Are you one of those who'll accompany us, Gimmel?" she asked.

"Of course."

A small victory of recognition. "You say 'of course' as if you had a choice."

"I did."

Esther accepted her packet of wrenches from him—how had he known she'd require them?—and untied their leather thong. "You have a will? I'm confused."

"Does your horse have a will, mistress?"

She shrugged.

"Despite that she's a machine."

"Well, it's complicated." She knelt down, chose a socket wrench, and began loosening the access bolts.

"This mechanical horse and I, we are not so different. Except that I am aware of our similarities, and I believe she is not."

The hatch swung free into her hands, and she peered up into the machinery to see if everything looked right. She felt for the exhaust pipe, which jiggled in her hand. "Loose," she said to no one in particular, and traded her wrench for a larger one. How did anyone with larger hands work on these machines? In some hypothetical, progressive future, Esther thought Khazaria might train women to be mechanics. Once she'd tackled the leak, Esther closed the hatch and circled Seleme to open her neck. She couldn't see anything wrong—all the connections were intact—but she asked for the oilcan and began lubricating the joints and tie rods. If this didn't fix the grinding sounds in the beast's neck, some more serious repair would be needed, but there was no way to know until they were moving again. Esther passed all the tools back to Gimmel, who handled them deftly. "You seem familiar with these," she said.

He replied, "Not familiar. Adept."

She continued to wonder. From the corner of her eye, she saw that Amit had returned with a small rucksack high on his shoulders. He'd made an effort to comb his hair, which only made it fluffier.

"Do you have everything you'll need?" Esther asked. For reasons she couldn't articulate, she was desperate to dissuade him from coming. "The steppe is bitter cold at night. You'll need a bedroll and warm garments."

"I know the steppe as well as you do."

Gimmel tied one last bag of provisions onto a packhorse. Esther mounted Seleme and started her engine. The horse watched with what appeared to be interest as Itakh climbed onto someone else's back. The golem had misestimated the length of Itakh's stirrups—he was small—and stood working the belt in its buckle while Itakh fidgeted, making the saddle creak. Amit had little experience riding, that much was clear. The way he sat his horse, the thing might pitch him off at the first step. By contrast, Esther felt tall and proud atop Seleme, ready, despite her misgivings, to lead this expedition.

Shelomoun came back to make the priestly blessing over all the assembled, and Esther tried to take it into her heart and her bones. She wondered what kind of a blessing, if any, the enemy's warships and aeroplanes received before making their way to Khazaria and the other nations of the east. Surely their nation had a god, though none was as powerful as the Name. She sat her horse in the midst of a crowd of people, yet this was her only chance to ask him.

"Shelomoun?" she started, as if he wasn't already looking at her. He waited. "When we arrived, you said you'd met our father long ago." He nodded. "His family." All the golems and golem horses waited, their patience seemingly inexhaustible. "Did you also meet his brother?"

"The whole family, yes," Shelomoun answered.

"What was his brother like?"

He regarded her a moment. "You never met him?"

"No." Each moment they spoke burned fuel.

"He was big and gruff like your father. Destined for a career in intelligence, and he had a passion for pigeons. An easy laugh. I'm sorry your family lost him before you got to meet him. I think you would have liked him."

Esther nodded. She couldn't correct his assumption. She had known Matityahu as nothing more than a name as unlikely to be spoken as Haman the Agagite's. Now he resembled her father, but with a better sense of humor. "Thank you." She eased Seleme into first and used the handlebars to swing her neck gently from side to side. Seleme's head pivoted without a sound.

They headed west out of the town gate into a warm, bright morning. Esther, Itakh, and Amit rode abreast in front, with three rows of golems behind them, the last of whom each led a string of horses, tied bridle to bridle with long ropes. Some were laden with supplies, others empty. When Esther glanced back toward them, they all seemed at ease, in contrast to her own mind, teeming with questions about her family and what awaited them all in Atil. For a while, the party walked without speaking, the only sounds the steady clop of the horses' hooves, the rumble of Seleme's engine, the buzz of insects, and the swish of grass. As the sun rose higher overhead, one of the golems began to mark time with a song in his low voice. Soon others joined in, and the song's rhythmic refrain made the walk to the river pass swiftly.

"We can hire boats," Amit said, his voice a counterpoint to the low, sad singing. "We'd reach the capital sooner."

"But we'd lose our opportunity to gather volunteers. We need to visit every possible village en route."

"Hasn't the bek been through? Gathered everyone he can?"

He had a point. "He's taken conscripts. I don't know about volunteers. We'll try too."

"Even the Uyghur village?" Itakh asked.

"For fuel if nothing else."

Itakh shuddered, which caused him to slip sideways in the saddle. Bad as he'd been at driving Seleme, he had better luck with this golem horse. There were fewer things to manage—his feet in the stirrups and a pair of reins, unfamiliar tack to him, as he'd never ridden a natural horse—and his restless motion didn't trouble the beast as it plodded along. "I miss Nagehan."

"She'll be back soon, *Barukh Hashem*." If her uncle lived, perhaps he would send some bird of her father's back home. It would mean he had kept it all this time, waiting for a message. "How long can a pigeon live?"

"Why are you asking?" When she didn't answer, he went on, "It depends. Most seem to live five or six years, but our loft has a couple who might be older than you." So it was possible, if not probable. She didn't know how long ago Matityahu had defected, but she gathered it had been before she was born.

When they stopped for lunch by the riverside, Esther looked around at all the golems and golem horses, and thought how they had been made from this clay, this water. Did they feel nostalgia when they returned to the banks? She didn't want to ask, though she yearned to know. The golems untied the horses as if for a rest such beings did not require. Some lay down, while others performed their pantomime of nuzzling the grass. She wondered if the kabbalists had taught them this ornamental gesture as a way of making them appear more like natural horses, or if kabbalists and mechanical horse-makers alike had, to their surprise, found this behavior intrinsic to horselike beings. As the three humans in this company stretched their legs, two of the golems unpacked bread, cheese, and figs, while another dispensed water from a water skin into three earthen cups. They handed Amit a small jug for *N'tilat Yadayim*, then held out scraps of towel once the prayer was done. They waited for Esther, Itakh, and Amit to seat themselves in the tall grass, and held still while together they said the blessings over bread and fruit. Then they retired to a distance, one stopping to pat Seleme on the nose—an attention she received with more grace than Esther might have anticipated.

No food tasted better than the food one ate traveling. Whether the sweaty smell of sunshine or the fresh breeze or the exertion stoked Esther's appetite, the bread had a savor like none other.

While he chewed, Itakh leaned back on one hand and looked up at the sky, his sleepy expression like that of a cat basking in sunshine. Amit, hunched over, smiled at him and said, "You look happy."

Itakh shrugged and sat more upright to pick up his cheese. "Everything is so much easier than it was coming here, now that the golems are doing all the work."

"No question."

"And we've been out all morning, and not a single *volkelake*."

"*Barukh Hashem*," Esther said. "I think they're nocturnal." She looked around. "Should we invite the golems to sit down with us? They look uncomfortable, standing around."

Amit said, "They don't experience discomfort."

Some wandered, some stood with the horses, some sat on the ground in that odd posture in which they whiled away the nights, their legs straight in front of them. "Are you sure?"

"Ask them."

But Esther felt awkward haranguing them with questions in front of Amit. "How can they have the power of speech but not need sleep or sustenance?"

"Speech has to do with thought, not digestion."

"They can think?"

"In a rudimentary way."

Did they mind if someone called their thinking "rudimentary"? If so, she didn't see any change in their expressions. She took another bite of bread, cheese, and fig, so sweet and savory. How did they live without the power to enjoy such things? Could they be said to be alive? "Thinking is more complex than eating. Worms eat, after all, but it's a measure of our superiority over worms that we do more than that."

"It's too bad the *mikvah* didn't work for you. You would have made a fine kabbalist."

He regarded her with a faint smile. She couldn't tell if he was trying to goad her on. "If it had worked, I would have become a soldier. Exactly as I'm doing now." It was hard to believe the kaganate was at war on this balmy morning. As if to illustrate this point, two white butterflies gamboled past, spinning circles around each other. A golem who stood a distance off, watching them, said, "Beautiful." She wondered what beauty meant to a nonhuman. Amit took a long drink from his cup, his eyes on her the whole time. Esther stood and began looking for a place to relieve herself—not easy to find on a broad, flat plain in sight of the river. Finally she squatted, sure that if the tall grass didn't hide her, Amit would have the decency to look away.

Had her prayer worked differently, she would have urinated standing up. Probably that was the main reason men fought wars: because they could do this on the march. Her relief at being unchanged notwithstanding, she remained curious about what it would be like to be a man. When she squatted down, all she could see was grass and sky and the creatures that inhabited them. From such a vantage point, she knew better than to believe she understood the mysteries of creation.

When she returned, both boys were lying back in the grass, Itakh unaware that an ant meandered across his forearm. "We have a war to fight," Esther said. "We have to hurry." Impossible to know it from here. Even the traffic in naval ships seemed to have slowed. A tranquil day on the Atil. The boys stood and brushed themselves off, and soon they all arrived at the ferry.

The ferryman was poling his way across with two women, both in colorful Mongol garb, one with a clucking brown hen in her arms. Her face darkened at the sight of the men and horses on the river-bank. During her short time in Yetzirah, Esther had grown accustomed to the golems' appearance, but she remembered how strange they'd looked on first view.

The ferryman called out something unintelligible as he ran the barge aground and sloshed in his boots to make fast his rope to the cleat. The women spoke to each other in a dialect Esther didn't understand, but the one with the chicken clutched it to her breast and spat on the ground as she hurried the short distance to Malinky Yatsa. There was no mistaking what that meant.

The ferryman looked over the group and shook his head. "You'll have the wrath of the Name upon you. They'll mutiny in the night."

Esther glanced at Amit. She wondered if that was why she'd been given instructions on how to—Shelomoun had clearly said "kill them," though they could not be said to live. Amit spoke up. "We know how to control them. All the classical texts warn of their independence, but we've had no difficulty with them in Yetzirah."

The ferryman wiped his big, rough palm over his mouth and chin. No doubt, living at such close proximity to the kabbalists, he had seen *golemim* before, but perhaps never in such numbers.

"We all need passage," Esther said.

"It'll cost you."

"We are familiar with your rate."

Already, a crowd had begun to gather from the village—traders and workmen, a few women who'd been beating their wash on the rocks, and a gaggle of children, jostling one another aside to get the first, best look. One chubby toddler, his wispy hair still uncut, opened his gap-toothed mouth in a mask of fear and ran away, both arms straight out for balance. A larger boy, his forelocks swinging, shouted, "What are those?" to whoever might be listening.

"We are the *golemim* of Yetzirah," one said in its spooky monotone. "What are you?" Esther glanced over; it was Gimmel. They were so like one another in most particulars, yet she was developing the ability to pick him out from a crowd.

"I'm a boy," the boy said.

"We are raising an army," the golem said. Was it allowed to speak before it had been spoken to?

"A real army? With guns?" another boy asked.

"With whatever weapons we can muster," Gimmel answered. "We seek recruits to help us push back the foreign menace. Do any of you wish to join us?" A human's tone might have changed inflection somewhere in this statement, but Gimmel's remained flat and calm.

The second boy glanced around. "The bek requires a man to be a bar mitzvah, or the equivalent age, if he's not Jewish, to fight. Do you?"

Without hesitation, Esther said, "We take any brave-hearted volunteer."

The child's parents seemed not to be in sight, but a man with a large wineskin slung over his back said to Gimmel, "Are you the leader? A made thing?"

"Not I." If the comment had been meant as a slight, Gimmel gave no hint of having understood this. He raised one solid finger and pointed to Esther.

She girded herself for a disparaging remark about her sex. None came. Instead, the small crowd that had gathered looked her over. An old woman, her back bent under the weight of a bale of laundry, said, "And who are you?"

"Esther bat Josephus, the kender's daughter."

She was ready to defend her right to lead, but all the old woman said was, "We've seen warships, and received useless papers from the sky. Yet our village hasn't heard we are at war. Does news take so long to travel from the capital?"

They should have sent Nagehan off sooner, though there was no guarantee she'd return with information. "When we left Atil a few days ago, the enemy had crossed the Dniepra and were headed toward the Don. We don't know how far they've progressed since then, but we know they're coming for us just as they came for the Jews of Polonia and Ukraina." She thought again of Rukhl's parents, and wondered if her uncle, having renounced the faith of his birth, had escaped punishment.

By now the children stood still to listen, all except the toddler, who ran in a tight circle, either in glee or in fear.

The old woman set her bundle down, saying, "We have heard of the refugees."

"We seek anyone willing to fight, men and women, children old enough to bear weapons and whose parents will let them go." She could not refuse children if Itakh was prepared to fight. "We ask those who join to bring provisions and shelter if they have any. We have golem horses to help carry." Where they would get weapons, she couldn't guess. The bek must already have deployed his armaments to the front.

People spoke amongst themselves, and at last a woman scooped up the toddler, who said something unintelligible and spread his wet, open mouth around the top of her shoulder. Esther still couldn't tell if he was excited or upset.

The man who'd last addressed Gimmel said, "How soon do you depart?"

"As soon as all of our party have crossed."

He nodded. "I'll be ready."

Off the man went with his burden to gather supplies. Many of the assembled turned to watch him go, then two more set off after him. In their wake, a boy older than Itakh but younger than Esther sprinted off, perhaps to ask his parents. It was that simple? She'd thought she might have to *hondel*: sit like a rug trader, drink so much tea her hands

190

shook, engage in the elaborate dance of convincing the other person to do what you wanted. But she had stated her case and people had responded to it according to their will. No back and forth. Perhaps the *mikvah* had made this possible.

The ferryman loaded on a first group, including Esther, Itakh, and Amit, with Seleme and Gimmel. The horse stood pastern-deep in the water. Slowly he began to pole across, swearing oaths to the Name, sweat dripping from his hair and darkening his blue shirt.

Itakh said, "Could the rest of the *golemim* swim? We could go faster."

"They can," Amit said, "but it's best if they don't. They're like earthen flower pots; they get waterlogged."

Esther shivered. She would have been more comfortable with golems if they'd been either more or less like people. Gimmel watched the ferryman. Then he walked over and stood behind and over him in that disconcerting way they had, close enough to make one's skin creep. The ferryman stood upright to bark at whoever was interfering with his work, but when he became aware of the golem's stature, he quieted. The creature pointed toward the pole, and the ferryman handed it over without a word.

The raft now glided through the water at a fast enough clip to raise a slight breeze. The ferryman mopped his brow and the back of his neck, and crossed his arms to watch. He glared at his human passengers as if willing them to comment. Then he caught Esther's eye and said, "These things could put me out of business."

"They're coming to fight the war. After that, they'll return to serve the kabbalists."

"Perhaps one would like to stay on and work for me."

"One would not," said Gimmel. "But we will help you for the rest of this journey."

He kept his arms crossed and paced in the small space afforded to him.

On the western bank, the ferryman disembarked with his passengers. "I'm not needed," he said. The raft rode high in the water, and with Gimmel manning it, skimmed across the water toward the waiting troops like a fleeter craft. In a few minutes he returned with a number of his kind on board. She wondered if another golem should relieve him, then realized they didn't tire. By the time he'd gathered most of their party, the three men and the boy had returned to the far bank and were ready to cast their lot with the golem army.

It hadn't been necessary to be turned into a man, at least not to drum up a few recruits. Depending on how the attack progressed, she and Itakh might have been at the front by now if they'd chosen that course of action. But the two of them on a mechanical horse could never have gathered an army without the golems. They made an impressive sight, guiding the raft across the river with as little visible effort as automata. The golems convinced these people to join. She shouldn't fool herself, thinking otherwise.

Soon the three men and the boy joined the rest of the company on the western bank. One man had a trader's wicker basket suspended like a backpack from two straps on his shoulders. The others carried their possessions in bundles, one slung across the man's body like a baby in its sling. The boy kept looking back across the water at the village.

"Did you get your parents' permission?" Esther asked him. Was he a boy or a bar mitzvah? She couldn't tell.

He shrugged one shoulder and the other in succession. "I couldn't find either of them, so I—assumed." He watched to see how she'd respond, so she tried to keep her face still. "I left word with a neighbor."

"If we wait for everyone to have ironclad permission," Amit said, "we'll never reach the front." He was, she recalled, despite loving the Law, someone who'd run off in the middle of the night to change his own sex.

"He's right," said the man with the trader's basket. "Asking the father's permission? The usual way is not even to ask the soldier's. You scoop him up from the field, stick a bayonet in his hands, and make him fight."

Even mounted on Seleme, which made her head and shoulders taller than any of the human men around, Esther felt unsure of herself. A fire burned in her to defend Khazaria. She knew more than most girls did about history, she'd listened with care to her father's conversations in his room of state. Still, she remained ignorant of military tactics and strategies, and this was no time to admit that.

The ferryman wouldn't let them pay for any but the first passage. "How can I take money, when someone else did all the work?"

Esther fished ten dinars from her neck pouch and offered it to him. He reached up for the large coin, then nodded to Esther and placed it in his purse. "I wish you luck in your endeavor," he said, with none of the sarcasm with which he'd remarked on their desire to find Yetzirah. "I expect I'll hear about its outcome."

Esther regarded her few human troops and the many golems and said, "We must hasten to the capital, but we'll stop in every village along the river to gather men. If we hear of an encampment inland, we'll detour to visit it. And we should go to the oil refineries."

"They're not even Jews," said the trader.

Some golems shifted their stance.

"But they're Khazars." The trader himself looked part Uyghur or Mongol. So many steppe tribes had swept down over the Khazar plain. People of many nations had come to trade, found Atil cosmopolitan and tolerant and the soil of the surrounding countryside rich, and settled there. It was impossible to tell by looking what a person might consider himself to be. "What's your name?"

"Benyamin ben Gershom."

That sounded Jewish enough, though one never knew. "It's as much because we're a Jewish nation as because of our strategic position that the Germanii wish to conquer us." Now that she'd started naming the dark kaganate, the harsh word rolled off her tongue. Pronouncing its syllables didn't make the heavens open. "But we fight for all Khazars, Jews and non-Jews alike. We take any soldiers who wish to join us."

"And if they don't keep kosher?"

Gimmel drew nearer to Benyamin. "We observe all of the six hundred thirteen *mitzvot* that a nonperson can perform. When we slaughter, we use the prescribed methods, and we would not boil the calf in its dam's milk. But if some of you wish to hunt the wild boar and eat it, we will not stop you." Esther marveled that this creature with, she understood, no soul and some kind of mechanical intellect could insinuate that there were, in fact, other tasks with which the golems *would* interfere. Benyamin seemed to arrive at a similar interpretation, because he stopped talking, hiked up his shoulder straps, and fell into line. Mounted on Seleme, who puffed black smoke into the air behind her, Esther led the way back downriver toward the capital.

She learned the names of the other recruits as they walked: Aviv, Mikhael, and the boy—not even a bar mitzvah—Natan. She could remember these, but as they gathered more, they'd need a roll. She also realized, with a warm flash of embarrassment, that she hadn't learned any of the other golems' names yet. As for the horses, she doubted they even had names. Knowing such things might help to prevent mutiny. Did a kabbalist ever need to kill a golem horse?

As they walked, Natan worked his way up through the ranks until he was nearer to Esther, Itakh, and Amit on their mounts. He seemed small, on foot and without his pack, now hitched to one of the golem horses. "Excuse me, Esther bat Josephus?" he said, as if she might not have noticed his approach. "How many of them are there? The golems, I mean?"

"Thirty-six man-golems. Twice *khai*."

"That's what I thought," he said. She looked at him. "*Lamed vavnikim.*"

Amit laughed. "Don't you think if there are thirty-six righteous men holding up the world, they're actual men?"

"Golems aren't men?"

"Created by men." His shoulders hitched up, as if he feared being struck or mocked. No doubt he had participated in creating some of them. What did that feel like? "*Lamed vavnikim* are created by

Hashem. In addition to which, if they really do hold up the world, the Great Name might want to spread them out a bit. That way, if something happened to one of them, the world could remain aloft."

Whoever Natan was—Esther couldn't guess his family's business from his linen work shirt and loose striped trousers, sun-faded but clean—he wasn't a kabbalist. He couldn't out-argue Amit. But as they trekked in their solemn rows toward the next river village, she imagined that all the just of the world followed her. They sang in their low voices. The word *Emet* marked their brows, the sign of their goodness. They prepared to keep the sky up a little longer.

This land had looked the same when her ancestors had gazed up at that same sky and seen Tengri there, imagined him in the form of a white goose flying over the waters. Had his been simply another name for the Name of Names? The fact that it was forbidden to ask the question aloud could not keep her from wondering as they rode.

CHAPTER 17

At each encampment, they picked up a handful of recruits, and soon Esther's army had as many human soldiers as golems. Amit begged a ledger book and two pencils from the schoolteacher in a large village. In his spiky, cursive hand, he wrote down the name, parents, and home village of each man who joined them. The rest of each line stretched leftward, blank: waiting, Esther grimly supposed, to record injury or death.

"Or honor," Amit added when she voiced the thought aloud. "Bravery or daring."

"*Barukh Hashem.*"

Benyamin spat, seconding her desire not to offend the Almighty. So probably Jewish. Though perhaps other people spat for this reason too.

When they started up again, Seleme seemed eager to move, so Esther allowed her the freedom of a third-gear trot. Itakh and Amit, on their golem horses, soon caught up with her. "We've enlisted dozens of men," Amit said, speaking loudly over the roar of Seleme's engine. A golem horse ran silently. "But not an army."

"We'll gather more," Itakh said. "And you'll see—when we get to Atil and Khazaran, we'll get lots of volunteers."

"It's true," Esther said. "We need larger numbers. But do you know where we're going next?"

In the shimmering midday heat, Itakh waited.

"Göktürk."

Amit hissed over his teeth, while Itakh said, "Who?"

"Göktürk, you remember, the—"

"Don't say his name!" Amit cried out, and raised a hand as if he might strike her. It didn't matter that he had only one hand on the reins. The docile horse would continue forward until given some other command. "Holy Shekhinah! Don't you know anything?" He brought his fist down on top of the golem horse's head. It didn't even wince. This was one way it differed from Seleme. "No one names him, like, like the person we call Haman the Agagite. He hunts people down." He lowered his voice. "Any of the men we've picked up—any one of them—could be his spy."

"I doubt it."

"I wouldn't be so sure. Benyamin has that look."

"Are we talking about the old Uyghur with the long white hair?" Itakh asked.

"Shh," Amit said, harsh and loud. Then, "You saw him?"

Itakh grinned. "They told us to lower our eyes, but I stole a glance anyway."

"I did too."

Amit's eyes flickered over Esther in admiration. She sat taller.

"You should have seen her," Itakh said. "She spat at one guy's feet."

Amit let out a short whistle. Seleme startled at the noise. Her ears swiveled, though she continued to trot. "When we get there, you'll do the talking."

In her short sojourn in Yetzirah, Esther had forgotten how the integrated saddle made her tailbone ache, forgotten the tang of Seleme's exhaust on the roof of her mouth, forgotten the hunger and sunburn and bitter thirst the open steppe bred. Such travel was both rough and exhilarating, though Itakh was right, their journey would be easier now that the golems could make camp and prepare the food.

When the shadows began to lengthen, the army's human soldiers stopped to bicker about the best route to the Uyghur stronghold. Benyamin thought they'd overshot it and would need to travel northward as well as off to the west. Esther believed it lay southwestward. She had, in favor of her argument, the fact that she and Itakh were the only people among the assembled who'd set foot in the village. But the local men had lived in the area all their lives and knew the terrain better, despite its unrelenting sameness, grass and more grass. The logical thing would be to trust their judgment, but Esther couldn't. "The truth is," she told them, "if we're anywhere near them, they'll find us. They don't want visitors."

Golems, as it turned out, said nothing in such a situation. Instead they awaited orders while the people weighed their options. After a moment, Benyamin said, "We all agree they're to the west. We should follow the sun, and if you're correct, Esther, they'll lead us in."

So they set out in search of a place any sane person would avoid. But traveling in convoy with thirty-six golems, each more than a head taller than the tallest man, and with golem horses, they would attract notice.

They'd traveled westward no more than an hour, not even long enough for anyone to have broken rank to make water, when in the distance, Esther spied three of the Uyghurs' miraculous aerocycles. From far off, their only sound was a tremendous *whoomph* each time the wings beat down. One couldn't hear any gears or chains ticking, which made the wingbeats ominous. "We've been seen," she said to no one in particular. She wondered how long before the aerocycles themselves or someone they informed of the threat closed in on them. As she squinted up at them in the hazy sky, they drew nearer.

Only a few minutes passed before a troop of horsemen galloped out of the northwest, their machines aiming for Esther's party. At first they seemed to waver in the heat, but they resolved into solid beings as they approached. Esther still wasn't sure what model of horse they drove—her knowledge of them wasn't as sophisticated as she'd believed it to be a week earlier—but they shot like arrows across the landscape of green grass and pale blue sky. As they hove into view, the thirty-odd human men behind her quieted and stilled. The dozens of golems stood with their large hands alongside them, relaxed but ready to fight. One golem intoned the *Shehekhiyanu* under his breath, and Esther wondered what a clay thing meant by giving thanks. The Uyghurs tore across the steppe, the same conquering horde they had been for centuries. They knew how to strike fear in people's hearts despite small numbers. This was a skill that Esther and her miniature army should cultivate, particularly when as yet they had so few weapons. Seleme's ears drew back and her gleaming eyes began to scan.

Riding abreast, they charged until one of them saw what he approached and braked hard. Though he managed to prevent his horse from stalling, it reared, pawing for purchase on the ground, and came down turned to the side, its teeth bared and one yellow eye regarding them. The other four riders swerved to avoid him, then drew their horses to a halt. All five machines bobbed their heads as they looked at the people and beasts they faced. They had not been designed with golem opponents in mind. Their riders conversed in rapid-fire, guttural Uyghur.

After a brief interchange, one gestured at Esther with his chin and said, in Khazar, "You're the one who traded with us for fuel."

"I am. Who are you?"

He kept his chin raised. "Where did you get these?"

"From the kabbalists of Yetzirah. I asked your name."

He walked his machine back and forth in front of the group: a blatant intimidation tactic and a waste of fuel.

"We're in search of your village," Esther continued. "We hope to speak to your leader."

The Uyghur grinned openmouthed, and translated for the others. They laughed.

"Will he speak to us?" She preferred Chuluun's outright threats to this showmanship and mockery.

His grin faded slowly. "He speaks to no one. Like your kagan." It had never struck Esther as strange that Khazaria's supreme leader kept himself cloaked in mystery like the Holy of Holies while everyone went to the bek for military affairs and matters of state. (Meanwhile, in the West, they printed photographs of their leaders in the newssheets.) Yet hearing these words from the Uyghur's mouth, the kagan's secrecy seemed odd to emulate.

"Your kagan too. Chuluun told us that henceforward, he would be our protector."

This he also seemed to translate, in sharp bursts. Without saying anything more, they turned their horses and began walking in first gear. The horses farted out exhaust at Esther and her party.

Itakh said, "What just happened?"

The band of Uyghurs kept walking. At a certain point, one man cast a glance back in their direction, though he didn't gesture or say anything. He did take a small radio device from his pocket, call in a command, and wait through the static for a reply. A single syllable returned to him. He switched the machine off, and a moment later, the aerocycles performed a graceful turn to head toward the city of derricks. "Holy Shekhinah," Esther said.

Amit said, "It's just as Benyamin imagined. They mean us to follow."

"Or to kill us," Natan offered.

Amit patted his golem horse on the neck and it started off. Having no will, it understood such gentle cues. Everyone fell into line, with Esther taking the lead as soon as she could. "They could have done that already if they'd wanted to."

"Are they good cooks?" Natan asked. "Because I'm hungry."

Someone hushed him.

Amit said, "They don't want to make trouble, with the *golemim* behind us." This was where a human soldier might have glowed with pride. The golems simply walked, their eyes turned toward the ground. Esther kept watching the flying machines. She longed to encounter a grounded one, to take it apart and see how it worked.

Soon the city of tanks and derricks came into view, clouded by the blue-gray haze of heat and distance. Another party of riders out on patrol must have seen them coming, because they galloped toward them. Their fellows, leading Esther's troop, shouted out to halt them. She heard them mention Chuluun's name. He rode at the second party's head. Esther's body flooded with relief as if he were an old friend.

Her face opened in a smile. He smiled back, the long creases forming around his mouth. All together, they slowed and entered the town. Men armed with rifles and pistols, as well as some with pikes and scimitars, met them. Though the men were dusty, their heeled boots caked in mud, the weapons glinted in the late-day sun. Esther shivered at their menace, and at the same time wondered if the Uyghurs could arm her forces.

She couldn't make out most of Chuluun's conversation with the other group's leader. Uyghur shared its roots with Mongol and Hun, while Khazar was a hodgepodge of Turkic and Hebrew. "Golem" sounded similar in every language she'd heard. They barely moved their hands while they spoke, unlike Khazars, who used them for emphasis. Rukhl sprang to Esther's mind, her brassy curls leaping out from beneath her faded kerchief, her features so expressive. Esther clutched at her shirt and felt the *hamsa* beneath it, on its cord. For a moment she felt as if the amulet itself, or her friend's love, which had made her bestow it, could protect her from harm. But lest she be struck down right then, Esther referred the thought to Hashem and His Holy Shekhinah, the true protectors.

When their conversation ended, Chuluun, still mounted, approached Esther. Seleme revved her engine in a mechanical growl, and though he chuckled at her, he also stopped. "If we present you to our leader, you go alone, without your"—here he paused to look crossly at Itakh—"deputies. You speak only when he invites you to speak. If you mention the meeting to anyone beyond those assembled here, we assure you a death so gruesome, it cannot be described." Esther saw kind Tselmeg among those who'd gathered at the group's periphery. She couldn't risk greeting him. "Do you accept these terms?"

"With gratitude." From the murmur that went around the assembly, she couldn't tell if they admired her pluck or were amazed at her stupidity. But leaving Seleme's engine running, she dismounted, feeling small without the machine's added height. To Amit she said, "See that they fuel her. I'll be back."

"*Barukh Hashem.*"

She felt grateful for his blessing and troubled that he thought she needed it. The aerocycles began to drop toward a nearby landing field.

The city kept on about its business as Chuluun led her through. Men filled blue barrels, each about the size of Itakh if he squatted down, from massive petrol pumps. Others loaded these onto small, spike-tired mechanical carts, the only kind that could run over Khazaria's barren, nearly roadless terrain. (If the enemy had not yet overtaken the Rus's impressive railway system, much of this oil would, Esther knew, travel into their territory to Tsaritsyn and Moskva, thence to be distributed throughout the nation.) Some carts lacked their own motors. These, to Esther's surprise, were hitched to mechanical horses. "Holy Shekhinah," she exclaimed before she could stop herself. When Chuluun glanced sidelong at her, she said, "They aren't oxen."

"They work better than natural horses, once you've broken their spirits."

"Mine would never submit."

He shook his head. "It's a machine, little Khazar. It does your bidding, not the other way around."

He could think what he wanted. Seleme didn't possess a soul—even less of one than a golem did—but she had some other thing, very like one.

At the center of town stood a metal tower, a grain silo with windows around its top. Around the outside, a metal staircase spiraled. Though it was silhouetted against the setting sun, she recognized it at once as the place where she'd seen the man with the yellow-white hair. Chuluun led her upward, his boots chiming a hollow reverberation on the stairs and making the whole structure quiver. The stairs had treads but no risers, so as they ascended Esther had the vertiginous sense she might fall through. There was also no handrail, as if on purpose to frighten the faint of heart, or to make it easier to push them off. He left her standing on the small, open platform while he went inside. A breeze blew up here, and one blackbird flew past with a second, a rival or a mate, in pursuit.

When Chuluun returned, he held open the door for her. He said nothing, but looked so stern she bowed her head as she entered.

The door closed behind them with a metallic thud. Despite the windows, the room was dark by contrast with the outdoors. All she could make out was a patterned rug at her feet.

"Take off your shoes," a voice said, a man's voice, matter-of-fact.

Esther dreaded the smell of her feet after traveling, but complied. Though she tried to stand her boots up by the door, they were soft, and flopped over. Chuluun's riding boots remained upright when he took them off and lined them up.

"You can look up, *bubeleh*." The man used the refugee word with ease—more easily than Esther could have—but gave it a guttural, Uyghur pronunciation. "I'm not the kagan."

This was the same man she'd seen descending the staircase. His white braid shone, clear and precise. As her eyes adjusted to the indoor light, she saw his immaculate black suit, a charcoal pinstripe now visible in its weave. He wore a black shirt with no collar, buttoned all the way up to his neck. He cracked a one-sided but friendly smile. The apples of his tanned cheeks were smooth, but a web of wrinkles spread out around them. "You're the little Khazar who came before to fuel your horse. What was your name? Ephrat?"

"It's Esther. I lied before."

"You lied?" Chuluun said.

She licked her lips. "I'm sorry. I was afraid if I told you who I really was, you'd take me prisoner and try to get a ransom."

"And who are you?"

Would he still do it, at this point? She had to tell the truth. "The kender's daughter."

Chuluun snorted. "The kender's daughter, a common liar."

"I said I'm sorry."

The boss sat quiet, his open face inviting a longer answer.

Emily Barton

"I was on my way to Yetzirah, hoping they would change me into a man. I figured Ephrat could work for both."

Chuluun grunted a laugh. "So they couldn't do it."

"Wouldn't. I don't know. Here I am." She held her palms open at her sides to display herself. Had she been made a man, she wouldn't have looked much different: broader, perhaps, sprouting a wispy beard like Amit's.

The boss said, "Esther."

"Sir?"

"You're my guest. Sit."

The rug was soft underfoot, woven of silk. She sat down on a flat cushion across from him. Chuluun padded around to stand behind the man's left shoulder. Because both Esther and the big boss were seated on the floor, Chuluun seemed tall.

"Sit down," the man said, glancing toward Chuluun over his shoulder without actually looking at him. Chuluun shook his head no and folded one hand over the other before him. "Will you have a drink?" their host asked Esther.

She nodded. The law of the steppe—greater, she thought, than the law of the Khazars, greater, perhaps, than the Law—was the law of hospitality. If a traveler appeared at your door, you fed him, as Avraham had done. If you entered a person's tent, you did so with deference. This man had before him a clear, sweating pitcher on a silver tray with copper cups. Probably some exotic liquor. Esther's heart sank as he filled two vessels full.

"*L'khaim*," she said, having no idea what the local toast might be. Then she took a sip. It was water, cold as a winter lake. She kept drinking.

His smile returned. "What did you think it was?"

"I don't know. Why is it so cold?"

"Where are you from?"

"Atil."

"Don't they have ice in the capital?"

"Not in the summer, and only for special occasions."

"Spring water. The most healthful beverage. Your people love wine," which was true, "but it's water that keeps us fit to conquer." He watched her as he drank, his eyes on hers. Chuluun, behind him, remained almost golem-still. "You hardly needed the kabbalists to transform you in order to become a warrior. You're a Sarmata, aren't you?"

Esther wished she were. Among the Sarmatae, one of the tribes who'd long ago conquered this steppe, women fought alongside men. The early Khazars had subdued them. Any number had been converted in the Atil's holy waters. Many Khazar Jews carried their fierce and warlike blood. Perhaps there had been some among Esther's ancestors. But the Sarmatae, like many of the tribes, had been tall, fair-haired, light-eyed; Esther's family was dark-complected. "Not by birth, I don't think. I wish I were one."

"You are in spirit. My men tell me you've come on a military mission." Though his eyes remained on Esther, he indicated Chuluun with a slight gesture of his head. Chuluun was the one whose presence made her uneasy, alert. This man, so widely feared, seemed surprisingly gentle. Esther remained on her guard.

She explained about the breach of the Dniepra—he'd already heard—Khazaria's inadequate defenses, her journey to Yetzirah. She told him about the thirty-six golems, and her need for men and weapons. "Weapons most of all. I don't know the bek's arsenal, but I assume he's sent most of it to the front."

He considered what she said. "Why should I help him? He merely tolerates me, although I bring him great wealth." He took another long drink of water. Sweat rolled down the glass and onto the neat black trousers from which his manicured feet protruded. He wasn't who she'd expected: a gruff warlord, rich with oil money and ordering his men to torch villages for sport. This fellow had an urbane polish Esther had rarely seen in the capital. Perhaps this was part of why people feared him.

Esther knew her face could betray her. Nevertheless, she prepared to lie. "You should help us because the Angel of the Lord sent me to you." She kept her eyes on him as she finished her water, though the Angel of the Lord might show up right then and strike her dead. "He appeared in a blaze of light while we stayed with the kabbalists. To my knowledge, everyone else was sleeping, except the golems, who don't sleep. And he said to me"—this was where she might dig her own grave, but she couldn't back out now—"'Esther, go to Göktürk, the scourge—'"

Before she could finish, Chuluun exclaimed something in Uyghur and pulled a gun from his holster, aimed it at her forehead. Esther also shouted, and ducked by instinct into a ball. Her rational mind knew this wouldn't help, but as her heart raced her body took over. "Please don't shoot," she said.

"I heard you say something!" Chuluun barked. He spoke close to her ear. She could smell his breath: fennel. "Turn over! Let me see your face."

Her body didn't want to unclench. She uncurled onto her side and opened her eyes. Chuluun straddled her, crouching over her with the gun. She rolled onto her back and he aimed it at her mouth.

"What did you say?" he asked, his temper back under control.

"I said the Angel—"

"You. Spoke. A name." He was enunciating so viciously, a fleck of his spittle grazed her cheek. She didn't dare wipe it off.

"Hold, Chuluun," the boss said. Esther's breath rasped. "Let her sit up." Chuluun straightened, backed off a step, kept the pistol aimed at her mouth. "Whom did this angel tell you to look for?" She continued to breathe. "Sit up. Speak."

Chuluun tracked her movements with the gun, so she tried to be slow and steady. He braced the weapon with his other hand so his shot would be true. Esther found the voice to say, "Göktürk, scourge of the steppe. The Angel said, 'Only he is powerful enough to help you in the battle to come.'"

The boss blinked, and drew a breath in and out through his nose. "This angel told you my name?"

"How else could I have learned it?"

"The punishment for speaking it is death."

Chuluun cocked the pistol. "And it would be my pleasure."

Göktürk poured himself a new glass of water and drank it down without even looking at Chuluun. He said, "Someone told you."

It was difficult to control her face. "Who would risk it?"

"What did this angel look like?"

Esther glanced down the barrel of Chuluun's pistol before willing herself to hold Göktürk's gaze. "Taller than the *golemim*. Made of fire." This was the line on angels, yes? "He had six wings, two reaching for heaven and two for the Earth, two more shielding his body. His face was terrible."

Esther didn't know if Uyghurs believed in angels, or what Göktürk and Chuluun were likely to know about Jewish celestial beings. He took his time thinking about what she'd said, or torturing her the way a cat toyed with a cornered mouse before pouncing on it. Then he said, "Put the gun down."

"She already lied to me once."

"Put it down."

Chuluun didn't respond at once. He weighed his options. Then he lowered the barrel toward the floor, depressed the hammer with his thumb, pulled the trigger, let the hammer back into place. Though he'd disarmed the gun, Esther still watched it, alert and nervous. He replaced it in its holster without looking away from her.

"Now, sit," Göktürk commanded him. Chuluun bent down and sat on his heels, both hands splayed as if he might reach for the gun again at any moment. To Esther, Göktürk said, "I don't believe you, yet can't think why you'd risk telling such a lie. You know the penalty. If I send my men to fight alongside yours, to train them with guns and swords; if I supply you with weapons and ammunition, how will I be paid?"

The conversation had turned rapidly, while all her senses remained pricked to danger. She had no idea how much money they were talking about. All that she had was what she'd stolen from her father. When she reached the capital with her fighting force, there was no saying how her father and the bek would receive her. "Bek Admon will pay."

He gave a short, sharp wave of his hand, a dismissive gesture.

Her mouth was dry, despite the big glass of water. "I think your chief payment would be in continuing to be able to do business," if that was what one called what he did. "If the Germanii take Khazaria and Rus, industry will stop dead. No one will purchase fuel. They'll have nothing to heat or operate with it."

"The Germanii will." His expression remained bland. "They have aerocraft, naval ships and submarines, tanks, automobiles."

She could feel her heart beating in her ears. "You wouldn't," she began.

There was Chuluun's mean smile.

"Because of my great loyalty to the kagan?" Göktürk's tone remained mild, but she knew she'd have to take another tack.

"You can think what you will of the kagan and the bek, but they do fair business with you. They don't persecute you."

"Because we fill their coffers."

"Yishmaelites and Tengri-worshippers live at peace with Jews in the capital, practicing their trades and religions unmolested. This would not be the case, with the Germanii in power." Her stomach gurgled with embarrassing impropriety. She placed a hand over it to try to make it stop.

His calm smile once again appeared. "Who appointed you to this task, to muster an army and to seek me out?"

"I appointed myself. The Angel of the Lord sent me to you." She was glad Khazar Judaism didn't bother much with angels. Otherwise, she felt certain the flaming thing would kill her in its fury. El of the Mountain—one never knew when the Name of Names would turn from the God of Mercy to the God of Wrath.

He nodded. "The sun is about to set. You'll be our guests to eat, and you'll pitch your tents within our encampment. I'll make my decision by morning."

"Thank you. We'll leave at dawn."

"Don't tell anyone you know my name. Or I will have Chuluun kill you."

Esther didn't doubt it. She didn't trust them enough to turn her back on them, so she shuffled backwards toward the door, fumbled to pull her boots on, and let herself out. Outside, the broad sky was awash in a pink and orange glow. The work of the place still went on, the derricks pumping, noise all around. No one looked up amazed to see her standing, alive, on the precarious deck. Chuluun followed a moment later. At the top of the stairs, he said to her, "You lied to me."

"Out of fear. I knew nothing of your character then." She knew little more now, and what she did know frightened her. He seemed to accept her explanation, however, and let her go down the stairs alone.

She walked up behind Amit as he stood with his arms folded, watching the golems. The recruits and Itakh were nowhere in sight, but the golems had fallen in with a group of workmen in their indigo trousers. Two by two, the humans stacked full drums of oil onto trucks. A golem could lift one of the gigantic barrels by himself. "What are they doing?" she asked.

Amit shivered, startled by her voice, and turned to face her. "They're made to work; they said they needed to. You're all right, I see."

"Barely," she said. "I almost got killed." Some of the workmen glanced over at them, so she leaned in closer to him to talk. He was warm from the day's travel. His scent wafted off him like a perfume. "Now he's offering to shelter and feed us and to make a decision by morning."

"Then it sounds like you did a good job."

Her face was as close to him as it could be without impropriety, yet she wished she could bury it in his shoulder and inhale. He wasn't as handsome as Shimon, and was also less agreeable. Still, he filled her with desire. Knowing that he'd once been a girl didn't change that. She was trying to figure out if it might also be part of his appeal. "I guess I would have liked a decisive victory or a quick defeat."

"Be glad it wasn't the latter—you'd be dead. You need a book on military tactics."

"Don't tell me what I need. I wanted to win."

"He's considering your proposal. You did win."

Esther glanced up at him. His brown eyes twinkled behind his dirty glasses, so she looked away again. She did need a book on military tactics. And, while she was at it, she would have liked to see what was in Zohar, but she couldn't, because she was a girl. For the first time since her trip to the *mikvah*, she was able to think that with something like a sense of humor.

Uyghur food, it turned out, resembled Khazar food. Legumes and rice, fresh vegetables in this season, some roasted goat. Because they didn't observe kashrut, there was also soft cheese on the table, mixed with an herb. Esther's camp politely declined it, though if pressed, she would have added some to her bowl. The laws of hospitality outranked dietary laws in theory, though in practice, she'd never seen their relative importance tested. As everywhere in Khazaria, there were grapes and so there was wine. No one blessed it here. Esther had long thought wine was part of why the first kagan, fifteen hundred years before, had chosen to convert his nation to Judaism: because this land abounded in vines, and Judaism was the only religion with so many opportunities to bless their fruit. Imagine, if he'd chosen to become a Yishmaelite, what would have become of all the vineyards! Eating in the Uyghur camp, observing their customs—they eschewed utensils, used their long-fingered hands with grace—she understood that any number of things she thought of as Khazar had as much to do with the soil from which they grew as with anything particular about the people who ruled the land or with their religion.

Göktürk didn't eat with his men. No doubt it was part of his menace and mystique to go unseen. She wondered if he ate special, richer food up in his tower.

Before the meal concluded, word came through Tselmeg that their leader wished to offer his guests access to the bathhouse, a luxury. Benyamin and the other men grunted and clapped with pleasure. When they quieted, Esther asked, "Is there a separate one for women?"

Tselmeg looked over one shoulder, then the other, before wiping his nose on the back of his hand. "We don't have women here." He stared at the pointy tips of his riding boots. "Except for prostitutes. They bring them in a few times a week."

Esther's first thought was, Jewish prostitutes? Who were their fathers?

"Late in the evening, we escort them into the baths so they can wash. If you'd like to do that?"

"Yes," Esther said, not looking at him because she felt equated with a prostitute. "Thank you."

She was battling to keep herself awake when he came to fetch her from her tent. As she followed him, she saw the last stragglers heading home from their bath, their faces less grim, scrubbed clean, and their wet hair catching the moonlight. Tselmeg didn't say anything as they walked. The bathhouse to which he escorted her was nothing like a *mikvah*: a wooden building resembling a barrel. Inside was a large wooden tub, in which one both soaked and washed oneself. Steam rose off the water, which smelled like a pond, and petrol torches burned in wall sconces, wafting acrid smoke. After Tselmeg left, she pulled the wooden door to, then took off her clothes and climbed in.

Esther discovered a bench running around the tub's perimeter. She sat down, the hot water lapping her chin and her earlobes. It was filthy. A film of soap bubbles floated on the surface, gray in the grime, and the water's sheen had to be scrubbed-off oil. Still, the bath felt wonderful. Esther reached up to the edge for one of the slimy, gray-tinged bars of soap that lay scattered around. She worked up a dirty-looking lather. It felt good to scrub her scalp, a pleasure she hadn't noticed at home. She tipped her head back into the water to rinse her hair. As she worked her fingers through to untangle it, she thought about what distinguished a *mikvah* from a bathing tub. Though there were other specifications, she knew all *mikvot* had at least to touch a supply of rainwater, which was why, in a pinch, a person or a whole society could use a river or sea for purification—assuming one could get to it, clean and naked, at night. Could she use this as a *mikvah* if she had to? The pure, holy one of Yetzirah hadn't worked. She pinched her nostrils shut and dove under, knowing there would be no transformation.

When she hoisted herself onto the tub's wooden lip, her body still ached from the day of riding. She squeezed water from her slick rope of hair and began pulling on her clothes.

Before she was halfway across the compound, however, she heard shouting in Uyghur—a guard relaying information. As men called out the news to one another, one word cropped up three or four times: *güvercin*. Esther ran toward the commotion. Three guards had left their posts and gathered, arguing. One held a bird gruffly in his hands while another shone his electric torch into its red eyes, making it blink and ruffle its white feathers.

When they'd set out on their journey, Esther had been blind to a bird's merits or attractions. Willfully blind; uninterested. Now, without even thinking, she shouted out, "Nagehan!" though no one could have been more surprised than she to discover that she thought of the pigeon by name.

Startled to hear her voice, the guard let the bird go, and it fluttered to the ground and pecked at something.

"Nagehan," Esther said, crouching down to her. "You found us." Maybe the bird was smarter than Itakh realized. The portable loft was no larger than a pair of men's shoes, yet the pigeon had managed to find it, on the open steppe, at night. They had stopped in this village before. Did she remember it? Esther scooped the warm, jittery creature up. "It's my brother's bird," she said to the guards. "She homed to us." She struggled to hold the animal still while she screwed the top off the bullet case.

Inside, a tightly rolled piece of paper. Esther pinched it out, afraid it might be the same paper she'd packed in early that day. Her fingers grew thick and unwieldy as she flattened it.

This was not the note Esther had written. On a thinner, finer sheet of paper, someone had written in a hurried cursive hand: *Enemy breached Dniepra all the way to Kyiv. Western refugee camp decimated.*

Some taken prisoner, others seeking refuge in east. Bek and troops de-fending Don. Enemy gaining ground. Panzer armies. You're leading an army? You're in trouble. It was not signed, and the handwriting wasn't Shmuel's, the person in her family likely to intercept a pigeon. The writing most resembled Elisheva's. But she'd never shown an interest in pigeons, or in anything that might get her dirty. Esther felt alarmed that the news was so dire, and wondered why the writer hadn't signed the note.

"Rouse your master," Esther said to the guards.

One grunted; the others continued their conversation in Uyghur without responding.

"Amit! Itakh!" she shouted. In the quiet camp, her voice would wake them. When the first guard seemed startled, she said, "I told you: Rouse your master."

He reached out a hand to shush her. "He does no one's bidding."

"This cannot wait until morning."

Once again, the men conferred. Esther still had the pigeon in her hands. She screwed the cap back on its message case. People began emerging from the barracks around the camp. Still dressing them-selves, Itakh and Amit ran out, and Esther thrust the paper at Amit. Before he'd read it, she said, "We're leaving for the capital."

Itakh grabbed his bird and held her to his chest, where she nestled, cooed. "You found us!" he said to her. "Are we that close to home?"

Without even thinking, Esther called out, "Göktürk!"

All around her, the commotion ceased. A guard hissed, an eerie sound in this darkness, this foreign place. The Uyghur guards took a step back. After a long silence, one whispered, "Where did you learn this name?"

A light came on at the top of the tower. A moment later, the Uy-ghur leader appeared silhouetted in the open doorframe. He was too far off to see clearly—recognizable only because his hair was so bright—but Esther intuited that he might have gestured to her. He stood still, waiting. "Come on," she said, grabbing Itakh by the sleeve.

"No!" he said, with a familiar, irritable recoil. He was small, but could make himself heavy when he wanted to. Esther pulled harder to drag him along. Amit followed.

Göktürk disappeared from the doorway before they reached the top of the stairs. By the time they'd taken off their shoes, she saw that he was fully dressed and sitting on his soft rug, as she'd left him that afternoon. She had the fleeting, spiteful thought that he might be like a golem: animate but nonhuman, requiring neither food nor rest. Then she saw that his face was puffy, as if he'd woken too soon from sleep. "Who are these?" he asked, his voice as gentle as before.

"My brother, Itakh ben Josephus, and my"—what was the word?— "adjutant, Amit ben Avraham."

He nodded in greeting. "I told you not to speak my name."

"I apologize. The guards said I couldn't see you until the morning, but it's urgent." She wrested the paper from Amit's hands and held it across the rug to Göktürk. Even as he bent his eyes to it, she blurted out, "We need to leave now. We need men and weapons." There was a deliberate calm to his movements. He bent his head to read the message a second time. "Please," she added, at once rejecting her own supplicant tone.

"How did this reach you?"

Itakh held the flustered Nagehan up in front of him. "A miracle she was able to find us."

"Filthy," Göktürk remarked to no one in particular. He pressed his lips together, nodded once before he spoke. "My operations are secure no matter who wins this war." Esther prepared to be refused. "May I ask you a question?" He went on, "I cannot see why, instead of sending my assistance directly to Bek Admon, I should send it through you."

Esther's mind raced through explanations, from her army's need (her people were volunteers, ill equipped in every regard) to her own (she feared her father's contempt, and wanted to bring firepower to prove her worthiness for the cause). What left her mouth was simple: "The bek controls his armies. But only I have killed a *volkelake*. A were—"

"I speak your language, and that of your refugees."

215

"I killed one."

"That cannot be true."

She sat still and held her gaze steady.

Again he pressed his lips together as he considered her silence. "You killed a werewolf. How?"

"When Itakh and I were traveling to Yetzirah. She looked like an ordinary wolf, except that she didn't have a tail. I didn't know until she—changed." How. He'd asked her how. "I killed her with a knife."

His eyebrows lifted and lowered.

"Our horse trampled her first. She was wounded, so I thought I should do the merciful thing. I slit her throat." A chill shook Esther when she thought of how the fur had resisted the knife, when she pictured the lifeless, dull skin of the transformed dead woman.

He poured them all water, which his guests accepted with mumbled thanks. All the time he watched Esther. "About the werewolves, my people say," and then he recited a musical phrase in his own tongue. "It means that he who can kill one has power over death itself." The hair on Esther's forearms stood up like grass. She knew she might as well have killed it by accident. "Do you have proof?"

"I saw her do it," Itakh said.

"Proof," Göktürk repeated.

The lock of hair, wound in its coil, burned against her chest. She touched her breastbone to see if the leather pouch actually was hot, then worked open the cinch of its closure, damp with sweat and dirty bath water. She took out the lock of hair and handed it to him, careful not to touch his fingers as it changed hands.

He regarded the rank lock of dull brown hair. He held it to his nose and inhaled. His grunt signaled pleasure or assent. He worked it between his thumb and fingers a good long moment. Then he passed the hair back to her. She felt his scrutiny as she reclosed the pouch.

"I saw her," Itakh said. "And I saw it transformed."

"As did I," said Amit.

Esther's mouth was so dry she had to peel her tongue from its roof. She took a long drink of water in case she had to talk.

"I'm uncertain I believe anything you say, yet I admire your tenacity. I will give you men, mechanical horses, and fuel. I will arm you. But I cannot guarantee my men's allegiance to anyone but me. And if your campaign succeeds, I expect payback."

"Of course."

"Large-scale payback."

Esther nodded, though she didn't know what he meant.

"More land to drill, down into the oil-rich Kavkas, and a more favorable taxation rate. Your father is a powerful man. He can arrange this."

Esther continued to nod. Her father, the third most powerful man in Khazaria, did not bargain with the Uyghurs under ordinary circumstances. But these were new times. She wished she could negotiate with the kagan herself.

"Do fifty men help?" he asked.

"Yes." She imagined the Germanii, somewhere in the steppe between the Dniepra and the Don, with thousands, tens of thousands of men, and superior firepower. But fifty was better than none. "It doubles our human numbers. More than that. Thank you. I also want to ask for your aerocycles."

He looked as if she'd spoken an unfamiliar language. "They aren't weapons. Mere surveillance tools. A folly of my predecessor that has turned out to have use."

"Can you perform your surveillance without them? They could help us." She wasn't sure how.

Göktürk continued to regard her, then again nodded once. It was as if he lacked the time or patience for redundant nods. "You must tell no one outside the camp where they came from, or that you've seen me."

"On my honor." Not, she thought, such a valuable oath from someone who'd tried to do magic in a *mikvah* and had already lied to him, but she meant it.

"Now go," he said. "And tell this boy, the next time he enters my chambers, to leave his bird behind."

"Yes, sir," Itakh said in a small voice. Esther hoped this would be his last time in Göktürk's presence.

The guards and a small crowd had gathered at the foot of the stairs and stood looking up, as if they expected her lifeless body to be flung to earth. All they got was Esther, Amit, Itakh, and a tired messenger pigeon. Esther looked at the bird in Itakh's hands and wondered how far the other one had made it on its long journey, if it still lived. The vertiginous stairs vibrated and made the faintest sound, like a mouth harp, under their soft boots. Seeing the expressions on upturned faces, Esther thought, was this how Moses felt, coming down from Sinai with the Law in his hands? It couldn't be. Moses had been chosen. Esther had been—she didn't know what. Two golems stood amidst the crowd, head and shoulders above everyone else. At once she recognized Gimmel, as she had recognized Nagehan a short while ago. She thought she saw curiosity in his dull brown eyes, then told herself it had been a trick of the torchlight.

When Göktürk appeared behind them, his men fell silent. "Fifty volunteers to accompany our sister, the Sarmata, on her journey. As many mechanical horses as are needed. All of the aerocycles. Chuluun?"

He stepped forward from the crowd.

"Take her and ten of her creatures—"

"*Golemim*," Gimmel corrected. People hushed him.

"—to the arsenal."

Gimmel went to gather more of his kind. When he returned with them, Chuluun led the group to a large, concrete building on the outskirts of town. Amit followed behind. Itakh went to feed and water Nagehan and to pack their bags.

Chuluun walked ahead of the group with an irritated twitch, as if some pest were nipping at him. When he turned to Esther, she expected him to yell at her. Instead he said, "Do not tell the bek I brought you here. We don't want him to know what we have."

She nodded. There was much these men didn't want told. Esther supposed their mystique and power depended on it. He took a ring of keys from his trouser pocket, and used three in succession to work the locks on a huge iron door. It rang hollowly as it opened, and let them into a cool, cavernous space. When Chuluun pulled a chain for a string of overhead lights and the room sprang into focus in their yellow glow, Esther saw the building was immense—spacious enough to house multiple acrocraft. Plain steel shelves lined the walls and, in neat ranks, filled the center of the room. The shelves were as tidy as those in Atil's Great Library, but displayed weapons of every description. Just like a library, the stacks in the middle of the room had labels on their short ends, though Esther couldn't read the Uyghur script. She saw what must have been thousands of short knives and slender stilettos, swords and scimitars, their blades the same blue as Seleme's flanks. Shelves of snub-nosed pistols, more of larger handguns, some automatic. One whole set of shelves housed the weapons the steppe's warring tribes had used against one another for a millennium: maces, slingshots, picks, whips, crossbows as big as Itakh, bolts of every length and thickness. One shelf held electric torches, so new their aluminum sides gleamed. Stacked haphazardly atop one another on the far shelves sat horrible, evacuated faces: flat, goggling eyes, steel cans where noses and mouths should have been. They resembled the fossilized skulls in Atil's natural history museum. "What are those?" Esther asked.

"Gas masks. You may need them."

Their expressions were frightful.

Chuluun waved one hand in the air around his head, as if battling off flies. "It's a Western aberration. They fear to ride up and disembowel you with a sword. Instead they release a poisonous chemical into the air to kill you slowly from afar. That way, they can stay back and hide between their mothers' legs. You'll need a large supply." The bek must have known this and supplied this equipment to soldiers at the front.

He led them into the room's far right corner and began to pull weapons down and lay them into the golems' waiting arms. As he did so, he said the name of each item. When necessary, he showed his audience how to release a safety latch or work a mechanism. The golems' faces betrayed neither strain nor interest as he piled their arms high with instruments of death.

"Pay attention," Esther commanded them. "We'll all have to learn how to use these."

One golem coughed. Another said, "You'll have to learn. We understand machines."

When their arms were full, they turned as one and carried their burdens out the door. A few minutes later, they returned, ready for another load. When choosing weapons for men, Chuluun gave a wide variety. To arm golems, however, he chose the big and primitive weapons. Clearly he expected the creatures to bludgeon their combatants to death. He also gave one golem two small, heavy instruments. "Microscopes?" Esther asked.

"Don't be ridiculous," Chuluun said. "Theodolites. To determine your coordinates. I'll instruct your men in how to use them."

Amit's eyes grew round as he watched this. Esther couldn't tell if he felt fear or a desire to work the machines. Though Chuluun wasn't watching Amit, he must have sensed his interest, because he drew down a machine gun and slapped it into the kabbalist's open hands. Amit staggered under the weight. Chuluun laughed his mean laugh. "You'll have to grow stronger to use it," he remarked.

Back in the square, the golems packed much of the weaponry onto golem horses. The rest they distributed to the old and new recruits— many of the Uyghur oilmen wanted to join, to terrorize the steppe, to hunt and kill. Other than Amit, the people assembled knew their weapons. They hefted them with a bravado Esther admired. The guns, swords, and crossbows appeared sinister in the moonlight, the wavering torchlight, and the cold gleam of the few arc lamps someone had illuminated high above the square. Every inanimate object suggested threat. Itakh, carrying Nagehan in her mobile loft, stood in line to get a pistol from Chuluun, but when he approached the front, Esther kicked him hard in the shin.

"Ow!" he yelled, doubling over to grab his leg as if that would ease the pain. Still he was careful to set the bird in her box down gently. "What's wrong with you?"

"You're too little to be trusted with a gun."

"I'm your lieutenant! I'm not little!"

He'd grown in the days since they'd set out—his wrists and ankles protruded from his cuffs—yet he remained a boy. Back home in Atil, if he'd been highborn, he wouldn't even have begun the training to become a bar mitzvah. "Here," she said, and took a solid hunting knife from one of the golems. Itakh frowned as he turned it this way and that to examine it, watching the light dance on the blade. When he stowed it in his boot and turned his leg to admire it, he seemed appeased.

"Little Uyghur," Chuluun remarked casually. "Give him a chance with something more deadly, he'll be fine."

Itakh reached down to adjust the knife in the boot. He looked torn between asking for a gun or crossbow and asserting once more that he was a Jew. He held his tongue. He could be both, Esther knew.

Amit said, "We have to keep track of the distribution of weapons as carefully as we keep track of the new recruits."

"Right now," Esther replied, "our priority is to get to the capital." She was glad he'd chosen to come, however, and wondered in passing what would have become of him if he'd had to live the rest of his life as a girl. If his home village bordered Ukraina, maybe the enemy would already have herded him toward a death camp. She pictured his parents and brother marching there on this cold night.

Chuluun said, "Out on the road, my men and I will provide lessons in the weapons' use."

"You're coming with us?" Esther asked. She tried to scoff or at least sound unconcerned, but heard her excitement leak into her tone.

He blew a sharp breath out of his nostrils. "Against my better judgment."

She knew he meant this as a personal slight. Still she said, "Thank you," her body flooding with relief to know he'd make up one of their number.

221

"Some of us will remain here to guard the fort. Those who head off with you have the chance to kill and pillage. I know which life I choose."

"Not to pillage," she said.

He took a breath as if to say something, then didn't.

Some of the oilmen had led golems to where the aerocycles were kept, outside the city limits. She heard the slow rhythm of their great wings *thwoop*-ing toward the ground. Then the sound would stop, perhaps as the Uyghurs explained some aspect of the machinery. A few minutes later, a deep hum erupted from the field: a number of them gaining speed and beating their wings until they gained altitude. They made their slow way toward the Uyghur stronghold, fifteen or twenty of them. Esther could see that some were manned by people, others by *golemim*, whose frames fit awkwardly into the machines, but who could power them tirelessly as the night wore on.

The Uyghur volunteers more than doubled their human numbers. Most wore the blue uniforms of the workers. A few dressed in the black, Western riding clothes and drove mechanical horses. No matter their other garb, all the Uyghurs wore somber black skullcaps. The warlord horses swiveled their sharp ears toward Seleme as a Uyghur boy rode her, against her will, from the stable. Esther could not tell the vintage of these machines. Their build was more aerodynamic than Seleme's, yet the ghastly suicide shifters jutted from their left shoulders. On the other hand, Esther had seen how the riders maneuvered them on the steppe. Seleme's green eyes scanned them, then returned to an expression of studious disdain. "Where did you get those?" Esther asked Chuluun.

"I asked you a few days ago where you got yours."

"I stole her. You?"

He gestured ambiguously with his chin toward his shoulder and began to inspect the horses.

As Esther prepared to lead her army out into the darkness, one final volunteer came charging into the square, his black-jacketed form struggling under the weight of his baggage. "Wait!" he called. It was

Tselmeg, breathing hard. As Esther swung herself up into the saddle, he halted beside Seleme with a grin on his face. "I'm coming too."

Esther smiled back. "But you're a—" What was the word? Few of the horse-riding marauders had volunteered. She assumed this was because their lives were already good.

Tselmeg looked around at his brethren before responding. "The youngest and the least respected. I'll cast my lot with you."

Some nearby men snickered, and Esther shifted Seleme into reverse, revved her engine, and wheeled her around. The men quieted with the mean-eyed, rumbling machine watching. Tselmeg called out to one of the snickerers, then tied his bundle to an available golem horse and badgered a man off a mechanical horse that might have been his own. Only once they had marched out of town and toward the dark river did Esther ask him what he had said. "I told him that when the war was over, I'd come back to slit his throat." When he recounted the threat, they both laughed.

In the dark of night, away from the city, they could see no other settlements. Neither could they see or hear or smell the battle as it pushed its way eastward. Yet it was there, the only question how distant. The acrocycles' wings beat so hard and slow, they raised a wind over the army, chilling them as they traveled. Esther shouted up an order for them to hold farther back, but the machines weren't as easy to control as mechanical and golem horses, at least not for novice cyclists. As the army moved forward, the mechanical horses' engines purred and growled in turns. The aerocycles made a deep, threatening rush overhead. Esther thought, this night might have been any night in the past thousand years, her army (with a few technological exceptions) any of the armies that had traversed this land to ravage and conquer. But their purpose in traveling back to the capital held steady in her mind. She hoped Atil and Khazaran would still be untouched when they arrived.

CHAPTER 19

The nearly hundred men and the golems traveled all night. When dawn broke, Esther could not have said at what point the sky lightened. Gimmel strode up beside her in the front of the line and said, "We must stop."

He might have overtaken her if he'd wanted to. "Why?" She scanned the horizon—the broad, flat river, the scrubby terrain, the distance shrouded in a purple mist—but could see neither friend, enemy, nor inclement weather.

"Human soldiers must eat. There is plenty of cold food. And Jewish soldiers must pray, as it is morning. We do not know the Uyghurs' customs, but perhaps they need to pray to their own god."

His argument about the prayers was unassailable. As a girl, she had never tied on tefillin, but it would be difficult on a moving horse. "Prepare the quickest meal you can." Then she shouted the order to halt. The aerocycles slowed their wingbeats and glided overhead, outpacing the army before each slid to a stumbling stop in the tall grass. Though the landing appeared awkward, the pilots, both human and golem, unstrapped themselves and stepped out tired but well.

Without the mechanical horses' rumble and the din of the aerocraft, Esther could hear the sounds of birds, insects, and running water. Nagehan cooed in her cage. As the golems unpacked supplies, Esther saw that many—not all—of the men she'd believed to be Jews were taking *tallitot* and tefillin from their bags to pray. Itakh was too young. Regarding the others, she wondered if they only appeared Jewish or if it was possible to be a Jewish man without performing these *mitzvot*. The idea had never occurred to her.

Amit, she noticed, was off his horse, digging angrily through his bag. "What's wrong?" Esther asked.

He flung a spare piece of clothing on the ground as he pulled out his holy articles. "At home, they prepare the food and make the Sabbath at our command. They have never before reminded us to pray."

Esther slid to the ground and gave Seleme a pat on her steel flank. Though the horse was turned off, she was warm from the night's exertions. "Maybe all this time, they've kept track too. Since people are fallible."

"Not about prayer. And I don't know how they'd do that. They're not human. They shouldn't have any more sense of time than a dog."

"A dog knows enough of time to tell the difference between morning and night." She said this despite having no firsthand experience of dogs. The *volkelake* must, she thought, have known day from night: during the daytime because of her human form, at night finding herself a wolf.

"Well, *golemim* aren't dogs." He walked to where the men had gathered to pray. His shawl and boxes spilled over his awkward arms. She wanted to like his smell less. It lingered in the air after he passed.

Esther said her own prayers, then observed the men. Though they did not pray in unison, they all stood together. The golems, gathered at the outskirts, chanted the prayers under their breath, just as the men did.

Amit, noticing this, raised his eyebrows, causing his round glasses to slip down his nose. As if thinking they might only have picked up key phrases here and there, he sped up his own prayers, but the golems kept pace, their sonorous voices lending gravity to the words. The boy Natan came to watch this spectacle, and smiled to himself as he did.

After Amit removed the shawl from his head and the phylacteries from his arm and brow, he turned to Natan and said, "That's enough. No."

But the boy continued to smile.

"Don't laugh. It's forbidden for them to pray." His voice wavered, though, as if he weren't sure if it was forbidden or simply not done.

"We observe your *mitzvot*," one golem said evenly. "The rabbis teach that if one's neighbor lives and practices as a Jew, one must not question that he *is* a Jew. We heard Shelomoun say this."

"One's neighbor is human." Though this was a simple statement of fact, the words sounded harsh in this beautiful morning, this evidence of the Lord's goodness in creating the world.

"We desire to praise His Holy Name. How can this be forbidden?"

Amit pushed his glasses up. The force of the gesture seemed to spin him around. "I can't believe we're talking about this."

The golem stood still.

"This is no time for discussion," Amit said. "It is your job to prepare our food. Go."

The golems went back to the horses and began their work. When the men folded their holy garments and walked away to return them to their packs, Esther hung back to speak with Amit. "Why does it upset you so?" she asked.

"Shh."

"Don't hush me," she said. "I'm asking you a question."

He exhaled a quick breath before answering, "Because it goes against nature."

"So does raising golems from the dirt."

He didn't respond.

The golems had already put out enough dried fruit and cheese to feed all the people. Drinking water was in short supply. They'd have to find a spring and replenish their provisions before they reached the capital. The army was back in motion only a few minutes later, the aerocycles beating their wings in the air behind them.

As they traveled along the river, Esther thought how, back home in Atil, her father and the javshigarim spoke of the steppe in the same tone of reverent horror they used for discussing the Evil Impulse, eating pork, or one's child marrying a non-Jew. Esther's imagination had painted this place—which until this journey, she had not seen—to resemble a desert, monochrome and barren. Now she was moved by its richness, the yellow green of the grass wavering bluer toward the horizon, the willow trees along the streams, the myriad creatures. Itakh had befriended the other young boy, Natan, who now rode his golem horse at the front of the line so they could talk. Amit, riding beside Esther, remained in a temper.

"What harm do they do if they pray?" she asked him.

His eyes widened as if the answer should be obvious. Then he faced forward again. He wasn't a good enough rider to steer without looking. "What if they did needlework on the Sabbath? Would that do any harm?"

Natan said, "Wouldn't it depend if they were doing work—darning socks, or something like this—or doing it for pleasure?" She had thought him too far away to hear their conversation.

"And if I wanted to light a fire for pleasure on the Sabbath? The Law isn't interested in intent."

"Sure it is." Natan looked around for support, but only she, Itakh, and Amit appeared to be able to hear him. He was smaller than Amit, the only one who was, besides Itakh. He could still have won a fight had it come to that. Amit had such a tentative way with his body. "And anyway, they're not Jews. So I'd think they could do anything they like on the Sabbath."

"Aren't they?" Esther asked. If not, what were they?

Amit relaxed his posture on the horse. "The Law applies to them because they coexist with us. It would be wrong of us to permit them to work."

Gimmel must have been close enough to overhear, because his low voice addressed Amit. "Do you think that's why we don't work on Shabbat? Because you don't allow us to?" Esther was either beginning to pick out his individual tone or beginning to imagine it.

"Of course." When Gimmel didn't say more, Amit added, "We made you. We give you your rules."

"No." The golem increased his pace until he walked abreast of Esther and Amit. He stood as tall as they were seated on horseback. "No. You formed us. For this we owe you gratitude. But we do not work on Shabbat because our conscience forbids it."

227

Seleme swerved toward Amit's golem horse, and Esther feared she might bite its shoulder. She drew the machine back on course, though she wanted to stay close enough to hear every word. As she righted Seleme, she saw the aerocycles chugging along behind them.

Amit said, "You don't have a conscience. A conscience comes from having a soul."

"No. You think that because you have both. If you look at the world around you, you'll see it is not the case. A house cat contains the spark of life, but there is no arguing that it has a conscience." He moved his ponderous head from side to side as if thinking. Was he thinking? "We, who possess only the breath of life that you breathed into us, nevertheless can judge between right and wrong."

"Because we have taught you to." Whether because of the noise of the engines or because of anger, Amit's voice sounded high and tense.

"Because we thirst for justice and the good."

Amit, always ready for disputation, seemed to have nothing to say. He rode on for a moment, his hands tight on the reins. Natan and Itakh watched him. There was no chance the golems in the aerocycles could hear this above the din of their wings, yet Esther imagined them listening.

"You made us without souls," the golem said, an impossible trace of reproach in his voice.

"We're men," Amit replied. "Only Hashem can create a *neshamah*."

"Despite this, we have an unquenchable thirst to know our Maker."

The soft hairs on Esther's forearms tingled.

"You mean us?" Amit asked.

She knew this was not what Gimmel meant.

"Him who made you. El of the Mountain. The Great Name."

"He did not—"

"You plant the wheat in the fertile soil, harvest it with your own hands, bake the loaf. Yet before you eat the bread, you thank the Lord who gave you the seed. Likewise, Hashem made the clay and the animating breath, which you shaped into the image of a man. Some praise is due to you. More is due to the Maker of all. We keep the Sabbath holy in His honor, and our hearts sing out to Him in praise."

Amit sat his horse. From his expression, he might have thought this golem was Balaam's Ass, talking out of line with his expectations of its species.

"We desire to participate with our human brothers in prayer."

Amit's mouth opened before his mind prodded it to speak. "Only people can pray. Only a Torah Jew addresses the Lord in His holy tongue. Our Uyghur troops cannot join in the prayers."

Esther glanced behind her. None of them was close enough to hear. From a distance, she could see how comfortable they were on their horses—a few seemed to know how to keep the throttle forward with the right knee, so that both hands were free to whittle or pack a pipe. This skill had value on the battlefield. She would ask them to teach it to the others.

"That's not true," Natan interjected. When Esther and Amit turned to him, his freckled cheeks blushed. "You don't have to follow every rule in the Torah to address Hashem." Esther couldn't see Amit's expression, but imagined his eyes burning holes into Natan, who blushed more deeply. "My family—my father's a fisherman. When it's time to haul in the catch, you have to do it, or you could lose a whole season's earnings."

Amit took a moment to process this. "You haul fish on Shabbat."

"If we have to. We gut them too. One day can ruin everything. We could starve." He wiped his palms on his thighs. "But we are Jews. We keep kosher; we fast on Yom Kippur; we have a mezuzah on our doorpost. We may not be Torah Jews, as you speak of, but we recite prayers."

Amit's eyes widened with amazement.

"What were you, raised in a box?" Natan asked. "No one in your home village ever inadvertently carried outside the *eruv*, or ate a piece of meat from a dairy plate? The Lord forgives transgressions."

Amit said, "No."

"And what of the righteous gentile, the *ger toshav*?" Gimmel asked, raising one stiff hand in the air to indicate the Uyghurs behind him and up in the air. They didn't look so righteous. "What of the Mongol who saves a child from drowning, or the Yishmaelite who gives from his table to feed the poor? Surely the Lord is pleased with these *mitzvot*, even if those who performed them would not call them by that name. When they give their prayers of thanksgiving, He hears them."

In the din of their travel, the sounds of Atil sprang to mind: the muezzins' melodic calls to prayer, the song—off-key and joyful—of the Nazarenes' carillon bells on the morning after Shabbat. When a child whose parents followed the Nazarene Rabbi whispered its bedtime prayers, its voice must sound as sweet to the Lord's ear as the *Sh'ma*.

Gimmel continued, "We are Jewish golems. Because you have not made us to eat, we observe no kashrut. Because you have given us no wives, we cannot be faithful to them. But we observe *mitzvot* to the best of our ability. We believe the Almighty hears our prayers. We ask that you allow us to offer them in your company."

Amit rode in silence for what seemed a long while. Then Esther saw his breastbone seem to retreat inward. Without looking at Gimmel, he said, "I need to think." What he needed, Esther thought, was a minyan of other kabbalists with whom to argue the point. No doubt that was how he'd done most of his thinking in Yetzirah.

Gimmel stretched to his full height. He towered above everyone and everything around him on the ground. Esther had grown more accustomed to being around such large creatures, but she noticed his size now. "Of course," he said, his voice low and even. "That is reasonable. Know, however, that we are not required to fight for your cause."

"Yes, you are," Esther said. She didn't see how Khazaria would survive without them.

"No, Esther," the golem corrected. Nothing in his face or voice changed—nothing could—but when he addressed her by her given name, she read his tone as less aggressive. "We have, thus far, obeyed our makers' commands because we have found them to be wise and just. But we are not compelled to do so. We may cease at any time. We have free will, as do your other volunteers."

Amit, beside her, looked up to the sky, his mouth open. "We did not give you free will."

"But He who made you—"

"Had nothing to do with it."

The golem walked along, his arms straight down at his sides. A human would look stiff in this posture, but he appeared comfortable. Esther realized this was an irrational judgment. A being immune to sensation felt neither comfort nor discomfort. "Take your time. Consider our request. But if we cannot pray as your equals, we will convene to discuss our further participation in your cause." He slowed his pace to allow the horses to get ahead of him. When Esther turned back, she saw him walking with his own kind. Only walking, not eagerly blurting out the results of his conversation, as a person might have done.

Esther asked Amit, "Have they ever done anything like this before?"

He kicked at his golem horse. It continued on, not feeling the assault. Only when Amit shook his reins and called out to it to speed up did it do so. He had gone a few necks ahead of the group when Itakh said to Esther, "I think you'd better go after him."

Esther saw Amit's determination in crossing the rocky, grassy plain. "Want to come with me?"

"I'm too little to have a gun. What use could I be?"

Itakh was rarely sarcastic, and his tone worried Esther, but she had to catch up to Amit. She upshifted Seleme. Soon the machine neared the tail of Amit's horse, and stretched out her neck to bite the fixed clay tail. "No," Esther said, yanking Seleme's head to the side with the handlebar. "Amit?" she called out. "Amit, slow down."

He continued as if he heard neither the roar of the approaching horse nor Esther's entreaties.

She tried to catch up without driving Seleme berserk. Her frustration rose, stiffening her chest, and she leaned far over the side of the horse to try to grab Amit's sleeve. He pulled away, swift as if she'd touched him with a glowing ember.

"Amit," she called out, irritated at how loud the engine was, "slow down. I want to talk to you."

"Don't touch me." He kept moving at the same clip. "Don't you practice *negiah* in the capital?"

Esther's head grew so hot with rage, her vision blurred. Just calm enough to calculate a response, she said, "You're not really a man anyway."

Now he pulled back on his reins. His horse stopped, and Esther lurched forward on her machine. He caught up to her a moment later and said, "How can you say that?"

Esther already regretted it. "It's true."

Amit glanced behind him at the rest of the party. Esther doubted anyone could hear them. "The Lord, who made Heaven and Earth, made me a man. He answered my prayers. Unlike yours."

Two or three smart retorts sprang to mind, but Esther knew that to make any of them would be unwise. She was embarrassed at how quickly she'd leaped to say the thing most likely to wound him. She wanted him to talk to her. "I'm sorry I slighted you," she said.

He didn't respond.

Esther rolled Seleme's gearshift back toward herself and brought her down into second. This would mean they had only a few minutes to talk before the rest of the army caught up with them, but also meant she wouldn't have to shout. Once the engine quieted, Esther's breath came easier, and she noticed some long-horned sheep in the distance, lifting their heads at the approaching sound. They bounded a few leaps away.

"Why can't you let them pray with us?" she asked.

"Because they aren't people."

"You wouldn't drive your horse away from morning prayers."

"The horse wouldn't try to participate."

He might have an answer for every argument. "Rabbi Kalonymos teaches that birdsong and a cow's low are the way they praise the Creator."

Amit continued on without speaking. Itakh, Natan, and the aerocycles were gaining on them. The sheep had somehow disappeared. "Creatures worship in the manner appropriate to their station. Golems," he said, as if beginning some longer statement, though he didn't finish it until moments had passed. "Golems don't have a station."

Esther didn't know how to respond. "Did they ever do anything like this before?" She meant more than one thing, so clarified, "Make threats? Ask for things they didn't have?"

Amit glanced sideways at her, his mouth pressed tight. "No, no. I could never have imagined this would happen. At home they just did their work."

"But these can't be the first golems to possess a religious impulse."

"It isn't natural to their kind."

Esther thought "natural" an odd word to choose.

"It isn't in their nature," he repeated. "It makes me fear what else they might be capable of." He cast a worried glance her way.

Esther wondered if this was why Shelomoun had told her how to kill them. Her heart skittered in her chest. "You don't know?" Their eyes locked, but she couldn't read his expression. Even in her panic, even given his bad temper, she felt the hot stab of desire. "You wouldn't kill them just because they want to pray?"

"It isn't killing. They aren't alive."

"Shelomoun called it killing. You can't take away someone's life for disagreeing with you." After a moment, she added, "It isn't bad to want to praise the Name. It's never bad." Certain as she was, she wanted his reassurance. Only he knew why Shelomoun had told them how to wipe out their names and the name of Truth. "This can't be what your elders were talking about?" Itakh and Natan were close now, close enough to hear. She said, "I can't imagine it pleases Hashem if some who desire to worship Him are forbidden to."

"You need to read your Maimonides."

"Why?"

"Because he'll teach you the Creator is too big to fit in your imagination."

In Atil, she might have argued—the whole world visible, contained within the city walls and its bustling streets. This wilderness seemed to stand closer to the infinite, not only in the way it stretched out in all directions but also in its mystery. She had not, before this adventure, witnessed such an expansive dome of sky, marred now by heavy black clouds in the south. In Atil, she had believed herself to have an appropriate, Jewish sense of the Great Name's vastness. Yet it was difficult to conceive of vastness when one's immediate surroundings were small. There, in that moment, she felt vastness within her. At some level, it was an understanding of the Name.

"Did you change his mind?" Itakh said as he rode right in between them.

Looking at him on his docile clay horse, she understood, at once, that he was not the brother she'd been telling everyone he was, but a *slave*. Her family's slave, just as the *golemim* were the kabbalists'. Whenever this thought had insinuated itself into her consciousness before, she had shooed it away like an impertinent child. He was not, she had told herself, a slave as the Yisraelites had been to Pharaoh, or as Ifrikians had once been in the far-off West. The family loved Itakh, treated him well. But she saw now that he lacked freedom. Had he run off alone, Josephus would have had the legal right to capture and flog him. Itakh could not choose either to learn their father's profession or to make a case for some other line of work. Upon their return, if Atil still stood, he would help Kiraz in the kitchen and dust and sweep the house. He would purchase the groceries and truck them home in bulging net bags. "I want to ask you something," she said.

He looked puzzled by the urgency of her tone.

"Do you want me to ask you in private?"

He shrugged.

"Fine, then. Tell me what you make of your condition as a slave."

He winced, and tried to hold her gaze steady, but his eyes darted around. "Esther."

"I asked if you wanted privacy." Did this excuse her? She wanted to think so.

His dark eyes began to glisten, and he reached back to place his hand on Nagehan's cage. Esther felt an immediate stab of remorse—he seldom cried. She felt shocked and ashamed to make him do so, but she wanted an answer. One tear crested his lower lid and spilled down his cheek. "How can you ask that?" he said.

"I need to know," she said, willing herself not to understand his question.

"How can you ask with everyone listening?" Only Amit rode close enough to hear. Perhaps Natan as well. "Ever since we left home you've told everyone I'm your brother. What's the use if you drop it now?"

Esther would have liked to go off somewhere alone. Despite the vastness of the landscape, this was impossible. "I wasn't thinking."

"No."

For all her annoyance at Amit, she saw he had the decency to avert his gaze. "But I needed to speak with you about this."

"Why?"

The golems weren't close enough to hear. She wondered, if they were, if they'd take an interest.

"I have never thought of you as a slave. I think of you as my brother."

A few more tears escaped, and he brushed them away. "But at the end of each day, you, Elisheva, and Shmuel go upstairs to sleep in the family bedrooms, while I stay in my closet off the kitchen."

"The warmest spot in the house." As soon as it left her mouth, she knew it hadn't been wise to say. His shining eyes glared at her.

"You have your tutor. I learn how to soak and prepare different kinds of beans. I don't even know how to write Jascha a letter for Nagehan to carry." Itakh let go the reins of his golem horse to wipe both hands over his face. When he pulled them away, dirt smudged his cheeks. "Why have you never cared until now?"

She could think of nothing in her own defense. "Because I was blind. I wasn't thinking." It might have been nice if he'd denied this. "I'll make amends now."

"By freeing me?"

"Haven't I already done that?"

"Officially, I mean."

She paused, felt the rumble of Seleme's engine, the strain in her hands from working the controls. She couldn't believe Itakh would leave her. His companionship was a constant. What would she do without him? "That's not within my authority."

Riding beside her, he snorted and lifted his chin in surprise or disgust. "You steal money and Seleme, you run off to muster an army, but you can't ask your father for one thing. I understand."

All of the humans on the ground clustered behind them, many trying to get close enough to hear the conversation. Who wouldn't? The masters were fighting, always of interest to those who lived in the huts outside the main house. There was no way out of the situation except through it. She had no power to free Itakh. As the leader of this army, she had authority to give Amit orders, yet sensed that his dealings with the *golemim* were outside her domain. Still, who were any of them to deny a being the right to worship its god? And what would become of her army if the golems deserted or turned against them? "Amit?" Esther said, her voice choked. "I demand you free your slaves."

Amit looked as confused as if she'd addressed him in a foreign tongue.

"If you deny them their freedom to worship as they choose, then that's what they are."

"They're practically automata."

"No, we're not," one said nearby.

Esther said, "I don't know what they are, and I don't think you can claim to either. But we'd best treat them with respect."

"I need time to think about this. I said that. They've never acted like this before, and I have no one to ask for advice."

"Choose," Esther said. Her voice sounded stronger than she felt in the moment. "I command you as the leader of this army. Choose now, and stand by your decision."

Amit stared. His expression might have meant anything from that he wanted to hit her to that he loved her. She had to make herself stare back, keep the horse moving forward. They had covered ground before he said, "Fine."

Her left hand let go the gearshift and gestured to heaven. "Fine?"

"They sing with us. They praise the One who made their creators."

Esther sometimes wished she'd been alive in Torah times. Had Amit made such a pronouncement then, a great storm would have gathered, a thundercloud spoken. The Angel of the Lord might have appeared with those six or however many fiery wings. In the given world, the mechanical horses' engines chugged, the beasts' hooves clopped. Then a golem, Esther couldn't tell which, raised his voice and shouted out, "Holy, Holy, Holy is the Name of the Lord!" The low sound reverberated across the open plain, and Esther shivered. One by one, others began to call out, their voices overlapping, "*Kadosh! Kadosh!*" "And you shall praise Him when you rise up in the morning and when you lie down at night!" "*Sh'ma, Yisrael: Adonai eloheinu, Adonai ekhad!*" Before long, their voices boomed so loud, the aero-cycles' wingbeats diminished and the ground reverberated. Esther closed her eyes to hear better, to feel the sound's intensity even over the horse's rumbling engine, to feel its beauty and ugliness ring in her stomach and her breastbone. With her eyes closed, the sound dwarfed her. The sensation hovered between fear and awe.

When their voices died down, the engine roar and wingbeats and faint twitters of birdsong sounded different—paler and thinner, by comparison—and Esther felt she'd witnessed a miracle, though she couldn't say what that miracle had been. Her body was hollowed out, as it had been for months after her mother died. All the people in their party regarded one another, wondering who would speak first, and what that person would say. Amit broke the silence by asking the golem nearest him, "Do you need to be instructed in the prayers for daily use, for Shabbat, for Havdalah?"

"We do not," the golem replied. "We have every one by heart."

When the golems' voices joined in a quick *berakhah* for the humans' cold lunch, the blessing, praising Him who had made everything, sounded richer and fuller than it had before. When they returned to Atil, when the war was won, she would have to speak to her father about Itakh.

CHAPTER 20

As they finished their hurried meal, the dark clouds rolling in from the south overtook them, and a steady rain began to fall. The grass glowed vivid green in the dim light. The hot day cooled. As Itakh placed berries in his pigeon's cage, he asked, "Can we stay put and see if it passes?"

"We're an army, not a pleasure cruise," Esther replied.

"For an hour?"

"The Germanii won't stop heading eastward because we're afraid to get our feet wet," Amit said.

"They might," Esther opined. "Mud on the steppe can stop a tank, and the rain grounds their aeroplanes as well as ours." She was beginning to think like a tactician. No one seemed impressed. "How well can aerocycles maneuver in this kind of weather?"

None of the Uyghurs was close enough to hear, so a golem called for Chuluun. By the time he rode forward, someone had conveyed the question to him. "The wings repel water, but in a downpour, they'll soak through," he told her. "They'll falter before they stop outright."

She glanced back. The aerocycles were flying fine, though the human riders appeared sweaty and flushed. "And how long can golems withstand the rain?" she asked Amit.

"A while," Amit said. "We should make haste, however."

As they traveled downriver, they met the storm, and the rain intensified. The mechanical horses' transmissions whined as their hooves stuck in the mud. Soon the rain fell so hard they could see only a short distance ahead. Esther's clothes had tripled in weight and clung to her skin. The horses' hooves now sank into the soggy earth, and spattered mud everywhere as they made slow progress. When she turned to look, the aerocycles' top wings sagged under the weight of the water they'd collected. Though the riders pedaled as hard as before, the machines hung lower to the ground.

"We need to stop and wait it out," Amit said.

"Where?" Benyamin called out from behind them. "It's the same rain everywhere."

"We could set up camp, or shelter in a grove of trees."

Most of the Khazar speakers laughed at this. They hadn't passed a stand of trees all day.

"At what point will the golems be in trouble?" Esther asked.

Amit thought a moment before replying. "When they're soaked, thoroughly soaked. Only then might they begin to break apart."

"When Shelomoun told me about erasing their names, he mentioned a wet cloth. They're all right if they're damp?"

"It would take hours to do it that way. People normally use a chisel."

She shivered, as much because of the gruesome image as because of the sudden damp. "We should go until we find a village to shelter us. I don't see how we can pitch our tents in this." As if helping her to make the point, Seleme walked through a puddle so deep, it sent rivulets of mud up Esther's soaked legs. She drew in a breath, waiting to hear if Seleme's vents had flooded, but the engine rumbled along.

Soon, however, a village did appear, one Esther and Itakh had steered a wide course around on their journey out. No one saw it until right before them stood cozy roundhouses with thatched roofs. Thin smoke tried to curl from smoke holes. In their fields, the villagers grew large-leafed squashes and something with weird purple flowers. Brown goats roamed a distant pasture. The aerocycles plopped down to land, one after the other, in the mud around the village wall. The golems climbed right out, but the human riders remained, sheltered somewhat from the downpour, to catch their breath.

Esther leaned down from her seat on the horse to push open the town gate, and she called out, "Hello?"

For a moment, no one answered. Then a young woman stuck her head out from a near doorway. "*Shalom!*" she cried. "*Shalom aleikhem!*" She was happy to see a drenched army? Esther couldn't decode what the woman wore—a long blue dress with an apron, as if she'd stepped out of some nineteenth-century woodcut from the West, and a knotted, striped headscarf—but felt pierced by her odd beauty. Her skin was dark, olive, while her eyes were a pale green. Esther had never seen such coloring. She couldn't associate it with any of the myriad tribes she'd encountered.

"*Shalom,*" Esther said after a pause.

The woman looked out at the long line of wet people, machines, and golems. She nodded as if some long-held suspicion had been confirmed. "You must—goodness. What are those?" She lifted her nose toward the aerocycles.

"Flying machines."

"And are those *golemim*?"

"They are."

"I knew it!" Her broad smile revealed a full set of teeth. "Come, we must shelter you till this passes." She seemed not to consider the army a threat: excellent for their current circumstance, if an unfavorable assessment of their ability to intimidate. She ducked inside the house and returned draped in an oilcloth cloak. Her feet were bare. She stepped out into the mud and opened her mouth in a high-pitched, warbling call that sent the mechanical horses into an uproar and drew forth the neighbors, most clad in rain gear, some with enviable rubber boots. A sensible village. The golem horses sat by and waited for the next thing to happen. The woman addressed her fellows in a tongue Esther didn't recognize—an experience she had been surprised to have so often on this journey. The language, like Khazar, was mainly of Turkic origin, with a smattering of Hebrew worked in, but Esther couldn't understand how the verbs worked, and many words sounded strange. The woman's auditors agreed with whatever she was saying. Some darted into the rain to lead groups of sodden men to shelter. The woman beckoned to Esther. Itakh dismounted. Unable to undo the

damage of what she'd said earlier, Esther regarded him with momentary panic about what to call him. He caught her eye, almost a dare,
and she said, "This is my brother." The woman ducked her head and
lifted it again, like a swan. One of the golems was up beside Seleme,
its enormous hand on the throttle. "You can't take her," Esther said.

"I know how she is ridden. I can guide her."

How had he learned this? There had been no mechanical horses in
Yetzirah. "And where will you go?"

"We can repose with the machines and beasts. The villagers will
help us bring them in." He took a calm look at the aerocycles, each
tilted to one side with its lower set of wings tipped into the mud. They
looked defeated. "For those, I fear there's little we can do." A rivulet
of water ran off his clay nose.

"Leave them, it's fine." She looked at the work and hurry all
around. One of the golems untied Nagehan's cage from Itakh's horse
and sheltered it under his huge arm. Before following the woman, she
asked the nearest golem, "How did you communicate with these villagers? What language do they speak?"

"Karaite."

Esther startled at the word. These were the famed heretics? They
seemed so friendly.

The golem added, "We have not yet encountered a language beyond our comprehension."

"Good, thank you," Esther said, flustered, wet, and uncertain if
she could give Seleme over to this thing. In the end, she hurried off the
horse and followed the now-even-more-mysterious woman indoors.
No mezuzah on the doorpost. The woman hung her cloak on a hook
by the door and dried her muddy feet on a scrap of towel. Esther's eyes
adjusted to the darkness and smoke in the small, round room. A man
in a draped headdress and two girls in long dresses rose to greet them.

"Welcome," the man said, extending his hand toward her. Despite
or because of how wet she was, Esther felt a sweaty chill run down
her whole body. A Jewish man didn't shake hands with a woman
who wasn't his sister or wife. She wasn't sure that was his intent and

wondered if he thought she was a boy, long hair and all. Then she thought, these people were called heretics for a reason. She left his hand dangling in the air and returned his smile.

The wife said something to him in their own language as she leaned over a large basket and fished inside. To Esther, she said, "First we dry you." She took two homespun smocks from the basket and handed them to Esther. "Here." Then she gave her two worn pieces of fabric, old tea towels. "We'll turn our backs while you dry off and remove your things. Yehudit, Esther, come."

"My name is Esther too."

The woman gave an emphatic nod. "What a coincidence. You were meant to come here." She gathered the children in and the family turned to face the mud-daubed wall.

Itakh shrugged, then began to remove his clothes. They squelched as they hit the floor. As if she could see him flinch at the sound, the mother said, "Not to worry." Her Khazar was fluent. They must have used both languages. When Esther removed her boots, rivers of muddy water spilled out and pooled on the dirt floor before beginning to sink in. She wrung water from her hair and tried to dry her limbs. She was caked in mud. The towel came away heavy and brown. The smock felt velvety from long use and smelled like sunshine. "All right," she said, once they were clothed.

The woman bundled all the wet clothes over to the door, which she opened, revealing a world veiled by vertical stripes of gray rain. She began wringing the wet clothes out into the street.

"I'll do that," Esther said, trying to snatch the wet bundle from her hand, but the woman said, "Did King Shelomoun ask his many guests to wring laundry?"

Though the woman was small, her hands were strong and knobby from hard use. She made short work of the arduous task. She brought the heavy, twisted bundles back inside and shook them out to hang over a line strung high around the periphery of the room. "They'll dry, with the fire. You'll be ready to go once the storm lets up." As she moved around the room draping things, the house began to smell of damp and exhaust. When she finished, she wiped her hands on her dress and said, "I'm Ya'el the Karaite. You said your name was Esther?"

"Esther bat Josephus, and my brother, Itakh. I'm the leader of this army."

Ya'el clapped. "A true woman of valor!" She smiled at her husband as if a long-contested point had been proven.

Then Esther explained their mission. She was getting good at relating it. Itakh surprised her by bursting in with an explanation of the golems, to the little girls' delight. As they spoke, Ya'el passed around fresh flatbread and an earthen bowl of bean dip, fragrant with garlic. "Do you take Karaite volunteers?" she asked.

Esther's eyes widened. Elisheva would not have eaten the food in a heretic's house. Their father wouldn't be happy to know she was there. But the army had to be more tolerant than Khazaria's leading citizens. "We take whoever will come with us. More than half the men we've gathered thus far are Uyghurs."

The man of the house, who hadn't introduced himself, shook his head. "Who knew they could do more than rampage through your village and extort money?"

"We think they wanted to kill us at first," Itakh offered, "but after that they were generous hosts." He chewed for a moment, then said, "Why wouldn't we take Karaites?"

Their host said, "Other villages won't have us. We aren't allowed to serve in the government."

"That can't be true," Itakh said, looking to Esther for confirmation. "You're Jews, aren't you? All Jews can serve the nation."

"All rabbinical Jews," Esther corrected him, embarrassed. If he thought for a single moment, he'd realize they'd never met a Karaite in their lives.

Itakh said, "I don't understand."

"We follow the Law of Torah," Ya'el said. She sent around a second bowl containing some kind of grain with fruit and nuts. Only now did Esther notice that no one had blessed the food before eating it. She wondered if there would be some immediate consequence, a bolt from the sky or a fatal illness. She raced through a blessing under her breath.

"So do we," Itakh said.

"You follow it through your rabbis' interpretation. We read from the text."

"I can't read," said the littler girl.

"But you will."

Itakh shot Esther a glance.

"We reject rabbinical authority," the father continued. "You read your Talmud. We do not."

Esther said, "But that's where most of the rules are."

Itakh said, "I still don't understand." As an afterthought, he wiped his bread through the grain and fruit and said, "This is delicious."

"Well, we don't tie on tefillin or hang *mezuzot* on our doors, because we believe those commandments to be metaphorical." Esther hadn't been concerned that there was nothing to kiss on the doorpost. It was amazing what a day among the Uyghurs had done to inure her to different practices. "We don't light candles on Erev Shabbat."

"So how do you do anything?"

"We don't," Ya'el said. "We rest. When it's dark, we sit in the dark."

To Esther, this sounded strange. At a loss for what to say, she felt relieved when the younger child said, "I want to ride your mechanical horse." The elder one hushed her. In this brief moment, Esther composed herself enough to say, "A Karaite soldier can fight as well as another. If some from your village wish to join our cause, we'll take them. We leave the moment the storm ends, though. We have to hurry."

Their host stroked his beard. "I don't know how many will volunteer. Khazaria extends few rights to our kind."

"The bek allows you to live here. He doesn't persecute you, or convert you. This is more than the Germanii will permit you, if we become an occupied territory."

She hoped she hadn't said anything offensive, and felt relieved when he replied, "True enough."

The rain continued to blow northward, and tapered off as quickly as it had come. The tempest hadn't even subsided when the sun burst forth. "There'll be a rainbow!" the older daughter yelled, and something else, unintelligible to Esther, in Karaite. When they drew open the door, Esther thought this must have been what the world looked like to Noakh when first he stepped out of the Ark. Sunlight glinted in the drops hanging from eaves and doorposts. The ground was so sodden, water pooled on top of it and sparkled. "Look!" the children cried, pointing up to the east. Indeed a rainbow shone there, vivid and luminous, broad in its arc and touching the earth on both ends. Others came out from their shelter when they heard the commotion. They turned to the east as if greeting Shabbat (did Karaites observe this same ritual?) and exclaimed with joy. Esther, Itakh, and Amit, who soon appeared, recited the blessing for rainbows—"Blessed are You, Adonai our God, King of all that is, Who made the covenant, and remembers Your covenant, and keeps Your word"—and heard it echoed back to them from around the camp, if not from their Karaite hosts.

The rainbow and her thoughts of Noakh reminded Esther of the dove with the olive branch. All of a sudden she thought of her uncle's gray pigeon on its mission, its chances of success so tenuous, and of Nagehan. "We should send her back out to try to gather more information," she said to Itakh. "Do you think she's rested?"

He nodded. "But a golem took her. I'm not sure where."

Before he could find her, the air began to hum far off to the west. When Esther looked that way, the sky at the outermost edge of the horizon was dark, not with the storm, but with exhaust. Others heard it, heads turned in that direction. A few Uyghur fighters somehow already had their crossbows at the ready, their heavy bolts trained at the western sky. Others ran to stand up the aerocycles, water pouring off their righted wings. Aloft, they'd get a better view of what was coming. But after a moment's observation, there was nothing close enough to shoot. If the KAF was fighting the enemy in the west, they had no plans to hurry toward the steppe. As Esther took her bearings, she

245

saw a troop of men marching downriver. "Soldiers approaching!" she called out, and the Uyghur fighters moved toward the north-facing town wall to take aim.

Tselmeg, however, squinted at them over the wall. "Not soldiers, golems," he said. His companions lay down their weapons. Some spat.

Esther's army and the Karaites streamed from the village to meet them. Their feet sank into the slimy mud. Were the golems in their party eager to meet more of their kind? It was impossible to tell. She wondered if anything could make them run.

The new golems were a group of twelve, three rows of four each. They came near the village, then stopped still, as if uncertain to whom they should present themselves.

"Are you our master?" one asked Amit, perhaps finding his dress familiar from the home village. His damp kaftan clung to him.

Amit pointed at Esther. The golems' dull eyes regarded her without surprise or interest. "I am," she said.

In unison, they bent from the waist.

As they stood again, Esther said, "Who are you?"

"We are your new troops," said one in front, "created and sent by the masters of Yetzirah."

"*Barukh Hashem,*" someone said in the crowd. Someone else said, "*B'rukhim habaim,*" blessed are they who come.

All the old golems gathered to meet these new ones. Esther said, "But we took all that Yetzirah could spare."

"So our masters toiled in the night after your departure, and sent us downriver to find you. When they complete more, they will send them."

From where Esther stood—an ordinary-sized, nearly grown person—the golems' size and numbers seemed miraculous, impressive. Against Haman the Agagite's forces, they were smaller than a speck of dust. Yet Esther's imagination leaped to see herself leading a hundred thousand golems into battle. Then she returned to the moment. "We are glad you've come. How did you make it through the deluge?"

"We covered ourselves with cloths and waited."

Perhaps Esther's army could have done the same, but then, they would not have gathered Karaite recruits. "We are preparing to make the final march toward the capital. Men, ready your horses and gather your supplies. Gimmel," the only golem she could call by name, "bring Itakh's pigeon. Good Karaites of this village, thank you for sheltering us. If any of you wish to join our cause, we will be glad to add you to our ranks."

Her soldiers dispersed to gather their things. A number of Karaite men and boys did the same. To Amit, Esther said, "You need to make more golems."

Amit blinked. "That's impossible."

"I know you can."

He looked around, as if some other person might talk sense into her. "I know how it's done, but I can't do it alone. It isn't a task for a solitary man, and no one else here knows how." The way he said this sounded like a challenge, as if he dared her to admit that she'd crouched in the grass to watch the kabbalists create.

But Esther knew this couldn't be. She and Itakh had hidden themselves well. And to her continual surprise, Amit was, despite his mystical profession, a legalist: He would have brought the transgression up before now if he'd known of it. In this way, he reminded her of Elisheva. "What a shame."

"It's like how you can't recite certain prayers without a minyan. It can't be done."

Esther sighed and said, "I should return these clothes."

When she reentered Ya'el's hut, no one else was there; the family was still out talking with their neighbors. She pulled off the borrowed smock and put her own damp tunic and pants back on. She folded the garment and opened the two brass latches on the wooden chest to replace it.

Fragrant cedarwood lined the chest. The sweet wood had to be a luxury in this remote, treeless village. Esther lay the smock on top with the other everyday clothes, large and small. She thumbed into the pile and found some scratchy embroidered fabric. When she lifted the other clothes clear, she saw heavy cotton, embroidered in bright colors and metallic thread. Wedding clothes. Beneath them, some old Bukhari *kippot*, needlepointed in wool. Beneath those, a small, thick scrap of paper. This Esther pulled free to read.

But it wasn't paper. Instead, a square of dried, scraped animal skin, the size of Esther's palm. She lifted it to her nose and breathed in its sharp barnyard smell. Its letters and figures meant nothing to her. There was a diagram of—something—with interlocking ovals and an equilateral triangle. Points on the diagram were marked with letters in an unknown *aleph bet*, while groups of these traveled in a jerky scrawl down the right side of the page. Esther knew it was some kind of talisman. Her breath seized in her throat, wondering what it might mean. The breathless sensation could, she realized, also have come from browsing uninvited through Ya'el's possessions. A familiar yet potent combination of elation and fear rattled around her insides as she knelt on the floor. One thing was certain: Having found this talisman, she had the powerful, immediate sensation of needing to take it. There was no logic to the explanation, but she felt it was hers by right, just like the *volkelake*'s hair. A prize. Careful not to crease it, and shaking from the rush of deceit, she rolled it into a tight little tube. She saw no scraps of ribbon or string in the dark trunk, so she pulled a smarting strand of still-damp hair from her own scalp and wrapped it a dozen times around. Then she tucked the scroll into the leather pouch around her neck, with the *volkelake*'s hair and the money, and beside Rukhl's *hamsa*. Fingers adrenaline-quick, she smoothed out the folded fabric, shut the chest, and replaced its tarnished clasps right before Ya'el came through the door. Though the room was dark, she had a fire in her eye. Esther was afraid she already knew of her misdeed. "Esther?" she said.

Esther stood before her, heart racing, commander of a small army, prepared to be labeled a common thief.

"Do you take women as recruits?"

Esther had so little expected this question that she thought she had misheard it.

"You don't, do you," she said. "That's why there are none in your party."

More than she knew, Esther thought. "None have volunteered," she found the voice to say, "but if they did, how could I not take them?"

"I wish to enlist."

Esther shook her head. "You're a mother. Your daughters—"

"Already help in the fields and cook for their father. They can survive without their mother, but not without Khazaria."

Despite the moment's gravity and her racing heart, Esther's mouth shaped itself into a grin. She did her best to hold it back. "There will be fighting, bloodshed. You'll have to train to use weapons."

"I have brought two children into the world. I can endure hardship and pain."

Esther looked at her in wonder. Her green eyes seemed translucent in this dim, smoky space. Her headscarf shone bright as grass. "Then pack what you need. I'll give you a horse to ride on."

As Ya'el gathered her goods, Esther wandered into the bright day in a mental fog, seeing many people bustling, but unable to observe them. Her mind and heart felt buoyant, full. Ya'el's enlistment brought the same giddy joy Amit's had when he'd announced his intention to leave Yetzirah and seek his fortune with her. She could argue that her joy was due to their righteousness. But it wasn't their piety that thrilled her, but Amit's scent, his particular way of going about things; simple interest in Ya'el, a desire to know her. Her feelings toward Ya'el did not concern Esther. After all, she had felt a similar curiosity about Rukhl, from which both had benefited. But Amit was a mystic, dedicated to Hashem and His Holy Consort's mysteries. He had nothing to do with women, other than that he'd begun his life as one—a fact that thrilled and excited her. Who could say, without empirical evidence, to what extent this had changed? She yearned to touch him, to know for sure if Hashem had made all of him a man or left some a woman. She hated herself for this same yearning, and for feeling desire toward anyone other than Shimon. And she wondered what it meant to feel such attraction precisely because Amit was or had been—she couldn't fathom the difference—female. No girl at court had ever enticed her so, but then, women married men and that was that. A single line in *Devarim* instructed men against lying with other men, yet Esther had never heard Rabbi Kalonymos explicate it. Perhaps he considered it unthinkable. In this moment and this place, Esther understood differently, though the great, burning question remained whether Amit was all man or part woman, *niddah* in every way or only *niddah* because she was promised to someone else.

Reason told her there were too many obstacles. He was not hers to have; she was Shimon's *bashert*. And she loved him, so she should not think of Amit. Yet she did.

Someone had been speaking to her: Benyamin, with a question about loading the nine new recruits' possessions. He repeated himself more loudly. Esther barked out an answer as if he had been the one not listening, and he backed away, puzzled, to finish his work. Gimmel then appeared with the pigeon in his huge hands. He dwarfed the bird. Esther took a scrap and pencil stub and scrawled a note asking for more detailed news of the enemy's location and of her father, and for the name of the person writing to her. Despite his huge hands, Gimmel worked the message into its capsule and tossed Nagehan up into the air. Esther watched her circle and fly off, a prayer in her mind for the bird's safe return and for the gray one making its way across Europa.

The horses were soon loaded, the riders mounted, prepared to press on to the capital. A group of Uyghur soldiers stood together casting dark glances at two golems who, with unhurried, practiced hands, checked levels and tightened connections on mechanical horses. Golems also now sat prepared to ride all of the aerocycles. This would give a few Uyghur soldiers the opportunity to rest from that labor, yet none appeared pleased at the prospect. Ya'el's daughters hung on to the side of her golem horse, both children clinging to their mother's leg. Her face set in a pained frown, she reached down and pried each child's fingers off her. Once disentangled and held back by their father, they hovered close, pleading with her in Karaite. The ground still squelched from the deluge and the sun was racing toward the west, but they had to press on. When thanks had been given to the Karaite village and to the Name, the enlarged caravan moved off toward the capital, the battle continuing as a glimmer in the western distance. The waterlogged aerocycles were slow to rise. Esther saw how hard the golems pedaled to keep them aloft and following behind the army.

As they rode, Amit brought his golem horse abreast of Ya'el's. "I wanted to say," Amit said, "that I think it's very brave of you to join up with us. It cannot be easy for a mother to leave her children."

Ya'el smiled a little, her mouth closed. "You flatter me, Amit. I already miss my daughters. But a woman's lot is harder than you know."

"No," he responded, "I think I can imagine."

She shook her head. "I know the life of a soldier will be hard, but no more than that life to which I am accustomed." Ya'el added, "And I want to serve my country."

It wasn't Ya'el's country as much as it was Esther's. The law afforded her some of the same rights, not all. Esther pondered this as she watched the new recruit riding on Amit's other side: her proud stature on the horse (she had experience riding), Amit's fumbling shyness. She thought of the story in Torah of Ya'akov seeing Rakhel for the first time: so struck by her beauty, he fell off his camel. She wondered if Ya'el could unhorse Amit, if she herself would lose control of Seleme for watching him. There was no time for thoughts of this kind. They had to reach the capital and prepare for battle.

CHAPTER 21

As the army—perhaps six score motley golems, Uyghurs, Jews, heretics, women, children, a kabbalist, and a slave—continued on its way, they stopped in villages. Though there was no time to wait for recruits to gather their things, each time they left a place, Esther saw the line of stragglers following the army lengthen. Talk reached her, up the ranks, of who had joined: three Turks, a handful of Huns, six Nazarenes and a dozen Koptikim, and dozens more Jews, of every kind—some observant, some nonbelievers, some who did not themselves keep the Sabbath holy but who agreed to abide by the army's customs.

"Jews who don't keep the Sabbath?" Itakh had marveled when this news reached them at the front of the line that night. "I thought— I thought that was what made a Jew a Jew. You light candles on Shabbat."

"We're Jews, and we don't light," Ya'el said, extending a regal hand into the air behind her to indicate the other members of her sect.

"You don't have to believe in anything to be a Jew," Amit lectured him. "You don't have to do anything either." His tone made clear how little he thought of this course of action. He could be so peevish, she had no idea what drew her to him so forcefully.

Itakh, in over his head, said, "Huh."

When Esther looked down the line as they walked and rode, she thought her troops seemed ready to build the tower of Babel. The songs and snippets of conversation that rose in bursts over the tattoo of hoofbeats and the purr of engines and the spin of aerocycle chains represented myriad languages and dialects—some so exotic, she couldn't believe they'd been spoken on her home soil all these years without her knowledge.

That night, as they traveled with golems holding torches to light their way, the Uyghurs called out instructions in the use of weaponry to those nearby. Esther heard one man bark orders about rifles; another, pistols; a third, automatic guns. One taught a group of humans to shoot arrows from a composite bow while Chuluun taught those golems who weren't aloft the mighty crossbow. All his men had the knack of driving their horses right-handed while performing complicated weapons maneuvers with their left. To fire a crossbow or a machine gun, they had to stop the horse without stalling, fire, then brace the weapon to move on. When Esther glanced back at Chuluun's crossbow tutorial, his agility amazed her. The crossbows were better proportioned for golems, who looked fierce wielding the huge contraptions. Hand-to-hand combat with bayonets, knives, and heavy, swinging maces would have to wait until the army had stopped in the capital and the men could spar with one another without impeding the army's progress.

"The women need to learn to fight too," Esther called to Chuluun when he announced the next training.

"A woman doesn't stand a chance in a fight," he replied.

"I will defend myself and Khazaria," Ya'el said, sitting proud on her golem horse. "You'll teach me the same as the men."

Esther didn't hear Chuluun respond, which made her suppose he'd said something under his breath. He could think what he wished, but they needed to learn.

Later that night, Chuluun rode up between her and Ya'el and slapped a pistol into each woman's open palm. Dizzy with exhaustion, Esther felt a rush of power from the thing. She turned it this way and that in the flickering torchlight to examine it: a slender, snub-nosed gun of foreign manufacture, its name etched in tiny Roman letters. "You can't kill much with it," Chuluun said, evidently keen to damper her excitement. "A fox or a dog. But you can wound a man with it, and it's light, easy to manage. A good place to start." She liked its weight, and imagined she would soon feel the same pride in her ability to use it that she felt knowing how to open up Seleme and change her belts. "I'll give you bullets and a holster next time we stop. Teach you how to use it."

When the sun rose in the east, the caravan slowed, the aerocycles gliding and then stumbling to a halt alongside the men and horses. Those of the Jewish soldiers who prayed, prayed. All the golems joined them. Atil and Khazaran soon sprang up at the edge of the horizon, and as they did, a new group of golems from Yetzirah arrived. These they'd sent downriver by barge to catch up with the army. Marching all together in a steady row, they looked fearsome, no matter how small their numbers. When they'd greeted their brethren and been told the customs of the army—the new privileges golems here enjoyed—they made no sign of surprise or delight. They joined the line and kept marching.

Esther wondered about them. In their very first conversation, Amit had admitted his own lack of clarity about their ontological status, and he had seemed genuinely surprised by their desire to pray. His grudging decision to let them had not made things clearer. If even he had no real sense of what they were, what they were capable of, what they might become, how were ordinary people to understand them? They were model soldiers. Yet Esther's unease about them remained.

As the army approached the twin cities, divided by the gleaming river, a haze shrouded them both. It might have been only the heat. She did not think the enemy could already have set them ablaze.

"Fires, furnaces," Itakh said. He was chewing on a piece of grass he'd picked at their brief morning stop. Esther couldn't smell it above the mechanical horses' stink, but imagined it giving off the sweet odor of fresh hay. "It never seemed dirty before."

Nor had it ever looked so large. They hadn't been gone a week, but compared to the open steppe on which they'd been traveling, Atil and Khazaran seemed a megalopolis. As they drew nearer, elements of the familiar city came into view: the sprawl of the great northern refugee camp, whose borders had expanded with more tents; the once golden onion dome of Kalonymos's synagogue, now painted black; the domes, minarets, and spires of Khazaran's many houses of worship. Dwellings large and small. The long-roofed building of the Central Market; the hulking Great Library and Museum of Natural History.

"I had no idea it was so large," Ya'el said.

Tselmeg said, "Who wants to wager the price they'll place on our heads?" Some of his tribesmen grunted their agreement. "We're not welcome here."

"You're under my protection, for what that's worth," Esther said. She wasn't sure she herself would be welcome. "I feel sure whoever comes to defend his country can enter this city."

"It's not my country," one of the Uyghurs called out. She glanced back—she didn't know his name. "It's never done anything but tax me and hunt me."

"Then why are you here?" Esther snapped.

He shrugged, picked something out of his brown teeth. "Get to kill some people."

Esther kept her mouth shut.

"How should we let them know we're here?" Itakh asked.

Chuluun laughed. After a long pause, he lifted his crossbow from where it rested across his mechanical horse's withers and drew one of its bolts back into its notch—all of this with his right knee on the throttle. Itakh didn't question him again. Others began drawing their motley weapons. The golems continued to march, and the city dipped out of sight.

When the army entered the camp with the aerocycles overhead, what seemed like thousands of refugees streamed toward them, shouting in their language. Esther understood intermittent words. There was no place for the aerocycles to land, so they swung in a wide arc northward to land in the fields at the camp's edge. All along the line of soldiers came the tiny clicks of guns' safety mechanisms unlocking. Arrows rasped as they came free of their quivers, crossbows drew back and locked into firing position. Someone's sword rang like a metal bowl as he pulled it free of its scabbard.

"Hold," Esther called out.

The refugees swarmed around and among them, not a single one armed. No doubt they had traded whatever weapons they had for turnips and boots during their trek eastward. Esther's army was road-weary and covered in the same red dirt that tinted the golems auburn, but still she noticed how dirty and tired the refugees looked and the relative homogeneity of their appearance, their fair skin and light hair. In a short time, she had grown used to the sight of her own army, not all of whose soldiers were even human. As the troops streamed among them, some children ran shrieking in the opposite direction. They had to battle their way through the tight crowd and duck between people to gain ground. A few returned drawing adults by the hand, but most kept running deep into the camp. The aerocycles excited only interest, but when people saw the golems, some screamed, in words or open-mouthed exclamations of surprise, while others ducked their chins or covered their eyes and began to mutter prayers. Esther could see Chuluun waiting for a reason to shoot someone.

In the midst of this, a woman's voice called out, "*Barukh Hashem,* Esther?"

Esther scanned the mass of gray and brown clothes, of crushed hats and tattered headscarves. Then she saw Rukhl. Esther and Itakh had been gone less than a week, yet Rukhl looked more worn than Esther remembered—smaller, with fans of wrinkles around her pale eyes. Her apron bore a new striped patch. Esther couldn't tell if Rukhl's expression indicated shock or displeasure at seeing her.

"Esther, *mein Gott.* What is this?"

Without meaning to, Esther felt for the *hamsa* around her throat. "I've begun to raise my army."

Rukhl took a breath in and out, her mouth frozen halfway to a frown. "Just in time," she said. "Our *landtzmen* have fled from the Dniepra camp. Bombs aren't far behind them. We received a shower of leaflets on Shabbat, in the enemy's language, exhorting us to surrender." She cast a timid glance at Ya'el, proud on her horse, then tipped her head toward one of the *golemim*, unable, it seemed, to look straight at one. "These—these—"

"Golems. The kabbalists of Yetzirah provided them to fight for us."

She held her hand on her breastbone and nodded. Esther glimpsed a few freckles above the high collar of her dress. In a louder voice, Rukhl translated what Esther had just said. In her own tongue, the word was *goylemim*. Cacophonous responses burst forth. One refugee said, clear as day, "Holy Shekhinah!" and people laughed and said, "*Sha!*" Esther had gathered that the refugees either didn't believe in Hashem's Consort or at least never invoked Her as an oath. So someone had picked up the phrase on the streets of Atil. She wanted to question Rukhl about the Shekhinah, so central to Khazar Jews, who believed she symbolized His Bride, His People, *Yisrael*—this was no time. And when Esther paused to consider it a moment, she realized that she felt uncomfortable broaching such a subject with her friend.

"Are they," Rukhl began, her hand still at her throat as her eyes flickered over the nearest golem, "are they people?" She didn't seem able to say the word again.

"That is the great question," Gimmel responded from where he stood, holding Ya'el's horse by the reins. "The question not even our makers can answer."

Members of the army looked to Amit, mounted on his golem horse and blushing. Some slung their packs from their shoulders and let them thud to the ground. His silence stretched on.

"We don't eat," Gimmel offered. "We don't sleep. But we bless the Name of the Holy One. If that helps you decide."

Amit still didn't say anything, while people shifted their weight, children wandered away. Rukhl stepped forward and touched Esther's leg—the part she could reach, with Esther mounted on the horse— and Seleme swung her head around with a mechanical growl. Esther jerked on the handlebars to keep her from biting. Rukhl stepped back. "I thought she knew me," she remarked as if her feathers had been ruffled. Then she said, "May heaven help you."

The refugees made way for the army to travel through their vast encampment. Watching people step aside, Esther felt powerful, as if she'd raised her staff to part the waters. She also noticed the desperate misery through which she strode aloft. Itakh rode up beside her, careful to keep his horse behind so Seleme wouldn't bite. For the first time since leaving Yetzirah, Esther missed him riding pillion, his reassuring presence close by. Nagehan came flying in low over the heads of the refugees, and when he saw her, he whistled his call at her. She alighted on his arm. "You're late," he said to her, stroking her head. "And you're a very good bird. Do you have a message?" He unscrewed her tube and passed a piece of paper to Esther.

Troops across Don, it said. *Preparing to defend capital. You're still in trouble.* Again no signature.

As they picked their way through the camp and toward the city walls, Esther wanted to lean forward, click her shifter, and burst into a gallop, so excited was she to be home. She hadn't known she felt such fondness for the sturdy beige and gray stones that had protected generations of her ancestors from Huns and Alans and Uyghur hordes. She had only ever wanted to drive out and be free, never to see the vivid life the walls protected. The guard atop the city's northern watchtower called out *"Salaam!"* and pressed his right hand over his heart as she approached. The aerocycles slowed, hovered overhead. A moment later, she heard the scrape of the large bolts drawing back, the pleasing creak of the gates opening on their old hinges. The aerocycles flew right over the walls. And Atil—smelled. The market was all the way across the river in Khazaran, but fresh turmeric, cinnamon, and coriander hung so thick in the air Esther could taste them. The scent of dog and goat excrement rose from the paving stones. The laundry on wash lines smelled like river water. A small troop of Khazar soldiers, *kippot* on their heads and bandoliers strung across their bodies, marched past on patrol. Civilians on the street wore clothing as bright as a midsummer garden. The din of different languages being spoken, by people in close proximity, spooked the mechanical horses, though the golem horses appeared blithe as ever. People took interest in the army. Amit sat so tall in his saddle, his shoulders nearly touched his ears. Even with the vibrant street noise, Esther heard him sing the *Shehekhiyanu,* the prayer for a novel experience. When he caught her looking at him, he smiled for what seemed the first time in days. Her body flushed hot.

Seleme knew the way home without guidance. She led the army, now at least a hundred fifty strong, counting people and golems, through the cobbled streets. They pressed against the sides of buildings and forced pedestrians to duck indoors. The aerocycles' wingspan was almost as wide as a street, and the tips of the broader upper wings sometimes scratched against the walls of tall buildings, brushing shutters and tangling in the leaves of upper-story window boxes. From a distance, Esther saw Josephus's stuccoed house with its grand balconies. She tingled with pleasure at the sight. The messages suggested he was angry, and she could imagine his stream of invective, but she could also imagine his pride at her great accomplishment, pictured him holding back tears at its magnitude. She wondered if her retinue would fit in the house's inner courtyard, and felt a thrill at the possibility it might not. Esther wondered if Shimon was waiting for her, and what his reaction would be to her desertion and the nature of her return.

Yet when the gatekeeper called out "*Salaam aleikum!*" and drew back the outer gate, Esther did not fall into her father's welcoming arms. Neither was he waiting there to yell at her. The two browsing milk goats only made way the instant before the army trampled them, and when a servant opened the inner gate, Esther saw Josephus standing on the steps of the portico, his arms at his sides, his broad face unexpressive. He did not walk forward to meet her. His hair had grayed in the few days she'd been gone.

"Father!" she called out, and trotted Seleme to him across the dirt yard. He stood there, Shmuel bouncing with excitement beside him, a couple of attachés behind them with startled expressions on their faces. Esther braked Seleme and shifted into neutral as the aerocycles began to alight in the outer courtyard. The engine guttered. Shmuel looked as if he might jump out of his skin with delight.

When Josephus spoke, it was to say, "That's my horse."

This was not what Esther had expected, and she didn't know how to respond.

"You stole her. You also stole money. But here you are, back again, so the damage can be repaired." He stepped forward to take the near handlebar. Seleme bared her steel teeth at him, so he dropped his hands to his sides again and drew back. "This is not the only thing you've stolen, but you're young. Much can be forgiven." Even from her vantage on horseback, her father seemed larger than she remembered. He nodded as he looked down the line. Either he didn't see the golems or was too angry to remark on them. She might have thought the aerocycles would pique his interest. "Traveling in the company of men, I see. Men and Uyghurs and"—he glanced at Ya'el's attire and took a longer look at some of the men's head coverings—"Karaites? I will not ask about the creatures." He continued to nod in the abstract way he sometimes did while thinking. "What will Kalonymos make of this?"

She said, "They're golems."

"I knew it!" Shmuel shouted. Their father raised his hand as if to strike him, and Shmuel fell quiet, though his eyes continued to dance.

A thought raced into Esther's mind. "We're at war, Father. Why are you here and not at the front?"

Though Josephus had never hit his children, at this moment, he looked fearsome. Anger sparkled in his dark eyes. "I'll speak to you indoors. Itakh, go tell Bataar there is work for him in the stables."

Itakh kept his seat. "I will not."

"A runaway slave?" Now Josephus's tone was heating up. "You'll do as I say. You're lucky I haven't flogged you already."

Esther reached over, grabbed Itakh's golem horse by the mane, and drew the beast closer to her. She hadn't touched the substance before. It felt tacky and thick, like the oil-soaked twine used on fishing boats.

"My adoptive brother," she said, not quite able to look her father in the eye.

Itakh yanked on his reins to try to turn the horse. But the inner courtyard was packed tight with people and golems. He couldn't storm off. Esther kept her grip on the golem horse's mane. Itakh blushed deep as a plum, she guessed in fury.

"Good," Josephus said. "You're keeping silent, as you should." While Itakh glowered, Josephus kept examining the army. All the aerocycles were down now, their golem riders streaming into the yard. Then he turned and walked into the house, his long blue robes billowing behind him. Shmuel's eyes grew large as a cat's. He stood on the steps a moment before pushing through the crowd toward the outer courtyard and shouting, "Bataar!"

Esther dismounted and Itakh slid down, his expression still apoplectic. Esther tried to see the army through her father's eyes: the sexes mixed together, Jews among nonbelievers and heretics. "Amit, come," she said. Together the three of them climbed up the creamy stone steps, a slight, smooth dip in the spot where people most often walked. Esther had never before noticed how the steps shone. Whose job was it to clean them?

They glanced into the kitchen, where Afra measured rice and red lentils into a cauldron while Kiraz chopped through a heap of garlic. Someone must have told them there was an army to feed. *"B'rukhah haba'ah,"* they greeted Esther. The main hall, with its vaulted, blue-tiled ceiling, stood empty. Josephus had to be behind the door to his quarters.

"This is your house," Amit said. When Esther didn't reply, he said, "The kagan's house is even grander?"

"No one knows." This hardly seemed germane. She knocked on her father's coffered door, so thick her fist made almost no sound. Itakh, beside her, fumed.

The latch clicked and the door drew inward to reveal an assistant, who didn't look at them. Maybe they smelled bad—exhaust, sweat, fear, mildew from the rain in the Karaite village. Her father sat at his desk, Avigdor and Menakhem pacing as they spoke to each other. Why weren't *they* at the front? The shine of Josephus's polished desk, the black Bakelite telephone, the two parallel fountain pens on his blotter appeared unfamiliar to Esther, as did the saturated colors. Her eyes had grown used to yellow-green grassland brown.

"You have no idea how worried I've been," her father began from the swiveling chair at his large desk. He didn't seem to notice Amit. "Search parties brought back nothing."

Avigdor stopped by the hearth, his hands folded. "Try explaining that the kender and the javshigarim can't locate a girl and a runaway slave on a stolen mechanical horse." She saw Itakh bristle at the word.

"An embarrassment," Menakhem added.

"I'm sure we could have found you if we hadn't had more important business to attend to," Avigdor remarked.

"More important than your own children?" Itakh said.

"You keep out of it." Josephus sat forward in the wooden chair, both forearms on the desk, his stillness disconcerting. "We are fighting a war. I cannot waste time and resources chasing after a child." Two children, Esther thought. Though the facade of Itakh being her father's son was crumbling.

Had he himself written the messages Nagehan brought them? That couldn't be. The handwriting looked most like Elisheva's, though she had never shown an interest in pigeons. "You're losing this war," she said. "The Germanii"—Menakhem hissed through his teeth as if she'd activated a curse—"have crossed the Dniepra and are already on their way across the Don."

"I am the one who receives intelligence," her father said. "There's no need—"

"How long before they reach the capital?"

"We don't know." At the same time Avigdor added, "Keep out of it. Undutiful—"

"Are they putting people in camps?"

Avigdor, cut short, shook his head at Josephus as if no Jewish man had ever before raised such a defective daughter. Neither answered her. Josephus said, "Where were you going?"

She shouldn't answer him. Itakh spat out, "To Yetzirah."

Josephus barked out a single laugh.

"We've come back with golems and golem horses," Esther said. "Don't scoff."

"And a kabbalist," Amit added in a soft voice. He bowed his head as he said it.

"With hardly even a beard," Josephus said. Amit reflexively ran one thumb down the wisps on his cheek. "Who is this person?"

"Amit ben Avraham v'Sarah."

Her father didn't notice the odd name. "You knew about their golems?" he prodded Esther. "How did you know?"

"Did you know? I didn't. You never told me." He'd never told her he'd met a kabbalist either, but his unconcern at meeting Amit corroborated Shelomoun's story. Esther's tongue felt too thick for her mouth. She took a deep breath and said, "I asked them to change me into a man so I could join the army."

"Akh," Menakhem cried.

Her father studied her a moment. "They refused."

By an effort of will she kept her eyes fixed on him. "They gave me the golems instead."

"The Lord gave you a woman's *neshamah*," Avigdor said. "If the kabbalists changed you, what would happen to Shimon?"

Menakhem was saying something under his breath, but Esther caught the word "*bushah*," a scandal.

She wondered if when he'd been a girl, Amit had had a *bashert*, and if so, what that young man was doing now. Perhaps the Holy One had made Amit solitary. Even as a girl, he must have been dogged, argumentative. There was little hope for difficult women in the marriage market. "Shimon inherits a high-ranking office. It would be easy to find him a wife."

Josephus leaned farther forward in his chair. "You go to our holy men with this ridiculous question. They say no. Why do you not immediately return home?"

"It's complicated." Her father waited for elaboration. This had to be part of how the family had long ago risen to such prominence in the government: As angry as he was, Josephus remained cool. And as well as Esther knew him, she couldn't tell what he was thinking. "Though they couldn't change my form, they believed my," she struggled to explain, "my nature suited me to serve. So they entrusted the golems to my care to aid Khazaria."

"A *bushah*," Menakhem repeated more loudly.

"We also made her more of them," Amit volunteered. "Powerful fighters."

"You'll turn them over to the bek today. And where did you get the Uyghurs? And whatever those flying machines are?"

"Their leader volunteered the men and armed us, for a price. They patrol their oil fields with the aerocycles. I thought we could use them."

"A price."

As Esther steeled herself to tell her father what she'd promised Göktürk, Avigdor saved her. "Enough," he said, quitting his spot by the empty grate. He shook his head as he approached Esther in the middle of the room. Because he was bald on top, his *kippah* slipped to one side. "Esther. Don't tell your father that you met with the leader of our most powerful crime syndicate, that he kitted you out with weapons and machines, and that you're here to talk about it." He sounded incredulous, though still calm. "What you've done is bad enough without that nonsense."

"It's not a crime syndicate," Itakh said, his tone still irritated. "It's a business."

"I called him by his name," Esther said. And because she couldn't stop herself from continuing, "I told him I'd killed a *volkelake*."

"Akh!" Menakhem cried out, and covered his ears. He glared at her father as if she was all his fault.

"It's true!" Itakh spat at him.

"Esti," Josephus said, "I did not raise you to—"

"You're not listening!" She reached into her shirt and pulled out the leather pouch on the cord. Damp with sweat, the pouch tinged her fingers orange as she worked it open. No doubt her chest bore the same stain. She drew out the foul-smelling lock of hair and held it up before her, a charm.

Josephus spread one broad hand across his forehead. "Put that away." When he drew his hand down, he stopped with it over his mouth, as if her misdeeds had exhausted him so completely he couldn't move it.

"The *volkelake*'s hair," Esther said. "I cut it off before the golems buried her."

Amit said, "No." She couldn't look at him.

"You cut off part of a body?" Menakhem asked, his tenor creeping higher.

"Werewolves aren't Jewish," Josephus said into his hand.

Itakh glanced at Esther, his eyes sparkling in triumph.

Josephus made a lazy, dismissive wave, then went back to rubbing his face. "Send these men home. Who knows where she even got that thing."

"No."

He took a deep breath and released it. "I command you to." She noticed that he was so sure of his right to do this, he didn't even raise his voice.

She tried to do the same. "I command my army. I determine what to do with it."

"Terrible," Menakhem remarked, as if beneath his breath, though everyone heard him.

"You," Josephus said, pushing back in the creaking chair and standing, "are a girl scheduled to be married in less than two months, if your bridegroom's father will still have you. You'll do as you're told."

"Bringing shame upon her father's house," Menakhem continued to no one in particular.

The kagan and the bek cherished her father's sage counsel. She'd always thought it her duty to do the same. All she could reply was, "It won't be up to Kalonymos."

"Disband your little army," he said, his tone growing sharper, "repay me what you've stolen, and return to your former life."

"We're at war!" Esther shouted back. "My former life is gone!"

"*Barukh Hashem*, it is not."

As if at least willing to acknowledge her, Menakhem said, "Excuse us, but we don't discuss matters of state with runaway children."

"Where is Bek Admon?" Esther asked.

Her father blinked at her as if she made no sense. "At the front, of course."

"I asked before why you weren't there, and you didn't answer."

"Because I am the kender." At the same time, Menakhem said, " 'Honor your father and your mother.' How did you raise her?"

"Why aren't you there?" she asked Menakhem. The javshigarim should have been leading troops.

Avigdor said, "That's none of your concern."

Josephus said, "You'll disband your army and return the golems to their rightful owners."

Amit said, "They aren't property." Which only made it the more galling that Itakh was.

"This audience is finished," Josephus said.

"And you will obey your father," Menakhem said, angry on his behalf.

As if he hadn't spoken, Josephus continued. "Despite everything, I'm glad you're safe. The cooks will offer the men food before they go." He looked around a moment as if for another thing to say, then walked with purpose out of the room.

Esther wanted to pull out the amulet she'd stolen from Ya'el—to wave it at his retreating back as the flag of her ill behavior, to ask Amit if he knew what it signified. Instead, avoiding Menakhem's and Avigdor's eyes, she went outside and announced to the hungry people in the courtyard that there would soon be lentils. Afra and Kiraz had filled two large tubs with clean water and rinsing cups. The men gathered around them to wash their faces and hands before eating.

Amidst the commotion, Amit said to Esther, "That was no good." She nodded, and he watched other people bustle and talk. "What will you do?" he asked.

The dirty men looked fierce. "Attack the bek's palace. If we bring it under our control, he'll know we're a force to reckon with."

Itakh, who hadn't seemed to be listening, snapped to attention, and Amit's eyes widened. With his wire-rimmed glasses, he resembled an owl. "There has to be a better option."

"What is it?" She regarded him closely. "It's that or send them home."

Amit continued to watch the men jostle one another. Then he looked at her, his eyes twinkling through the smudged glass of his lenses. "I don't know if it's the best choice. But by El of the Mountain, I don't see a better one."

She stifled her grin. She walked into the yard, and as Tselmeg raised his hand to greet her, whispered, "There will be a military action late tonight. Be circumspect in how you alert people. Tell them to be ready after dark."

When he smiled, he showed his buckteeth. She understood the allure of his life.

CHAPTER 22

A s Esther and Elisheva prepared for bed, Elisheva kept silent, her glance and her gestures respectful or even afraid. She let Esther sit at the vanity table, while she herself hovered over it, darting in and out for whatever she needed. Her moralizing had always irritated Esther, as did this visible effort to refrain from it.

"I won't infect you," Esther said.

"I know." She sounded as if a "but" was forthcoming. This was another reason she frustrated Esther. That and her cleanliness. As she sat at the table, Esther looked at her sister's buffed fingernails, her skin—darker-hued than was preferred in Khazaria, yet unmarred by the sun—and wondered if she herself had ever appeared so smooth. She glanced at herself in the mirror. Suntan, freckles, puffy gray circles beneath her eyes. She had hung her leather pouch and the *hamsa* over the edge of the mirror while they bathed together. The ugly items still hung there as the day's sweat dried. Esther looked more like a kender's daughter without them. "I'm glad you're home," Elisheva said. This made Esther feel worse for thinking ill of her. "You don't believe me."

Esther picked up a pot of some kind of cream, put it back down again.

"We're all glad. Father's too preoccupied to show it."

"Preoccupied" was not how Esther read him.

Elisheva had never been warm. From her, this was a barrage of compliments, a shower of kisses. Esther should encourage her. Yet all she could bring herself to say was, "I'm going to fight this war."

Elisheva took a small breath in and out. Her expression: She'd expected more from Esther. "Father says you're not. Your wedding is soon."

This too stabbed at Esther's conscience. "You don't think that's still going to happen?"

"Shimon loves you. He'll make it right with his father." Esther must have startled or made some kind of a face, because Elisheva put down her brush and watched Esther comb through the knots in her hair with her fingers. "You shouldn't be so rough with it." Esther made a noncommittal noise. "And we should go to bed."

"Is Shimon at the front?" Esther asked. She wanted the question to sound casual, but pitched her voice too high.

Elisheva's nostrils widened. "He won't have to fight."

"All the men will."

"Except those of a certain station." She rubbed a drop of jasmine oil between her palms and ran it down her braid to perfume it, then rubbed the remainder into her elbows. She performed these actions as naturally as Esther mounted a horse or shifted its gears. "He's been training to become chief rabbi since before he became a bar mitzvah. I don't know what would happen to Judaism without him." She took another drop of oil and anointed her feet, balancing on one while she rubbed the other. "Are you eager to see him?"

"Of course." The first straightforward answer she'd given her sister. Esther tied her wet hair back into a braid, then pushed the button on the wall that turned off the overhead light. They climbed into bed together. The air hung heavy with jasmine.

It was time for evening prayers, but neither began them. Esther listened to Elisheva's breathing and tried to keep her own sounding normal. The effort made it ragged and forced. The house's clock ticked past a quarter hour. At last Esther said, "Was it you, sending messages by pigeon post?"

With the shutters closed, the room was stippled with pinpricks of light not bright enough to illuminate her sister's face. She rustled in the blankets, turning toward Esther. "I wouldn't touch a pigeon."

"It looked like your writing."

Elisheva laughed, a wave of delight rolling off her tongue. Esther shot awake at the uncommon sound.

"How did you even know she'd arrived? You've never paid attention to the loft."

"Neither have you."

It was too dark to see, but Esther was sure Elisheva was smiling. She'd been replaced, in a few days' absence, by a friendlier version of herself.

"Itakh's friend from the camp came pounding on the gate for admittance. Shmuel and I went out."

Had she known about Jascha before? Did she know about Rukhl? She had shown no interest in the refugees until now. All Esther could ask was, "You touched a pigeon?"

The laugh again. She'd had one as a child, but Esther had seldom heard it since. "The boy touched it. But he can't read, so he passed the message along."

"Itakh can't read either."

"Really?"

"Where would he have learned? All his years at yeshiva?"

"You're always angry at me."

This was true.

Elisheva rustled in the sheets. As Esther's eyes adjusted to the light, she saw that her sister had propped up on one elbow and rested her head on her palm. "I tried to disguise my handwriting. Not very well, it seems." Esther made herself listen, wait. "I didn't think you'd believe any news that came from me."

"We acted on it right away."

"I'm glad. You're doing a brave thing." Esther should have thanked her, or at least responded, but didn't know how. Elisheva said, "*Laila tov.*"

They resettled themselves, drew the covers high up to their ears. Esther listened as Elisheva recited her evening prayers by rote. The *Sh'ma* had such an odd structure, if she thought about it, telling the person praying what she should do even as she did the thing spoken of. "Don't you pray anymore?" she asked once she'd finished.

Esther tried to say the words with more care and attention than her sister had used. She'd learned more about Elisheva that evening than in a long time, which didn't erase her sense of competition.

It took stamina to remain awake in their beautiful, soft bed while Elisheva's breathing grew shallow; even more to wait for the sounds of the household to subside. Soon after the hall clock struck eleven, Esther rose, dressed in clean clothes (her closet was full of them), and slipped down the broad staircase. Perhaps hearing her or perhaps on a mission of his own, Shmuel came down behind her.

"Go back to bed," she whispered.

He shook his head no.

Together they went to Itakh's door, where they found him dressed, waiting cross-legged on his mattress. "What's he doing here?" he whispered, pointing at Shmuel.

"I know you're off to make mischief. I want to come."

Esther hushed him. His high voice was too loud. "We're not doing anything."

"I can help." When neither of them accepted his offer, he said, "I'm older than Itakh, and I can do archery."

Esther could spare no energy to argue. Her army did have bows and arrows. "You can come with us, but stay out of harm's way," she said. To Itakh, she said, "Has a pigeon returned from Praha?"

"I haven't seen one yet. It's a long journey—I'm not sure how long it would take."

As soon as they were outdoors, their army began to stir in its encampment, which filled Josephus's grounds. The servants slept in their roundhouses at the far end of the outer courtyard. Everyone seemed to understand the need to keep quiet and not wake them. Men and golems began to muster, their faces gray in the moonlight. Itakh stole off toward the pigeon coop. Esther let out a low, descending whistle in case anyone had fallen asleep. But she doubted anyone had. Some of these men had joined up to protect Khazaria, but many only wanted to fight. This would be their first chance. Those who had already armed themselves faded into the background behind their weapons, which glinted in the dim light.

"Are we going to kill the bek?" someone whispered. A few chuckles, approving murmurs.

"No," Esther replied. "He's at the front. But we'll take his residence, thus the kagan's. We want to show them we're serious. We want them to meet our demands."

"Which are what?" Shmuel asked.

Natan asked, "Who's he?"

"My brother," Esther said. "My other brother. To let us fight."

"So we don't kill your bek," said one of the Uyghurs, the one with a black front tooth, in a gravelly whisper. "Whom do we kill?"

"No one. These are our own men. We simply want to show them our strength."

"But if we run at them with guns and swords," the Uyghur continued, "they'll try to kill us first."

Esther let out a sigh. "Wound if you must, but only in self-defense."

"No way to win a war."

"We do not harm our brethren," spoke a golem voice from the group's fringes. It had to be Gimmel. "We do not betray our God, nor those whom He has set to govern over us."

"The bek has betrayed the Name by not letting us fight," Benyamin said.

But he hadn't, really. To her knowledge, her father had issued his order without consulting the bek. Still, she couldn't attack her own house. To Gimmel, she said, "The palace is guarded. I doubt we can take it without your help. But if your conscience forbids the action—"

"Conscience?" Amit repeated, with evident scorn.

Gimmel closed his eyes. With a human, one could see that even in moonlight, because shutting the lids blocked the eyes' reflective brightness. But a golem's eyes were no more lively than the clay around them. Esther knew Gimmel's expression had changed because she saw his huge form begin to sway. He was praying, she realized with an emotion halfway between horror and delight. Praying to his god, their mutual God. The silent rocking went on what seemed a long time. When at last he intoned a low *"Ameyn"* and opened his eyes, Esther wished the kabbalists had given them facial expressions, so she might guess what he was thinking. He folded his hands before him.

"We will kill no one."

"No one is killing anyone." Nevertheless, Esther heard the quiet rip of more swords being unsheathed, the soft double click of guns' safeties unlatching. She raised her right hand straight up in the air, and everyone began to move toward the gate. Weapons clanked, though feet were silent. Two of the golems opened the doors to the stables. One of Bataar's helpers was sleeping in the hayloft, and Esther heard him gasp as the golems walked in and began leading out the golem horses. Uyghurs mounted them immediately, bareback. They nudged the horses toward the outer gate with their knees. It seemed too risky—too loud—to start up Seleme in the dead of night, just as it would attract unnecessary attention for anyone to pilot the aerocycles. The golem horses would be their only mode of transport to the bek's palace. Esther climbed onto one, Shmuel clambering up behind her. She marveled at its docility as it began to walk. Though the unfamiliar creature made her nervous, she knew a golem horse was easier if she needed to fire her new pistol, now holstered on her left leg. She'd practiced loading and aiming, but still feared that, in a critical moment, Seleme might stall. The gatekeeper did not even call out as they approached, so awed was he by the sight of them. He opened the gate, and as she passed, Esther thought she heard him praying under his breath.

She made her way to the front of the line, pleased to notice that the golem horses' clay feet made soft, muffled sounds on the cobblestones. Itakh soon came up beside her on his own golem mount. "There aren't any new birds," he said.

"Maybe tomorrow. Does it seem possible?"

"I don't know! Yes. Probably."

The streets were deserted, lights out in every window. Many

homes, she realized, had blackout shades to make the capital less visible to enemy aeroplanes at night. One lone drunkard, asleep in the arched passageway to a courtyard, awoke to see them pass. He muttered something, then stumbled into the darkness behind him. Esther was used to riding with Itakh, who sat a horse well. Shmuel gripped her rib cage so tight she found it hard to breathe.

They arrived at the bek's palace. She couldn't see the ground floor beyond the high walls, but the gray stone of the second and third stories massed above. On each side, a lower wing of private quarters stretched back into the court; from an aerocycle, the palace would have the shape of the letter *vet*. Seemingly a whole *parasang* behind the bek's residence, deep into its manicured grounds, she knew the kagan's mirror palace stretched back like a dream or a memory. No one ever entered it, but she knew it connected to the bek's palace via the side wings. She had been there other times at night, for state dinners and lavish concerts, at times when all the windows had been illuminated, festive. With blackout shades in the upper stories, the palace looked dead. Its huge gates were shut and barred. On her foreign beast, Esther sat, uncertain what to do. An army, arriving by night, couldn't knock for admittance. She pointed back into the crowd behind her, a gesture which drew forth a golem whose name she didn't know. He threaded through the crowd and came to face her. With Esther mounted on the golem horse, they stood eye to eye.

"Your job," she whispered, "is to make that guard open the gate for us, or to open it yourself. You're not to harm him."

The golem nodded. He patted his *kippah* down onto his head, as if the great danger were for his clay hair to be uncovered before the Lord. Then he went to the base of the guard tower, looked over its brick surface, and began to scale it.

A person would have been unable. The guard box sat higher than the surrounding wall, itself two stories high. There was no ladder. It must have gone down the inside wall of the compound, or it was made of rope, so the guard could draw it up behind him. The golem, despite the thickness of his hands and work boots, found finger- and toeholds in the brick, and ascended with as little apparent effort as a squirrel. At the moment his broad face came level with the open window, the guard called out in surprise. The next moment, the golem vaulted through the window. A pistol reported, followed by a hollow thud and the golem's deep grunt. Esther expected a scuffle to ensue, but after a brief silence, she heard conversation, more heated on the guard's part, calmer and more direct on the golem's. Twice he explained that they came on a peaceful mission, and that if the guard would open the gate, they would give their word not to spill blood. The guard said something about the golem's mother and an elephant. Then came another thud. Esther heard someone climb down a wooden ladder. The heavy bolt shot and the gates drew open.

The golem stood inside. "What did you do?" Esther said.

"I hit him. Not hard enough to cause lasting harm."

"Thank you," she whispered as she hurried past, unsure how he could judge this.

Had no one in the palace heard the guard's first cry? Did he not have a telephone or system of pneumatic tubes to inform them of what he saw from his vantage? He hadn't called for help. As her troops massed in the yard, Esther felt a sudden bubble rise in her chest, a pop of elation as she realized they were about to do something very, very bad.

Her golem horse's gentle feet walked through grass on which she had played croquet, spun in circles with Elisheva, rested and watched the sky. She took a good look at the palace, the tall windows along the gray stone front. All were dark, and dimly reflected her own mounted form and those of her soldiers. "The great danger, I think," she said, hoping her words wouldn't dissolve on the light breeze before reaching her troops' ears, "is that we can't risk even the appearance of endangering the kagan. But I believe we can take the bek's palace. We'll enter through both the center and side wings."

Men began to dismount. Some of the Uyghurs lifted up their cruel swords.

"Do not draw blood. Not even in self-defense, if you can help it."

One Uyghur said something, and others snickered. These were some of the most feared people in the land. Most Khazars considered them criminals. She should have prayed earlier. Now it was too late. She made up something inarticulate inside her head, hoping the All-Knowing would hear it. She lost her train of thought halfway through, forced herself to say *Ameyn*. Then she pulled her short knife from her boot and raised her arm. Crouching and quiet, the men began to swarm across the yard. The unarmed golems did not conceal themselves. They just walked, one softly intoning, "*Kadosh, kadosh, kadosh,*" as he passed her. Ya'el squeezed Esther's arm as she ran past, the moonlight glinting off faint metallic threads in her headscarf. Shmuel followed his sister like a shadow, as he had so often done in other contexts.

In her lifetime, Esther had read the few novels from Gaul, Rus, and Old Britain available in translation. Unlike her sister, she had not skimmed over the battles and fox hunts for parts that featured the odd, un-Khazar ritual of men and women courting. Yet no prior experience in body or the imagination had prepared her for this scene.

The moment her men entered the bek's palace, the night's silence exploded. The bek's guards did not know that this Khazar army came on a mission of peace. In an instant, they sent up an alarm, barking out commands and springing to bar doors to defend themselves as someone pushed the switch for the electric lights. Esther felt momentarily paralyzed when she saw all these men leaping at one another in the sudden brightness. Then she had to act. Many around her in the entrance hall had dropped their weapons and struggled hand to hand, though one of the bek's guards held what appeared to be a cricket bat poised to strike the golem who approached him with arms outstretched. Isolated shouts and oaths reached her, but she couldn't piece together a coherent narrative of what was going on: whether they were making progress, whether anyone was hurt. In a corner, Amit argued with one of the guards, who reached out to slap him across the face. Amit raised a hand to his jaw. Shmuel, obeying Esther's command, crouched behind a potted hibiscus to watch. Nearby, a golem had pinned a guard prone on the floor and bent over, trying to reason with him. The guard continued to kick him; the golem paid no mind. Esther stood with her knife gripped in front of her. She was uncertain what to do or how she'd know when to do it. Then a guard ran at her screaming, a curved sword raised in his striking hand. Esther prepared either to swipe at him or to leap out of the way, her body a bright adrenaline haze. Midway through his swing, he stopped as if stunned.

"What's this?" he said. "A girl. A girl."

Her body still raced, expecting the blow. "I'm Esther, the kender's daughter."

He relaxed his stance and lowered the sword. "I've seen you here before."

Some atavistic drive to self-preservation seized Esther, and before she could think, her left hand shot out and grabbed his sword. Despite how easily he'd wielded it, it was as heavy as her own arm. It threatened to drop to the ground before she steadied it with her right hand, which still held her short knife. She managed to raise both weapons aloft. In his expression she saw him wonder if she'd carry through. She herself didn't know. She could picture the weapon cleaving his skull, but didn't know if she had the will to bring it home.

A new group of intruders burst through the doors, whooping like steppe warriors: a small band of Atil police in their black kaftans. Had they been out on patrol and seen the fracas? They fired warning shots in the air and began to surround individual golems.

"Who are you? What are you?" one shouted, his voice hoarse with anxiety.

The golem, with no idea how to respond, stood with his hands up, demonstrating that he represented no threat.

"Like you, he is a man," another golem said for him. Because their voices could not modulate to show emotion, his words sounded eerie, calm.

With an almost casual air, the policeman raised his gun and fired into the second golem's shoulder. The sound upon impact was dull.

The creature started, and raised his other hand to the place, but his expression did not change. When he took the hand away, no blood flowed, though there was a hole in his shirt and some pieces of clay, like pottery shards, scattered to the ground. He went on about his business. All around the room—and elsewhere in the palace, Esther could dimly hear—battles continued, but the area surrounding this event stilled.

"Holy Shekhinah," the policeman said. He kept the gun raised, but his stance looked less sure than before. The bullet hadn't harmed the creature at all.

Because Esther had taken her eye off him, her guard snatched back his sword, though she managed to hold on to her knife.

Where was Itakh? As she looked around and failed to see him, she hoped his small size afforded him the same protection her sex gave her. He might have been hiding, as Shmuel was. While she was distracted, someone snuck up on her and yanked her arms behind her.

Esther cried out and folded over to try to get away, but the person tightened his grip. Esther struggled to free her hands, scratching him with the knife as she did so. He swore and kept holding on. Somehow he got the knife away from her and held it along with both her wrists, which he bound with something smooth and slippery. She couldn't pull free. He dragged her through the melee to an ornate door, and then into a dark, cavernous room. He slammed the door behind them, and Esther waited in panic to be able to see. One moment, she wished someone would notice what was happening to her. The next, she felt a stab of shame for wanting anyone's help. The man stood catching his breath for what seemed a long moment, then punched the button to turn on the light. Though Esther hadn't thought her eyes had adjusted to the dark, she now squinted in the sudden brightness.

"What do you think you're doing?" the man yelled.

The first thing she noticed about him was her knife glinting in his hand, a trickle of blood. The next thing she saw was that this was the bek.

"Esther!"

She took a moment to collect her thoughts and felt the tail end of whatever bound her hands fluttering behind her. When she turned to look at it, she saw it was one of the guards' decorative sashes, cobalt blue. "You're at the front."

He opened his mouth to explain to her, thought better of it.

"Why are you—"

"It's none of your business. Have you no shame? Your father—"

"Unbind my hands," Esther said.

"After you invade my palace with a battalion of—heaven knows what they are! You'll be lucky if I don't imprison you for the rest of your days."

"They're under orders not to harm anyone. The police have fired guns; we have not." She could tell him what the golems were, and the Uyghurs and Karaites, but he didn't deserve the explanation.

The bek raised both arms to heaven, and the blood ran down his forearm toward his elbow. "How am I and my men to know this? Orders not to harm. Your father should banish you. You're unworthy of him."

"Look how well we fight," Esther said, willing herself not to hear him. "We gained your palace without shedding blood." Though the thick door muffled the sound outside, some large glass thing shattered, a mirror or a window. "We want to join your forces."

"You have no right to act outside your father's authority."

"Admon?" said a slow, quiet voice. Esther spun around to see its source but saw only the intricate trellis of vines and flowers carved on the walls. All of these were painted. The peonies appeared so lifelike, she imagined ants tumbling over their petals. In the center of one flower, an eye blinked. Esther looked away, though holding her gaze elsewhere was as difficult as forcing herself not to wonder in what specific regards Amit was male or female. She was sure the green eye was the kagan's. The voice cleared its throat and continued. "A well-born girl. A kabbalist as her lieutenant, and an army of golems behind her."

"Automata. Infidels," the bek said. He took a deep breath and lengthened his neck. He too turned his gaze from the hole, though he was the one man permitted to look upon the kagan. Esther took her lead from Bek Admon, straightening her posture despite the uncomfortable position of her arms, and fixing her gaze on him.

"I was hardly any older than she when I was named to my position. Like her, I had no beard. But no one challenged my wisdom or my right." He cleared his throat again. His voice must have felt rusty from disuse.

"Think of her father. She must be punished, or every girl in the land—"

"We are about to read the final chapters of our history. It won't matter what every girl in the land does." When Esther eavesdropped through the ear trumpet into her father's study, she could picture the space and the people within. The invisible kagan spoke as if from the heavens. "Is the enemy at our gates?"

"As you know," the bek said. Esther didn't know if he meant this literally or metaphorically.

"I command you to deploy her forces."

"They won't make a difference."

Esther had never dreamed of being in the kagan's presence. Only the bek could speak to him, and a woman could not be a bek. She felt calm and electrified at the same time, as she might if Hashem Himself addressed her from a burning bush: aware that this circumstance was unusual, yet finding herself in it, sure this was where she was meant to be.

"Appoint her the head of her own army. Let her join you in battle. Let her sweep up any able-bodied sons that remain to our families, highborn as well as low."

"Daughters too," Esther said, aware that she should append an honorific, but unsure what it might be.

The bek glared at her. After a moment, the voice said, "If they wish to volunteer, I will not stop them."

A smile took over her face. The more she tried to suppress it, the wider it grew. She hadn't even had to show him the *volkelake*'s hair— then she noticed that her leather pouch and *hamsa* were not around her neck. She had embarked on this mission unprotected. She had left them on the mirror after bathing and failed to put them back on, dressing in the dark. Outside, men continued to shout, objects continued to break. For minutes, she hadn't heard these sounds, though they must have been ongoing.

As if he too had only then begun to hear them again, the bek said, "Call off your men and your creatures."

"Untie my hands."

He used her knife to slice between them.

Shreds of silken sash wafted down—an embarrassing, delicate thing to have been bound with. When she opened the door, a chandelier lay smashed in the entry hall. The light from the others revealed a confusing mess. Both her men and the bek's had taken prisoners by tying some of the other side's men to one another. All the golems remained free, and some were still fighting with the guards on the floor, which was littered with shards of crystal and broken Chinese vases.

"Stop," Esther said, raising her arms. No one looked at her. "Stop!" she shouted. "We've reached a truce." Men from both sides glanced up. "The bek gives us permission to go westward with him. We'll all be fighting together."

"There will be no westward journey," the bek said. "They're no more than a hundred *parasangs* distant."

Esther's heart leapt. "Then we have to head out to meet them."

Two golems went around and tore apart the straps that bound people. Men patted themselves down and searched the floor for missing weapons. Itakh and Shmuel unfolded from their hiding places.

Then she saw Amit with blood streaming from his nose and mouth. "Holy Shekhinah," she said, and ran to him.

He wiped blood from his mouth and gave a single nervous laugh. "It looks bad?" He examined his red fingers.

She nodded.

His mouth opened in a gruesome grin. "It's kind of exciting." To Esther too. Exciting and repellant in equal measure. "Did I lose a tooth?"

To try to look into his open mouth, Esther lifted onto her toes and reached her hands toward his shoulders to steady herself. Amit drew away as if she'd burned him, and she lost her balance.

"What's wrong with you?" he asked, still rubbing his lower face with one hand.

It wasn't a question she could answer. "I wanted to get a better look." The heat of exertion poured off him, carrying the sweet scent of his sweat and the tang of blood. "I'm sure you did lose a tooth. We can try to call a physician once we're home."

His hand still to his face, Amit went out into the yard.

Esther's army left in some disarray. Day was already dawning. She felt wide awake, giddy with dread and delight. Whatever came next, they had won their first battle.

CHAPTER 23

E sther's pouch was gone from the mirror. The *hamsa* still hung there. Esther clutched at her throat, as if the mere gesture might return the precious object.

"Sheva, wake up," she said, pulling the covers off her. Elisheva stirred, but didn't wake. "Sheva!" At this she stretched and opened her eyes, which squinted against the daylight pouring through the open shutters. "Did you take my leather pouch?" Esther patted the sheets around her sister, then ran to look at the floor. She yanked out each of the vanity's creaky drawers in turn, all stuck fast from humidity. The old piece of furniture jumped at each jerk, but the pouch was gone.

"I wouldn't touch that thing."

Esther's heart thudded in her throat. "Where is it, then?"

"How should I know? Maybe one of the servants took it."

Esther couldn't think why any of them would have come in. Nothing had been cleaned. "Lord," she said, getting ready to voice a complaint. Invoking the Name, however, only reminded her that neither of them had said morning prayers. She began speeding through them. Elisheva sat up and did the same.

That morning, the bek sent messengers with trumpets all over the capital, both Atil and Khazaran, to announce the call to arms. All able-bodied men who remained in the city should prepare to leave for battle later that day. Though a recent bar mitzvah would not be conscripted, he could volunteer, as could a woman over fourteen. With no system in place to check ages, Esther expected boys and girls as young as Itakh to offer their service. Though she feared for their safety on the battlefield, she also feared for it if they remained in their homes. There was no simple way to tease out right from wrong in this circumstance.

Within hours, conscripts and volunteers began arriving by the hundreds, pouring in through Josephus's wide-open gate. As each reached the portico, Esther or Amit took the person's name, age, and birthplace, and asked if he or she had a natural or mechanical horse, a weapon of any kind at home. Each they recorded in ledger books, turning almost none away. Before midday, a fresh contingent of golems arrived from Yetzirah, thirty-six more. "Can there be two groups of *lamed vavnikim* holding up the world?" Amit asked Natan in passing. The physician had come to tend to his nose and his broken tooth, and now he went about with his head high, proud of his war wounds.

"I should ask you."

"I'm kidding. I already told you, I think they're men, if they exist at all."

Esther began enlisting her next soldier, a lanky, dark-skinned man. She thought he might be an Ifrikian Jew, one of those speculated to belong to the Lost Tribe, though Esther had never understood how they were lost when everyone seemed to know where they were. When asked, however, he declared his faith: "Yishmaelite."

"*Salaam aleikum*," Esther said, bowing.

He broke into a warm smile as he returned the gesture. "*Aleikhem shalom.*"

In the moment between when he stepped aside and the next man strode up, she ducked her head toward Amit. "When the golem was shot last night, what happened to him?"

He glanced around to see if anyone was listening and shrugged his shoulders. "The bullet must either have passed through its body or lodged in it."

"Little pieces flaked off." There had been something gruesome about it. "Did that hurt?"

Amit's next recruit fumbled to tie up his pack on the ground.

"They don't experience physical sensation. The shot didn't harm him. Though it's possible to maim them past use, by lopping off their arms or feet, for example."

"You can't put new limbs on them?"

"You know that. Not even a fingernail."

"A prosthetic, then?" Esther's next person had arrived, a curly-haired refugee she recognized from the camp. The bek had not sent word to them because they were not Khazar citizens. The man must have wanted to join on his own. He possessed neither weapon nor mount. The wonder was he had a sturdy enough rag to tie his few extra clothes in. She tried to pay attention, but felt impatient to get back to the question. When he left, Amit's recruit was finishing up. She would have shooed him away. The moment he left, she asked, "So what do you do if one is incapacitated?"

He didn't look up from his ledger. "Decommission it, of course." He passed his hand across his calm face, then went back to writing. "As Shelomoun instructed."

"He said 'kill.' "

"I wouldn't use that word, because they can't be said to live."

Esther couldn't keep up the conversation in snippets. She settled down and tried to concentrate. But she kept wondering what it meant to be shot when you couldn't feel anything, what it could mean to kill something that wasn't alive. If for a moment she managed not to puzzle over this question, her mind darted to what could have happened to her leather pouch, to the *volkelake*'s hair and the money and the amulet she'd stolen from Ya'el. Chuluun and Tselmeg took over their posts for a short time so that Esther and Amit could wolf down some food while they observed target practice and drills. Natan was being trained in the use of one of the bek's field telegraphs, two other men in using the theodolites Göktürk had given them.

As they ate, Itakh ran up with a paper in his hand. "A bird came in from Praha," he said. "It flew in this morning." He didn't seem excited, didn't even meet her inquisitive gaze.

"It found us!"

He shook his head as if affronted by her stupidity. "No matter how long ago your uncle brought it there, it's one of our own birds."

"Was it old?"

He shrugged, handed over the scroll, which was thicker than those they'd received before, and walked away.

Usually, the message in a pigeon's case was brief, written on a scrap or small piece of paper. This was a whole sheet of onionskin, folded and rolled so tightly, Esther thought it might rip as it unfurled. She worked each crease open with care. The paper was covered with tiny letters in dark brown ink, a flowing hand, but Esther couldn't read them. "What is this?" she said, passing it to Amit.

He put his bowl on the ground so he could hold it in both hands. "Looks like Bohemyan. I'm not very good at reading it. And right now—" One of the bek's assistants waved to beckon them. "Later. I'll try later."

Esther had no choice. She had to wait. But her heart thundered in her chest to know who had sent the news, though intuition told her that Matityahu would have written in the mother tongue even if it had been a long time since he'd used it. Amit kept the paper as they went to meet the bek on the portico.

All the bek's forces had gone to meet the enemy, taking the Khazar arsenal with them. Any weapons the Uyghurs could not supply would have to come from Persia, the Rus, and the Ottomanim, since nations normally accessible across the Pontus were now cut off. The bek had requisitioned food from all the nation's farmers. Luckily it was harvest season. The numbers they discussed—the amount of food, the weapons the army as a whole required—boggled Esther's mind, yet the enemy outnumbered them. Germania had more, newer, and fleeter aerocraft. Their Panzer armies could decimate Khazar ground forces. Bek Admon's red hair and beard had developed a sprinkling of gray in the past week, and his skin bunched when he spoke. "We'll do what we can," he told Esther. "I don't know if it will suffice."

"We have a weapon our enemies lack," she said. When he didn't respond, she named it: "The golems."

"Cannon fodder," he said quietly.

"No."

"And mechanical horses and aerocycles," Amit added.

"Twenty of them?" said the bek. He couldn't deny the horses' efficacy, though he appeared to want to.

"And the Great Name's blessing on the Jewish people."

Notoriously unfathomable as *that* had always been.

More than five hundred people had reported for duty that morning, and more continued to stream through the gate. Much of Khazaria—including the great forts at Sarkel and Kharkov—was already under enemy control, but men were making their way to Atil from all over the fertile delta. Soon, Esther hoped, they'd arrive from the north and the Kavkas.

As Esther and Amit crossed the yard to take over the work of enlisting recruits, Esther kept an eye on how Amit was holding her letter, to make sure it didn't blow away. In her peripheral vision she saw Itakh in a group with Natan and other boys, playing a game with sticks. He looked up from it to watch her pass, but didn't acknowledge her. "That's odd," she said.

"Hmm?"

She shook her head. "Do you know what we need?"

Amit paused. "I can think of a lot of things."

"More golems."

As they sat down at the table, Esther watched him tuck the delicate piece of paper under his ledger. How he could focus when it held such portent, she didn't understand. "My brethren are making them as fast as they can."

"More than that."

"Esther," he said, then opened his ledger book, examined his pencil points. "We've discussed this. I can't do it alone."

"Then maybe you need to teach someone to help you."

Scores of people waited. "It's not like teaching someone a song. It's the crown of a course of study, not a set of tasks you can undertake to master."

"How do you know?"

He picked up a penknife and began to sharpen a pencil.

"How do you know? Have you tried it any other way?"

Amit watched the shavings peel away. "My teachers in Yetzirah became Masters of the Name through privation and long study." Esther wasn't so sure about the privation. They lacked women and wealth, yet had golem servants. "If there were some easier way to do it, they would have found it by now." When all three pencils were sharp, he lined them up in a row. "You don't believe me."

She shook her head. "We have work to do."

When a man enlisted, she focused on him. Everyone behind him was background, at most a faceless body. So when she looked up and saw Shimon and Kalonymos standing before her, her heart flipped in her chest. She stood up so quickly, her chair tipped back and pencils rolled to the ground. Amit, following her lead, also stood. Kalonymos appeared imposing as ever in his purple kaftan. Shimon's sudden arrival and what she could only describe as his polish unsettled her. His hair was freshly cut, his beard trimmed. He wore loose trousers tucked into shiny black boots. She wanted to leap across the table into his arms.

"Esther bat Josephus," Kalonymos said, bowing. This was an ordinary, polite greeting, but also allowed him not to look at her. She knew that despite her bath last night, she was road-worn.

"Rabbi." She introduced Amit to both of them. Kalonymos's face grew lively and inquisitive at meeting a kabbalist. Still, he could not seem to look at Esther.

"*B'rukhah haba'ah*," Shimon said to her.

People spoke to each other. She'd done it countless times. But having Shimon before her and Amit beside her was too much. With everything happening in Khazaria—events of true consequence, events of the greatest importance—their nearness shut her cognitive faculties down. There stood Shimon. As long as they'd been engaged, she'd tried to ferret out reasons to dislike him, coming up each time against the simple facts of his decency and her attraction to him. And Amit, who must in some way or another still have been female, and who had dedicated his life to the mysteries—but for whom she nevertheless longed. Shimon had greeted her, this much she understood. Each second that she failed to reply, his lopsided smile grew more delighted. All she could think to say was, "Why are you here?"

Kalonymos had always been firm about *negiah*, not rigid. He spoke to Esther and Elisheva, just as he had once conversed with their mother. Now he seemed to have become as inflexible about it as his strictest followers, or those of the Yishmaelites across the river who kept their women in purdah, allowing them outside the home only when veiled from crown to feet. He didn't even register that Esther had spoken. Perhaps something about her really had changed in the *mikvah*. Shimon replied, "Your father invited us to break bread with you before you leave to fight."

Had the whole day passed? She glanced at the sun, dipping westward. "I should put on clean clothes."

"You don't have to." His smile hadn't faded.

Esther and Amit found people to man the enlistment table while they went in. Afra and Kiraz were cooking for the kender's table and to feed the troops. Everyone would get couscous fragrant with spices and fruits, but only honored guests would have chicken with leeks. Esther went to her own bathroom to wash, and considered changing her attire, but found herself too eager to see Shimon. She galloped down the stairs, slowing her pace when she saw Kalonymos at the bottom.

Josephus's house had two dining rooms. One, seldom used, had been outfitted for foreign dignitaries, with high, Western-style table and chairs. No native-born Khazar knew how to sit in them. One was supposed to keep both feet flat on the ground, an uncomfortable position to people who sat cross-legged or on their heels on the floor. The other formal dining room had a Khazar-style table, low to the ground and inlaid with tesserae of rosewood and ebony. Silken cushions surrounded it on a soft, patterned rug. Josephus already stood before his place at the head of the table. Kalonymos, Shimon, Bek Admon, Amit, Avigdor, and Menakhem accepted directions to their seats, as did Josephus's three children. Esther noticed that whatever might have changed during her adventures, her seat at the table had not. And Itakh would still eat with the servants, in the kitchen. Josephus asked Kalonymos to recite the blessings.

At first, the dinner conversation was topical, tense and formal. As twilight descended, the blackout shades were drawn. Itakh sulked in to turn on the electric chandeliers, and the conversation splintered. Elisheva was drawn in by Shmuel, who sat on her other side. This left Esther, with Shimon beside her, watching her food while she ate. Then Shimon said, "It's so loud in here."

She nodded.

"Do you think anyone can hear us?"

"I can barely hear you, and I'm right next to you."

"Hmm," he said, and went back to eating. She noticed he'd taken a third helping of salad. "Then it's safe to tell you how proud I am of you." She glanced over to see if he was being facetious, but he took another bite of salad and chewed. "No one else has dared to do what you're doing. When my father told me you'd attacked the bek's palace, my jaw dropped."

As much as his praise pleased her, she didn't deserve it. Lowering her voice and leaning toward him, she said, "I tried to turn myself into a man, Shimmy." An expression flickered across his face. "I asked the kabbalists. That's how I got Amit." He looked her over. "It didn't work, if that's what you're wondering."

He ate some more salad, checked to see that the leaders were still engrossed in their own conversation. "Why did you do it?"

"It's complicated."

A servant knelt down beside him with the chicken, and he served himself more. After thanking her, he said, "I would release you from the match, if that was your reason."

Esther kept silent a moment, stewing in her own mortification. "Not that."

He thought for a while. Elisheva directed a question at Esther, who dispatched it quickly, as if it were a fly on her plate. When she caught Shimon's eye again, he said, "I'd like to come with you."

"On the campaign?"

He nodded.

"People like you get an exemption. People the country can't do without."

"I don't want an exemption. Khazaria *will* be able to do without me if the whole nation falls."

"You could get killed." She was trying to whisper, but found herself hissing with vehemence.

"My *bashert* can put herself in harm's way, but I cannot?"

Esther's cheeks prickled with heat. "Your father will never—"

"I'm a grown man. I don't need to ask his blessing." The fact that she did momentarily enraged her. She held still, waited. He finished his food and laid his fork across his plate. "You're sure you're not telling me you've changed your mind?"

She wanted to reassure him, but her mind was changeable. She couldn't tell him she entertained thoughts of Amit. Shimon was poised to become the next chief rabbi, if Khazaria as a kaganate with a spiritual leader continued to exist. She felt certain that, unlike herself, he didn't kill things, or steal things, or try to trick the Almighty. "I'm sure."

Partway through dessert, Esther noticed a pressure against her leg. Shimon's knee resting on top of her thigh as they both sat cross-legged. His knee was bony; she felt its weight. Her heart sped up, and as it did, it beat throughout her body, in every limb. His scent, whatever it was that made him smell like himself, wafted over her, just as the scent of jasmine hovered around Elisheva. Esther felt afraid that the slightest movement would startle him away, yet sitting still filled her with anxiety. What he was doing was a flagrant infraction against *negiah*. She would have thought him too obedient to try it.

During the after-meal prayers, an attaché came in without knocking. Esther's back was to the door, so she only saw her father stand abruptly with his heavy brow furrowed. He continued to sing until the prayer was finished. To stop in the middle was unthinkable. Esther and Shimon turned to face the door, which lifted his knee off her thigh. She didn't dare move toward him to let them touch again. The attaché's face was florid, and he held a telegram in his hand. "Bek Admon."

The bek and Esther's father hurried to meet him. Both let out despairing sounds as they read. Avigdor and Menakhem rushed forward. "What? What is it?" Elisheva asked, her voice high.

Josephus looked startled to see his children in the room. "Sheva, Shmuely, go to bed. Esti, prepare your men. You'll leave at dawn." Had he accepted what she was doing? She couldn't think.

"I'm going with you," Shimon whispered. Shmuel had no intention of going to bed. Shimon shooed him out the door. Esther peered around Avigdor to see the telegram. Its smeary, blue type conveyed terrible news: General Boulos's Ninth Army was now crossing unobstructed, open steppe en route to the capital.

The bek's face pinked with rage. "We have nothing left to fend them off," he shouted at Menakhem. "Nothing." Esther's forces couldn't stop an army of tanks. "Dogs!"

Esther knew about this because her father thought it so laughable. Some of the bek's men had trained dogs to take their dinner beneath tanks abandoned on Khazaria's borders during the Great Europaean War. In a conflict, Khazar soldiers could strap bombs to the dogs' backs. They'd run to the enemy tanks, crawl beneath them, and detonate them from below.

"Esti!" Josephus repeated. "Go inform your troops. They'll need some rest, but you'll leave *before* dawn."

Amit followed her as she hurried out the door and relayed the news. Though the men were weary from travel and the previous night's attack, Afra and Kiraz had fed them well. The Uyghurs relished the fight. Esther led Amit into the mechanical stable, where Seleme stood, her engine off, alone in the stalls except for broken-down old Leyla with her suicide shifter. Josephus's more modern horses had already gone to fight. Seleme's access hatch hung open, some wires dangled free. Bataar must have been working on her, though at present, he and his assistants talked to the recruits in the yard. Esther lit an oil lamp hanging from a hook. It cast a golden circle of light that didn't penetrate the stalls. "Amit," she said, "we need to make more golems."

"I've told you, it's not possible."

"Then read me my letter."

He had folded the paper into a pocket of his kaftan. When he unfolded it, he breathed a sigh. "I don't know all the words, but I can get a sense of it." Esther nodded, waited, tried to keep still. "The writer doesn't know who you are, can't read Khazar, but recognizes the *aleph bet*." Her heart sank. She had held on to a shred of hope that, unlikely as it was, her uncle had written the letter. "'Mattei,' does that mean anything to you?"

"No." She thought. "It's his name, my uncle's name."

Amit read through a long chunk. "Mattei and his family were taken months ago. On a train."

"To their deaths."

"It doesn't say that, I don't think." He watched her face, then the letter. "This neighbor is caring for his birds, though some have died. They don't have much food. He saw the pigeon fly in, found one with a Khazar leg band to try to send this message to you. Smart." He kept reading. "He wishes he could read what you wrote. It's been years since Mattei received news from home."

"No answers. No help." The bad news sat like a leaden weight in her chest.

"He's asking you for help, actually. He says if Khazaria can send troops, we can help save the Jews and all the other people who've been taken."

Esther shook her head.

"There's a little more." He chuckled to himself.

"Nothing's funny."

"But it's about a golem."

"Don't be ridiculous." If he were her brother, she would have hit him.

He held the paper out in front of her and pointed to a word, unintelligible in its foreign script. "Right there." She couldn't tell. "A golem that protects a synagogue? He says it's an old story." He read along. "And he wishes it were true; the Jews of Praha would be grateful for it now. There's no signature, I suppose—"

The door creaked open and Shimon kissed the mezuzah and slipped in. He drew up short when he saw Amit. "Oh. I'm sorry."

Esther and Amit backed away from each other. "He's translating a letter for me," she said. When Shimon didn't respond, she added, "We're talking about golems."

Amit crossed his arms, which pushed his narrow shoulders up toward his ears. "Were you hoping to find her alone?"

Shimon said, "I didn't know you were here, that's all."

"Because I'm surprised that our future chief rabbi would violate *negiah* so casually."

Shimon drew in a breath. "I don't know you, Amit ben Avraham."

"Don't mind him," Esther said, waving a dismissive hand in Amit's direction. She didn't want to arbitrate a dispute between them. Her uncle was dead, and she felt the poignancy of his loss. Her father had called him dead all her life, but to be cast out was different from being killed. She wondered if he even knew she existed. Her message, stuffed into Lyubomir's case, had been her chance to let him know, but it had arrived too late for him to receive it. She mourned the missed opportunity as well as the man himself and his family, so unknown to her. "He's angry because I'm asking him to make more *golemim*."

"How many times do I have to tell you it can't be done?"

"That isn't true."

"It can't—"

"Teach Shimon." She gestured toward him with such force, he took a step back. "He's almost a rabbi. Do you need a minyan? Somewhere in this army we can find you eight more Torah Jews."

"Years of study," Amit said, his tone clipped. "That's what it takes."

"Not that many years. Didn't you say you're sixteen, just like me?" He didn't respond. Esther sat down beside Seleme and dropped her head into her hands. It was that or scream at him, or knock him down and kiss him, or do the same to Shimon, or weep for the uncle her father already considered dead, and none of those was possible. She teetered on the edge of telling Amit that she and Itakh had crouched in the grass by the banks of the sacred river and witnessed creation. Her heart was breaking for this uncle she had never met.

Shimon said, "I'm not sure I want to know how to make golems. To be frank, I always thought kabbalists were *bubbemeitzen.*" She could count on him to use a word in dialect—the only other person in their sphere who would. "We need more soldiers, but more will volunteer."

"We can't make people," she said into her hands.

Someone knocked at the door and said, "May I come in?" A woman: Ya'el. She opened the door and stepped through without reaching up to kiss the mezuzah. Even in the depths of despair, Esther found this odd. Why was everyone coming to the mechanical stable? It was her private domain. She'd thought she and Amit would be safe there. "I'd like to speak with you."

Esther gestured for her to sit on the fresh straw. The men remained standing, as if to guard them.

Ya'el looked uncomfortable, but seemed to make up her mind to take a seat before she lost her resolve. "I have something for you." She reached into a deep pocket in her long skirt and drew out Esther's pouch.

Esther made an involuntary sound of surprise and snatched it. Her heart blazed with joy as if an old friend had reappeared. Her first instinct was to smell it. There it was, the pleasing stink of old, dyed leather and her own sweat. "Thank you! Where did you find it?"

Ya'el picked at something on her skirt. "I took it."

Esther held the pouch close to her heart. She worked open its thong and stuck her fingers inside. There was the *volkelake*'s brown hair, its stench starting to dissipate. There was a wad of folded money. But the parchment amulet was gone. She dug her fingers into the small space as if something could still be inside.

Ya'el produced it from the same deep pocket and kissed the outside of the tight roll. "I reclaimed this."

Amit and Shimon looked to Esther for an explanation. She blushed hot.

"You took it," Ya'el said. "I had it buried in our trunk. You must have had to search to find it."

"Is this true?" Amit asked. At the same moment, Shimon chided her, "You wouldn't."

Esther doubted either of them had ever been so gripped by the Evil Impulse. "I can't explain myself. When I was alone in the house, changing my clothes, I went to put your clothing back and browsed in the trunk. The amulet called out to me. Once I'd touched it, I couldn't let go, even though I don't know what it says." This didn't fix anything. "I apologize."

Ya'el nodded with her eyes lowered.

Amit asked, "May I see it?" He crouched down and Ya'el handed it to him. He unrolled the small document with care.

"What is that?" Shimon asked, bending toward it.

Ya'el said, "A magical amulet that belonged to my granduncle. It has protective powers."

"No," Amit said. "No, it doesn't." Her eyes looked skeptical. "It contains instructions."

"Pictures."

Shimon leaned closer. "Some of it is in Aramaic, but some, I agree with you, is diagrams."

"It tells you how to recite the *Shem Ha-Mephorash*," Amit said, "to breathe the spirit into a golem."

They all examined the runic characters. This was why the object had called to her. Some part of her had known.

Shimon held out his hand for it, and Amit gave it to him. Shimon cradled it in his two palms. "All this time, I thought this was hearsay."

"What you're saying is not what my granduncle told us," Ya'el said.

"He didn't know or didn't want you to know. Neither of you should be looking at it."

"It's a sign, Amit," Esther said. "It's a sign that I found it, that I felt compelled to take it when I've never stolen anything in my life." Itakh would have reminded her of Seleme, her father's candlesticks and knife, and a lot of money. But she could not admit these thefts in front of Shimon and Amit. Relieved as she was that he wasn't there to shame her, she wondered where Itakh was. "You have to gather a minyan. You have written instructions, a sign from Hashem."

"The Holy One, blessed be His Name, hasn't given signs since the days of the prophets."

"Maybe we're the new prophets."

He spat three times onto the clean hay. Esther felt glad Bataar hadn't seen. She said, "We watched you, by the river."

Amit looked back and forth from her to the amulet in Shimon's hand. "What do you mean?"

"Itakh and I. We snuck out at night and followed you down to the river. You all prayed fervently. You didn't notice us."

Amit licked his lips. "What did you see?"

"We saw it rise up."

"Where is Itakh, to corroborate this?"

"I don't know."

He closed his eyes, pressed the heel of one hand against his forehead, and let out a long breath. "It shouldn't have worked," he said.

Ya'el said, "Pardon?"

"With a woman and an uninitiated boy watching, it shouldn't work. This is part of the reason we kabbalists live alone in our village. So that our holy work cannot be disrupted."

For Esther, his words glimmered. "Then," she began, "there's no reason Itakh and I can't make up part of the minyan."

"Don't—" he began, then calmed himself, started over. "A minyan is ten men."

"So gather nine more and let us make eleven and twelve. A minyan is at *least* ten men. It won't be that hard, you already have Shimon."

He might unvolunteer himself at any moment, but until he did, she needed him for her argument.

Amit shook his head. "It's too risky. If it doesn't work, I'll need to know if it was because the men were untrained or because a woman attended. We can't try both at once."

"You're one to talk: born a girl, and a few days ago, willing to help me become a man."

The moment she said these things, she wished she had the power to stop time. In the lamplight, Amit's and Shimon's faces mirrored each other: dark eyes blank, jaws slack as if they'd been struck. Ya'el looked down at her legs. Esther could see only her nose and her striped headscarf.

Amit said, "Oh, Esther."

No words sufficed to apologize. She was mortified. All she could say was, "Holy Shekhinah."

"You were—a girl?" Shimon asked. His tone remained gentle. He seemed to want to know. "Amit," he said, as if trying on the name, weighing the number of times he'd seen it bestowed on a man or a woman.

Amit nodded. Shimon did too.

"So it wasn't your own idea to make yourself into a man," Shimon said to Esther. Ya'el continued to look shocked.

"It *was* my idea. I thought the kabbalists could do it. But when they wouldn't, Amit gave me the idea to try it myself."

"Why, though?"

"So I could lead this army." That was the simplest answer. Not un-true.

Shimon sat down on the floor and leaned back against the near-est rough-hewn post. "Though as it turns out, you can do that well enough as you are."

"As it turns out." He didn't seem convinced. "I didn't know how it might work. I thought that if I didn't want to stay a man, I might be able to change back."

"Because the Holy One has nothing better to do than flip you from one state of being to the next, the way one makes a coin appear and disappear to amaze a child."

For some reason, Ya'el laughed. When no one else joined in, she stopped.

"Amit," Shimon said. "Why did it work for you and not for Esther?"

"I don't know."

Shimon's eyes sparkled in a way Esther hadn't seen before. She felt sure he took a prurient interest, like her own, in Amit's transformation. This stirred her. If Amit and Ya'el would leave, she could teach them a thing or two about violating *negiah*.

Shimon said, "All this being the case, I see no reason why an untransformed woman cannot participate. If she had succeeded, you would have let her, wouldn't you?"

Amit lowered his face and shook his head.

"I too would like to help," Ya'el said.

Amit's head kept shaking. "No. No, I'm sorry. That's impossible."

"Why?"

He checked the rafters for a polite answer. "A woman, perhaps. A boy not yet a bar mitzvah?" He shrugged. "But everyone must be a Jew."

Ya'el widened her strange green eyes. "I am a Jew."

"A Karaite," Amit corrected.

"A Karaite Jew!"

Shimon blew a breath out of his nostrils like a nervous horse. "Excuse me for saying this—you seem nice—but the rabbinate considers Karaism a heresy. You don't accept the teachings of Talmud, am I correct?"

Ya'el blinked a few times in quick succession. Esther doubted she'd grown up expecting to be interrogated by the future chief rabbi. "We accept the teachings of Torah. We accept the Lord as our only God." When she said these things, her accent grew more pronounced.

Shimon had no response. No one they knew had met a real Karaite before. Weird dress aside, Ya'el didn't look like a heretic.

"Changing the very nature of what the Lord made you!" Ya'el added, indignant. "That's not a heresy?"

If only Esther had never spoken. If this one time, her thinking brain had moved more swiftly than her tongue.

"We must all work together then," Amit said. "The work can only be done at night, by the banks of a river, which gives us the clay for the beings. Where there's no *mikvah*, it also provides the water to purify ourselves."

"We have both a river and a *mikvah*," Esther said. "We could go right now."

Amit rubbed his jaw where the tooth had broken. "I need sleep."

"We leave for the front tomorrow. If you don't start teaching us now, it'll be too late."

He threw up his hands, but didn't say anything. This counted as agreement.

"Shmuel will want to join us, you know," Shimon remarked.

Esther didn't care. She tingled so with excitement, she leaped up. "Who chooses the minyan?"

"All of us together, I suppose," Amit said. "I am so angry at you."

"I'm sorry," she said.

"Sorry doesn't help."

Esther caught Shimon smiling at her as she made her way out into her father's courtyard, jammed with tents. She crouched down between three of them, and whispered that they needed at least eight pious Jews to begin the study. (Eight in case the Name, whose ways were inscrutable, didn't want to count two women, one a Karaite, and a boy as part of a minyan. Shimon and Amit clearly belonged.) Her companions split up to spread the news throughout the yard. Esther had expected her army's human soldiers to rise up, shouting, "*Kadosh! Kadosh!*" but the announcement rustled up only faint interest. Some had questions: Was it dangerous work? Would they be paid? (In some currency other than the priceless knowledge of how to make golems? Esther wondered. She wanted to shoo the man away.)

They took all nine men who volunteered. Including themselves and Itakh, they were now thirteen students and a teacher. They were too many to fit in a tent, besides which Amit didn't want others to overhear their lessons. So after Esther roused Itakh from his old bedroom off the kitchen, they left Josephus's compound, walked down to the banks of the river, and lit a tiny brush fire for light, though Esther knew it could attract a bomb if an enemy aerocraft flew near. The rest of Atil had its blackout shades drawn, but occasional lights dotted the landscape. A few vagrants happened by, found that the gathering had no food and discussed abstract concepts, and wandered off again. Thus the group commenced its study.

CHAPTER 24

A mit began with the most basic yet complex of subjects, the kabbalistic view of the universe's structure. All Creation was divided, he told them, into ten spheres, ten *sefirot* or sapphires, ten gleaming jewels. Each governed its element, its area of human affairs, and its mystical properties. Angry as he was at her, Amit relished explaining these arcana. At first, Esther listened with her body alert as a mechanical horse straining forward to kill. This was like nothing she had learned from her tutor or in shul: a new way of looking at things large and small. After the first two *sefirot*, however, Esther's attention began darting off in all directions. Her posture sagged. In the flickering light, she saw others blink repeatedly. Shimon's jaw tightened as he swallowed a yawn. Itakh was continuing to keep himself apart from her—otherwise he might have curled up in her lap to sleep. As it was, he lay down on the hard, damp ground and tucked his fist under his cheek. She saw his breathing slow and quiet. She would have liked to touch his brushy hair and tuck the loose pieces back underneath his *kippah*.

When she realized she'd lost track of what Amit was telling them, she waited for a natural pause in his exposition and said, "Amit? We may have learned all we can this evening."

He sat up straighter, as if brought to sudden awareness. "There's much more."

"But half of what you said has already escaped me," Benyamin said. "More than half." He wiped his broad mouth. "I don't know what you're talking about."

Another man pointed to Itakh and said, "He's asleep."

Amit drew taller still and pulled his shoulders back. "There's a great deal I'll have to teach you if this is going to work."

"We'll be tired no matter when we do this," Shimon said. "I wonder if some other teaching strategy might engage your pupils in a more immediate way? Demonstration, for example." Esther heard that by "more engaging," he meant "less dull."

"What kind of demonstration?"

Shimon shrugged.

"It's a great privilege to study Kabbalah. One sacrifices to do so. One gives up his claim to the things of this world. This is an honor I'm bestowing on you." He looked around. His students perked up at the hint of argument.

Shimon suggested, "If you could demonstrate one of the principles you speak of, instead of describing it?"

"You could make something," Ya'el offered. "A little something." When he didn't respond, she said, "Perhaps a sparrow."

Itakh woke up enough to suggest, "Make a pigeon."

Amit shook his head. "A sparrow or a man, its size doesn't matter. I can't do it alone."

"But if you told us what to do?" Ya'el said. Her eyes sparkled. It took pluck for a Karaite housewife to leave her duties behind and join. She looked mild, but in some ways she was fiercer than the Uyghurs.

"I don't think it will work."

"There's much you think won't work," Shimon remarked.

Itakh sat upright. "I know. We should make *volkelaken*."

All around the fire, people booed him and spat.

"Itakh," Amit said, pronouncing the good Khazar name like a command. "A *volkelake* isn't one of Hashem's creatures. It's an ordinary, unfortunate human on whom someone has done dark magic."

Itakh rubbed his eyes. "Maybe we could do the dark magic. We have a war to fight. *Volkelaken* would help." Then he said, "Wait." All of a sudden he was alert, crouching on all fours like an animal, one ear near the ground. "Something's coming," he whispered.

Men drew their knives and guns. Esther's ears were primed for

303

stealthy enemy troops. When she heard the sound, however, it was the deliberate footsteps of a group of men, not trying to hide themselves. The enemy was still west of the city; she expected an intrusion from the police.

The small fire blinded them to the darkness, but Shimon shone an electric torch out toward the path. Its weak beam didn't extend far. Soon, two large, heavy-booted legs walked into it, then four, then many.

"What are you doing here?" Esther asked them.

"We wish to study," Gimmel said.

They stopped still, respectful, silent. They stood with their hands clasped in front of them or loose along their sides.

In the warm firelight, Esther saw the set of Amit's jaw. During their time together, she had come to expect that his response to most questions would be "no." No, he would not let the *golemim* worship. No, he would not teach laymen or women Zohar's secrets. This was because he loved the Lord, as the injunction went, with all his heart, and all his soul, and all his might. He wanted to uphold the Law. But he was not closed-minded. He would have been a hypocrite to stand against change. He would refuse this request too, and perhaps later, when his Good Impulse had had time to consider it, he would recant. She watched him fill up his narrow chest with breath, and waited for his stream of invective.

But Amit surprised her. He let the breath go, then said, "Everything else has happened. I don't see what harm could come." She was not the only one surprised by his response—no one answered him. The golems continued to stand there. "I'm saying yes."

"*Barukh Hashem*," they said, and "His Name be praised." One said, "Bless you." They sat down in groups around the edges of the gathering. Having neither sensation nor the notion of personal space, they bunched close together.

Amit looked flustered, but continued his lesson where he'd left off. Itakh interrupted him: "Aren't you going to make us something?" People made noises of support.

"To what end?" Amit asked.

"Having us sit here bored isn't good for much," Benyamin said.

"Then come to the riverbank." He stood up, turned on his electric torch, and shone it toward the water. Ordinarily, the starry lights of ships would be visible, but the bek had ordered these too darkened. One could still see naval ships on the water, but they were black shapes in blackness, more threat than comfort. Once everyone had joined him on the riverbank, Amit scooped up a handful of muck. "It won't work," he said to no one in particular. "We haven't purified ourselves, and only I know the method." The golems crowded around the outskirts again.

Amit squeezed water from the clay until it formed a workable mass. He molded it into a pear shape, then began to pinch a slender tail from its wide end. Using both his fingers and his unpared nails, he sculpted legs and feet, eyes and ears, the filaments of whiskers. Esther had never thought much about mice, but saw, from this work, that Amit had observed their particulars. Before long, he held a fine clay replica of a mouse, larger than a natural one, but otherwise realistic. With a tiny twig, he scratched the word "*Emet*" across its brow.

He cradled it in his palms. He could have done anything at that moment and Esther would not have been surprised. He could have ululated, begun a wild dance. Instead, he closed his eyes and instructed them all to do the same. Esther wanted to watch him, but obeyed. In lieu of a ritual purification, he asked them to say a silent prayer. Esther thought something vague about becoming worthy, then felt awkward saying such serious words for a clay mouse. Soon Amit instructed them to begin reciting the *aleph bet,* then of letters in groups of three, just as he and the other kabbalists had done when Esther and Itakh had spied on them. People seemed reluctant—it seemed a ridiculous exercise—but Esther recognized the triads right away. Each combination spelled one of Hashem's secret names. She didn't know what each meant, or even how, if you put those three consonants together, you would pronounce the resulting word. But she felt their resonance: *tet* striking the palate, *mem* buzzing behind the nose.

As when she and Itakh had eavesdropped, the long cycle's repetition began to make sense. With each cycle through the names, the group's pace increased, as did the volume of the call and response. Esther soon found herself swaying. When she opened her eyes, she saw the whole group teetering on the edge of dance. By the time they shouted the letters as fast as they could, they clapped along with each one, the golems' hands making big, dull thumps. At this point, Amit did not initiate a new round of recitations. Instead, he fell silent. Esther, breathing hard, stopped and stared at him. All his attention wrapped in toward his palms, cupped like a bowl and quite still. Almost as one being his students drew toward him, straining to see. The little brown mouse twitched its nose, looked around.

"*Emet*," Amit whispered.

"*Emet*," Esther repeated, and others around them too. A lump of awe—disproportionate to the size of the thing they'd created—clogged her throat.

Amit set the mouse down at his feet. A natural mouse would have run. This one stuck close to its maker, like a pet. Though the motions of its face and paws were mouselike, its apparent comfort with its present circumstance made it strange.

"It worked after all," Esther said. They hadn't danced, either—not in the ecstatic way the kabbalists had. "With women and a child helping, and with the golems looking on."

Amit gave a slow nod, as if the creature before him were not the proof she supposed it to be.

All around them, men shook hands, patted one another on the backs and shoulders, laughed short bursts of laughter from embarrassment or relief. Someone lifted up a wineskin and made a quick, ironic kiddush. They emptied the skin in celebration.

"Time to begin, then," Shimon said.

Amit said, "Begin?"

"Making our golems."

"We're too tired," one man said.

Shimon didn't acknowledge him. "We need to rouse everyone.

As many people as we can. Golems, return to Josephus's grounds and gather more makers."

"Our own kind as well as yours?" one asked.

Shimon looked to Amit, who appeared dazed, defeated. He raised one hand, lowered it again. After a silence, he said, "We can rest until they return."

Esther sank to the ground, lay down upon it, closed her eyes. She was giddy with exhaustion. Her eyes burned, and she thought she would never be able to sleep. A second later, the clamor of voices awakened her from a deep slumber. She might have been asleep for six hours but guessed that only a few minutes had passed. She struggled to figure out what was going on around her. Most of the rest of her army had gathered by the riverbank, including a handful of Uyghurs. Chuluun stood at the outskirts, tamping tobacco into his pipe.

"What are you doing here?" Amit asked him.

Chuluun glanced back and forth between Amit and the pipe, as if the object might provide the explanation. "We were told you needed help."

Amit shook his head. "Help making golems." Chuluun didn't look up again from what he was doing. Esther saw Amit's jaw tighten with the effort to hold down his anger. "I've made too many concessions already. Non-kabbalists and golems: that's enough without initiating pagans."

Chuluun spat and walked calmly off, the packed pipe unlit in his hand. Over his shoulder, he called back, "Animists."

Shimon was dusting himself off from a few moments' rest. "Animists who fight for our cause," he mused, "provide our ordnance, and double our numbers. That could double production."

"This is not a factory," Amit said, as if it were a dirty word. "We are not trying to—" he groped for an expression, "maximize our profits."

"Perhaps we are. In a sense."

Amit turned one questioning palm upward. "What will become of Khazaria when you're its chief rabbi?"

Shimon, still brushing at his pants, smiled at him, a curt, tight upturn to his lips. "Nothing at all, if we lose this war. You should know I have more to say to you about your history."

Amit shook his head, avoided Shimon's gaze.

A few minutes later, scores of people—laymen, women, and children, all Jews—gathered at the waterfront, surrounded by golems. Amit stood at the semicircle's center. "The prudent thing," he said, "would be to try, as a group, to make a single one, to see if it's even possible. But if it does work, we need to make as many as we can, and we will have lost time with the experiment. So I think we need to break into groups. Groups of ten, so that each is," here he paused, "well, not exactly a minyan."

They began to sort themselves. Though Amit hadn't offered instruction about how to do so, a natural order asserted itself. No group contained only humans or only golems. Shmuel separated himself from Itakh. Esther and Ya'el split up as well. Esther found herself in a group with Itakh and with Gimmel, whom, she noticed, she no longer had difficulty picking out from his brethren, even in the dim light. At Amit's command, everyone began to scoop handfuls of wet clay from the riverbank, and to deposit these in loaf-shaped piles a short distance away. Because the golems prayed under their breath as they worked, a low rumbling, like bullfrogs, filled the night air. Esther had sometimes seen the Nazarenes across the water in Khazaran perform their ritual immersions. They gathered along this river's banks or in its shallows, their priest intoning words in their holy tongue before leaning the person he blessed back into the purifying water. As she slopped clay from the riverbed, Esther pictured the orange robes of a man she'd once seen blessed, billowing out upon the water in the shape of his savior's cross before being sucked under.

A single handful had sufficed to create a mouse. The form of a man, taller than a man, and with a man's heft, required far more. For all her hard exercise riding Seleme over the steppe, Esther's back felt the labor.

Before long, eight loaflike forms lay in a row by the riverbank. Though they glistened like fresh butter, their size and shape made them resemble new graves. In his central group, Amit prayed, then used his hand to cleave apart what would become the creature's two legs. Because the clay was heavy and thick, this was time-consuming, inelegant, like working a flimsy knife through a dense cake. When he'd finished, he made similar incisions higher up the body to separate out what would become the arms. In their groups, his apprentices followed suit. Esther, pushing her hand clear through their loaf to create an arm, worried she would deform it. There was no going back. Once a part was cleaved from the whole, there was no pinching off an extra bit to fill it out. Like Havdalah marking off Shabbat from the rest of the week, her hand was an impermeable boundary. And how thick was an arm, how deep an armpit? She had been human, and had observed people, all her days, but had never scrutinized a body's construction.

A moving scrim of cloud obscured the moon at times. Amit pushed in and up from his being's shoulders to narrow its neck. Displaced clay became a blocklike head. This he began to shape, rounding the skull, pulling out the buds of ears, drawing a rough triangle forward for a nose. His movements were economical and sure. The other groups hung back. When Esther tried to will Itakh to begin this delicate process for their group, he said, "Don't look at me."

"Someone has to start."

"It ought to be you."

She shivered. But when she looked around, all the humans avoided her gaze. The golems, incapable of such avoidance, nevertheless declined to volunteer.

Gimmel said, "The boy is correct."

Esther couldn't disagree. She tried to draw in a breath, but it hitched in her collarbone. She straddled the mound of clay near its as-yet-undifferentiated top end and squatted, bent over. She swept her hands along what would become the shoulder line and up around the giant melon of a head. As Amit had done, she began by shaping the golem's basic facial topography, its hills and valleys. Already, the thing looked wrong. The nose was too high up the head, the ears too far forward. She knew she could not pinch off and reapply the features any more than she could do this to her own face, so she massaged them until they began to appear more regular. Still she doubted her judgment.

All around, she heard quiet praying and the soft squelch of hands passing over clay. The moonlight wavered, so that at some moments, Esther could see well, while at others she had to work by feel. When she glanced up, a layer of patchy clouds raced in front of the moon.

Back at the beginning of Creation, Hashem had chosen a form for each creature. But how? Two eyes were useful for judging distance, but must they of necessity sit above the nose and mouth? They did so in all beings Esther had observed. As she tried to sculpt a human face, she saw the magnitude of the task.

Gimmel squatted over one of the arms, which he shaped with skill, giving the figure the appearance of muscles under the skin. He shaped a blocklike hand similar to his own.

"You'll want a reed or a quill," Amit said, his voice loud enough for each group to hear but quiet enough not to startle anyone from concentration, "to help with the finest features—drawing eyes and eyebrows, the outline of finger- and toenails. You'll pry the mouth open carefully to form a tongue. And you must drive the reed twice up into the nose to form nostrils."

Esther looked at the ill-formed face taking shape beneath her hands. The idea of burrowing into its insides turned her stomach, but none of her companions volunteered to help. Each bent over his area of study. Gimmel and another golem worked on the hands. Itakh and a human recruit whose name Esther didn't know shaped the feet. Four more worked at the places where the limbs met the trunk. And one poor soldier stood with his feet close together near the apex of the golem's legs, staring down at the creature's blank crotch and not knowing how to proceed.

"Not like a human," Gimmel offered, without looking up from his own work. "Taking in no physical nourishment, we have no need to eliminate waste. Our earliest masters used this means to keep out the Evil Impulse."

Esther at once wondered what the Evil Impulse would be for a golem. Had anyone ever made she-golems? She had to concentrate. The man crouched down and smoothed the area.

Itakh went to the riverbank to pluck reeds. With their dark, furry tails, they were darker than the river behind them. It was as if Itakh were picking slivers of emptiness. He returned with a bouquet, which he distributed to all those who were sculpting. Esther accepted a small handful, certain that the heavy clay would bend and snap the delicate stalks.

These simple implements helped her give the thing a more lifelike appearance. With the fine tip, she delineated eyelids and tear ducts. She etched crow's feet at the outer corners of the eyes, hoping, as she did so, that this might give her creature a chance at wisdom. She could think of no way to create eyelashes, and could not see any of the current golems well enough to determine if they had any. As she prepared to drive the hole for the first nostril, her own nose tingled in sympathy. She worked the reed slowly up into the clay, careful not to puncture the sides of the nose, then began to wind the reed in circles, widening the hole. Her eyes itched and teared. After she bored a second nostril, she shaped their outer edges to be rounder, more human. Looking at the thick, provisional lips, she could not see how the reed would be able to slice a hole wide enough to admit a free-moving tongue. She drew her knife from her boot. The blue steel gave a dull glint in the moonlight.

"No!" Amit hissed. Her action had not made a sound, yet he appeared at her side, his hand on hers to stay her. Esther felt the contact as a shock, a jolt of electrical current from his body into hers. She held still, feeling the good warmth of a living person after the cold of wet clay and night air. Her own Evil Impulse, never far off, goaded her to move toward him and kiss him. The light flickered as if she were about to faint. Yet when she looked up, she saw it was clouds scudding across the moon, obscuring it at one moment, the next letting it glow like plankton in the Atil. Distracted by this phenomenon and by her own body, Esther took a moment to realize that Amit was in fact squeezing her wrist and hand hard.

"Put it down," he said. "You can't touch the clay with a weapon, with anything crafted or forged."

Shimon said, "Amit," in warning. Ever since Esther had so foolishly revealed Amit's secret, she had dreaded what Shimon might say about it, though thus far he had kept his temper.

"Let me go and I'll put it away."

He released her hand and it throbbed, her whole arm tingled. She contained so much energy, she felt she no longer required sleep. She replaced the knife in her boot, then massaged the wrist with her other hand.

"The reed comes from nature, crafted by the hand of Hashem. A manmade implement will destroy your work."

The urge to strike him rose from her feet up through her trunk and arm, but she resisted it. He had touched her, yet this didn't mean the wall of *negiah* had come down. "I can't see how to form a tongue with a reed."

"Using patience," Amit said. "And care."

He went back to his own half-formed golem. All around, people had stopped their work to watch, but now turned back to it.

"Doesn't anyone else want a turn?" Esther asked her group. But of all of them, only Itakh looked her in the eye, and even he wouldn't volunteer. "Holy Shekhinah," she said under her breath, and crouched down again to try to solve the problem of the thing's mouth. The oath was just something people said to express amazement or frustration, but at this moment, the help of Hashem's Holy Consort was the very thing Esther needed—the fertile, creative force of life itself. She pushed the reed deep between the thing's lips, then tried to force it toward one of the cheeks. Of course the reed didn't budge. Patience, she told herself.

By degrees, she made a hole, then worked it open into a cavity.

Then, with a slow steadiness she had not known her hands possessed, she pried open what she could now call the golem's lower jaw to begin to sculpt a tongue from the material inside the mouth. Tongues were long and wide, she reminded herself. She wanted to give it enough of one to speak.

Soon the huge golems were formed. When she stood back, Esther saw they were all misshapen. Some had one foot larger than the other, some a withered arm. Her own had either a short neck or hunched shoulders, she couldn't be sure which. She hoped that the Holy One, by whose grace these creatures would come to something like life, would smooth out their deformities in the process.

"You must write the word *'Emet'* on each brow," Amit said, "and scratch a name into each left wrist. Their numbers are one hundred nine through sixteen."

Esther's was 115, then. And as another person bent over its brow, she took her reed to the left wrist and turned the soft, weighty arm to reveal its underside. The name that popped into her head, however, was her uncle's, Matityahu. This thought was inappropriate; the golem was supposed to have a number. But the image of a person she'd never met haunted her. If he had children, they too must have been taken to the camps. The neighbor had written that he'd been taken with his family. Esther couldn't guess how many people that had been; more than just her uncle and a foreign wife. Who would honor him by using his name if her father had so long ago proclaimed him dead? At the same time, while people did name babies to honor dead relatives, no one named horses or housecats after people, let alone made things. Yet now that it had occurred to her, the name stuck. The letter from Bohemya had said something about a golem protecting that far-off place Matityahu had chosen as his home. It seemed fitting to name a golem after him to protect the land of his birth. No one was watching her. She scratched the six characters, *mem tav tav yud hay vav*, into the still-damp clay of its inner wrist.

Then the real work began. They all joined, humans and golems, into a great, elongated oval with the eight supine forms of the new golems in the center. Amit solved the problem of men and women being unable to touch each other by grouping Esther and Ya'el together and placing a child on each woman's other side; Esther held Itakh's hand, Ya'el held Natan's. Esther's mouth felt coated with paste. She didn't know how she'd chant. Yet together, they began the slow recitation of the *aleph bet*. Each time they came around to *mem*, it shone with new meaning as the first letter of her golem's name. *Mem*, the first letter of Moshe, of his sister Miryam, of the *mayim*—the waters—she had drawn forth from the rock. As they began to recite the triads, the names that together formed the Great Name, she saw that many of the Uyghur, Yishmaelite, and Nazarene soldiers had gathered around the periphery to watch. Their presence carried her outside herself, as if she could see through their eyes the foreignness of what she and her companions were doing. But before long, as the chant gathered in intensity, she lost sight of the observers. She saw only the clay shapes before her and the fervent expressions of the other golem makers. As the chant increased in volume and intensity, the makers began to dance. Esther felt an animating shock in her lower belly, an unpremeditated outpouring of Hashem's gift of movement. Her hips swayed, which made her feet step in rhythm. Her arms undulated in time. Everyone danced and shouted, faster and faster, until at last the clouds parted and the moon shone down in her glory. The supine forms jolted, then began, each in its own way, to move. One placed its forearm over its eyes as if startled by the light; another rolled onto its belly, then pushed up on all fours. The ecstatic shout of *"Emet! Emet!"* went up all around, men whooping in joy. But amidst the jubilation, which increased as the creatures made their unsteady way to their feet, Esther paused to watch them. Their lurching gait concerned her, and what troubled her more was that the Great Name and His Holy Shekhinah had not seen fit to smooth them over in their transformation from dull matter to something like men. Hashem had made the universe in six days, but He had not made right these creatures' malformed limbs. No part of them had grown, shrunk, or become more beautiful. Some had arms that stuck out from their sides like turned-up wings. On one, the makers had failed to craft knees, so he tottered as if on stilts. Her own golem, with its secret name, limped because his legs were so different from each other. When he gave an experimental turn to his wrists, the hands didn't match. One eye hung lower than the other, and she had left the imprint of her thumb on his crude nose. He hunched. Hot shame flooded her head and coursed down her. She sensed that all the people around her felt it. If the *golemim* who'd participated in this work were capable of feeling emotion about what they'd done, the blank repose of their faces revealed nothing. The Uyghurs and other non-Jews who stood watching remained still and quiet.

Gimmel approached one of the new golems. His bearing had never looked so fluid, humanlike. "*Barukh habah.* What is your name?"

The new golem struggled like a beached fish to open his narrow mouth, not sculpted wide enough for use. "W-w-one ten," he piped at last in a reed-thin voice.

Esther's stomach flipped and squeezed in on itself. He did not sound like the other golems. Then again, for all his ugliness, he could move and speak, which was perhaps more than one could assume.

"Yours?" Gimmel asked their own golem.

As if feeling the letters, it touched its wrist with the fingers of the opposite hand. "Matityahu," he said. His voice sounded normal, normal for a golem. She had dug his mouth cavity deep enough.

Amit came to investigate. "What did you say your name was?"

"Matityahu."

The answer diverged so far from Amit's expectations, he seemed unable to hear it.

Esther remained silent. Now that she stood looking at the terrible thing in the moonlight, she was sorry.

"Numbers! They have numbers!" Amit shouted, close to her face. Shimon hurried toward them. In a quieter tone, Amit said, "On the next one, do it correctly."

Esther felt as if he'd kicked her in the stomach. In the moment before she regained her voice, Itakh said, "You can't mean tonight?"

"We have an army to raise, Itakh. We can make one more round before dawn, two if we're quick about it."

Itakh was too young to prosecute an argument. But Natan jumped in to say, "Those we've already made remain naked. Surely someone must attend to that?"

Amit looked around. He was no fool: He had to know that Itakh and Natan spoke for many. But he said, "They do not suffer from the cold night air, nor from modesty. They can wait."

"You say this," said one of the older, clothed golems, "as if you were sure."

"I am sure."

It shook its blocklike head. Lacking a full human range of motion, the golem's gesture appeared mechanical.

They had to experience physical sensations. Otherwise, they couldn't walk without falling over or judge when the sun was setting. But their inability to eat or drink must have left them insensible to thirst or hunger. And surely they did not experience emotions as people did. Though they had expressed their desire to worship the Name and to participate in making more of their kind. These yearnings—there was no other name for them—must have taken root in some kind of emotional experience.

Amit looked to the outskirts of the gathering. "Could some of you, I wonder, escort them back to the camp?"

Tselmeg stepped forward. "I will." Some companions joined him, perhaps as eager to sleep as to be helpful.

"Our golems carry extra clothing. You can distribute as much of it as is necessary to the new creatures." Some golems opened their mouths to protest, but Amit raised both hands to silence them. "You cannot tell me that you have any sense of personal ownership. We ourselves have so little belief in it, we could not have imparted it to you."

Gimmel said, "For a man who has given his life to the study of all that is holy, you have a high opinion of your own powers."

A coughing sound erupted from a few golems, an abortive throat clearing like a mechanical horse's engine trying to turn over on a cold morning. Once again Esther thought it must be laughter.

Over the face of the moon, which was setting toward the southwest, a fine haze had arisen, tinged reddish. Esther observed it a long moment before realizing it was the haze of the battle they were on their way to join or that was coming to overtake them.

Tselmeg and two of his Uyghur companions led the eight new golems back toward camp. Perhaps the uniformity of their loose-fitting garb would help them look more regular.

"The rest of you should sleep," Amit said to their audience, his tone softer now. "Who knows what awaits us tomorrow."

Many soldiers trudged off after their fellows. A few sat or lay down in the grass to continue to watch.

Esther did not know where she'd find the energy to continue this work. Yet the moment she bent over and reached into the cold, wet clay of the stream's bank, her body tingled with anticipation. Although they all remained novices at the craft, the possibility glimmered before her that, as the night progressed, their skills might improve.

CHAPTER 25

The night's third set of new golems had begun to stir when the sky lightened over Khazaran. To the west, the firmament remained hazy, with clouds and the dust and debris of battle. She still couldn't hear it. Amit hurried the new creatures to their feet. Esther didn't know what would happen if the work remained incomplete at dawn, but Amit seemed unwilling to risk this. As they all walked back to her father's compound, Esther watched the naked, lumpy bodies of the new golems ahead of them. They looked better than the night's first attempts. No sooner had she thought this than Shimon, beside her, commented, "Hashem have mercy on these misfits."

In an instant, his words disfigured them further. They were so uneven. Some were lame in one leg. "I don't know if the Holy One spares much thought for machines."

Shimon glanced at her from the corner of his eye. Though his lids were puffy, his brown eyes danced. "You know as well as I that they aren't machines."

"Yes." Yet Seleme was a machine, and there was no denying she possessed some kind of animating spirit. "I wish I could say what they are." All she wanted was to rest her head on his shoulder.

Exhaustion fogged her thoughts. She believed she had said the evening *Sh'ma* at some point during the night, but could not recall if she had merely intended to. She said the morning prayers now, saw others' lips doing the same. The golems prayed in unison. Back in camp, as the roosters crowed, Amit and Shimon removed their tefillin from their packs and tied them on. They pulled their fringed *tallitot* over their heads. Other observant Jewish men followed their lead, but the golems possessed no phylacteries and could not fulfill this mitzvah. Surrounded by people who did not perform the ritual, Esther saw these blessings with new eyes, as something foreign, lovely, strange. If her immersions had managed to transform her, she herself could pray with them right now. She couldn't name the feeling this realization gave her, since it wasn't possible to experience nostalgia for something that had never happened. But nostalgia was what this felt like: cold in her long bones, hollow in her belly. She wondered if, as with so many things she'd learned since leaving home, she could simply choose to tie on tefillin. Everyone said a woman could not lead an army or study Kabbalah, but men and women together had made golems from the stream's clay. Perhaps other acts relegated to one sex or the other worked the same. Perhaps Amit had not had to change his destiny to say this prayer in this way.

By the time the sun had risen, the tents were packed, the golem horses tacked up, the golems in ranks, even the new misfits ready to march. The milk goats had been locked inside the barn to keep them out of the way, and they bleated in confusion or discontent. Seleme waited, riderless and idling, at the foot of the portico's steps, along with rusty Leyla. Bataar had replaced a belt and oiled gears, so the old thing sputtered along. Shimon had gone home to bring back his own late-model horse, Tolga, and had a servant drive in another, with his pack hitched to the cantle. Esther didn't know its name. Shimon kept Tolga back a safe distance from Seleme. He sat the machine with an easy grace, his spine tall and his boots polished, though he himself looked tired.

Josephus stood at the top of the steps while she mounted Seleme. From this vantage, she saw the Uyghurs' mechanical horses ranked in the outer courtyard. They swung their boxy heads, stamped their metal hooves, grunted in irritation at their proximity to one another. All together, they were fearsome. She imagined them thundering across the steppe toward an unprotected village. Then pictured them running toward a Panzer unit, and thought how small their forces remained after all this work.

"Amit?" Shimon asked from his mount. He gestured with his hand toward his other horse.

"I don't drive," Amit said.

"You'll learn." He held his hand open long enough that Amit had to climb on. His kaftan bunched up around him, and he leaned down to straighten it. "His name is Akbar."

This left just one mechanical horse without a driver—Leyla, the least desirable. Ya'el had been put on a golem horse, since she was already familiar with them. Josephus, from the portico, beckoned to Itakh, who'd been kicking the dirt near the front ranks of the foot soldiers. Itakh slouched forward. A rooster kept crowing though its work for the day was done.

"Can you drive?" Josephus asked him.

"Esther taught me." He sounded neither proud nor excited. "But not on this. It has one of those." He pointed to the old-style shifter, protruding like a spear from Leyla's withers.

Josephus's large jaw twitched. "I command you to ride, my servant and my son." As if he had any control over Esther's army.

Itakh sulked toward the machine. Though he could barely reach his foot to the stirrup, he was limber, getting himself up. Esther tried to look him in the eye. He avoided her gaze. A golem came forward to raise the stirrups. Another had Nagehan in her mobile loft, and attached her to the back of Itakh's saddle. Half a dozen of his other pigeons were already caged on golem horses' backs, in case the army needed them to communicate with Josephus.

"I'm joining," Shmuel said, coming down the steps toward where Esther sat mounted on Seleme. He had packed his things in the rucksack he carried to yeshiva. Slung across one shoulder, it looked laughably tiny.

Josephus came forward. He towered over his son. "You'll do no such thing."

With one thumb hooked into his shoulder strap, Shmuel stood up straighter.

"Go back inside and put down your bag. You will not follow your sister."

"I will. I want to fight."

Josephus did not allow conversations like this to occur in public. He knit his brows, developed an angry flush, kept his temper. "You're the future kender. You'll protect Khazaria with your wits, not your life."

"I want to do this."

"You're too young."

"And I'm not?" Itakh said from atop Leyla. The golem had finished adjusting the stirrups, and he sat ready to ride, his feet and hands on the controls. "I am also your son." Out of habit, he reached up and tugged the earring in his left ear.

Josephus drew his brows even closer together. His complexion darkened by the moment. Esther wondered how much the boys could provoke him before he exploded. "Fine then, Itakh," he said. "You'll stay home too."

"He will not," Esther cried. Her heart rushed out to him. "I can't go without him." Though in fact, he was speaking to her only when required to do so. When his silence didn't infuriate her, it felt as if it would break her heart.

Shmuel looked expectantly at all of them, his thumb still hitched in his strap like a schoolboy.

"If he goes," Josephus said to no one in particular, and resolutely avoiding Esther's gaze, "no harm may come to him." They were heading into battle. How could Esther, or anyone, guarantee his safety? Her father knew this. He blinked, his eyes red. She had never seen her father weep. He did not do it now, but said quietly, "My youngest child. My only son."

Shmuel blushed, fidgeted, looked for someone to tell him what to do. "Is there a mechanical horse for me?"

Their father didn't refuse him. He kept silent.

Amit or Itakh would have to be unseated for there to be one.

That or one of the Uyghurs, and Esther would not broach the subject with them. Shimon had insisted Amit take his horse. She didn't understand why or want to argue with him about it. Itakh: Her father had just admitted he was more slave than son, and the boy glowered. With another glance at her father to make sure he wasn't about to say no, she called, "Saddle him a golem horse," into the ranks. When a golem brought the beast forward, Shmuel regarded their father before walking down the steps. He mounted the unfamiliar creature with skill.

Josephus still refused to look at Esther. "The bek has placed great faith in you, despite my misgivings and your reprehensible behavior." Esther willed herself to keep cool. Her hand rose to her collarbone, to feel the *hamsa* and the pouch under her clothes. "He is making his lines of communication open to you, and his lines of supply." Esther thought her association with the Uyghurs might matter more in that regard. "I don't approve of what you're doing. But you are fighting for a noble cause." His eyes shone.

Esther shifted in her saddle, fiddled with Seleme's spiky mane. She wanted to tell her father she loved him, in case she never saw him again. Before she could, he raised one hand in the air, a signal, though not to her. Out of the house marched four men bearing two long poles. At the kender's signal, each of the rear men let go. Those in front stood the poles up on end. The flag of the kaganate—a crisp, bright flag, the sword and menorah a sharp display in gold and blue. "*Todah rabah*," Esther said, speaking the Holy Tongue because it seemed to fit the moment's solemnity. Some of her own soldiers stepped forward to receive the flags. She saw, as they adjusted them to rest against their shoulders, how heavy they were. When her father's eyes passed over her, she mouthed the words "*I love you*," which she could not recall ever having spoken to him. He paused a moment, then nodded.

She turned Seleme in a slow, precise circle, mindful not to let her bite other machines and creatures nearby. The crowd parted to make way. Behind her, the engines of other horses started up. Shimon fell in, Tolga's engine humming. Though Leyla was difficult to drive, Itakh lurched through first gear to a walking gait in second. When Esther looked back at him, she saw he had to lean off the horse to shift. She hoped he'd find a better way before they engaged in battle. He wasn't going to grow. Amit's only experience with mechanical horses was riding alongside Esther while she drove one. He stalled on his first few attempts to start it, and one of the Uyghurs pulled up beside him to offer advice. "What's its name?" he called out to Shimon.

"Akbar!"

Above the din of engines, the Uyghur ordered Amit: "Step on it harder!" Then, once the engine turned over, "Squeeze the lever on the left handlebar—left, left! Roll it toward you until it clicks." When Esther glanced back, Amit was pink and shiny, his horse jerking forward. The Uyghur mechanical horses rumbled menacingly. Behind these came soldiers on golem horses, foot soldiers, and last of all, the man-golems, marching. Before long twenty of them had climbed into the aerocycles. They ticked aloft.

People lined the streets of Atil to cheer them: women, children, the elderly. Some clapped and whistled, some blew trumpets. Others called out blessings or bowed. Judging from their clothes, they had come from all over Atil and Khazaran. Though the army headed toward the West Gate, refugees came down from the north to wish them well. Children tossed grains of cracked wheat as if blessing the harvest. Golem horses didn't seem to notice; mechanicals watched the grains as if they might be weapons, but kept moving forward.

"Esther! Esther!" cried a woman from farther up the avenue, most of the way to the Great Library. Despite the crowds and the distance, Esther picked out Rukhl's slight figure and the wisps of curly hair escaping her headscarf. Jascha stood beside her, waving to Itakh. Esther fished out the *hamsa* from inside her clothes so that Rukhl could see it around her neck. When they reached her, Esther halted the line. She heard Amit stall behind her and his Uyghur companion curse at him. "Esther," Rukhl said, "I'm glad I have this chance to greet you."

Esther was surprised to feel anger bubbling up under her collarbone. "I hoped you would enlist."

Rukhl's mouth opened and hung there a moment before she spoke. "I'm a woman."

"As am I."

"And a mother."

When she turned, Esther made out Ya'el's headdress, back where she rode one of the golem horses. The bek had not sent out the call to the refugees, but even so, some of their men had enlisted. As Esther sat her horse, her army behind her, the realization dawned that she had never known Rukhl. She'd admired her strength in the face of hardship, felt proud to be one of few people of her class to have a connection to someone in the camp. Giving food had let her feel useful and virtuous. But it was a misnomer to call this a friendship. Unable to express any of this, she ducked her chin toward Rukhl and said, "I'm glad to see you. Please stay safe," then released the horse's clutch and started off again. Rukhl said something as Esther drove away, and at once Esther wished she'd stayed long enough to hear it.

The crowd stretched past the public park and the courts. People pointed at the golems, and children crowed with delight at the aerocycles overhead. As they passed the bek's palace, his guards *salaamed* to them. Esther wondered where the kagan hid, where he watched from. She knew he was somewhere. All the way to the West Gate those left behind by the soldiers lined the streets and leaned out of windows and doorways—and when the army reached the gate itself, Esther noticed that, having lived her whole life in this city, she had seldom passed through it. Her adventures in the camp and to Yetzirah had taken her northward. Childhood vacations along the Khazar Sea had brought her whole family south. But west, toward Europa, she'd ventured only once. Past this forbidding barrier lay *parasangs* of cultivated fields, the great, stream-crossed grasslands, and the enemy.

But in the first moments of the trek westward, the landscape made it difficult to think of tank units. For a time, the army traveled a narrow, stone-paved road with a central gutter. It wound through a grove of ancient olives, their massive trunks gnarled and the undersides of their leaves twinkling silver in the breeze. Their branches hung heavy with fruit. Everything burgeoned in this temperate season: pea plants draped pods in wild abandon from their poles, and arbors sagged beneath clusters of grapes. Flocks of sheep and herds of goats dotted the rolling hillsides, the lambs and kids still frolicking with their rocking-horse gait as they had in springtime. Because the climate was more temperate here than in the north, the grass was taller, its whitish fronds brushing above the horses' knees. When the breeze blew, this grass rippled as would the sea. And when men and horses passed through it—for the road here had become no more than an ill-kempt track—they scared butterflies out ahead of them.

Though the army now numbered hundreds of men and scores of golems, they were neither loud nor rowdy. The day's beauty kept everyone calm. Amit disrupted the peace. He could barely control his horse. He stalled, ground his gears, and popped the clutch every few minutes. If he had ever in his—her—former life been prone to swear, his years with the kabbalists had trained this out of him, but his frustration and embarrassment leaped off him like beads of sweat. Shimon relieved the Uyghur and explained the horse's mechanics. He guided Amit, then critiqued the corrections he tried. Amit said little in response.

Shimon looked around as if searching for a new topic of conversation. To Chuluun, who rode nearby, he said, "I always wondered why, when our ancestors ceased living as nomads, they'd leave Atil in the warm months and set up camp in orchards and vineyards. Here, it's easy enough to see why."

Around his pipe, Chuluun gave his menacing smile, the long, parenthetical wrinkles framing his mouth. "I always assumed they did it so that my ancestors could sweep down from the plains and ransack their deserted villages."

Amit said, "My people still camp in the summertime." Itakh made a complicated maneuver to get himself between Amit and Shimon. Esther remarked on his skill—it was difficult to steer Leyla into such a tight space while downshifting—and thought he might be lording this ability over Amit. At any rate, she was glad to be trotting at an even pace. All Amit had to do was hold his throttle steady. It was a relief not to hear him grinding the gears.

In the distance, a herd of sturdy-boned wild horses galloped away from the army's approach. She awaited news by pigeon post or, more likely, the field telegraph her father had entrusted to the army. Until it came, and despite that beautiful landscape, her army and the front continued to barrel toward each other. The haze in the distance grew thicker, but perhaps the bek's forces still held the enemy back.

CHAPTER 26

A s Esther was deciding whether they should stop for a meal or press on, a rider on an old-model horse like Leyla hurtled toward them from the west. A few mechanical horses reared, but Seleme grew intent, her green marble eyes scanning and her sharp ears turned forward. Esther cocked her pistol with her left hand. She lacked the Uyghurs' finesse, but kept the horse moving forward. A hundred weapons trained on this moving target. Esther doubted this could be an enemy assailant. Knowing little of Germani culture, yet judging by Amit's clumsiness, she didn't think a foreigner could learn to maneuver a mechanical horse so well. As he neared she saw that he wore the blue and white uniform of a Khazar officer—though that could be a disguise. Someone picked off his cap with a bullet and the man ducked, putting his left hand up to his head and holding his right glued to the throttle. The horse continued at speed. "Hold your fire!" Esther called back, and slowed Seleme. If the rider didn't also slow, they'd collide.

The rider kept toward them at a gallop. Before he could hit any of Esther's horses, however, his horse lurched, stalled, and collapsed onto its forelegs as Esther had never seen one do. She braked Seleme to a halt, heard Amit stall behind her, heard someone swear at him in Uyghur. The rider's machine hissed like a boiling kettle. Steam plumed from its nose and slack mouth.

The rider, still with one hand on top of his head, stumbled to the ground. "Are you wounded?" Esther asked. She disembarked from Seleme, the ground shifting and buzzing.

"No," he said, out of breath.

327

"He lost his hat," Amit said. Getting down from Akbar, he almost fell, but he managed to pull a knitted *kippah* from the pack tied to his horse. He ran to the man, the cap held out in front of him. The man snatched it, kissed it, and pressed it over his crown with both hands.

"Thank you."

"You should have been wearing one underneath," Amit remarked. This was no time for a sermon.

"Esther bat Josephus?" the man asked.

She nodded and extended a hand toward the wounded machine. Heat rose from its skull plates and kept her back.

"By Hashem's grace I reached you."

"Are you a deserter?" she asked.

"No. Bihor ben Alp, of the Fourth Cavalry. The enemy is no more than twenty *parasangs* west. Prepare for battle."

Esther squinted at him. He looked and sounded like a Khazar, but why hadn't someone in the chain of command sent word to her? Natan was riding with the field telegraph lashed to his saddle's horn.

A Uyghur came toward them, unwrapping a greasy packet of wrenches as he walked. "Maintenance," he said, lying down prone beside the horse to get to the belly access panel. "Can't neglect it, even at war." He selected a socket wrench and began loosening the panel's bolts. Benyamin followed along to watch, a golem close behind him. In other circumstances, Esther would have pushed them all aside. She was proud of her ability to work on Seleme, and liked to exercise it.

"My unit commander sent me to inform you, on the bek's orders. He said to tell you to prepare for battle later today."

"Natan?" Esther called. He saluted her from a distance back. "Telegraph the bek to confirm this."

"In the meanwhile," Benyamin said, "we should hold him prisoner."

"Why?" the messenger cried. Again he pushed the *kippah* down on his head. He must have thought them a bunch of zealots.

Benyamin shrugged, and before Esther could see what had happened, he grabbed the man's arms and flattened him on the ground.

"Holy Shekhinah," the messenger said, and turned his head to the side.

Benyamin said, "Sorry," as he trussed him. "You could come in handy."

"Someone offer him water," Esther said.

The man with the wrenches remained sprawled on his belly alongside the horse, both his hands buried inside her though steam billowed out the access hatch. He yanked out a wire whose rubber casing had eroded, its copper end frayed.

"Is that the source of the problem?" the golem asked. Esther expected him to jump to the messenger's aid, but instead he remained near the Uyghur repairman. Meanwhile, Benyamin helped his prisoner to his knees, sat down beside him, and fished rolling papers and a pouch of tobacco from his coat.

"No. A bad connection in the power train. But this isn't helping." He reached into his tool roll for needle-nose pliers.

"It may be something more than that," the golem said. "Would you like me to take over?"

"No."

Another golem brought the messenger bread and water and knelt down to feed it to him. He repeated the first golem's question to the Uyghur, as if he might simply not have understood.

A golem could not threaten. It possessed no means to modulate tone, which meant it couldn't hint or imply. Nevertheless, the short hairs behind Esther's neck prickled, and the Uyghur pushed back from the horse and up onto his hands and knees. He walked away brushing his shoulders and shaking out his neck, as if the golems had wounded his pride. Benyamin offered his prisoner a puff of his cigarette. Wildflowers ran riot amidst the hummocks, splashes of blue, yellow, and red glowing against the grass, which had the crisp, salty scent of late summer. In the few minutes her army had halted, the fug of exhaust that surrounded them had begun to dissipate. They were so close to the front, but she couldn't hear or smell it from here.

Bihor's mechanical horse was soon fixed. Golems checked and

groomed the others. Their work seemed swift and precise. Natan brought telegraphed confirmation of Bihor's report. He provided the bek's coordinates, and Shimon unrolled their field map to mark them in pencil. The enemy was rapidly driving the Khazar forces back toward Atil.

As they resumed their march, they began to hear the front in the distance. At first, Esther mistook the sounds for thunder: far-off booms and cracks like the finale of a fireworks display. The haze hung heavy as if rain obscured the western horizon. But no foul weather was in sight on this peaceful summer day. The field telegraph went wild, sending them updates and coordinates every few minutes. Their own army, these told them, was in full retreat. In the distance, machine guns trilled.

"How long until we reach the front?" someone asked. But Esther had no answer. The front kept racing toward them.

People loaded bolts into their crossbows, unlatched the safeties from their guns. The aerocycles, behind them and overhead, would be the first to draw fire. At the same time, they could see farther out into the rolling landscape. So it was a golem—one of the old golems, she remarked, as the new ones were not sturdy enough to be trusted with these machines—who called out, "Aeroplanes ahead. Land-based vehicles arriving from the north."

Esther downshifted Seleme, and the army slowed behind her. When she glanced back, it wound a course through the tall grass like a fat snake. People, machines, and golems stopped, a trail of dominos in reverse. She left Seleme idling. "Whose?" she asked.

The golem didn't reply. Foolish to imagine it could discriminate between Germani and Khazar flying machines. Aeroplanes and insignia weren't part of a golem's experience, though that did not stop them from fixing mechanical horses, understanding languages. She couldn't yet see the aercraft, and felt more than heard their distant drone. The ground vehicles were a convoy of moto-trucks, their wide, studded tires sturdy on uneven terrain. They made a racket as they lumbered along. In counterpoint, she heard the calls of the various small birds that their progress disturbed. People began sighting toward the horizon and watching what approached on land to assess its intentions. The aerocycles turned and circled back to the army's rear, to give them more time to view what approached. Then the birds fled en masse toward Atil, away from the disturbance they no doubt felt more viscerally than humans could. Mechanical horses grunted and skittered on their hooves, sending puffs of scurf into the dry air. Their riders clicked their tongues to hush them, drew back on their handlebars. At the same time, those who were not already aiming at the western horizon did so now.

As the engines grew louder, the aeroplanes appeared, first as black specks, then as gray swallows with their backward-pointing wings fixed in menace. A squadron of enemy bombers. The Khazar Aero Force, with its beautiful, bat-winged craft, was nowhere in sight.

"Flying low," Shimon, right behind Esther, remarked.

The moto-convoy, Esther could now see, was Uyghur, its riders dressed in blue and black. She had only two weapons: the knife she'd stolen from her father and the snub-nosed, small-gauge pistol Göktürk's arsenal had supplied her. Both were meaningless against an aerial threat, but she drew the pistol, slid bullets into the chamber, clicked it into place, cocked the trigger. She held it out in front of her at eye level, bracing it with her other hand, and smelled its pleasant scent of metal and oil. Seleme's kin.

"What we need," Tselmeg said from off to the right, "is anti-aerocraft guns."

"Do you think they're bringing any?" Benyamin asked, lifting a shoulder in the convoy's direction as he steadied his crossbow.

There followed a low conversation in Uyghur. When it concluded, Tselmeg answered, "If not, we'll send the request back with them. And pigeon post our leader. It'll reach him faster."

The aeroplanes dipped lower as they approached the army, spread out before them, exposed. Esther's heartbeat and breath quickened, even as she held her laughable weapon steady. She should offer the men some command, but what? They could stand steady and shoot, or scatter and be picked off one by one. There was no place to retreat to, no cover of trees. They had been seen. The moto-suppliers sped toward them, she hoped armed to the teeth.

As the aeroplanes neared, they whipped the grass below into a frenzy. Their reverberation against the hard ground was so loud, Esther couldn't hear people around her though their mouths were shouting. She could see the aerocrafts' enormous twin engines, the machine guns protruding from the cockpits. These aerocraft were of the same manufacture as those Esther and Itakh had first seen in the refugee camp. Her first thought: panic about her inability to protect Shmuel. She had made her brother ride toward the back of the line, but this offered no real protection. She prayed for his safekeeping.

A blink of an eye later, the aerocraft began to fire. Bullets spat from the guns with shocking force, and though they hit the ground scattershot, each small trough and plume of dust marked a near miss. Her own men and those in the Uyghur convoy fired, but the aeroplanes had enclosed cockpits, some kind of isinglass, which made the pilots more difficult to hit. Still, every Uyghur moto-truck seemed to be equipped with a handlebar-mounted machine gun. Between these and crossbows, the two small forces inflicted some harm. The golems remained as calm as if they were cooking. Those aloft in the aerocycles took up their weapons and fired straight into the attackers. One managed a shot into a cockpit before being shot down himself. He had perhaps wounded the pilot, because the aeroplane veered off course and into its neighbor's wing, which it sheared off with its propeller. Their engines strained, and on two different trajectories, they crashed into the ground. Someone else drove rounds of machine-gun fire into one aerocraft's rear. Thick black smoke plumed from the holes, and the aeroplane wobbled like a wounded bird before banking in a wide arc to turn back. Esther saw men, including one of the supply trucks, gun their engines toward the downed aeroplanes. One pilot jumped out of his machine, both hands clutching a rifle, and began to run, shouting in his guttural tongue. The men gunned him down. As the aerocraft strafed the army with quick bursts of fire, men called

out oaths in various languages. Shards flew off golems' bodies here
and there. Some bullets hit perilously close to Seleme's hooves, but
she was designed not to spook or lose her footing. It would have been
easy enough to drop rockets on Esther's army and blow up the petrol
trucks, but the understanding dawned on her that they were not the
Germani aerocrafts' real target. They had been heading toward Atil,
and merely fired on whatever had presented itself along their route.

As the squadron moved on, someone in her company was squarely
hit. Esther heard his wordless cry, quieter than the swears of those
around him. A moment later, she heard Shmuel scream. When she
turned, afraid for his life, she saw him still on his horse, his mouth
wide in terror. A large man who'd ridden near him had fallen from
his horse, one foot still caught in the stirrup. The man writhed and
struggled to free his foot. His golem mount stood still and untrou-
bled, looking straight ahead with placid eyes. The man was Benyamin,
she now saw through the blood covering his face. A rider nearby him
jumped down from his horse and pulled Benyamin's foot from the
stirrup. The foot thudded to the ground like wet laundry. Shimon, on
his mechanical horse, got hold of Shmuel and quieted him.

Someone fired a passing shot at the last plane's near wing and hit
the fuel tank. First came the bright flash and heat of its explosion,
then, a moment later, the boom. All around, people ducked to avoid
falling shrapnel. Esther felt something sharp slice past her arm. The
aeroplane tipped one wing toward the ground and, like the twirling
pod of a maple seed, spun as it fell. It boomed again when it hit the
steppe—unlike Benyamin, whose impact hadn't made a sound in
the general din. Gouts of acrid smoke plumed from the aerocraft's
cracked-open shell. Inside the machine, fire burned an uncanny blue
and orange.

"Everyone back!" Chuluun shouted. People sprinted away, took
cover as the wing rockets exploded in a series of pops. All of the aerocraft's fellows were gone now, perhaps radioing in its fall.

Once the explosions ceased, the moto-convoy approached. Engines, loud voices. Beneath them, birdsong and insects, the sounds of

a summer day. The crackle of the aeroplane consuming itself in flames was the only unusual sound. The telegraph ticked. Natan called out, "The battle is upon us. The bek requests our coordinates." A Uyghur removed a theodolite from his saddlebag, set it up, and began to locate them; a man from the supply line shouted out numbers toward him. Meanwhile, supply trucks moved toward the mechanical horses and the fuel-bearing golem horses. Men forced open machines' mouths—a heartless-looking gesture—and jammed in fueling hoses. They dispensed the fuel with hand cranks.

"Pigeon!" Itakh cried, "One of mine!" It darted toward them like a missile. "Elif, Elif," he called out to it, and followed with his particular whistle. It slowed and circled, recognizing its loft and wanting food, then landed and began to strut, jutting its beak forward. Itakh snatched it up and removed the message from its cylinder. Before he reached Esther with it, Amit said, "We have to bury Benyamin." He was still perched atop his golem horse.

Esther took the message from Itakh, all of whose attention was devoted to the gray pigeon, which had settled in his hands. The same message arriving by different means. The bek must have had Elif with him in a tiny loft of his own.

"I said we have to bury him."

A man had a rubber tube down Seleme's throat. The petrol burbled as it poured in.

"In battle, that isn't always possible," Shimon said.

Amit said, "It's our duty to honor the dead."

Shimon rubbed one hand on the base of his skull. "There isn't time."

"We'll do our best to do what's right." Amit spoke with finality. To one of the golems he said, "Do you have shovels? Dig a grave." The golem did as he was told. Esther knew he didn't have to.

As she saw the specks of the enemy aircraft continuing eastward, Esther wondered if they should press forward to meet the battle or retreat the few *parasangs* to set up better defenses for Atil. Meanwhile, she did not stop Amit's golem from digging the grave. She noticed one of the deformed new golems alongside him, scratching at the dirt. Once Seleme was fueled, Esther rode over to inspect the third aeroplane, the one that had been so spectacularly shot down. The head of the Uyghur convoy stopped her en route.

"Almost finished here," he said, not making eye contact. "We could have found you hours ago if we'd had better coordinates."

"Chuluun hasn't been in contact?"

He cocked his head toward the telegraph. "Our leader wants to know where you are at all times. We're leaving you pigeons. Use the machine."

"You'll find us in battle."

His long nostrils flared. "He asks me to remind you that the question of payment remains."

The fueling motos had scattered themselves all through the army, a score of them. All her stolen money wouldn't pay for this. "Tell your leader to talk to the bek."

He shook his head, smiling as if with regret.

The burning aeroplane, so nearby, threw blistering heat. Esther wondered if Seleme was safe, if any of her parts would melt. "Tell him to speak to the bek," she repeated.

Still smiling, he extended one finger toward her like a pistol. She noticed that he wore dark leather riding gloves. Then he called something out to his men and turned to investigate the downed aeroplane.

As the fire burned, it left behind blackened struts and curled sheet metal, all hot and stinking of char. Shimon approached the wreckage, but flinched and drew back when he saw the pilot. Esther turned Seleme off, dismounted, and got close enough to see that much of the man's clothing and parts of his flesh had burned away. Flies buzzed around the body. One lit on his glassy blue eye.

Tselmeg, who stood close to the front, said to a golem, "Make it possible for people to get in, will you? It's too hot for us, but you can forge the way."

Gimmel regarded him.

Tselmeg looked up, his long face smudged and his hair lank. "There might be useful information inside. And things."

Gimmel walked over and Tselmeg backed off a pace. Two new golems hobbled up behind him. One, Esther realized with pleasure and horror, was Matityahu. "We do all this work," Gimmel explained to him. "We do not require purification if we touch a dead body." They were incapable of expression, yet Gimmel's lips appeared set, resigned. Humans around folded their hands, rested their weight on one leg and then the other. Uyghurs from the fuel convoy gathered in.

Tselmeg said, "I don't believe a dead body can pollute me. It's just too hot."

A nearby golem said, "They do. They wouldn't eat with you after you'd done it." Esther stood still, gauging the ripple of anger his words sent through her.

With Matityahu's mincing help, Gimmel pulled the lifeless pilot from the wreckage and laid his mangled body on the ground.

He wore a neat brown woolen suit with brass buttons, tighter than anything people wore in Khazaria, and an armband with the Hunnish insignia. A leather helmet with goggles pushed up over it obscured his hair, and someone was already stripping the good, lace-up boots from his feet. Tselmeg drew his knife.

"What are you doing?" Amit asked. Esther didn't know where he'd come from. She'd thought he was overseeing Benyamin's burial.

Tselmeg reached up under the helmet to grab a lock of hair. When his hand found nothing to hold on to, he ripped the helmet off. Everyone around stopped to marvel at the man's appearance. Some Khazar men, mostly non-Jews, shaved their whiskers, but few cut their hair shorter than their ears.

"He looks like a sheared sheep," Ya'el remarked.

Tselmeg ran his fingers through the brushy, flaxen hair—"Clean too," he mused—and lifted out the longer pieces at the top. He sliced through them, gathering them into a little sheaf and gripping tight as they fell free.

"What are you going to do with that?" Amit asked.

Tselmeg grinned, showing his rabbit teeth. He took an old red handkerchief from his pocket and folded the hairs inside. He kissed the dirty bundle and stuck it back into the pocket. Some members of the fuel convoy laughed and clapped. One came forward to pluck the brass buttons from the man's jacket.

"That's barbaric," Amit said.

"Do your dead need things in the afterlife?" the man said.

Esther had stolen the lock of hair from the *volkelake*. She had no right to speak. The foreigner now looked even more peculiar, a big hank cut from the longer hairs near his face.

"We should bury him as well," Amit said.

"We don't bury our enemies," one of the fuel men replied. "We leave them for the wild animals."

"He's a person. He might be a Jew." Here even Esther couldn't help glaring at Amit, the idea was so stupid.

"This is a war," the Uyghur said. "Get used to how we fight it."

"Or go home, little girl," another added.

Amit's face turned dark red, as if he'd choked on something. Esther reached out a hand to him in warning, trying to send the silent message that she had told no one of his origins beyond her impolitic revelation to Shimon and Ya'el—that the words were metaphorical. "Our war. Not yours," he said without looking at the man, and turned away.

The golems began to search the downed aeroplanes for equipment. They did this, as they did everything, without haste, and brought back two field radios, an assortment of pistols and knives, a heavy machine gun that could perhaps be mounted on an aerocycle. Soon the Uyghur fuel men clamored to rifle through the machines, and the golems made solemn way for them. First they emerged with documents in tubes and leather pouches, the print in that odd, spiky script. Amit was the only one able to decipher this, and had gone off to sulk. She kept the documents with her until he returned. Moments later, the Uyghurs emerged with leather stripped from the aeroplanes' seats,

337

pieces of navigational equipment dangling tentacular wires, lengths of copper wire cut free of their moorings.

"What are you doing?" Shimon asked no one in particular. "Don't scavenge."

"This all has value," one of the fuel men said gruffly. "Either directly to us, or on the market."

Shimon shook his head and walked away. The looters continued, methodical as hungry men picking clean the carcass of a lamb.

Golems buried the three downed pilots and Benyamin. Esther had not known him long or well enough to mourn him as a friend, yet felt his loss: one of her first recruits, and her first casualty. A minyan gathered and Shimon said Kaddish over all four men, not discriminating amongst them. In the meanwhile, Esther watched the golems as they shoveled spadesful of dirt back onto the graves. The meaning of this work did not seem to affect them. Esther could have sworn she saw something plodding, resentful in their deliberate movements. The fuel men gathered their spoils and packed them onto their moto-trucks.

When all was done, one golem said to Shimon, "We might have left already had we not had to bury those infidels." All around, from his own kind and humans, came murmurs of agreement.

"We know nothing of them," Shimon said, expression mild. "Not their religion, nor if they even practiced one."

"We know they tried to kill us," Natan said with a monosyllabic laugh.

"If you were killed in battle and your enemy found your remains, would you not want him to bury you?" Shimon's tone remained gentle, but his brow furrowed.

"They came to kill us. We're defending ourselves." Natan glanced around, as if for support. "It's different."

After a moment, Shimon said, "I feel less certain I know Hashem's will."

The fuel men's leader called out, and they mounted their moto-trucks with efficient swagger, just as they might have mounted horses.

The machines had starters and chokes similar to their mechanical equestrian brothers and sisters. The supply men revved their engines before bumping off toward the north.

As they receded into the distance, Shimon looked to Esther. "Do we go to meet the battle, or retreat to prepare?"

"We go back," she said. "Someone needs to dig in."

Until the army had stopped in Atil, Amit had been their spiritual leader. The moment Shimon had joined, he'd taken over. This was his right, Esther supposed. Nevertheless, she thought, then the thought petered out before she could complete it, replaced by the din of engines turning over and aerocycles beating their wings to rise up. Only now that the smoke had cleared did she notice that Bihor ben Alp, the bek's unlucky messenger, was still trussed, unharmed by the aerial assault though clearly rattled. She shouted for someone, anyone, to free him so they could move on.

Amit, mounted on his golem horse, held the roll of documents in his hand. "You want to know what they say?" he asked.

She looked at him crossly. The answer was obvious.

"Orders from Germani generals, directing their aero force on what targets to attack. They've taken Kharkov and Samandar, sent waves of prisoners westward from both. Atil is the final target on Khazar ground." She heard his pride in possessing information. "And a more general statement. They don't want Khazaria. Jewish prisoners are a secondary prize. They want unrestricted access to the Uyghur oil fields and the Atil, as well as a clear line of attack to Tsaritsyn."

"To shut down the Mensheviki war machinery," Esther said. She had known all along that Khazaria might be on Germania's way to Rus without being its target. Still, it was a blow to realize that all of them could be killed in battle or rounded up, their cities, crops, industries, and culture destroyed, as a sideline to some more important campaign. "What are we fighting for?" she asked aloud. "To protect Mensheviki steel?"

"The homeland," Shimon responded. *Eretz moledet*, she said in her mind. *Memleket. Haimland.* The other ways she knew to say what

Shimon had said, in the Holy Tongue, in Turc, in Rukhl's dialect. In all its forms, the word tugged at her heart, called to mind the vast grasslands, the waters of the Khazar Sea, the riches of the Great Library, the sword and the menorah, crossed. But it meant nothing to the enemy barreling toward them with tanks, bombers, Western motorcycles. Or it meant something different.

CHAPTER 27

Heading the short distance back to the capital, the mechanical horses raced across the uneven terrain in a fourth-gear gallop. They were built for this—their necks stretched out long before them and their hind legs aft, so they seemed to leap across the landscape. Their hooves pattered like hail on the dirt, and the grass made a sibilant swish against their legs. No one could talk while doing this. As the mechanical horses rushed onward and the aerocycles pedaled overhead, the machines pulled away from the golems and golem horses who, in turn, left the foot soldiers behind. The golems' disinclination to hurry surprised her. She would have imagined that, feeling no physical sensation, they would outpace humans, perhaps even machines, whose speed was limited by their engines' capacity. The man-golems—she had seen their discontent at the site of the conflict. But horse-golems had no cognitive faculties. Surely, seeing mechanical horses out ahead, they could run to be part of the pack. These thoughts raced through her mind as the ground streamed forward to meet her. Once the thoughts had sped on, she found that the steady rhythm of Seleme's hoofbeats and the rush of wind past her ears lulled her mind into a pleasurable, alert relaxation.

The army kept moving. Esther drank water from her water skin to assuage her hunger, then resettled into her spacious reverie.

What startled her out of it was Gimmel, who appeared, running without effort, alongside her. Esther's first thought was that she'd been correct: the golems could have kept pace with the mechanical horses all along.

"Mistress, we must stop," he said.

Uncanny to hear his voice so flat and ordinary while his body exerted itself. "Why?"

"Because Shabbat approaches."

Esther continued to ride at speed, her eyes trained on him. "Now?" She had lost track of the calendar. More had happened in the past ten days than in all of her previous life. Months seemed to have passed since she'd petitioned the kabbalists in Yetzirah.

"We must make preparations. There's no time to braid khallah, but even the fleeing Yisraelites could bake *matzot*."

She glanced at Shimon, charging ahead on her other side. He also appeared deep in thought. How could they stop to observe Shabbat now? The bek's army was right behind them, being driven toward the capital. If they stopped, they might not reach their destination in time to defend it. On the other hand, the habit of observance ran deep. She hadn't returned her father's candlesticks; she had them in her pack. It was forbidden to work or to carry on Shabbat, and what did her army do, at this juncture, but labor to move quickly and carry things from place to place? To do such things on the Sabbath was beyond imagining. Gimmel was right. The fact lodged like a lump of food in her throat.

"Mistress," Gimmel said again.

"We are almost back in Atil. We'll observe the Sabbath there."

Gimmel continued to keep pace with her, but did not say more.

Esther's army could wake the dead from their slumber. It choked a cloud of exhaust into the air as it galloped forward. The aerocycles, overhead, churned up a stiff breeze. As the army closed in on a sleepy village preparing for the Sabbath, livestock in the fields raised their poised heads to watch them. Sheep huddled together. Kids pronked this way and that, leaping like grasshoppers. Villagers watched their approach. Esther knew that behind her, some of her number flew the Khazar flag. There was no chance the villagers feared attack—though one would come imminently. But their stillness, as they stood outside their mud-daubed homes in their kaftans, headscarves, turbans, and *kippot*, told Esther how unknown to them was the possibility of anyone doing anything besides preparing for Shabbat. From their expressions, she imagined they would have been less surprised had men descended from the moon on ropes. She had never felt so loud, so uncouth, so unholy.

"The enemy approaches!" Shimon called out to them as Tolga rushed him past. "Join our forces to fight!"

They passed the onlookers too swiftly for Esther to hear if they responded. When she glanced back over her shoulder, however, she saw various soldiers call out to the townspeople. Perhaps they were urging them to join.

Guards stood alert in the watchtower of Atil's West Gate. Behind Esther, the Uyghurs let out a triumphant war cry, an ululation that raised the hair on her arms and neck. The guards in the tower sprang to aim their weapons. "Esther bat Josephus," she called out to them. "The bek is close behind us. We seek admission to defend the city from attack."

Within, guards drew back the great bolts that released the gates. Esther's father and the javshigarim waited in the wide plaza within, Avigdor and Menakhem wearing the blue military uniforms in which Esther had so rarely seen them. On ordinary days, they did not need an officer's high black boots or draped indigo trousers. She was startled now by the sight of them, their garb so Western in contrast to her father's. Arrayed behind them all were the rest of the city's guards and police and a ragtag militia, smaller than her own, yet looking more alert and ready to fight than her exhausted forces. "*Abba!*" Shmuel cried from somewhere back in the line. Josephus did not move.

"Bek Admon is no more than a few hours behind you," he said. "We're tracking the enemy's aerocraft by radar, and unless the bek can stave them off, they'll overrun him. What is your plan for defense?"

"To dig in and fight."

Her father's heavy eyebrows knit together, the deep furrow marking itself between them. "Get everyone inside."

Esther gave the order for her troops to move in. They swelled forward, spilling into the residential neighborhood near the western gate. A few civilians leaned out of windows or poked their heads around doors to see them. The rest were, no doubt, either on their way to synagogue or already conscripted. The city's non-Jewish residents all lived across the water. As the army moved back to defend the river, they would find more potential helpers there. "Take an hour to rest. After that time, report for duty. Bring your gas masks. We are told the enemy uses gas."

Hundreds of packs fell to the ground at once. Hundreds of buckles ticked as their harness leather squeaked and cracked. Everyone had received masks either when Göktürk first armed them or when the bek had issued supplies in the capital. Esther had given the equipment little thought since then, as gas was so foreign to steppe warfare. Her men had either been trained to hack their foes to pieces or spent their lives dreaming of the same: Kagan Bulan subduing the tribes with primitive weapons and bloodlust, his progeny defending their borders with the same savage spirit and the Great Name's help. As Chuluun had said when he'd first shown her the masks, Uyghurs looked down on anyone who'd poison an enemy from afar. A few men hung the masks from their necks by their thick rubber straps. Those on mechanical horses dangled the contraptions from the handlebars, where they could be of no use, but didn't make the rider look ridiculous. A few put them over their faces. To set a good example, Esther hung hers around her neck, but disliked both its weight on her chest and the sharp smell of the rubber fittings. As soon as the masks had been placed, most of the men turned off mechanical horses and lay down on the ground, their heads resting on their packs or the cobblestones. Those riding golem horses simply dismounted. The beasts had so little will of their own, they would not trample their masters or even wander into the streets.

Esther turned to Gimmel, who remained close beside her, and said, "We must ask you golems to prepare the *matzot* and a Sabbath dinner. The human troops need rest."

Already the golems detached packs from the horses. They hadn't been waiting for her command. A few people retrieved nets and string to fish in the river.

Some Uyghurs took the opportunity to check the mechanical horses while the golems were otherwise engaged. Any amount of preventive maintenance paid off. And clearly, they considered this work their own.

Amit came down from his horse, his lips pursed as he looked around for a task with which to occupy himself. He made an inept adjustment to his horse's near stirrup. Akbar growled and bared his teeth.

"Turn him off before you do anything," Esther said.

"At home, they do the work of making the Sabbath, but they wouldn't dare remind us of when it begins."

Esther patted Seleme's steel withers. The machine bristled as if Esther's annoyance were transitive. "I think they must be keeping track because people are fallible."

"We are. I myself had lost track. But I still don't know how they'd do that." He walked off as if with some purpose, but Esther saw he had nothing to do.

Some of the golems gathered brush and broken pieces of barricades for a fire, while others took out large bowls and flour from their packs and began mixing dough. Others unwrapped small clay ovens from the baggage and set them to warm in the fire. Matzoh would cook quickly inside them. When they unloaded yams from their packs, Ya'el poked them with holes and prodded them into the fire's embers with a bayonet. Esther unlocked the silver candle holders from each other and fitted them with a pair of short white candles. She removed the tiny kiddush cup from its carrying bag.

As the sun dipped over the battle to the west, the sky grew hazy and pink, like apple blossoms viewed from a distance. The golems retrieved fragrant *matzot* from their covered ovens, and set out the yams and a simple stew. One filled the kiddush cup with wine from a skin.

Amit changed into his white robe, though Shimon remained as he was. Esther had to borrow Ya'el's spare headscarf to light the candles. She wound her slovenly hair into a low bun and wrapped the long piece of fabric around it. Esther was surprised at how heavy the head-dress felt, at the weight of her own coiled hair. She had to hold her shoulders back and her chin high to balance it.

The whole army gathered to observe the ritual. Esther had won-dered how the Uyghurs and other non-Jews might react—how even Ya'el would view the proceedings, since she practiced *mitzvot* differ-ently. But they all stood silent, some not listening, others with their hands folded in respect before or behind them. Ya'el seemed keenest of all to observe. Esther lit, drew in the light, covered her eyes with her hands, and took a deep breath, her fear, exhaustion, and irrita-tion draining away that instant. She sang out the prayer. She took a moment to pray silently for their mission's success, then found herself standing still, eyes covered, with only the sounds of breathing and a quiet city around her. She listened hard for the approaching battle, but could not hear it. Then she said, *"Ameyn."* Everyone—the Uy-ghurs with their guttural accents, the golems in their basso voices—responded.

When she opened her eyes, she saw she was no longer in charge: Shimon held the flat of his palm against Itakh's and Shmuel's fore-heads as he recited the blessing for sons and the priestly blessing. Then he raised the kiddush cup in the air and sang the long prayer over the wine. "And there was evening and there was morning, the Sixth Day," he began. Many of the Jewish Khazars joined in. Some mouthed the words. The golems chanted along, clear on every syllable. Amit watched the ground. Esther wondered if he'd wished to preside in his fine white kaftan. At the prayer's end, the whole congregation joined in a hearty *"Ameyn."* Shimon sipped first from the cup, then passed it to Amit, who took it with his eyes cast down. It made its way from hand to hand, Itakh wavering before he passed it to the Uyghur be-side him, then making the gesture of fellowship. Having gone all the way around the circle—Esther thought it had to be empty by now—it reached the boy Natan, who turned and looked at the golem behind him, his expression questioning.

"No," Amit said.

Shimon put his hand on Amit's arm to stay him. Amit made a halfhearted gesture to shrug him off.

The boy continued to hold the blessed cup aloft. The golem reached out its blunt hand and took it. In comparison, the cup looked tiny, fragile as an eggshell.

"No," Amit repeated. "That's forbidden." His voice wavered in the uncertainty between forbidden and simply not done.

The golem raised the glass to his heavy lips and touched the wine to them. He did not try to swallow any. He could have eaten the cup in one bite, yet he handed it with care to his neighbor. All around it went, to all of them, old and new, each dampening his lips before passing it on.

Once the cup had made its way around the circle, the last golem handed it back to Natan, who tipped it back to drain the final drops and gave it to Amit. Amit looked it over, as if wondering if the golems had tainted it, while Shimon led them through *N'tilat Yadayim* and the blessing of the bread. Shimon held up one large cracker in each hand. When the prayer was through, they said, "*Ameyn*" and passed the *matzot* from hand to hand, each breaking off a jagged piece. The golems, Esther noticed, each took only a crumb. Some stood with them in their fingers, while others bent their faces to their upheld hands and touched the morsels experimentally with their tongues. This seemed hard proof of their otherness. As they had done in Yetzirah, they stood by while the humans ate.

Everyone sang the *Birkat Hamazon* after the hasty meal. Even those who had not been raised to recite these prayers had heard them enough, in this army, to begin by now to sing along. On an ordinary Shabbat in the capital, instruments would then have come out, and the evening's festivities—music and tame dancing—would have commenced. But the moment the prayers concluded, Esther stood up and said, "All right. That's enough rest."

Itakh groaned and dropped to the ground. Amit said, "It's *Shabbat*." At the same moment Shimon said, "We need to make more golems."

Amit shook his head at him. "Did Hashem make the world on the Sabbath?"

"Hashem wasn't at war," Shimon said. "The preservation of life is the highest good." He puffed up a little when given the opportunity to be didactic. Esther supposed anyone would. "I don't care for you lecturing me."

Ya'el said, "I don't believe in dispensations. Simply follow the words of Torah."

Amit's head shook at everyone and no one. "I can't believe I'm going to agree with a Karaite, but she's correct."

"Amit," Esther said, then waited for him to understand. The silence of his stubbornness stretched on, the army waiting for something to happen. "I wish to speak with you," she said at last.

She checked that her pistol was in its holster and took a heavy electric torch in case they needed to light their way. She stalked into the side streets without turning it on. The cooking fire and the dim moon illuminated their path. She did not turn to see if Amit followed her. Once the sounds of the army receded, she heard his feet and his kaftan, swishing against the cobblestones as they made their way toward the riverbank. She stopped to listen around them, and Amit crashed into her. She must have been harder to see than he was, in her dark, dirt-caked clothes.

"I'm sorry," he said.

His body lit hers as a match ignites kindling. Where he'd stumbled into her back, her shoulder, and the sensitive back of her knee, her flesh gave off sparks. She wanted to smash the torch down on his head. Instead, she kept walking until they stood by the Atil's banks. When she turned to face him, his white kaftan shone in the moonlight reflected off the water. She wondered if this exposed them to danger.

As they'd walked, she'd rehearsed a speech about his impeding their progress and endangering every Khazar. She'd planned to call him out for hypocrisy: so intent on upholding the Law, yet so eager to circumnavigate it when someone's sex—hers or his own—made that Law seem unjust. Now she couldn't think where to begin. He was sweating. She smelled the sweet fragrance that clung to him, Yetzirah's good soap still in his Sabbath clothes. A few days' exertion on the road had not yet changed him into a warrior. She herself didn't even have to catch her breath.

When she tried to gather the thread of the speech she'd prepared, it spooled away from her. Instead, she leaned toward him and kissed him.

Amit's first response was to call out "Aah!" and raise both hands to push her away. But for whatever reason, this didn't scare Esther off. She placed her palms on his and kissed him again. He wasn't much taller, it was easy to do. The second time, he opened his mouth and kissed her back, his tongue touching hers. Esther felt herself drawn toward him the way the Earth draws a falling body. She planted one boot between his feet and pressed herself against him. As when he'd knocked into her on the path, she lit up in each place their bodies touched: the sides of her thigh, sliding into the soft space between his; the tips of her breasts, alert to his bony ribs; her groin, which throbbed with delight to feel his hidden self stiffening against her. He had been transformed in the *mikvah*. He had become not the image of a man, but the thing itself.

Her hair was still bound up in the heavy bun and covered by Ya'el's scarf. Amit cradled the back of her head in his hand, relieving her of the weight of the hair, and drew her tighter against him with his other arm. She had the sudden, powerful urge to lie down with him. As she bent her knees, he followed, laying her out supine on the dust and releasing his weight on top of her. Her body pressed against him as previously it had rubbed only against her own clever hand. Amit—the weight of him, the particular way in which their bodies joined—

intoxicated her. Almost at once, she jerked and rocked in a spasm of delight. She let out a quiet cry of pleasure into his mouth. He pulled away and regarded her. She wanted to continue what they were doing. She reached one hand to touch the sparse beard on the side of his face.

"I don't—" he began, but Esther sat up and cut him off.

"Shh."

As they sat with their legs intertwined, he brushed at his face in irritation. "*Yetzer Ra.*" The Evil Impulse.

"Better or worse than breaking the Sabbath?" He breathed out through his nose, and she could see the faint shine of his oddly fitted teeth in the moonlight, a hint of a smile, so she pressed on: "Men and women are supposed to delight in each other on Shabbat." Her curiosity about Amit continued to color every thought of him. Her experience right then had been of a male body, and this satisfied some part of her interest. Yet she continued to wonder how much of him remained female, or feminine, inside. Although her attraction to him had no precedent, she was beginning to feel at home in it, her love— she had to call it that—for Shimon notwithstanding.

"Husbands and wives. I don't need to tell you." He closed his mouth again, and his features seemed to dim. "And your *bashert* is back in camp. Ordering people around, no doubt."

"His right."

"Yet here we sit together."

Esther's trousers felt wet, bunched up in her crotch. She continued to feel pleasure in her body's nexus. She let one knee fall to the side so that it could touch Amit's. He flinched, drew back. "Don't pull away like that." He didn't answer. She tried to imagine his expression. "We'll break the Sabbath one way or the other. Either we make golems, or, as soon as the enemy arrives, we fight. You prefer one to the other?" He continued to sit quietly. Esther listened into the darkness. Could she hear the approach of aerocraft? She wasn't sure. Nighttime insects thrummed.

"Why do you even ask me?"

She couldn't answer. When she disentangled her legs from his, she felt his magnetic pull. The bond connecting them broke only when she was far enough away to stand. "Brush yourself off." She began swatting at her own backside, then at her hair, bound so tight in Ya'el's scarf. Amit too smacked at himself, as if in punishment for his behavior. "Don't tell me you didn't enjoy that."

"It's difficult to explain."

As in silence they wound back through the streets, they saw their campfire in the distance, warhorses and aerocycles ranged around it as their ancestors' natural beasts would have guarded the encampment. Golems ranked around the perimeter, where they could keep watch. Had any of them seen her and Amit? She had no idea how keen their vision was or what they understood of human relationships. They did not, at any rate, blink or change their stance when the two people approached.

Nearly all the soldiers slept on the ground. To no one in particular, she said, "We need to prepare to fight at any moment, to take up defensive positions. Gather your supplies and load your weapons." She felt a giddy fear that anyone could see the wrong she'd done.

A few soldiers groaned and resettled. Golems began moving amongst them to rouse them.

To Amit, Esther said, "Perhaps you could take a small group to make more golems?"

She couldn't judge her own tone, but his response was to raise his two hands, palms toward her. "What is wrong with you? What is wrong with you?"

"What did I do?" She dreaded him answering. Her whole body shook, from exhaustion or excitement, she couldn't tell. A nearby Uyghur soldier said, "I would gladly help, if you do it." Amit huffed off, irritated. Esther heard the *"Barukh atah Adonai"* of him beginning a prayer, but not what he was entreating the Lord for. As the camp bustled into alertness, Esther thought how strange it was to see so much activity on Erev Shabbat. She had never dreamed of such a thing. She doubted any Jew had. The joy of transgression kept her alert. Amit lingered with her. She couldn't see him—he kept himself away, angry or mortified or frustrated or all three—but she felt the delight of what they'd done, the pleasure of thinking of herself differently as a result.

CHAPTER 28

Clouds blew in from the west, obscuring the crescent moon as Esther's troops dispersed, some to guard the river, some to guard the palaces, some to station themselves before or behind the Great West Gate and fight the enemy on arrival. When next Esther saw Amit, he said, "I'm taking a minyan down to the river." He didn't look at her. "We might as well."

"Amit," she began, then found herself unable to finish.

No sooner had some of those—humans and golems—who'd participated the previous night joined him than the Uyghur who'd asked before joined the group, along with another soldier Esther thought she remembered as being Koptiki. It was too dark to see Amit's expression, but Esther could imagine it. He had believed there to be all kinds of rules about who could make *golemim* and how. Many had turned out not to be true. She kept this thought to herself as he led his group toward the river. "By the Holy Shekhinah, I don't know if anything's sacred," he said to no one in particular. She could now see and hear the battle approaching from the west, the sky lit a dull red. No more than an hour had passed before one of Menakhem's adjutants came to usher her to a last discussion of strategy.

She roused Shimon from his rest, and when Chuluun saw them walking off, he strode to catch up with them. Shmuel saw the commotion and followed behind, saying, "Doesn't Amit have to come too?"

"When he's finished," Esther said, "you can go get him," though she knew her father would never allow Shmuel out alone at night, let alone in wartime. "Find Itakh, take him with you." Only a moment later she heard cries of "*Emet! Emet!*" followed by men offering shouts of praise to their own gods, in their own languages. *"Alham-dulillah!"* *"Mucize! Şükürler olsun ya rabbim!"* So it had worked. She felt amazed that they'd been able to make golems: filled with awe at the world's wonder, slightly sick. This seemed so Jewish a task, a communion with Hashem, not with any other god. Yet Esther reflected that some of her own ancestors had surely been Uyghurs or Alans or Huns. Göktürk had called her a Sarmata. Before Kagan Bulan's conversion, not one Khazar tribe had been Yisraelite. His conversion had instantly made many peoples one and tied them all to the ancient desert of Palestine. It was no more Esther's birthright to make golems than Chuluun's. It was no one's or everyone's. When she saw the new golems later, she thought them no more hideous than Matityahu and his peers. Esther hoped this meant they could be trained to fire a gun or hack an assailant to death. And perhaps after the war, some of them would join the kabbalists in Yetzirah, or journey to Eretz Yisrael to pursue their dreams of knowledge in the place from which all such dreams had come.

"I'll go," Shmuel said. She wondered if he was afraid as he ran off into the night.

Atil—usually so bustling—seemed eerily quiet even for a Shabbat eve. No festive lights were lit. The only people on the streets were soldiers and golems sandbagging buildings in the Central Square and erecting barricades before strategic positions. Shmuel, accompanied by Itakh and Amit, came running up as the group climbed the stairs to Menakhem's palace.

Esther had never been in his chamber of state. It was opulent, fitted with inlaid tables and patterned cushions and rugs. Staff bustled, as at home. The cushions beckoned, and Esther stumbled down onto them, rolling onto her back. Her eyes closed. She was too tired to sleep—her body hummed and her mind buzzed with thoughts—but too exhausted to be upright.

"There's no time for this!" Menakhem chided.

Avigdor laughed his low-pitched, easy laugh. "She can talk from the floor."

Though Esther feared she might fall asleep for a minute or a day, she couldn't make herself sit up.

"Bek Admon and his forces are nearly here," Menakhem went on. "Your father has been cabling Moskva nonstop, begging for help."

"And?" Shimon asked.

"Nothing." This was the voice of her father. "Radio silence. Either they are already under siege—"

"Unlikely," Avigdor interjected. "Our intelligence would know."

"Or they consider us beneath their notice."

"Filthy," Chuluun said, and something else in Uyghur that sounded like a curse.

"It's to their own benefit to defend us," Menakhem said.

"I'd like to know what you think you can do to help, Esther," her father said.

She realized, at a slight delay, that no one else had so much as sat down. She opened her eyes and forced her body upright.

"We have more golems than the enemy does," Shmuel said.

Their father glowered at him.

"Mechanical horses too," Itakh said. "They don't have any of either one, do they?"

"Unique to Khazaria," Shimon told him quietly.

"And I bet they don't have even one aerocycle."

Menakhem shivered and began to pace. "They can shoot ours down from their superior aerofleet. You're going on a suicide mission, you realize."

The telephone rang and one of the staff answered in a strident voice. He kept shouting into the receiver as if the voice on the other end were unclear.

"They don't have Uyghurs fighting for them either," Chuluun said. He ran his thumb and middle finger down the creases on either side of his mouth. There was some implicit threat in the gesture. Josephus and the javshigarim backed up.

"Sir?" the staffer called out to Menakhem. "The connection was breaking up and finally went dead, but I understood that the bek is closing on the western gate. His rear guard holds back an advance force of enemy motorcycles. Anti-aerocraft guns are at the ready. I couldn't make out the rest."

Menakhem continued to pace. "We don't stand a chance."

"We'll use whatever we have," Esther said to Chuluun, thinking as she spoke. When she stood, she felt as refreshed as if she'd slept. "Whatever our natural strengths. And our better knowledge of the terrain and the streets. We have that in our favor. And we're already in defensive positions."

"My men are the best drivers. We'll go first."

"The aerocycles," Shimon said, "give the advantage of surprise."

"Can the golems fire while they fly them?" Chuluun asked Amit.

He wobbled his head. "Thus far, they've proved capable of everything we've asked of them."

"Everything they wish to do."

"Human troops are guarding the riverbank, within and without the city walls," Esther said. "We can place snipers in my father's house, and high up in the *beit knesset*, and in the minarets of Khazaran." The golems couldn't join them at the riverbank. She had to keep them out of the Atil's waters. "We'll send the golems out in front of you, Chuluun." On no one's command, they all moved toward the door.

"Behind us."

"No." A few short days before, out on the steppe, she'd been afraid he'd kill her. "They're tireless, and they look more frightening."

He grunted.

"Don't argue. We have to make the best of every advantage."

"And even so," Menakhem said.

Outside, the fighting rumbled like a thunderstorm rolling in. They ran back to the encampment, mounted their machines, started up. Once Itakh had Leyla running, he maneuvered himself beside Esther, extended his hand, and rested it on Seleme's crest. Was he done avoiding her? She didn't know—she didn't know what the problem had been, or if there even was a problem. The horse, preoccupied, didn't notice, and this was no time to ask. Esther settled both boots in the stirrups, engaged and disengaged the clutch with her left hand to check it. Then she clicked her up into first, rolled the throttle forward, and shouted out, "Snipers take up your positions. Golems and aerocycles first. Then Uyghurs. Then cavalry. Foot soldiers? Half of you follow the cavalry. The rest, shore up our defensive positions before the synagogue, the palaces, and the riverbank."

People and machines fell into line behind the hulking gate. A number of soldiers broke off to head east toward Khazaran, the sharpshooters with their precision rifles among them. Guards once more opened the Great West Gate. Immediately beyond it now stood the bek's army. So many were mounted on mechanical horses, a dense black fog of exhaust obscured the machines' hooves in the night. Dark riders hovered in the darkness. At the rear of their line, almost touching the city walls, ex-Mensheviki tanks loomed and moto-trucks were scattered as if dropped from the air. A mechanical horse lay on its side, access hatches open, a foot soldier stripping it for parts by the light of an electric torch. Esther could not see the enemy army, though she could hear the KAF readying itself in the Atil behind her. At that moment, no aeroships seemed to be aloft. All the fighting was on the ground. Except that nearly all the machines she could see were petrol-powered, this might have been any front in any war in the past millennium. Esther thought of the Frankish general death-marching his ill-prepared troops into Rus. The Great Europaean War, which had thrown the whole distant west into turmoil and spurred the production of Khazaria's mechanical horse fleet. She thought of the myriad attacks, by hostile tribes and governments, her ancestors had beaten back from this soil. She quietly sang a *Shehekhiyanu*. Blessed was the Lord, her God, for sustaining her and allowing her to reach this season. She shouted the order for the aerocycles to rise and the golems to march forward to fight.

The aerocycles churned up a cloud of dust as they lifted into the air. Their menace grew at night, like bats. Through the gaps between horses and men, Esther saw the golems load bolts into their crossbows, lift their maces, point their bayonets forward as they began to march.

The enemy they faced was too far off, and too obscured by darkness and dust, to see clearly. Esther heard rather than saw their pointy-winged aerocraft overhead, and felt the impact of bombs dropping over the troops before her.

To Shimon, she said, "Menakhem is right. We're all going to die." He didn't answer. "I can't see anything."

"It'll soon enough be morning." Would it really? The evening and night had rushed past. "You'll be able to see more from the guard tower. I'll watch Seleme. Go quickly."

She cut the engine and slid down. No nobleman—no one of Shimon's acquaintance—would leave a riderless horse in the midst of battle. Not even on a busy street. Knowing this, Esther ran to seek admittance and climb the ladder to the guard tower. One of the guards grabbed her arm to pull her in; no worry about *negiah* here. He stared at her, as if he had not believed, until that moment, that the kender's daughter would take part in the battle. The less awestruck guard shoved a military field glass into her hands, and moved aside so she could crouch to the viewing slit.

The Germanii had devices to see in the dark. Khazar forces did not. Still, Esther's eyes were adjusting. The aerocycles' double wings beat, scattering debris on the ground. Esther could just make out the darker dark of another supply line snaking down from the north and the enemy army, through clouds of swirling dust and the bright blasts of weapons firing. In front, they had sent motorcycles with thick, studded tires. Then infantry, weary men in dark, ragged uniforms. Behind them cavalry, and in the far distance, in a broad swath, tanks. Aeroplanes above, flying eastward toward the city.

Aerocycles moved with a strange elegance. They reminded Esther of something she'd seen when her father had taken his children to an operatic performance, imported at great expense from some theater in Europa. Understanding none of the words, Esther had yet been enchanted when a queenly figure had dropped from the fly loft to hang upon a horned moon and sing. Later, the moon had glided across the sky with a ghost ship's stately grace. The aerocycles slid forward into the sky that same way. Of the golems on the ground, she saw one swing a flail above his head. His posture was casual, as if the flail weighed nothing. The weapon's proximity did not disturb other golems around him.

Esther's nose and throat burned. She wanted to put on the gas mask to keep out the fumes, but couldn't bring herself to. She couldn't see far enough ahead to witness her army's effect on the enemy—but she could hear it. Her own soldiers shouted oaths and taunts, raised weapons, knelt to fire. Though at that moment, she could not see how Khazar forces could defeat such a huge and well-equipped army, she imagined surprise and confusion in the foreign sounds of the Germani tongue. Now she could see the Germani infantry. Men in front looked at one another and shouted before backing up into those behind them. Esther thanked the guards, scrambled back down the ladder, and returned to remount Seleme.

Shimon craned his neck to spot her. All around him, troops had begun to move forward. Esther leaped onto Seleme and started the engine. She had never felt smaller than she did astride this powerful war machine, its engine even in repose thrumming so powerfully. Her body shook as if with palsy. Her unchanged woman's body.

"It's hopeless," she told him.

"Don't say that."

Ya'el sat mounted a little ways down the line. As if she had read Esther's thoughts about womanhood, she began to unwind the knot that bound her headscarf. She held both arms up, akimbo, to work at it. Once she untied the knot, the scarf's two long ends fell down her back and released the yellow hair, longer than the scarf itself. Both armies surged with motion and sound, but people around Ya'el paused to watch her. She folded the scarf. Ya'el's bright hair—the brightest object around—stayed in one place, plastered to her head by days unwashed in the scarf, sticking in a solid mass to her back, marked with ridges where it had been bound. This hair was dull, unclean. It didn't glint in the dim light like a field of ripe grain. Nevertheless, it seized Esther's breath in her chest. Ya'el was beautiful astride her machine, but what stopped Esther still was seeing her hair exposed. This was one of the great taboos for married Jewish women, apparently even for Karaites. To display one's hair in public was to tempt the eyes of men, to dishonor oneself and one's husband. Once Esther married Shimon, no one but he, their future children, and her siblings would ever see her black hair again. Some commandments a person might flaunt in rebellion, as when Shmuel had once slipped across the river to the market in Khazaran, stuffed his *kippah* in his pocket, and wolfed down a steamed pork bun at a Mongol baker's stall. But this was something a married woman did not do.

Even as the army surged forward, Amit drove Akbar toward Ya'el, the horse's engine whining at being wound too high in first gear. The machine shuddered and stalled when he braked. "What are you doing?" he barked more than asked. "Cover your head."

Ya'el leaned to her golem horse's side and stuffed the folded scarf beneath her saddlebag's flap. She sat upright again.

Esther called out, "Move forward!"

Amit jumped on Akbar's kick-starter. The engine didn't turn over. He needed to open up the choke, but seemed too angry to think of this. Ya'el kept one hand behind her on the saddlebag. Something far off exploded, a bomb in the city or by the riverbank. People shouted oaths in Turc and Khazar.

"Move forward!" Esther called again.

Amit struggled to start his engine. Shimon, who had stayed by Seleme all this while, said, "Blessed are You, Adonai our God, King of all that is," then fell silent. All prayers began this way. It wasn't unusual of him to say this, yet a handful of people near him stopped to listen. Artillery boomed loud around them. Then he started up again in the middle of one of the psalms: " 'But You, Adonai, are a shield for me; my glory, and the lifter up of my head. I cried unto Adonai with my voice, and He heard me out of His holy hill. *Selah.*' "

"*Selah!*" said someone nearby. Everyone around them was moving into the battle.

" 'I laid me down and slept; I awakened; for Adonai sustained me.

I will not be afraid of ten thousands of people that have set themselves against me round about. Arise, Adonai; save me, O my God: for You have smitten all my enemies upon the cheekbone; You have broken the teeth of the ungodly. Salvation belongs unto the Lord: Your blessing is upon Your people. *Selah.*'"

Another bomb went off.

"*Selah. Selah.*" The word blew around them like a breeze through a forest. Esther said, "*Ameyn.*"

Shimon's beautiful prayer: insufficient. When Khannah had begged Hashem for a son, no one knew what her text had been, yet the Lord had heard her and granted her desire. When Esther had knelt in the *mikvah*, her faith and words had been strong enough to achieve something, but too weak to achieve the change she sought. Fervently now, in her mind, she asked the Lord to grant them victory, and to keep her and those she loved safe. The other side's soldiers must also have offered prayers. But Hashem was *El Elohim*, the God of gods. No other nation's god could match Him. Why had He not given Khazaria an army that reflected His might?

Esther rode into the midst of her human troops as they went forth to join the golems and the bek's forces. Seleme lunged at people she passed. Esther thought she glimpsed the bek himself, his bright red beard, his short blue fighting tunic. Whoever he was raised a hand toward Esther, then disappeared amongst other people. Seleme bared her teeth, pricked her ears, her head high and taut. Esther kept a firm hold on the handlebars to prevent her biting their own troops.

The enemy's infantry volleyed forth barbaric yells as they plunged into the engagement, weapons held high in menace. Still, golems frightened the human soldiers. The creatures the kabbalists had made were much taller than natural men, and though Esther had grown accustomed to their looks in her weeks with them, she knew that to the enemy soldiers they must have looked uncanny, especially before dawn. Humans—even trained soldiers—backed up or ducked when guns confronted them at short range. Golems kept pressing forward. An enemy soldier might shoot a golem or stab him with a bayonet, and he might leave a hole or flake off bits of clay. Yet to superficial wounds, the golems did not respond, retaliating instead with methodical dispassion. She saw one bludgeon a foe long past the point at which a human would have given him up for dead. Meanwhile, as the enemy soldiers tried to fight these beings, the aerocycles overhead distracted them. Aerocycles moved slowly, and must have appeared laughably antique compared to the sleek Germani war machines. Yet their motion was unpredictable. Snipers on the ground tried to pick them off, but it was hard to disable the golem pilots. Even when rifle fire damaged the wings, the machines could wobble aloft. The airborne golems, meanwhile, shot at people on the ground. Their aim was good, their arms emotionless and steady and their vision unmarred by the many afflictions of human sight.

As dawn began to break, the enemy's cavalry, mounted on natural horses, closed in behind their infantry. Soldiers pressed forward through the dust-choked air, the fertile land to Atil's west invisible. A throng of bodies swarmed over it like a plague. Tanks massed behind the men and beasts to provide covering fire. Their treads creaked, clanked, shook the ground as the leviathans inched forward. As they became more visible, they swiveled their long noses, drew back, spat out volleys that whistled over the soldiers with tight tails of smoke in their wake. When the gunmen's heads popped out of hatches, they looked minuscule. To Esther, who compared the tanks to mechanical horses, these machines seemed awkward and slow, but the damage each shot could do was worth the ponderousness of firing it, what must have been the remarkable difficulty of moving the machine so far from its homeland. Men scattered like sparrows from their probable points of impact. Those not lucky enough to escape gave piercing shouts of pain, anger, surprise. Comrades hurried to pull those who could be saved to the back of the line. And did the monstrous treads simply run over people, beasts, smaller machines? Esther dreaded the sight, watched for it.

As Seleme walked in first gear through the chaos for which she'd been built, Esther heard a man's jubilant laughter. When she turned to look, she saw his left leg missing below the knee. He leaned back against a fellow soldier's fallen form, regarding the limb's novel relation to the rest of his body. Another man, hit in the groin, shouted in a hoarse voice as bright blood spouted in an arc from his leg. As the blood fell, it pooled and glistened on the dark mud, then seeped into the ground. Esther took her left hand off her shifter, freed her pistol, unlocked the safety and cocked it. She rested her hand on the shifter with the butt of the live gun between them. The weapon seemed meaningless compared to the destruction around her. At the same time, she hoped she wouldn't kill herself or someone near her by accident.

In front of the line of tanks, some of the enemy's rearmost infantry fired machine guns up over the heads of their front lines, their bursts like a chorus of deranged woodpeckers. Esther had not studied machine guns with her Uyghur teachers, but could tell that the adversaries had better guns: They seldom jammed, they fired faster, their belts of ammunition were longer. The bek's army had also set up machine guns on low tripods, behind sandbag embankments. The gunners lay sprawled prone as they shot. Spent cartridges cascaded from the guns' sides, a delicate plink. As the day continued to brighten, Esther realized she had lost track of everyone's whereabouts—she hadn't seen Shmuel since the engagement began. She saw how the enemy shrank from the golems and aerocycles even as their army continued toward the West Gate. To those near her, she called out, "Men with rifles and crossbows can slide in around the golems and pick off the inattentive. Now!"

Someone called back, "We should get the tank gunners if we can."

Soldiers with rifles sped around the golems to crouch down or take cover on their bellies. As the golems pressed forward, these riflemen sniped at the enemy soldiers they drove back. Some of the drab-suited men fell to the ground at once. Others paused, dazed or assessing the scope of their injuries, then continued on. One man kept firing after his ear blew off, his mouth frozen in a rictus. Crossbow-wielding Uyghurs stayed mounted on their mechanical horses, their weapons too heavy to aim and fire on the run. Yet they were such skilled riders, they could dart in and around, stop on a moment's notice, brace the crossbow between the horse's sharp ears, and fire a bolt. Each time, the man would shout an oath in his native language and let the bolt fly with a mechanical clank and a rocket-like rush of wind. The shots rose parabolically into the air, just missing the aerocycles' pedals, and returned with remarkable accuracy. One drove straight into a hatless man's exposed crown.

Esther had her knife in her boot, inaccessible to her right hand, and the six bullets in the chamber of the gun. A hundred more bullets in a pouch slung across her body. She had Seleme, who would kick or trample any opponent, human, animal, or machine. If she was to fight at all, it would be hand to hand, at close range. As she kept riding forward, she also skirted toward the side of the battle to try to see it better. All the way, she called out encouragement to her soldiers and the bek's, hoping her voice would carry.

The deeper she traveled into the thick of the battle, the less she could see. She glimpsed parts in motion, and bullets and bolts as they sped by. These missiles, and those the enemy fired at them, rushed past so close, she could feel the breath of their flight. Each shot that came close enough momentarily shut down her hearing in one ear. As the enemy soldiers joined with the Khazars, they looked warily around, trying to make sense of what faced them. Motorcycles might travel swiftly on Europa's paved roads, but lacking Khazar studded tires, they skidded on cobblestones and in mud. And they couldn't run right over the Khazar front lines—not in the way mechanical horses were trampling Germania's. The golems also made the drivers swerve, lose focus. When their infantry drew up behind and between the motorcycles, they stood close enough for Esther to make out individual features: a cleft in a chin, a nose once broken and ill reset, meaningless insignia on collars, epaulets. She was now close enough to fire on these people. But as she sighted a man between Seleme's upright ears, his expression changed from menace to bald interest, and he shouted at a comrade in a sharp, guttural burst. When Esther glanced to see what had excited him, she saw Ya'el approaching him on her golem horse. Filthy as it was, her hair appeared bright in the gloom of battle, more so as she and Esther were the only women in sight. One foreign soldier addressed Ya'el. Esther couldn't hear him. Ya'el lifted her rifle and shot him between the eyes.

Ya'el rode into the midst of soldiers running and firing their weapons. She guided her horse to walk right over one, which made her seem ruthless as a band of Uyghurs out patrolling their oil field. Her ferocity made Esther wonder why the bek didn't recruit Karaites, religious differences or no. Someone hurled a grenade at Esther. She ducked by instinct before she saw it coming. It exploded some distance behind her, throwing a rider from his horse. A man grabbed hold of her foot and she kicked him before thinking to fire the pistol. So much for the injunction not to touch a man outside one's family. Before he could yank her off Seleme, a troop of golems moved with their usual deliberation in front of her. One pried the man off her foot. "Get back," he said to her, his voice low and even. A foreign soldier startled, dropping his rifle, which a nearby golem calmly lifted before bringing it down hard on the man's head. Up close, the golems stood a head taller than the tallest soldier, twice as broad as the most solid. The savage effects of their maces and clubs seemed eerie, coupled with their inscrutable calm. They had been almost gentlemanly in their attack on the bek's palace. Esther didn't know what she'd expected, but felt half revolted, half elated to watch one club an adversary over the head until the man's knees buckled and he sank into the mud like a pile. The Germanii shot at the golems, swiped at them with knives, stabbed them with bayonets, and the golems kept moving despite superficial damage. A few soldiers tried to turn and run back, but their own cavalry kept closing in behind them, forcing them into battle.

Though these events unfolded over mere seconds, Esther witnessed them with the bright clarity of a dream. "Get back," the golem said again in his monotone, but she itched to fight. At such close range, her aim with the pistol was good, and she managed to wound a man in the arm and another in the shoulder while still steering Seleme.

But as she aimed to shoot her fourth bullet, someone came up from behind, grabbed Seleme's right handlebar, and torqued it hard to the right. Nothing like this had ever happened—under normal driving conditions, such a move was unthinkable—and Esther's mind seized with panic as she tried to think how to keep the horse from stalling as she banked into the tight turn and headed back toward the city wall. The person had acted so quickly, Esther lost her grip on the throttle, but whoever this was, he was an expert enough driver to keep both horses—Seleme and his own—in motion. She wondered if she should stall the machine to keep from being dragged away. Seleme was trying to bite the person, though she couldn't reach him with his hand on the handlebar. It would be undignified to call for help. Why weren't the golems watching her now, and why hadn't they intervened? Bullets whizzed overhead, people shouted in multiple languages, enemy aeroplanes shot eastward, low enough to churn up the dust and lift hats off heads. In the midst of this, Esther collected herself enough to take in who had grabbed her: one of the bek's own men, she was startled to see, a blue silk strip at the bottom of his tunic.

"Where are you taking me?" she yelled at him. By now, she had neither hand on Seleme's controls, her pistol aimed at the man.

"Put that away. I won't harm you. I'm under orders."

Though his voice was raised, his tone stayed calm. She noticed how he piloted the two horses at once: one hand on each throttle, none on a shifter. Both horses trotted in second gear, their engines in turn racing and guttering, on the edge of a stall. "Let me go and I'll follow you," she said, leaning toward him so he could hear. As he looked her over, his eyes narrowed, lingering on the gun. Then he let go and began to weave toward the city walls. Esther had a choice now. She could turn back. But she kept following him. She wanted to know why he'd grabbed her. All around, bullets continued to fire and shells exploded. These felt more threatening when she couldn't see them. She still had her gun at the ready.

They wove around skirmishes, around clusters of men strategizing and working together. To avoid them required skill and attention.

Esther wondered how Itakh fared on clunky old Leyla. The farther toward the gate they drove, the more men they passed rushing into battle. KAF aerocraft lifted off the carriers in the Khazar Sea, machine guns firing at the enemy's bombers, which dropped missiles seemingly at random. By Hashem's will, Seleme did not trot into the path of a bomb. Soon enough, they'd decimate the city. Where were all the old people and children? Hidden in cellars, Esther hoped, or fled to the countryside. The kaganate's aerocraft bore its blue and gold insignia, representing faith and the willingness to fight. Seeing this sign overhead lent her courage. "Where are we going?" she demanded, though she doubted the soldier, riding in front of her, could hear her words.

"The bek," he called back.

The last she'd seen him was in the battle. He had now, however, set up a base of operations outside the western gate. Under the open sky, he stood surrounded by uniformed men, shouting and gesticulating. A telegraph tapped away, a soldier hunkered down close to it so as not to miss a signal. Natan still had Esther's, but she had lost track of him. A field radio barked tinny words between stretches of static. Beside it, a man crouched, adjusting its tuner and cocking his ear toward it for improvements. The bek had brought her here to discuss strategy. Esther flushed with purpose and sat straighter in her saddle. Nearby, golems worked on damaged mechanical horses.

"Sir! Esther bat Josephus," her companion said. He turned off his horse. The battle continued loud around them.

"Good, good," the bek replied, not looking up from his map.

Receiving no further instruction, Esther turned off Seleme and dismounted. Solid ground seemed to vibrate, her legs wobbly. The KAF could not hold the enemy aerocraft back as they bombed the city and the carriers in the port. The ground shook, every minute anew. As if he couldn't feel this, the bek concentrated on the pins on his map.

"Sir?" she said.

His eyes ranged over the colorful document.

"The enemy is gaining ground," she said.

367

"I'm not a fool, Esther. I'm not blind."

She didn't understand his tone. "While you've been back here plotting, I've been in the midst of it. The golems and the aerocycles are doing good work. Despite their superior numbers, the enemy can't figure out how to fight them."

"That's something." He brushed his fingers over some of the pins. The telegraph operator raced up with a written message. The bek snatched it from his hands.

"And I saw a new Uyghur supply line arrive at dawn."

He didn't respond.

"There's the question of paying their leader." She knew it wasn't right to bring this up now, but neither did she think it was appropriate of the bek to take Göktürk's aid without arranging payment. The noise of battle distracted her, but she held on to the argument's thread. "Sir?"

He held up a warning finger. "Not now."

Esther bristled, but waited until he barked at the operator and lowered his finger, his eyes on her. "Why have you brought me here, if not to discuss strategy?"

He drew his head back on his neck, as if affronted. "I promised your father I'd try to keep you from harm. Someone is out searching for your brother." He scanned the written message again.

Esther heard his words without understanding them. She hadn't regained her land legs. Shells and grenades exploded, men shouted, bombs shook the ground, and part of the city wall toppled off, narrowly missing the telegraph operator's head. She heard the firecracker pops of small ordnance. Then she began to understand. She had raised this army and subdued the bek's palace with it, but that had not convinced him to let her and her forces fight. He was desperate, and he had struck a bargain with her father. She had begun to think that, if the God of her fathers had failed to heed her literal prayer in the *mikvah*, He had at least allowed a girl to do something extraordinary. Now she saw this was not so. The bek might not even pay the Uyghurs for their oil, men, and weapons. No better than a pickpocket.

"Enough," he said. "You've done good work. I'll have you escorted to your sister if there's a moment when it seems safe." He glanced around with the distracted, peevish air of a man accustomed to having his wishes met. "Someone bring the kender's daughter a pair of field glasses, so she can watch."

Tears stung like ammonia behind the bridge of Esther's nose, and a terrible rage burned in her breastbone. She had a knife in her boot— the knife with which she'd slain the *volkelake*—and the loaded pistol in her left hand. Still three bullets in the gun. Against her heart, she wore the greasy lock of the *volkelake*'s hair and Rukhl's tarnished *hamsa*. She could murder the bek. She was close enough, unimpeded. But this would not help Khazaria. And before she could act, the man who'd seized her at the front handed her a pair of field glasses. He was redheaded in a typical Khazar way, and he looked like his one desire was to do this task well, to please the highborn girl. She took the glasses without thanking him and sighted into the battle. When she bent the field glasses to fit her, it felt as if she were folding a small, heavy bird in half by its wings. She adjusted the geared focus knob and looked out.

Most of what she saw was chaos. Men from the two armies sped in bursts from place to place, grappled with one another when they met. A haze of smoke, exhaust, and debris hung over everything, as did the smells of burning fuel and saltpeter. Seen with natural vision, the battle was a panorama, a roiling, shifting scene of struggle unfolding. The field glasses narrowed her eyes to a single point, shutting out what lay beyond. This made the narrative difficult to follow. The twitching, muddy pant leg and boot of an enemy soldier—was it attached to a living man? She had to shift her view to see. The huge, severed right arm of a golem. A bomb would have had to hit him to detach it. She swooped the glasses up and down, but did not see the maimed being. One arm missing, it might have kept fighting.

Struggling with the device's narrow focus, she scanned the scene in search of those she loved. There was Amit, separated from his horse. He wielded a sword with two hands, struck at an enemy's rifle. The man tackled him to the ground and they struggled, a trained soldier and a person who'd devoted his life to esoteric study. Esther watched with the same horrified fascination with which she'd watch herself bleed. The whine of incoming bombers overhead captured her attention for no more than a second, after which she could no longer find Amit.

The glass focused her eyes on a golem, who shot an enemy at close range and did not balk when the soldier collapsed onto him. Even as he brushed the man away with one hand, he pulled a cavalry officer off a natural horse with the other. Another golem held an enemy soldier by the throat. Though the creature seemed not to exert himself, the man struggled, his face dark as a plum. One golem, shot in the shoulder, reeled from the impact as chips of him flew away, then continued walking forward as if nothing had happened. His assailant fired again, and the strange scene repeated. The soldier ducked to a new position. Yet another golem raised his blocky hand to fend off a bayonet. When the blade thrust clear through his palm, the golem stopped, yanked it free, and turned the weapon on its owner.

Esther might have expected this apparent lack of feeling. She knew the golems' behavior. Even so, it remained uncanny, something she'd expect from a machine. Mechanical horses really were machines, yet had been so well designed for malevolence, they exuded hatred and threat in their every movement. Side by side with mechanical horses, the golems appeared soulless. However the kabbalists had animated them, they lacked *neshamot*, the spirits that made people people. They lacked even the kind of spirit that made a bird a bird. At the same time, they yearned, as people did, to know Hashem. Esther struggled to square these facts with each other. This was Shabbat— the time to consider such questions. But the din all around prevented her from thinking the thought through to completion.

With the mud and gore, she couldn't always be certain which side men were fighting for. The enemy soldiers' round, brimmed helmets helped to distinguish them. She caught a momentary sight line into the distance, and an enemy tank exploded far off. By instinct, Esther jumped back from the yellow, orange, and blue flash. By the time the thundering boom ensued, she watched with her naked eyes, trying to see what had happened through the haze of black smoke. When she brought the glass to her eyes, she once again lost her bearings for a moment. "How am I to lead my army if I don't even know what's where?" she asked herself. She tried to shift her position closer to the bek's field radio, to see if she could glean any scraps of information. Far in the distance, she saw a man's head rise out of a tank into the open air and peer around. He wore epaulets and numerous insignia, no helmet, and his gaze was calm despite the chaos around him. Esther's heart leaped to think she might have spied General Boulos, the leader of this Panzer army. Before she could scrutinize his face, he retreated and the tank closed, now indistinguishable from all the others around it.

The field glasses stumbled on a view of Itakh. He sat astride Leyla, leaned to the left as he gripped her awkward shifter, and drove her hard toward the rear of the line. His clothing hung in tatters. Either he was covered in mud or dried blood stained his shirt. He bent low over the horn of Leyla's saddle. Even as Esther's heart hammered with worry for him, she felt their nomadic ancestors would be proud to see him. She raised her free hand and hollered to him, though he couldn't hear her from this distance.

Yet at that moment, he jerked upright. Whether he'd been hit and lost his grip on throttle and shifter, or whether Leyla had been struck or had stumbled, Esther couldn't see. For a moment, Leyla seemed suspended in a pitch toward the ground, and Itakh hung above and slightly in front of her, crouched and still. Then Itakh rolled forward over the horse, who spilled on top of him the next instant.

Esther was running before she had any sense she was in motion. She lacked breath the same way she once had after falling off a high garden wall. As soon as she could breathe, she shouted, "Itakh! Itakh!" though the wind and the noise of the battlefield pushed his name back in her face. She couldn't see him. The field glasses had given such a narrow view, it was difficult to tell where he'd fallen.

Someone called, "Esther bat Josephus! Esther bat Kender!" behind her, but she ran as fast as her legs and burning lungs would take her. She didn't look back. "Stop!" he yelled. When she didn't, he grabbed her arm and brought her tumbling to the ground. A sharp pain shot through her shoulder—he might have yanked it from its socket—and her knee cracked against a rock. Her kneecap was on fire. It might have been broken. She tried to stand on the painful leg, shook the man's arm off, and turned to face him. The same redheaded soldier who'd grabbed her before. His freckled face was flush with exertion, embarrassment. "I'm sorry I touched you," he said, his body coiled to spring at her again if she bolted. "I can't allow you into battle. Did I hurt you?"

Until the month of Av, Esther had been, despite her interest in mechanical horses and her trips to the camp, a person who prayed behind the *mekhitzah*, studied her tutor's lessons, would marry Shimon when the holidays all ended in Tishri. That person wanted to argue that breaking *negiah* was worse than letting her fight. But her heart wasn't in it. Any thought other than what had happened to Itakh and how she could help him stalled out. Her knee, bleeding inside her trousers, ached and stung. She tried flexing and extending her leg. This hurt, but nothing was torn or broken. A shell exploded, close enough to rain debris on them. They both ducked. There was a sudden stink of bad eggs. "I have to go," she told him.

She started off again, though she limped now and had lost her bearings. A quick, soft whistle sounded near her right ear, and a moment later, a shell hit a distance in front of her, blowing up a spray of dirt and gravel like a geyser. The force of its impact pushed Esther back. The adjutant must have been less fazed, less deafened by the impact, because he seized the opportunity to grab her long, dirty hair and pull her by it back toward the bek's command center.

The sharp, bright pain all over her scalp made Esther cry out.

"I'm sorry," he said, then prayed under his breath, she couldn't tell what for.

Her first impulse, as she stumbled after him, was to reach her hands to her head. This did nothing. Here she was, in the midst of the battle she'd longed for, and the pain of being dragged by the hair was too much for her? By instinct she groped into her boot and retrieved her knife. The hair was pulled taut. Esther began to slice through it.

Esther's hair was thick and greasy. It fell free in chunks, her scalp stinging anew in each place from the release of pressure. When she sliced through the last of it, she lost her balance, but soon righted herself and began to run. Her head felt strange, buoyant without the excess weight. The hair had never before been cut. She was surprised at how novel it felt for the ends to tickle her collarbone instead of the small of her back. The battle was a jumble of bodies, machines, powder, blood, smoke. But she would find Itakh.

The adjutant must have called for help, because two of them now closed in from behind and tackled Esther to the ground. Her chin thudded against the earth and her top and bottom teeth cracked into each other. One man drew her wrists together and bound them, just as the bek had done in his palace. She wasn't strong enough to break free. The one whose voice she recognized said, "May the Great Name forgive us."

He gripped her forearm as he steered her back toward the bek. Esther wondered if all this contact would mean he'd have to immerse himself later. Where did one purify oneself, in the midst of battle?

In the time she'd been gone, the bek had retreated to the guard tower. Somehow the Khazar forces had held the enemy soldiers back from the city itself thus far, but bombers were already maiming it and fighting would soon burst into the streets. The adjutant unbound her hands and jabbed her back until she began climbing the rope ladder toward the bek. Once she fell inside, her keeper bound her again, pressed on her shoulder, and forced her to sit down in the cramped space. He also pulled the ladder up behind them. The bek cast a dark glance her way and continued shouting out orders. "Inside the walls," he was saying. "Snipers in the high buildings. We'll have some advantage in our winding streets."

"I've already done that," Esther said. "I have sharpshooters positioned here and in Khazaran."

Bek Admon gave her a cat's peevish, dismissive stare, then turned back to the men he'd been addressing, gave his commands more quietly so she couldn't hear.

Would they open the gates to allow their own soldiers inside? They'd been built to keep Khazaria's innumerable enemies out. Esther couldn't stand the thought of opening them wide to admit their foes.

When she looked down, she marveled at how the odd chunks of her hair now swung free near her shoulders. The adjutant sat beside her and pulled something from his pocket: a squat wild apple, yellow and freckled, one cheek blushing pink. He unfolded a bone-handled pocket knife—Shmuel had one like it, one of his treasures—halved and quartered the fruit, and with two cuts, took out the seeded core of the first piece. He held it out for Esther to eat.

His gesture of kindness surprised her. Either from smoke or exhaustion, his fair eyelids looked itchy and red. Esther's own eyes teared in sympathy, though she knew nothing about this person, not even his name. She whispered the prescribed blessing for fruit, for the fruit of the earth: "*Barukh atah Adonai, eloheinu melekh ha'olam, borei p'ri Ha-eitz. Ameyn.*"

When she bit in, the apple was tart, mealy, nothing like the cultivated apples at the kender's table. She couldn't imagine where he'd gotten it. Despite its taste, she ate so hungrily she almost choked.

The adjutant, coring another piece, glanced at her and laughed. "More?"

"If you have it to spare."

He fed her each piece in turn, though he too must have been hungry. "Only a few weeks till we dip them in honey to celebrate the sweet New Year, *Barukh Hashem.*"

"*Barukh Hashem,*" Esther repeated, though the words caught in her throat. Without warning, her face grew hot and she began to cry. The New Year might bring apples in date honey and her *khuppah,* or the enemy that now clamored at the gate. If tales from the refugee camp were true, their conquerors might put everyone on Khazar soil to death. "*Barukh Hashem.*" Half-chewed apple drew saliva to Esther's mouth. She did not want to cry in front of this stranger and the bek, yet her heart ached for her homeland, for the Holy One's people, *Yisrael,* for her beloved friend Itakh. These must have been the tears that Khannah had cried at the Temple gates, the tears her own namesake had cried before King Ahasuerus, goading him to bring down Haman the Agagite, enemy of the Jews. These tears had flowed since Avram had heeded the Great Name's call in the desert—*"Hineni!* Here I am!"

But for Esther, they quieted. When she bent her head to wipe her face on her shoulder, the adjutant pulled a handkerchief from his pocket and held it out so she could blow her nose. Then he handed her his water skin. The water was warm, but she drank it down. After she finished, she asked his name.

"Tarkhan ben Yirmiyahu."

One rarely heard such an old-fashioned steppe name. "Esther bat Josephus. You knew that."

He nodded.

Together they knelt and peered through a slit as the bek's troops retreated and the enemy pressed toward the gate. In the crater left by a bomb, she saw blood, a severed head, a golem's upper body, separated from its legs and with one hand missing. She looked around in a panic for the rest of both beings. The human soldier must have been torn to bits, but she saw one of the golem's legs a distance off. Perhaps the rest of his body had shattered into shards. "Holy Shekhinah," she said under her breath. Though golems had seemed invincible fighters, no part of this one moved. A bomb could destroy one as easily as a kabbalist, she shuddered to see.

The leather pouch and Rukhl's *hamsa,* tucked inside her shirt, began to make her itch, both objects steeped in her sweat. Their tingle sparked two memories. First, the feeling of the *volkelake's* windpipe giving way under her hand and her blade. Second, the thought of Rukhl and her countrymen making the same trek these enemy troops had made to cross Khazaria and seek refuge in its capital.

"A word," she called to the bek. He glanced up from his map as if he'd forgotten she existed. "I need my horse. Have you been to the refugee camp to gather volunteers?"

He winced. "I command a regular army."

"I command one of people and golems. The refugees have all fled the menace of"—what to call him?—"may his name be obliterated, like Haman's. They can wield knives and guns." He looked pained. "If you won't let me fight, I can at least bring them to you. I'm no safer up here than anyplace else in the city, and with God beside me, I will not be hurt." Her whole body urged her to spit on the ground to ward off the Evil Eye, but if she did it, her case would be lost. As the bek delayed, the guard tower shook with the force of explosions and of Khazar troops streaming through the gate.

"Tarkhan," he said. "Accompany her. Stay inside the city walls until you reach the North Gate. You know where to find the camp?"

In telling her father that she'd stolen Seleme and his money, she hadn't confessed to everything. Perhaps her smaller thefts, and her many visits to the camp, remained unknown. She said, "I do."

He waved the back of his hand at Tarkhan. "Untie her." To one of his adjutants he said, "Find their horses. Be quick."

Tarkhan slipped his knife under the knot and pulled up to slice through it, as he had done with the apple. A dagger of cold shot down Esther's arms as they fell free, the bruised shoulder throbbing. Her wrists tingled. The apple had only made her feel lightheaded from hunger. Her knee was swelling. But she scrambled down the ladder into the chaos of the two Khazar armies choking Atil's streets. Before long, the bek's man came toward them riding Tarkhan's horse. "Yours is there," he said to Esther, pointing around a corner. She jumped up pillion behind Tarkhan, and they wove through the crowd. She slipped from his saddle straight into Seleme's, and felt a rush of pride as she let out the choke and the engine roared to life. A golem with a fuel can stepped back, respectful. As soon as she could turn Seleme in the press of machines and moving bodies, they headed north.

CHAPTER 29

Soldiers and mechanical cavalry clogged the streets. Every window had its curtains drawn or cardboard or wood nailed over the panes. High up on apartment roofs and turrets, snipers readied themselves, scoping out positions and camouflaging their guns. Seleme, her nerves on edge, nipped at every horse they passed. Esther tried to keep her moving in low gear, but progress was slow. As they wound through the streets, she saw that all the soldiers were human. The bek must have kept the golems back as a last defense against the approaching enemy. The Great Library and Kalonymos's synagogue, when they wound past them, had concrete barriers around their perimeters. These would be meaningless, Esther knew, against tanks. She thought of the library's hundreds of thousands of books on fire and swung around into a side street as aerocraft zoomed overhead. What unnerved Esther most about the state of her city was how empty it seemed of ordinary people. Everyone had fled to the countryside or taken cover. She'd seen not one pedestrian, not a single civilian moto-cart. Stray cats darted through the streets, their heads down as if afraid of being caught in a bad act. Across the river in Khazaran, Esther imagined the market stalls empty, still bearing the smells of rotten vegetables and day-old fish. Some houses were already falling in, craters bombed through their roofs or into the pavement. Throughout it, the bek's and Esther's troops moved into position as she and Tarkhan sped past.

One guard at the North Gate didn't want to let them pass. "You're safer inside," he told her.

"We're on a mission from the bek. We have to get to the refugee camp."

He scratched his nose with the back of his hand. "Every other time you've gone, you weren't supposed to be there."

She hadn't known the guards thought about what she did. "I am now." She saw Tarkhan wondering, but there wasn't time to explain.

He came down the ladder. As they passed, he said, *"Allah yardımcınız olsun,"* a blessing she was glad to accept.

From outside the gates, they had a better view of the river and the Khazar Sea, both full of warships and aerocraft carriers. Though aeroplanes continued to buzz overhead, the cloud of debris that had surrounded them on the streets soon began to clear. Beneath the exhaust that coated her nostrils, Esther could smell the fresh air. If she could just ignore the sounds of engines, the area north of the capital seemed as peaceful as it must have when her ancestors had left the city to enjoy the harvest landscape. She and Tarkhan shifted up to a fourth-gear gallop. He was a good horseman, she noticed as she raced on. He crouched over his machine with native ease.

Esther no longer marveled, as she had in the early days, over how the refugee camp looked, a hodgepodge of yurts, tents, and shanties, some built in the local roundhouse style, others to approximate the distant villages the refugees had left behind. But approaching it now from the city side, she saw anew how big it was. Thousands of dwellings spread over the Atil's fertile plain, thick as grass over the open steppe. Were Khazaria's smaller fortified cities this large? As they rode toward it, the camp stretched beyond the horizon.

"Holy Shekhinah," Tarkhan said, and downshifted to take in the view.

"You haven't been here?" She slowed her horse to match his. Together, they descended toward the sprawling camp at the speed of people in a hurry rather than invaders.

"I'm surprised you have."

The villagers saw and heard them coming. A crowd gathered at the encampment's outskirts. Esther left Seleme idling. There wasn't time to dismount or turn her off.

"Forgive our intrusion," Tarkhan said. "The bek sent us."

Someone snorted. From another direction someone said, "You can't drive such a thing on *Shabbos*."

Esther said, "There's an exception in battle."

"It's yours to judge when there's an exception?" a man said in his thick accent.

"At this moment, we're waging a war against"—she couldn't say it; she knew the refugees were as superstitious as Khazars—"against Haman the Agagite and his forces. They've breached Atil's gates. They're within the city walls."

"May his name be obliterated," one man said, to the approval of those around him. Another said, "Who are you?"

From the crowd came Rukhl's voice, forceful and clear. "Esther bat Josephus, commander of one of the bek's armies."

The title rang in Esther's chest, behind the *volkelake*'s hair and the *hamsa*. Esther tried to catch her eye to thank her.

"She brought the *goylemim*," someone remarked, then spat on the ground. Not a good sign.

"We need your help," Esther said. "We need more people to fight."

The crowd shifted. From up above, on the horse, the movement looked like wind rippling through grass. The same man, a shapeless brown hat over his gray hair, said, "Not on the Lord's *Shabbos*."

The thought sprang to Esther's mind that every dwelling in this camp had a morsel of khallah inside, left over from the previous day's baking. Nothing could have been less appropriate, but her stomach flipped and squelched with hunger. "We're fighting now. An alliance of Khazars and Uyghurs, Jews and non-Jews, people and"—what was their pronunciation? Someone had just said it—"*golemim*." They would know what she meant. "If we pause to observe the day of rest, they'll take our city and our kaganate."

All her life—before she'd stolen Seleme and left for Yetzirah—Esther had kept the Sabbath holy, according to the Lord's command. The practice was as natural as night following day. Shabbat unfurled like a clean coverlet over Khazaria, and while those of other faiths might go about their business in Khazaran, Atil rested from its labors.

"Observing *Shabbos* is the central fact of our lives," the gray-haired man said. "How can we do otherwise?"

"*A* central fact," she replied without thinking. "The Law also enjoins us to preserve human life. Mishnah asks the question about the pious man who sees a woman, a stranger, drowning. Should he observe *negiah* and keep walking past, so he doesn't pollute himself by touching her?"

"*Neyn, neyn.*" This was a man whose long, golden forecurls were streaked with worried gray.

Silence spread around them, punctuated by the far-off whine of aerocraft and the tympani of explosions.

"I too am a Torah Jew," she said. "I observe and obey the Law. But in this instance, I must break it." She'd broken a lot of other laws while she'd been at it.

"Your bek has done little for us," the younger man said. "Left us to starve here. To starve and now, because he can't protect your borders, to die."

"That isn't true, Yussl." Again this was Rukhl. A brown headscarf made its path through the crowd like a snake through water. As she approached, her margin of coppery hair sprang into view, as did Jascha, close behind her. The toddler clung like a monkey to her hip. She walked right up to the man but didn't touch him. Was this her husband, or a brother? She wouldn't call another man by his given name. "He gave us asylum when no other country would. Isn't this enough?" She meant Esther to understand her words, or she would have said them in her native tongue.

"No," Esther answered for him. "The way we treat you is wrong. I know it's wrong. I've tried to do my tiny part to redress it, but it hasn't been enough. I don't know how to fix it." The days of bringing Rukhl stolen food had been a lifetime before. "Who fights for a country that won't let him live in its cities?" she asked herself. Tarkhan, beside her, wrinkled his forehead in concern. She wouldn't gather recruits by arguing against their cause.

She reached into her shirt and drew out her pouch and the *hamsa*. "Look," she said, a last effort. She held out the *hamsa*, black with tarnish. "This belongs to my friend in the camp. She let me borrow it for protection."

"That's Magyar work," a woman remarked to her. "How did you get it?"

The blond man turned to Rukhl and quietly said, *"Es iz deyns."* That's yours.

Esther loosened the pouch's drawstring and drew out the greasy lock of brown hair. "This," she said, "is the hair of a *volkelake* I slew out on the steppe."

She heard people draw breath over their teeth. A few people spit. Someone said, *"Sha!"*

As if she remembered that night, Seleme shifted from hoof to hoof. Esther kept a firm grip on one handlebar while continuing to hold the hair aloft. "Since I killed it," she went on, her voice louder, "I've come to think that, if I—an ordinary person, a woman at that—could slay something that Hashem himself did not create, then surely all of us together can defeat this enemy army, whatever their numbers. Surely we can triumph!"

She'd hoped her emphatic tone might make the refugees cheer. Instead, their reticence continued. Meanwhile, by the time the sun set on this Shabbat, Khazaria might be conquered.

"Will the bek arm us, if we fight for him?" asked Yussl, the fair-haired man at Rukhl's side.

"To the extent he can. If you have weapons of your own, bring them."

He didn't leap up to volunteer. No one did. Instead their hats and kerchiefs turned and they spoke to one another in their language. She understood isolated phrases. Tarkhan's face was anxious, set. The horses rumbled as the ground shook with distant bombs. After a long pause, Yussl said, "I can't speak for anyone else, but I'll join you. I forbid my wife to do as you have done." He raised his chin toward Seleme, a dismissive gesture.

Bile and fight rose in Esther's gullet. She managed to keep her horse, keep her posture, and say, "Thank you."

He touched his hat before retreating toward their tent. Others followed his lead, while still more continued to talk and argue. Tarkhan caught Esther's eye and said, "We'll get a few."

She nodded. "Better than nothing. I wish we could ask them for food."

Rukhl approached, her toddler across her hip. With her free hand, she kept a grip on Jascha's shoulder—Esther thought to keep him from joining up with his father. Jascha tried to shake her off, without force or success. His too-big hands and feet moved in a jumble. Esther slid down, the horse still idling. "Do you want your *hamsa* back?" she asked.

"You still need it."

The toddler's eyes expanded to take in the horse. "Your husband might need it too."

Rukhl's face always seemed tired, but the corners of her mouth flickered up. "All of us could use one right now. We should have kept on to Palestine."

Esther had not heard a recent report, but it was true that Palestine had stayed clear of the conflict until now.

"I wouldn't have met Itakh then," Jascha remarked. "Is he well?"

"I don't know." Her worry for him blossomed afresh.

"I'd like to come with you," he said.

Rukhl's eyes blazed. Esther said, "Your mother wouldn't forgive me. And you're too young to fight."

"Itakh isn't?"

"Itakh is a Khazar. We're born for this." The words were true, but felt hollow. She imagined him lying dead, Leyla on top of him. Trying to convince herself not to do this only made her see it more clearly.

Men began to return, bearing kitchen knives, cudgels, axes. A few came with empty hands, prepared to fight with them. The camp possessed not a single mechanical horse, but coughed up half a dozen sway-backed drays. *Better than nothing*, Esther told herself, though logic said these few recruits could not affect the conflict's outcome. She kept an eye trained overhead to make sure bombers weren't yet targeting the camp. Instead: a small flock of birds. She wasn't sure of their species, couldn't tell if they had been scared out of some roost by the tumult. She saw, however, that they weren't flying in a migratory pattern—they darted and shot, the rearmost tipped to one side as if injured. "Pigeons," she said, before realizing she recognized what they were.

Jascha at once put a hand to his mouth and whistled to them, Itakh's same calm, descending call. Not all the birds responded— even Itakh, who loved them, admitted they weren't bright—but a few began to circle down. Was that Nagehan among them? All the others were brown and gray. One looked white against the sky.

"Nagehan?" Esther called out to her. To Jascha she said, "Does she know her name?"

"I don't know." He whistled again, and the white bird landed and strutted at his feet. He scooped her up, unscrewed the message case, and handed the scroll to Esther.

"Holy Shekhinah," Esther said to herself. It was a message from a unit commander to the home loft, begging for reinforcements as the enemy breached the river. Why had the bird flown northward before delivering it? Esther wondered if the ordnance had frightened her, or if her father's pigeon loft had been destroyed. To Tarkhan she said, "We have to get back." Tarkhan shouted an order to march into the crowd. Not all the refugees spoke Khazar, so the command rippled outward in translation. Esther handed the message back to Jascha, who replaced it in the case and cast the bird aloft again.

"*Ikh vill mit dir kommen*," he said to her. Then, after watching to see if she'd understood, in Khazar: "I want to come with you."

"But you'd break your mother's heart," Esther replied. She touched his shoulder. He had grown, in the sudden way boys do. All at once they stood nearly eye to eye.

When Esther mounted again and revved Seleme's engine, it rumbled in the quiet Shabbat landscape. Nagehan remained visible only a moment, then vanished into the battle-dirty sky. The new recruits fell in behind the mechanical horses. Every man carried something, and they'd soon pass beyond the *eruv* that encircled the camp. No one mentioned the holiday except to call *"Gut Shabbos!"* to friends and family. They shouted farewells, and those left behind asked Hashem's protection on those leaving to fight. When Esther looked back, she saw first scores, then hundreds of men in a ragged line, as if trudging across the steppe to found the camp in the first place. Back along the line, people talked to one another. Snippets of song rose, some from the Shabbat liturgy, others perhaps native to the home country. But as they approached the city, the sounds of the battle grew louder, nearer. And there was its acrid stench again, there the chaos of men fighting along the riverbank. Line by line, the songs died out. Snipers shot at any birds that happened past. One fell, but Esther hoped the pigeons would get through to their home loft, if it still stood.

"Barukh Hashem, may we all live to celebrate the next Shabbat," she said.

"Ameyn," Tarkhan replied. He pulled his horse up short and patted his body for his field glasses. Esther realized she still had the pair he'd given her earlier, slung across her like a bandolier. She stopped Seleme and lifted the glass.

Smoke billowed from all over Atil. In the black-camouflaged roof of Kalonymos's synagogue, a blacker hole gaped and steamed. The enemy surrounded the city, from the northern gate to as far south as Esther could see, and all the gates had been breached. Where her view extended over the city walls, she glimpsed people skirmishing in the streets. East of the city, between Atil and Khazaran, struggling people choked the waters of the mighty Atil River, and fighting extended into the port and delta. Esther thought of Pharaoh's armies pursuing the Yisraelites into the Sea of Reeds. The shock they must have felt when the Holy One's hand closed the waters over them. He did not show Himself today. From her vantage, Esther couldn't tell who was winning or losing this battle, but the God of Yisrael was as silent as He'd been since the time of the prophets.

"*Vas kan vir tean?*" someone asked behind her. What do we do?

She turned the horse to face them. "We join the battle. We kill as many enemy soldiers as we can." The Holy Shekhinah help her. "If any of the bek's commanders give you an order, follow it. They have blue stripes on their tunics, as Tarkhan does." They narrowed their eyes at him. Distrust, memorization.

She turned Seleme, put her back in gear, and began first to walk, then to gallop, toward the river. She lost sight of everyone she'd brought with her, and thought of Itakh, trampled in a ditch west of the city walls. Her brother, she hoped, was under the bek's protection. Let him keep Shmuel in a guard tower, spare her father a broken heart. She would fight.

When Esther reached the riverbank, she saw that the enemy's cavalry horses swam, their riders waist deep in the water. Infantrymen were submerged up to their necks, their guns and ammunition held high and clear. In places, the waters of the holy river could not be seen for the throng of bodies. Tanks, massed at the river's edge, provided covering fire. Snipers on the Khazaran shore picked off enemy swimmers in the water. Some of these sank like stones while others thrashed in distress. In the fray, it was easy to see golems, who stood head and shoulders above their human adversaries. Most fought on the western shore, where they kept the enemy back. A few battled in the shallows.

The bek didn't know where she was. Until he did, he couldn't stop her. She slung the field glass back across her body with the gas mask, took her pistol in her left hand, and pointed Seleme toward the riverbank. The horse had been made for this: her steel teeth bared almost in a grin. As they walked, she bit off part of an enemy soldier's arm, her teeth closing with an awful clank. While the man recoiled, Esther shot him, then moved on.

Once in the battle's midst, she sensed that the Khazar fighters were at that moment gaining ground. From their positions, most of them in the water, they pushed their enemies back onto dry land and toward the city, shouting curses in Khazar, Uyghur, Hebrew, Turc. Golems took the lead, unafraid of what enemy guns could do to them. Uyghur fighters hacked people with war swords the size of Esther's leg. Men on golem horses moved calmly between brown-clad soldiers and shot them point-blank into the water. Though mechanical horses could not swim or wade deep, they could travel well enough in the shoals. Like Seleme, they bit at assailants, trampled them, reared. The bones of a man's cheek crumpled like eggshell beneath a scrabbling hoof. Esther wondered how long she could control her mount under these circumstances. It was as if all Seleme's wildness, the dark truth of her nature, shone forth. Until now, Esther had liked the horse—or appreciated her own mastery over its precision and speed—but the biting and Seleme's metallic growl complicated things. A bomb went off in the shallows. Esther ducked and turned Seleme hard to the right. As they stumbled away, she wished she could catch a glimpse of Amit, Shimon, or Ya'el—anyone she knew—though this was impossible with two armies clashing in the water.

Even as she dodged fire, steered, shot, Esther thought of her ancestors. Almost every one of the males had entered Avraham's bloody covenant not as an eight-day baby, but as a boy or a grown man. All the many thousands of them, men and women, had gone down to the banks of the Atil by night and immersed themselves in its frigid black waters. She saw a thousand heads emerge glossy and dark from the water, heard a thousand voices murmur the prayer of conversion. The Hebrew words must have felt like a mouthful of rocks to her ancestors' Turc-speaking tongues.

The Atil was the great Khazar river. It flowed from its origin in Rus down to this fertile delta. It had transformed a warlike tribe into a nation of Jews, and it provided the basis for trade in the east. If any of the men in the water right now was praying, its waters would surely transform him. One person's ardent prayer might transform them all.

As she surveyed the scene, Esther heard a golem's basso voice, not shouting but singing. She couldn't hear his words until a few more joined in: *"Adonai malakh tageil ha-aretz, yismikhu iyim rabim."* The Lord reigns, let the Earth rejoice. One of the psalms sung on Erev Shabbat. Esther knew its melody as well as she knew her own name. "A fire goes before Him, and burns up His enemies round about." The golems had chosen their song well. Though they weren't people, they were righteous men. *Gerim tzedek*: converts, as all Khazar Jews had once been. "Confounded be all they who serve graven images, who boast of idols. Worship Him, all ye gods."

Some kind of missile landed a few feet in front of Seleme, and in the instant before it exploded, Esther leaped off the horse by instinct and landed splayed flat on the wet, sandy banks. Though she'd folded both arms over her head and squeezed her eyes shut, she saw the bright orange flash, felt the heat of the explosion. When she sat up, wondering if this was death and then surprised at her own safety, she saw that Seleme's front end had been blown off. No longer supported by her front legs, the machine's torso rested on the ground. Where her proud neck and head had been, loose wires gaped from a smoking wound. Esther's own legs, which had been nearest the horse, burned with what must have been hundreds of tiny cuts from shrapnel that had passed through her boots and trousers. Parts of the explosive, parts of Seleme. She wanted to tend to the horse—and to take back her thoughts of not liking her—and at the same time, she scuttled along the ground to a hastily dug trench with a barricade of dirt, perhaps twenty feet long. The horse could not be helped. The horse had never, for a moment, been a living thing, though Esther felt punched by her loss. The moment her feet skidded into the bottom of the trench, Esther knew she'd hit a body. She'd climbed halfway back out before she heard someone say her name.

Esther nearly vomited in fear. But when a hand reached out to grab her boot, she recognized it as Itakh's. She crouched down beside him. "Are you all right?" she asked. One of his legs was bent under him at an unnatural angle, the other flayed open below the knee. The body lay beneath them both. "How did you get here? I saw—I thought I saw Leyla fall on you. You were—you weren't here, you were outside the city walls." His clothes hung in dirty, bloody ribbons.

"She shielded me from the blast, and I got away to fight more. Now I don't know what happened to her."

"It doesn't matter."

"Our father won't forgive me."

"It's a battle, horses are lost." Seleme. A machine, her companion. She peered out of the trench. A Uyghur was already stripping Seleme for usable parts as if she were a thing. Back in the trench, Esther asked, "Are you in pain?"

"I don't know."

From the direction of the water, someone cried out, "Gas! Gas!"

Itakh at once fumbled for the mask still tethered to his neck. She saw his fear in the clumsiness of his movements, felt it in her own body. She wasn't certain whether gas posed a more immediate danger to the skin or to the lungs, but knew she had to hurry to protect herself. A smell like horseradish permeated the air. Esther untangled her mask from over her shoulder and put it on. It was too large. The goggles gave a view out the sides more than straight ahead. But once she tightened the strap, her mouth and nose were well covered. Her breath sounded loud and tasted of rubber. "I'll be back as soon as I can."

Itakh looked like a wounded animal as she clambered out of the trench. Her head felt heavy, vulnerable.

All the bek's and Esther's human soldiers had masks, and most had put them on. Not one refugee volunteer had received one. A few, she saw at a glance, were wearing them anyway, which meant they had stripped them from fallen soldiers. Others ran headlong toward the city. One who stood dazed, she grabbed by the arm, shouting, "Get back!" Her voice was trapped inside the mask. After a moment of confusion, the soldier ran. Some who'd been close to the detonation looked stunned, as if they couldn't tell if they should flee or claw off their clothes. Natural horses whinnied in frenzy. They ran in circles and stomped the mud of the riverbank as they tried to unseat their riders. "Cover your faces and run!" Esther yelled, though her voice collected in the warm pocket protecting her nose and mouth.

Amidst the chaos the mustard gas created, the golems remained as calm as if they'd been performing their duties in Yetzirah. They might have been weeding or cleaning plates. One stripped a mask off an enemy soldier and handed it to a refugee. Others followed suit. Their voices sang snatches of individual songs, then joined together for a line here and there. Golem and mechanical horses kept charging their enemies, as if no frightful yellow cloud hung low over the water. The enemy had unleashed the gas—Khazars wouldn't use such a cowardly weapon—but Esther thought it might harm them more than it did her own forces. Most of her countrymen kept fighting, despite that it meant continuing to expose themselves to the poison. Meanwhile, the golems exposed more and more members of the enemy army to the dangerous fumes.

The cloud of gas began to disperse, lift. If Esther left her mask on, she could get below the cloud and down to the river to fight. She ran straight into the water, feeling the cold, heavy rush as her boots submerged. The water numbed her swollen knee and the many small wounds on her legs. Esther plunged in up to her waist, barely able to keep her footing in the mucky shoals. The Khazar Army had driven most of their enemies up onto the bank, but a few still straggled in the shallow water. One crouched forward, his hands braced on his thighs. His mouth hung open, as if he'd seen something unexpected in the water or vomited. When he heard Esther's approach from the side, he turned his face toward her but did not close his mouth. His watering eyes reflected the sunlight.

Had he spoken? She thought she'd seen his lips move. Esther raised her gun in her left hand, steadied it with her right. "*Gnade*," he now said clearly. His expression pled with her, and she understood his meaning without knowing the word. She stood in the waters of the holy river up to her knees. She could spare this human life. Part of her believed she should. But she aimed at his chest and fired.

His slack mouth snapped into an O. As he tried to back away, he stumbled and fell, as if sitting into a Western-style chair. He sank beneath the shallow water, and Esther stood watching the place where he'd fallen.

Both armies began to recede toward Atil. Perhaps soon they'd be back beyond the city walls in the western fields. A lone figure splashed toward Esther in the water. She aimed at it, then realized from its attire it was a Khazar fighter, one of her own, not in the bek's uniform. No face was visible behind the animal-like mask. A moment later, the water-dark clothing resolved into Shimon's.

"Esti," he said, his voice muffled by the mask. "Get back."

"We have to fight."

"Get away from the gas."

She was struck by how normal this conversation felt. "It isn't affecting me."

"It acts slowly."

The battle was moving up out of the water, into the city streets. She could still help, where she stood; there were stragglers, waiting to be shot. But she turned toward the shore and began walking. Only now did she notice the water's resistance against her legs. Once she pulled her boots free of the riverbed and stood on the bank, a cool dusk wind bit into her bones. "What time is it?" she asked Shimon. "When does the Sabbath end?"

He shook his head. Perhaps the first time in his life he hadn't known this.

They walked into the city. Now it was easy to see how many had fallen. Twisted bodies of men and horses littered the ground, as did parts of both, and parts of mechanical horses, torn apart by bullets and shells. In places, piles of bodies clogged a narrow street, and they had to detour. As bombs continued to hit and bullets to fire, teams of medics combed through the wreckage for people to save. Across the crater-pocked Central Square, a golem, missing one arm, wandered. Around the corner, another stood quietly singing, his body riddled with holes. One, supine, struggled to right himself, although one arm and most of the opposite leg were missing. "Stop," she said to Shimon. She thought she recognized the spindly intact leg. She bent down close to the creature. With a person, one gauged life by the breath, the pulse, the blink of an eye. Esther didn't know how to judge if whatever it was that animated a golem remained in its clay shell.

Was this Matityahu? The left arm had been blown away, so she could not look at the wrist to see the name. "Matityahu?" she tried, her breath hot and stale in the mask. The golem didn't respond. She thought about the *Emet* still incised on its brow. It remained animate, but if the mark of its identity had been removed, could it hear its own name? Esther knew they should wipe out its *aleph*, but as she groped in her boot for the knife, she remembered Itakh in the trench. Living, breathing. "We have to go back," she said aloud.

Shimon gestured with his open hand.

"Itakh is wounded. I can find the place."

A man in a gas mask wore no facial expression. As if he were a golem, she had to trust to his words and actions to know what he thought.

"Quickly," he said, and they headed back toward the riverfront.

The landscape had been torn up by the battle, but Esther soon found the trench. Itakh rustled as he saw them approach. When she bent down, Esther smelled the horseradish smell, faint through her mask. The gas had pooled there, as mist clings to a low-lying bog. She turned her hidden face toward Shimon. He put his hand on her shoulder to hold her back, and climbed down into the trench himself. With one arm, he reached around the boy's back; the other he threaded gingerly behind Itakh's injured knees. Itakh groaned when the broken leg came forward. Esther couldn't see his expression behind his elephant mask, but even through it she heard him suck breath over his teeth. Doing his best not to jostle Itakh, Shimon climbed out of the trench, and the three of them began to pick back through Atil, avoiding the remaining skirmishes. They heard ordnance and shouts from various quarters, but the Khazar fighters were beginning to push the enemy back toward the West Gate.

As they entered the Central Square, a pair of medics in gas masks approached them, one almost leaping to take Itakh from Shimon's arms. "Rabbi?" he asked, either unsure of his identity because of Shimon's mask, or astonished to find him in battle because of his station.

Shimon nodded. "This is Itakh ben Josephus. He has multiple injuries, and was heavily exposed to gas."

"He has a mask, at least," the man said.

"Where are you taking the wounded?"

"The hospital was bombed into rubble. We've set up temporary quarters in your father's synagogue." He stood quiet a moment, perhaps looking at them. Being unable to see anyone's expressions was disconcerting. "Were you down by the waterfront?"

Esther nodded.

He struggled to hold Itakh's weight against his body, and pulled two small brown bottles from a pocket. "As soon as you can, strip down, throw away your clothes. Rub yourselves with iodine and clean yourselves with soap and water. If you were wearing the masks, your lungs are safe, but it can blister the skin."

Shimon snorted under his mask as he took the bottles and handed Esther one. "The idea of running a bath at such a time—"

"The river is clean enough."

"How long does it take the gas to clear the air?" Esther asked.

"You should be fine."

She peeled the mask away from her chin. Despite the battle, the air smelled rich and sweet. Her face had grown damp between the rubber gaskets, and now felt cool. Pushing the mask up to the top of her head, she leaned down to kiss Itakh's hair, bare for the first time she recalled in his short life. A sharp, chemical smell clung to her lips when she pulled away from him. She tried not to gag. She took the mask the rest of the way off, and Shimon did the same. "We'll come find you," she told Itakh. "Be brave." The medic began carrying him back toward the synagogue.

"We should go bathe," Shimon said.

But with her mask in her hand and the bottle of iodine shoved in her ammunition pouch, Esther ran toward the fight.

Khazar forces kept pushing the enemy back. Most were already outside the city walls. Though fewer in number, the aerocycles outmaneuvered any of Haman's aeroplanes. They swooped in light as hummingbirds, then fired on soldiers from above. Three closed ranks on a group of cavalry and together drove them westward. From Esther's vantage, it looked as if the force of the wind their wingbeats generated drove the horses back, though they may have been more spooked by the gunfire. Enemy fighters outnumbered Khazars, but the enemy had no Uyghurs or golems in their ranks. Both fought with tireless ferocity. Seeing a light machine gun abandoned on the ground, Esther grabbed it and held it to her chest. She put her own pistol away. She had only the one long ammunition belt currently in the machine, but she would spend it.

How she continued to evade the bek's notice, Esther didn't know. She darted among her countrymen, stopping to brace the gun and shoot at the enemy when she had a clear line of sight. As the soldiers retreated, she fired at their backs and didn't ask herself if this was honorable, if this action befitted a Jew. The bek's men shouted orders she couldn't hear. Once they had the enemy running, the golems and the Uyghur fighters continued to pursue them. Esther also saw some refugees following a distance behind, on foot. Whatever crude weapons they held in their hands, they wouldn't let their quarry go.

At a certain point, the motley Khazar forces had driven the enemy far enough back that, for the moment, they could slacken their pursuit. For a moment, they hollered, drank water from canteens, collapsed on the ground. Dusk had surely fallen; the lingering debris of battle made it difficult to tell if it was yet night. Esther scanned the sky for three stars, but none were visible. Still, Havdalah had to have come. Shabbat was over. Without anyone's notice, the world had returned to secular time. Esther's heart continued to race. Her body, deprived of food and water, seemed stuck to the earth each time she tried to move.

Though aerocraft still buzzed in the west, many KAF planes now headed to the carriers on the Khazar Sea for fuel and service. Soldiers turned back toward the city, some supported between pairs of their fellows. Esther followed them. On their return, the mechanical horses no longer emitted the roar of high-gear travel. Rather, Esther heard, all around her, the rumbling purr and occasional stutter of a steady, first-gear walk. She could hardly believe that Seleme's powerful engine did not add to this noise and never again would. Men shouted and sang songs, holy and bawdy. Medics scoured the field, gathering bodies and parts of bodies onto overloaded stretchers. When Esther avoided obstacles underfoot, she tried not to think what they might be. In the daze of her exhaustion and hunger, she looked around for people she knew, but had trouble distinguishing faces in the dim light.

Esther was stunned by her body's depletion, the physical and mental strain of the day, the tenuous wonder of being still alive, despite all she'd witnessed. When the Great West Gate stood open before her to admit the stream of returning soldiers, she wanted to collapse at its foot, kiss its stones. But she kept walking through. If she went back to her house, would it still be standing? Would her father and sister be there? She remembered the bottle of iodine in her ammunition bag and steered herself through the city and toward the river.

Atil had never been a buzzing metropolis at night. Restaurants, coffeehouses, music halls, and late-night shops and market stalls all stood across the river in commercial Khazaran. But when Esther had ventured out after dark in the past, the glow of ordinary life in houses and apartment buildings lit the streets with a tableau of warmth. Now, only a few citizens were beginning to emerge from hiding. The city stood gray, grim, pocked, abandoned. When Esther's ancestors had retired to the countryside to enjoy the warm harvest weeks of summer, the city must have looked ghostly like this. She followed the streams of people heading down to the river to bathe. Hundreds—thousands?—already stood neck deep in the waters, splashing and shouting from the cold. Esther walked north along the riverbank until the crowd thinned. There would be no strict observance of *negiah* to-night: The Holy One had not made a separate holy river for women, and Esther needed to get clean. But she could take steps to preserve her modesty. She walked until the heads in the water grew sparse, lay down her weapons, then stripped off her clothes and placed her leather pouch and Rukhl's *hamsa* on top. Shivering, she poured iodine into one palm and rubbed it into her scalp. She measured it out in small doses and tried to cover all the skin that might have been exposed to the caustic gas. When she'd emptied the bottle, she squelched down to the riverbank, her bare toes sinking into the clay. Bracing water lapped her feet. As she contemplated easing in, she heard a splash and an incoherent holler as someone else dove in, then exclaimed, "Holy Shekhinah!" Then whoever he was made a loud gargling sound and whooped.

"Is it that cold?" she called out.

"Cold and beautiful!" The man's voice echoed across the water. If he was surprised to hear a woman call to him, he didn't say.

Esther splashed out to where the water grew deep.

At first, the water was so frigid she couldn't breathe, but soon the pain of the river's iciness came as a kind of pleasure. She treaded water, her feet tangling in the river bottom's long grasses. She used each hand to scrub the opposite arm, dove under a few times to clean the iodine out of her shorn hair. Shimon might be bathing in the river this very moment, the same water touching their two bodies. This was the water that had transformed their thousands of ancestors. She could use it as they had if she chose—she now knew the *mikvah* prayer by heart. But she chose to say nothing, to swim three quick breaststrokes toward the shore and trudge the rest of the way up the slick undergrowth. By the time she emerged, she shivered so hard she could barely wring her hair. Clean clothes would have been a blessing. When she pulled her dirty shirt over her head, it stuck to her, soaked up water from her skin, and chilled her more.

As she stumbled into her trousers, she heard a boisterous chorus of "Adon Olam," and knew the army was celebrating its fleeting victory. She could choose, at this moment, to go find her family. But once she'd forced her wet feet into her boots, returned her pistol and knife to their places, and hefted the spent machine gun, she headed toward the kagan and bek's palaces.

CHAPTER 30

All the blackout shades remained drawn. Armed guards swarmed outside the palace doors. The bek had to be inside. Recognizing her, one guard saluted while another bowed his head. As faint as she felt, both gestures buoyed her spirits as she raced up the stairs. A third said, "I'll take that gun."

The machine gun was a sort of prize, but she handed it over. "Out of ammunition," she said, and walked in.

Inside, however, all was still. Though lights burned in the chandeliers, the chamber of state stood dark. "In the cellar," remarked a baritone behind her. The guard gestured toward the back of the house, where both the kitchen and the kagan's palace stood.

Maids scrubbed dishes as on a normal day. The smells of cooked onions and tomatoes lingered in the air. Esther stopped and inhaled.

"Here." One of the maids handed her a cool metal cup of water. The cleanest thing she'd touched all day. When Esther passed it back empty, the woman folded a flatbread into her hand. "They're eating downstairs." Esther raced through a *Motzi* and stuffed the food into her mouth, almost without chewing. Her fingers tasted like chemicals. The bread stuck in her throat, then settled as a lump in her gut. The stairs stood dark in the back of the kitchen.

Esther's eyes needed to adjust before she could descend. Soon, she saw light and heard the commotion at the bottom. Into this dank room, the bek had moved his telephone and telegraph, the staticky radio, the hulking typewriter, his staff. The room smelled of unwashed bodies, fear. Avigdor and Menakhem stood in military dress behind the desk. Esther's first question was, "Where's my father?"

Menakhem shook his head. "Military affairs are not his concern."

"They're everyone's, when we're under siege."

"We've driven them back."

"For the moment," Esther said.

"Your father and sister are in hiding."

Esther knew the spot: an excavated cellar beneath one of the servants' huts. Her father kept it provisioned with preserved food, candles, jugs of water. Ever since the early days of the kaganate, houses had had hiding spots, simple or elaborate, to protect against neighboring tribes' attacks. In Esther's lifetime, servant children had used the cellar for games to which they invited the kender's children on rare occasions. "How far have we driven the enemy?" she asked the bek.

He drew his brows together as if irritated to have to answer her. "They are outside the city walls. That was our first goal."

"They won't stay that way for long."

"The KAF is refueling. They'll follow the enemy on a bombing mission. Your golems are already on the trail." Sturdy soldiers, as Esther had known they'd be—no need to rest. "The human forces, yours and mine, are bathing to—"

"I know." Could they not see she was wet?

He paused. "We hope to delay their progress until the Rus or the Ottomanim pitch in with reinforcements."

Avigdor said, "Your father is working on that."

"From the basement."

Avigdor gestured to the walls around him. "He has a field telephone."

"You're staring at the food," Menakhem said. "Eat."

Fruit, vegetables, cheese. Esther began to stuff things in her mouth without regard to how they'd taste together. She picked up someone's cup of water and gulped it down.

"We also need the Uyghur warlord's entire arsenal."

"Göktürk's?" Esther said, her mouth full.

"*Sha!*"

Avigdor, calmer as always, said, "We know you know how to reach him."

Esther chewed and swallowed. "You haven't paid him for the fuel and arms we've already received."

The bek said, "We'll square our accounts once all this is over."

"I'm starting to worry."

Admon shook his head. Esther couldn't tell what he meant.

"I can send a message by pigeon post," she offered, not knowing if the home loft was hosting any of Göktürk's pigeons. If she could find Chuluun, he would have access to one.

"Through your father," Menakhem said.

Avigdor held both palms up toward his fellow javshigar, showing him to back off. "Already," he said to the bek, "the enemy is in retreat."

The bek scratched his ginger head. "Halfway back to the village of Buzgui already. Good news."

"We need more golems," Esther said. "Thousands more. We can make them."

"Go home and tell your father to contact the Uyghur leader. Then rest."

Esther said, "We already broke the Sabbath."

Through the wall, a voice said, "Nevertheless."

The kagan again. Esther couldn't see even the glimmer of his eye. Perhaps he had a listening trumpet like the one in her schoolroom. A speaking trumpet, facing her way. She said, simply, "Sir."

"Go home to your father, if only for a few hours," he continued. "*Golemim* must be made at night, yes?"

She nodded before realizing he might not be able to see her. "Yes." Could she do it without Amit? She doubted it. And how would she find him?

"You'll make as many as you can, and follow our troops westward in the morning."

"Have the medics carried any golems back from the field?" she asked the bek.

"There's no help they can offer them. They're bringing back men."

Esther didn't know how long a golem could lie wounded in the streets. They didn't bleed to death, as people did. They couldn't go into shock. Yet she worried about what they might experience, damaged and exposed. "Then someone has to tend to them. The injured— the broken ones, I mean."

"After you sleep," said the kagan, his voice buzzing through the wall. "Now go."

When Esther climbed the stairs, her feet weighed as much as her whole body had before. She hoped no one would try to ambush her on the short walk to her father's house. She'd be as easy to catch as a turtle. Outside, the battle boomed in the west. Esther asked for her gun back. The guard slapped it against her hands, then said, "Here." He had found another ammunition belt for it; she slung it across her body, wondered how she'd manage the excess weight in her exhaustion.

Refueled aeroplanes took off from the river. The streets remained dark. Figures darted from building to building, alone or in pairs.

Though her father's guard tower appeared deserted, she called out, "*Salaam aleikum.*"

A pair of eyes blinked in the narrow window. She could barely see them in the gloom. "Esther bat Josephus?" Hurrying down the ladder. The bolt unlatching. "We did not think to see you again."

She thanked him, though his comment unnerved her.

Esther and her siblings were seldom invited into the servants' huts. The outbuildings were a nearby, different world, without electricity or running water. A well with a hand pump stood in the yard. Nearby, the chicken coops, the goats in their barn, and the pigeon loft. Had the night been brighter, she would have stuck her head inside to look for Nagehan and for a Uyghur bird. She needed to wait for daylight. Tonight, she only hoped Itakh's favorite bird was safe, like its master. To Esther's surprise, Kiraz and Bataar were sleeping in their hut. They startled when Esther threw open the door. "I'm so sorry," was her first response. Then, "Why aren't you hiding in the cellar?" And in her mind, she questioned why Bataar—a strong, healthy man of thirty or thirty-five—wasn't fighting for his country.

Bataar said, "If we're bombed, we're bombed. And we have work to do in the morning. Your father's downstairs." He rose from the bed and dragged the low dining table across the rush-strewn floor. Beneath the rushes lay the wooden trapdoor with its iron ring, which he pulled up. The stairs descended into darkness, though a dim light shone, as of a covered electric torch.

"Thank you," Esther whispered.

Already her father was saying, "Esti?" his voice gravelly. Someone was laughing or trying to stifle tears, she couldn't hear which. An electric torch cast a cone of dust-speckled light onto the stairs, led her toward his pallet on the floor. When he stood, it rustled and crackled. Stuffed with hay. She put down the machine gun, the clanking ammunition belt. He gathered her into his arms, and he whispered, "You're alive." He smelled of sun-dried laundry, civilization. He felt hot. On the pallet, a man hunched, his face in his hands and his back heaving. Weeping. She didn't recognize his broad back and had never seen hair as matted and dirty. "We had no idea what had become of you. Bek Admon told us you'd escaped him, and that was the last we heard." He spoke quietly, careful not to wake people sleeping in the shadows. There were maps all around the floor, a field telephone.

"I was fighting. I'm all right. I saw Shimon ben Kalonymos." The man looked up. His hair was long, and clumped so tight it would have to be shorn to his scalp. His beard, more gray than the hair itself, grew wild. He looked like a *yethi.* "Who is this?"

Josephus kept his arms around her.

"Your uncle," the man said, digging the heels of his hands into his eye sockets. "I'm sure your father told you I was dead."

Esther pulled away from her father, knelt down. His red eyes regarded her. Up close, he smelled of sweat and urine. "Yes, he did." Her letter hadn't reached him, could not have summoned him. She believed the golem she had named for him had met its end. "But," she didn't know how to put it, "I have always, always believed you still lived. How did Wicked Haman not kill you?"

He rocked, still hunched. "I escaped my transport train. I don't know where my family is."

"Your neighbor said you were taken." When he and her father both waited for an explanation, she said, "I sent a pigeon to try and find you." To her father she said, "I'm sorry. I thought he might be able to help us."

Matityahu opened his arms to embrace her, and he continued to weep. She didn't mind the smell, felt his heart pound against her. "One of my daughters is your age. Or was."

"They might also have escaped." Esther glanced around the cellar, took in her sister, who rustled and sat up. "Where's Shmuely?" Esther asked, and at the same moment, Elisheva said, "*Barukh Hashem,* you're back." Esther had never been so happy to see her.

Josephus said, "No word of him, or of Itakh." Nearby, an adjutant slept. He rolled over and resettled without waking.

"Shimon and I took Itakh to the field hospital. He's injured, but I think he'll live." She didn't know how much damage the gas might have done. She hoped Shmuel was all right. To Matityahu she said, "Can your family find us here?"

He released her from his embrace, shook his wild head. "I don't know. When things began to get bad, we spoke of coming here. They know where I came from. But they know little of my homeland. They don't even speak the mother tongue." He took a deep, hitching breath.

Esther thought of Rukhl's parents, lining up to be shot. "We have thousands of refugees. They might already be here. And you made it." To have cousins who had lived all this time in Europa only now to be shot was too terrible to think of. "I'm so glad you came home." He had no shoes. His feet were bound with mud-caked rags. "Can we try to find them?"

He nodded. "I don't know, but your father has told me what you've done. I'll join you tomorrow in the fight."

Josephus said, "No. I need your help more."

"After all I've been through—"

"You need to rest. And you have strong ties now in Europa, ties we can exploit." He looked at Esther and said, "Praise Hashem you're safe. You must also need sleep."

Esther couldn't describe the way she felt. "Any news of Amit ben Avraham?"

"Nothing."

"I need to find him. We need to make more golems." They could do it now, in the artificial new moon.

Matityahu looked to Josephus, who said, "I'll explain." To Esther he said, "In an hour or two. There's still time."

She had to sleep, however briefly. "I have so much more to do."

Elisheva slid closer to the wall and said, "Come."

Her father shone his torch at one of the maps and crouched down to examine it. Esther curled around her sister on the thin pallet. Packed earth offered little comfort and its dankness rose through the hay, but the moment she'd whispered her prayers, she fell into a sleep so still and profound, she awoke without having moved an arm or a leg.

No place was darker than a hiding hole. She couldn't guess how long she'd slept. Everyone else was asleep. Esther had been grateful to receive her pistol from Chuluun, but what she really should have asked for was a timepiece. She groped on the floor until she found her father's torch, then covered it with her hand as she turned it on. The dim red glow helped her find the remains of a loaf of bread, which she blessed and ate from. She didn't know if she should wake her uncle. He wanted to help; he'd had the mettle to escape his transport train and make his way across a thousand *parasangs* of war zone to reach them. But she had never seen a person more parched, exhausted, and gray. She left him for now. When he awoke, he could help either her father or the bek. Esther strung her ammunition belt over her body, taking care to move slowly to quiet the clink of cartridges against each other, checked her holster for the pistol and her boot for the knife, took up the light machine gun, and made her way to the foot of the stairs. She left the torch behind; in that cellar, they needed it more than she did. At the top of the stairs, she pushed on the door, but Bataar must have returned the table to its position. She knocked, and after a few moments' shuffling, the hatch opened. Light didn't pour in, the upper world no more daylike than the lower. Kiraz handed Esther a peach on her way out the door. Esther said *Ha-Eitz* for it, and bit into the sweetest, wettest food she'd ever tasted.

The sky remained black, but birds were singing. She hadn't heard a single one the day before. She also heard the battle, far to the west. Closer to home, the chickens rustled in their coop and the goats in their barn. She would search for a Uyghur pigeon as soon as she could—it was still too dark to find one.

Just beyond her father's gate, she looked out, in the rising light, toward the North Gate and the road that led to the camp. Near the city walls, she saw men working and heard a rhythmic, rasping sound she couldn't place. A moment's observation showed her golems digging graves in rows. Though their hearing must have been better than men's, they did not turn from their labor at the sound of her footsteps. As Esther looked from her high vantage around the city, she saw that the medics had labored all night to gather the wounded, the golems to carry off the dead. Few bodies remained. All appeared still. The battlefields were pocked with holes, littered with rubble and what must have been torn bits of fabric and spent shells. Here and there she saw the shape of what might have been a finger or a hand, ghastly gray against the earth.

Esther dropped her peach pit on the ground, wiped her hand on her filthy trousers, and set off for the waterfront holding the machine gun across her body, in both hands. She had squandered this precious night, but soon enough, she would report to the bek and find Amit to figure out how to start manufacturing golems on a grand scale. But her time in the river the night before made her want to see the holy waters once more before she began the day's work. As she neared the riverbank and began to take in the wreckage, she saw Amit and Shimon crouched together over some kind of task. From behind, they resembled boys setting fire to a pile of leaves with a magnifying glass. Seeing them together reminded her with a jolt of her misdeed. She felt she had kissed Amit a hundred years, a lifetime, before. At the same time, she recalled the feel and taste of him vividly. She wondered if, as they worked together, he had told Shimon anything, if Shimon had questioned Amit about being born a girl.

As she swung around to their side, Shimon drew his gun, and Esther leaped back. The moment he saw who it was, he threw it down. "Holy Shekhinah, don't sneak up on people," he said. "I might have killed you."

Esther's heart raced. Beyond the minarets and spires of Khazaran, the lowest strip of sky had turned a deep, luminous blue. With his knife, Amit hacked at a maimed golem's brow.

"Stop!" she called. She put her gun down and reached to grab his arm. Shimon yanked her back by both shoulders and she stumbled into his lap. He wrapped both arms tight to contain her, but she'd lost her fight by then. "What are you doing?" she asked.

Shimon said, "Shh."

Amit continued his work, now with a more gentle, scraping motion. His eyes flickered over her and Shimon before focusing again on his task.

"Stop that," she whispered. She leaned forward and turned over the wrist to see who it was: Shv'im v'Shnayim, Seventy-Two, a golem from Yetzirah. Both his legs were missing.

He paused for a moment and also read the name. Then he went back to gouging shards from the golem's forehead. Its flesh chipped off like a shattered flowerpot. The *aleph* at the start of *Emet* was nearly gone.

"Are you there?" Esther asked Shv'im v'Shnayim. He didn't respond. To Amit she said, "We can't wipe the letters away?" As if he might not have understood, she made a frantic rubbing gesture with her hand. She noticed she was still in Shimon's lap, encircled in his arms. She didn't know what she thought of this, and couldn't guess the complexity of what Amit might think.

"I told you, it would take too long. There are too many."

She looked around. Half a dozen more lay on the field. She'd seen more the day before in the city.

"They can't feel anything, you know."

But in her heart, Esther refused to believe this. They heard and spoke and yearned for the Holy One. Surely they felt, if not in a way people understood. "We missed a precious night to work, Amit. We need to make more. They're Khazaria's best fighters."

"Right now, I need you to help us."

This was no time for sentimentality. As Khazaran's sky lightened an inch at a time, the enemy was not running home toward conquered Europa. They'd been pushed back, not defeated. Esther pulled her knife from her boot and prepared to help. She caught his eye and this time, he looked right at her. What she read in his expression might have been sadness, regret, or mere exhaustion. She sensed, however, that he hadn't divulged anything to Shimon. That he would leave that revelation—momentous in her mind, so small compared to everything going on around them—to her, if she had the courage to make it when the time came.

As she walked along the shore, Esther saw two *golemim* that Shimon and Amit had already killed. She wondered again what that meant, when the golems had never truly lived. Farther along, a severed golem foot. She averted her eyes. In the distance, one of the giants lay facedown in the mud. At first glance, she saw nothing wrong with it. Then she saw that someone had hacked clear through its middle, a jagged diagonal line extending from its left rib cage to its right hip. Whoever had attacked it had done gruesome, spiteful work. The golem could have done him little harm once prone.

She knelt down and pushed on one shoulder to try to turn it over. It didn't budge. She wedged the toe of one boot beneath its near shoulder, and managed to raise it onto her foot. "Shimon?" she called.

He jogged over. Together, they gave a strong shove and flipped it.

A living person, separated from his legs, would bleed as a river flows. He might holler in the instant before he lost consciousness. But this golem was calm, as if he had not noticed the grotesque separation or the mud on his mouth, nose, and chin. His features showed no displeasure.

It was Gimmel, regarding her mildly. Esther's stomach lurched. He said, "Hello, Esther," in the same low tone as if they'd passed in the street. "I'm glad it's you who've come."

She didn't know how to respond.

In a quiet voice, Shimon said, "I can do it."

She shook her head without looking at him, though she wanted to flee. Shimon walked farther along the torn-up riverbank to find another wounded one. Esther and Gimmel regarded each other.

"I understand what you must do. I heard the rabbis talking." He lifted one huge finger as if to gesture toward Shimon, but quit halfway through the gesture.

Esther sat down cross-legged beside him and put down the knife. Then, in despair, she lay down next to him, swinging her legs out to the side to avoid touching his. The sky had continued to lighten, and looked clearer than she might have expected. At this moment, it was free of aeroplanes. "Does it hurt?" she asked him.

"Nothing hurts. We're not mortal."

"A human would soon die of such an injury."

"Humans are fragile."

She watched a sparse wisp of cloud pass overhead. Amit called out, "Esther, we have work to do."

"Are you afraid?" she asked.

Gimmel remained silent a long while. A nearby thrush sang a tuneless song. Then he said, "No. I am made of this clay. I assume I'll return to the riverbank." When Esther didn't respond, he went on, "Did not King Dovid sing, 'Yea, though I walk through the valley of the shadow of death, I will fear no evil; for You are with me'?"

"He did."

" 'You anoint my head with oil; my cup runs over. Surely goodness and mercy shall follow me all the days of my life: and I will dwell in the Lord's house forever.' "

Esther's eyes stung. "But when he sings, 'He restores my soul—' "

"He restores my soul as well." A moment later, he repeated, "He also restores my soul."

But what was that soul? After days and nights in Gimmel's presence, Esther had a sense, but didn't know for certain. She was glad Amit stood far off, unable to contradict him. It was Gimmel Esther wanted to believe. Did believe, in her heart.

The golem said, "You have work to do, Esther bat Josephus."

She closed her eyes, drew in a breath, then let it out in a soft, slow stream. This was not hers to reckon. What was she to say? She opened her eyes and sat up. She looked into Gimmel's dull brown irises, and the brown whites surrounding them, and at his eyelids, sculpted by a master: the same color. She thought, not for the first time, she saw a glimmer of—something—there. She picked up the knife again and turned it over in her palm. Its mother-of-pearl handle fit her as if it had been shaped to her hand. "Are you ready?" she asked him.

At first, he remained quiet. Esther couldn't proceed until he spoke. He regarded her, then lifted his blocky right hand and placed it over his eyes. In his low voice, he sang out, "*Sh'ma, Yisrael, Adonai eloheinu, Adonai ekhad,*" giving each word, each note, its time to unfold. Beneath his breath, he said, "*Barukh shem k'vod malkhuto l'olam va'ed.*" A moment later, he removed his hand as slowly as he'd brought it up, looked into her eyes, and gave a single, slow nod.

The bridge of Esther's nose stung. She swallowed to hold back tears. Still her vision clouded. She could not do as Amit had done, and hack at the forehead of this being, her friend. Instead, she lay her left hand flat over the place where a human's sternum would be. A heart would have beat behind that bone. With the tip of her knife, she scratched at the *aleph* on his brow. She had never noticed what a fine hand his creator had possessed, with what flourish the word had been written. As she worked, she kept pausing to look in his eyes. She could not determine when whatever had animated the clay departed. When she'd scratched through each of the *aleph*'s dynamic, animate limbs, he indeed lay *met*.

Behind her eyes and nose, fire still burned. There were other golems to attend to. The sun had nearly risen; sky-wise, the day appeared ordinary, though she knew this would not turn out to be true. Esther could not bury Gimmel. Amit and Shimon left the others where they'd fallen in the field. Over time, they would turn back to dust. But she wanted to mark him, to leave him something. She needed her knife, pistol, and machine gun. If she lived through this war, she would have to return Rukhl's *hamsa* to its owner.

She reached into her shirt, pulled out her pouch, and extracted the *volkelake*'s brown hair. In addition to its own animal stink, it now bore the spicy tang of mustard gas. This wouldn't harm Gimmel. She squeezed her prize once—it was hard to give it up—lifted the collar of his worn blue shirt, and tucked the hair over where his heart would have been. She patted the shirt down to seal it, held her palm over the cool clay a moment longer. Then she tucked her pouch away and her knife into her boot shaft, picked up the gun, and stood up again. Amit and Shimon still needed her help. She set off along the shore to find the next golem.

Once the sun was up, she and Amit made plans to gather every person they could—all the remaining residents of the refugee camp, if possible, and any soldier whose hands were free—after sundown to make golems by the Atil. She watched him a moment after they'd concluded their plan, waited to see if he would speak of their transgression, but it was as if it had vanished. He seemed determined to help Khazaria in the way that he, as a kabbalist, was best able, nothing more. For now, he went into the city to look for more broken or wounded golems that might need to be killed. Esther once again hefted her gun, and she and Shimon headed toward the bek's palace. Her limbs continued to feel leaden, her heart a dead, cold weight in her chest. So much had taken its toll: physical exhaustion, grief for Gimmel and Seleme, worry for Itakh and Shmuel, the miracle of her uncle's return, the terrible reality of the previous day's battle. A temporary victory, many dead and wounded, and no guarantee that Khazaria would still stand in a week's or even a day's time.

"Still," Shimon said as they passed through the bek's gate. "We have reason to hope."

Esther nodded. "I look forward to having a reason to celebrate."

"Such as our wedding."

She tried to calculate in her head. It might be Rosh Khodesh, the first day of Elul. The High Holy Days approached. She longed to have one more chance for atonement.

The bek, they found, was already out in the field, west of the city. Esther and Shimon would join him there to strategize the day's fight. En route, they stopped at the synagogue.

Shimon stumbled backward the moment he stepped inside. His eyes widened, and he seemed to struggle to take in breath. "What is it?" Esther asked.

"I knew they were using the synagogue for a hospital. But I didn't expect to see it completely transformed."

Half of the great dome was gone, open to the sky, as was part of the eastern wall. Patients lay on the men's hard pews, each with at least one arm or leg dangling off. A folding screen surrounded the bimah: now an operating theater. The air smelled of camphor, alcohol, blood. Esther put her hand on Shimon's shoulder, and he reached his other hand up to hold it. Had they abandoned *negiah* or transformed it? Esther didn't know. But no one noticed.

They found Itakh lying close to the bimah. Blisters marred the clean little-boy skin of his neck and hands, and a cast encased his left leg from ankle to hip. Esther fell to her knees, handed Shimon the machine gun, and wrapped her arms around Itakh. He gave her a half-hearted hug with his arms only, keeping his injured hands clear. "Are you all right?" Esther asked. She felt him nod against her shoulder.

"They gave me medicine for pain. It's going to be a long time before I can walk again, but the doctors expect the leg to heal." Esther didn't know how the family, crouched in a cellar, would care for him. As if he could see her thoughts, Itakh said, "The doctor said I can be transferred to a hospital out of the city. But I want to go home."

Home, where his warm room off the kitchen sat abandoned, waiting to be bombed. Esther pulled away and looked at him. The flesh beneath his eyes was puffy, ashen. He wasn't even ten years old—how could she let him travel to a distant city on his own, especially when no one could say if the hospital would still be standing when he arrived? "Father and Elisheva are in Bataar's basement. I don't know if you'd be comfortable there." In wartime, and with his injuries, the distinctions that had kept him in the kitchen might no longer apply.

"Have you seen Nagehan?" he asked.

Esther had seen a pigeon shot down without knowing which one it was. "Jascha intercepted her in the camp last night. We sent her home with her message."

He let out a small sigh. He loved his bird the way she'd loved Seleme. Perhaps more, since the bird had a beating heart. Yet Gimmel's lack of one didn't keep her from mourning his loss. "If I agree to go to the other hospital, will you come with me?"

Esther couldn't accompany him now, and at the same time didn't know how to refuse him. "Once we've repelled the enemy, perhaps."

"I have to leave sooner than that. They want the patients who can to move out of the city, so the doctors here can tend to the fresh wounded." When she didn't respond, he went on, "I came with you, on your adventure. And I don't want to go alone."

She kissed his forehead, believing she'd never go. "I'll check on Nagehan for you, as soon as I'm able. Are there any Uyghur birds in the loft?"

"I'm not sure. Sometimes there have been."

She kissed him again, as if this would make amends. "Itakh, why have you been angry with me?"

"I haven't." His glance flickered across the ceiling. Shimon stepped away and greeted another wounded soldier, whose voice gained strength when he saw that the future chief rabbi had come to the hospital.

"You've been avoiding me for days."

He continued not to look at her. Esther's mind swerved toward the moans of the wounded, the pews creaking, the quiet talk of patients and medics. "You've said some foolish things. You betrayed my confidence, and Amit's."

"I didn't mean to." In the heat of the moment, sure. But she'd meant no one harm. And she believed she'd apologized.

Itakh shrugged his thin shoulders. Esther could tell from his expression that he didn't consider this explanation enough. She said, "I'm sorry," kissed him again, a meaningless gesture, then pulled Rukhl's *hamsa* over her head. She gripped it in her fist before holding it out to him.

"To protect you," she said, "in case I'm not able to make it back."

Tears welled in his eyes. "You have to."

"If I don't, promise me you'll return it to Rukhl someday?"

"You're coming back."

"You can't lose it."

"I wouldn't. You said you'd give it back to her." The blisters on his hands made them awkward as he tried to loop the leather thong around his neck. Esther did it for him, freed the hair at his nape from it, fluffed the pillow under his head. "Tell me when you've made up your mind," he said. "They want to transfer me out tomorrow."

"Yes," Esther said. "You know, I think when Chuluun calls you a little Uyghur, he means that as a compliment."

The corners of his mouth lifted, a dazed half smile.

She didn't say goodbye. After a long moment looking at Itakh, she beckoned Shimon outside.

They passed a guard unit on patrol. A squadron of Khazar aerocraft buzzed the rooftops while heading westward. Close on their tails came a larger unit, bearing the red and gold emblem of the Menshevikim. Under ordinary circumstances, Esther would have run for cover. Today she knew this was her father's good work. West of the city, the landscape was as gouged up as the riverbank. In the night, soldiers had built defensive barricades before the gate. Far in the distance, tanks lumbered away from the city behind the troops who stretched to the horizon. "We need mech horses," Esther said. "I lost Seleme in the tumult yesterday." She felt a cold stab of grief when she thought of the horse's destruction. Still, her thoughts returned in an instant to Itakh and to what she would do for him.

"A golem was working on Tolga, but I don't know if he fixed her."

"We need more of them." She didn't know how long it took to build one. The bek must have had the factory operating around the clock, since horses, unlike golems, did not depend on magic or the sacredness of any particular time of day.

As far as she could see, there were no horses they could borrow or commandeer, though not everyone had gone into the engagement. Behind each barricade, a few men crouched, loading their weapons before moving forward or filling their pouches with ammunition. Some medics had set up stations there at the rear, while others even now moved toward where the casualties would be. Esther and Shimon jogged to one barricade, then the next, making erratic progress toward the battle. Behind one barrier, they found Tselmeg sharpening his sword against a portable whetstone in elegant, ringing strokes. "*Ässalamu läykum*," he greeted them—in Uyghur, but this was close enough to the usual Yishmaelite greeting to understand. A dust-stained bandage bound his head, and dried blood had seeped through to darken a spot over the temple.

"*Aleikhem shalom*," Esther and Shimon replied.

"Nice gun," he said. Shimon still carried it.

Chuluun darted over from the next barricade. A distance behind him, as a bomber whizzed past, a shell hit, throwing a spray of dust into their backs as they all ducked. He grunted his hello, took Tselmeg's sword from him, and tested its blade against his thumb. Whatever he remarked in Uyghur, disapproval laced his tone. Esther tried to make a mental tally of people she knew who were still alive, but lost count each time an explosive detonated. "We needed to find you," she said to Chuluun. Tselmeg grabbed the sword back and continued to sharpen it, his face dark. "The bek needs to ask your leader for help."

Chuluun smiled his long, devious smile.

"All the help he can offer."

He nodded. "When payment has not yet been arranged for what he's already done."

What could she say? A few weeks before, she had thought Göktürk a warlord and her father, the bek, and the javshigarim the most honorable men in Khazaria. Now she rated them all about the same. "If Khazaria falls, all our debts will be forfeit. If it stands, I trust the bek to pay them."

Chuluun's eyes made calculations. He glanced dismissively over his shoulder. Esther read this as assent.

She asked, "Do you need access to a field telephone?"

"Or find me a pigeon."

"Whichever I can get you faster. Have you seen the bek yet this morning?"

Chuluun rose to survey their position, then quickly crouched back down. "Some of his men, in their skirts," he spat the word out, "confer with each other a *ghalva* distant." Esther didn't know his unit of measure, but it couldn't be far. He gave a sharp, threatening point to the southwest.

Shimon nodded and wiped his hand over his face. "Let's go."

With each move, they came closer to the engagement. Esther drew her pistol and kept it in hand as they traveled. At one point, they rested while Shimon offered her a drink from his canteen. The water bore the tang of metal, as delicious as the clearest stream. "You're not going to go with Itakh to the other hospital, are you?" he asked.

She shook her head. "I didn't know what to say. I don't know what to do. He's just a little boy, but I can't abandon the fight now."

Shimon took a swig. "*Barukh Hashem*, we'll drive the enemy back."

"*Barukh Hashem.*"

"'Rejoice, O ye nations, with His people: for He will avenge the blood of His servants, and will render vengeance to His adversaries, and will be merciful unto His land, and to His people.'"

"Are we His land?"

Shimon snorted and smiled. "I suppose. Until we return to Palestine."

She didn't know if his "we" was personal or referred to *b'nai Yisrael*. If the world persisted and their marriage came to pass, Esther wondered if it would be a pleasure or an annoyance, his ability to quote Tanakh and Talmud for any occasion. Instead of voicing this question, she said, "*Ameyn.*" For the first time, she hoped without reservation that she would someday be the *rebbetzin* of Atil.

"May the Great Name be praised."

The Great Name: all 212 letters. Something she herself, with her mortal, woman's body, had pronounced and used to alter Creation. She looked at Shimon's kind brown eyes in his exhausted face. Before she could think what she was doing, she spread her hand in the gesture of priestly blessing and pressed the heel of her palm to his brow. "May Adonai bless you and keep you. May Adonai let His face shine upon you and be gracious to you. May Adonai look kindly upon you and give you peace."

Her hand didn't belong on his forehead. She held it there a moment longer, understanding that this blessing would protect him in death as well as in life. When she pulled her hand away, he took it and kissed the palm.

"Let's go," he said. "We're getting close."

Esther rated Khazaria's chances soberly. The enemy's armies outnumbered the bek's, and had more and better equipment. Not all of Khazaria's forces were professional soldiers. Yet they had golems, Uyghur oilmen, and aerocycles on their side—all of these conferred some advantage. The refugees Haman himself had driven onto this soil. Matityahu among them, they would avenge the loss of their homes and brothers. Even now, Khazar fighters had pushed the enemy back from the sacred river and the capital. And Khazaria would fight until its final person died fighting. That was how they had held this territory for the last thousand years. The war would continue until art and the Holy One's grace transmuted all of this many-rivered nation's clay into golems. Until the enemy hacked every one of those golems to uselessness on the field.

Esther took a deep breath, full of fear and wonder, and looked around at the battle she now stood so close to. In the far distance, beyond sight, rose the snowcapped mountains that had protected her homeland as best they could for centuries. Without conferring, she and Shimon darted for the next barricade.

To my editor, Tim Duggan, his assistant editor, Will Wolfslau, the whole team at Tim Duggan Books, my agent, Eric Simonoff, and his colleagues at William Morris Endeavor: Thank you for believing in me and in this work, and for all you've done for us both.

I'd like to thank the institutions at which I taught while writing this: Yale, Columbia, NYU, Princeton, Bard, and most of all, Smith, where I felt so supported in completing this project. I'd also like to thank my students, who have inspired me with your creativity and your dedication to craft.

I am grateful for the support of the Guggenheim Foundation, the National Endowment for the Arts, and the Sustainable Arts Foundation. You made this book possible.

This novel required research as well as imagination, and I want to thank the many people who helped along the way, starting with Michael Chabon, who at the very beginning offered advice about embarking on a project outside my comfort zone. Kevin Alan Brook answered questions about (real, historical) Khazar history and culture when this novel was still in its earliest phases. Twice a week for a year, Paul La Farge met me to write at the public library. This discipline and camaraderie made it possible to finish a draft. Adam Snyder and Marshall Curry gave me thoughtful, intensive first readings. Stewart Waldrop of the Royal Pigeon Racing Association patiently answered questions about trained pigeons, while Robbie Rhodes of Scooter Bottega and my friend Max Leach helped me find my way around a Vespa, the machine on which Seleme is based. Horse questions went to Sarah McFarland Taylor and Lauren Harrison. Rabbi Marc Katz answered many questions about Halachah, while Rabbi Jonathan Kligler read the whole book through with thoughtful attention to details of Jewish thinking and practice. Rabbi Moshe Yosef Firrouz and Dikla Bandah-Rozenfeld answered questions about modern-day Karaite practice. Brian Buckman got the wrenches right. Many friends and family contributed Hebrew and Yiddish phrasing—Edie Scher, Judith Frank, Rabbi Riqi Kosovske, Amy Meltzer, Erika Dreyfus, Liz Kubany, Adina Kopinsky, and Ethan Stein—while Nagehan Bayindir helped with Turkish idiom and phrasing, and Susan Bernofsky with German. When I couldn't recall whether a saying was attributed to Hillel, Noach Lundgren found me the reference in Mishnah. Susan Ray typed the entire first-draft manuscript without complaining about my handwriting and, when she'd finished, told me she'd really enjoyed the novel—a benefit I hadn't expected.

I would never have been able to finish this book without school, daycare, and most of all, babysitters. To the teachers at Smith College Campus School, George Washington Elementary, Fort Hill, Aunt Jenn's, and Country Meadows: Thank you for letting me write. Jerusha Kellerhouse, Cassie Pruyn, Chinyere Davis, and Rosie Alig: My children are fortunate to have you as exemplars. May they grow up to be as principled, driven, creative, and fun to hang around with as all of you are.

I owe huge thanks to my family, especially to my dad and stepmom, J. D. and Millie Barton. And most of all I want to thank my husband, Thomas Israel Hopkins, and our sons, Tobias and Emmett. I love all three of you "up to da 'ky," as Emmett would say.

February 2016
Kingston, New York